MW01227663

A PACK of STORMS and STARS

A PACK OF STORMS AND STARS
BOOK 4 OF THE BOULDER WOLVES SERIES

Copyright © 2021 by Olivia Wildenstein

Cover design by *Ampersand Book Covers*
Editing by *Anna Joy Missa*
Nikki & Liam artwork by *@elionhardt*
Proofreading by Rose at *Griot Editing Services*

Be heart-smart.

PROLOGUE

18 MONTHS EARLIER

My favorite smell in the world was the wild during springtime, when the wind bent the evergreens, the rain softened the soil, and the sunshine buffeted our pelts.

A close second was that of summer break. No more weekends spent cramming for exams. No more sitting out pack runs because of homework. No more rising at the crack of dawn to make it before the first bell.

As Grant gunned his brand-new motorcycle out of the compound's gates, I wrapped my arms around his middle and tipped my head back. The blistering sun poured through my helmet's visor and licked my shoulders and bare thighs while the wind tangled in my long hair.

Grant sped up when we reached the end of the private road and turned, leaning so far sideways our bodies became parallel to the asphalt. I let out a little yelp of surprise. Although this wasn't Grant's maiden voyage astride his rumbling beast, it was mine.

"Is that normal?" I yelled over the motor and wind.

"Is what normal?"

"Tipping so much."

"Yes, babe! Totally normal."

I willed his confident thrill to settle my pulse which was currently thumping as fast as the wings of the magpies I'd unintentionally spooked a couple days earlier. The poor birds had taken one look at my wolf and sprang off the deer carcass they were feasting on. To think I was on the scrawnier side of the lycanthropic spectrum. What would they have done had our Alpha, Cassandra Morgan, surprised them? Dropped dead from heart failure?

Could birds suffer from heart failure?

Another bend in the road banked our bodies and snuffed out my mental ramblings.

I clamped my thighs around Grant's and hugged him so tightly my forearms dented his six-pack. For all my love of speed in fur, I wasn't a fan of it in skin. Especially when I wasn't in control.

When he righted the motorcycle, I yelled, "Hey, can you slow down a little?"

Grant turned his head and shaped the word *relax* with his lips. Fat chance I could relax, especially with his eyes off the road.

Even though I wanted to stick my palms on either side of his bright orange helmet and redirect his attention, there was no way I was releasing his middle, so I settled on screaming, "Watch where you're going!"

He chuckled as he finally rotated his head back on its axis.

When the road straightened again, my shoulders loosened. Not my grip, though. As long as the engine rumbled and the wind tore around our bodies, I'd choke my boyfriend's body like a vine.

He turned the death trap again, tilting us harshly, before twisting the handlebars the opposite way. I really wished he'd slow down, but since he didn't, I cinched his ribs and shut my eyes. Not looking proved more frightening, so I peeked over his shoulder just as we dipped sideways again.

"Grant, come on. Just a little slower."

He stroked my forearm, probably to reassure me. Instead, it made my heart vault into my throat. I wanted both his hands on the grips where I could see them.

Just as I gritted this out, the front tire slammed into a deep pothole and caught. Grant's palm flew off my arm, but too late. The handlebar jerked to the side, and then the bike skidded, veering off the road and over the shoulder.

His orange helmet joggled. Became the only thing I could see. Until the tree.

I saw it right before impact.

The crash tore my arms from Grant and sent me soaring. I landed with such a violent thwack that I thought my helmeted head had unhooked itself from the rest of my body and my spine had snapped. My senses dimmed and then awakened when thunder clapped against my eardrums.

It was hot. Blisteringly so. And so damn muggy I could hardly breathe.

"Nikki!" Grant's voice sounded like it was coming from a mile away.

I attempted to prop myself up, but my legs wouldn't move.

I blinked, trying to clear my vision, but everything remained blurred and gray.

And the smell . . . Lycaon, the smell.

My stomach churned at the reek of burning kerosene and barbecued flesh, and then it hardened when I realized it was *my* flesh that was on fire. Arms gripped my underarms and yanked me away from the blazing heap of metal.

"My leg," I whimpered.

Grant rolled me onto my front to extinguish the flames. The slick grass and damp soil cooled my broiled skin but did zilch for the pain.

"My phone's gone, Nik." Grant peeled off his muscle tee and tossed it aside. "I'll run back to get help." His shorts dropped next.

I rolled my mouth off the forest floor. "Don't—Don't leave me here."

"I'll be right back." He fell to his knees and morphed into his wolf.

"Please, Grant," I croaked. "Please don't leave."

But he did.

CHAPTER 1

PRESENT DAY

Cell phone pinned between my ear and shoulder, I rooted through my bag to locate my car keys. *Ugh.* I needed a better system. I had so much crap, from tissue packets to two—no, three—chapsticks to loose change, tampons, and headphones that were forever getting tangled.

Pouches. I was going to buy myself a gazillion pouches. "Where can I buy pouches?"

"Pouches?" Adalyn sputtered.

"Like with zippers and—"

"Babe, I know what pouches are. I was just wondering how we got from *girl murdered in the woods by a wolf*"—she hissed the last word even though the blow-dryers in the background were on full blast, so I doubted any of her customers could hear a thing, especially considering the median age at Hair of the Wolf was seventy—"to pouches."

I set my supermarket bag at my feet. "Because I can't find my keys." To think Mom had gotten me an outsized leather and rabbit-fur cherry charm to facilitate the entire process.

"How about I ask Grams to bead you a lanyard with a clip? You'll never lose your keys again."

"Funny, Ads, but I'm not hanging my keys around my neck. My love life sucks enough as is." I started taking things out of my bag and placing it on my Jeep's hood. The car had gone through all four of my brothers before it got to me, but heck, I had a car, so I wasn't complaining.

"Did Nate say if it was one of us . . . or a real one?"

"He didn't say." Okay, this was getting ridiculous. I took my tablet out and plopped it on the hood, then squinted into the dusky interior of my bag. "Shit. They're not here."

"Who's not there?"

"My keys. Keep up." I upturned my bag and shook it.

"Don't you have like, three key charms on that thing?"

I growled, sounding a lot like Niall when he'd come across a skunk two summers ago. Instead of leaving the poor creature alone, he'd had to go and taunt it. He'd smelled so bad our three other brothers booted him out of the house during meals for a full week, and our parents apologetically agreed he should eat outside. I'd carried my plate to the porch and sat with his sorry, stinky ass.

"Did you check your jacket pocket?"

I blinked, then patted my black winter jacket and bingo. "You're a genius, Adalyn."

"Still getting you that lanyard."

I rolled my eyes as I started shoving everything back inside my bag. "Careful. I'm in charge of your bachelorette. You get me a lanyard, I'll get you a subscription to dildo-of-the-month and put it in Nash's name."

Adalyn roared with laughter. "Perv."

"I did grow up with four brothers. One of whom you're marrying."

"I know. I can't wait."

I made a gagging noise even though deep down, when Adalyn and Nash got together it was the best day of my life, second only to when my first digitally painted book cover sold for a grand. "Bye, *chica*."

"Bye, Nikki."

I tossed my phone into my bag, then dug my keys out from my pocket and was about to unlock my car—there used to be a fancy remote control, until Niall—when someone tapped my shoulder. Pulse ramping, I shoved my keys between my fingers and spun around.

A guy wearing a baseball cap in spite of the sun having set an hour ago held up a tampon. "You dropped this."

Even though his face was steeped in shadows, his gorgeous maleness didn't elude me—straight nose, dark eyes, full mouth, defined jaw, evening stubble, strong neck. He was the sort of guy I drew on book covers. Tall, dark, and obscenely handsome.

But then my gaze snagged on something that made my lust shrivel up. On the upside, my fear expired at the same time. He had a baby carrier strapped to his middle. It's not that I didn't like children, but they usually meant a wife.

His nostrils flared out slightly as he wiggled the plastic-covered tampon. *Right.* The reason he'd approached me in the first place.

"Thank you." I took it from him and chucked it into my bag.

Out of all the things that could've rolled out . . . I *really* needed pouches. Wait. Why had he sniffed the air? Only shifters did that. Or pervs, but he didn't strike me as a pervert.

I took a long inhale—musk, mint, wolf. How had I missed that he was a shifter? "What pack?"

If only I possessed my brother Nolan's sharp sense of smell. I would've been able to tell the man's pack affiliation instantly.

The guy took a step back as though to thin out his smell. I was very tempted to say, *you smelled me first*, but I was nineteen. I might've shot that out at eighteen, but now I was mature and unflappable and—

"Yours."

I stopped enumerating my qualities, which were all aspirational anyway, to give the guy another once-over. "Visiting from Boulder then?"

I knew all the shifters in the area, but fifteen months ago, our pack had been annexed by a tiny pack when our Alpha, Cassandra Morgan, lost a duel to this arrogant male named Liam Kolane. I'd never met him, because I'd been stuck in the hospital when it all went down. And when he'd visited Beaver Creek for a couple of our full moon runs, I'd been hopped up on too much Sillin to shift, or back at the clinic because of an infection.

I had a serious love-hate relationship with the werewolf drug. All at once, it allowed my bones to mend since it prevented shifting, but it fragilized my werewolf magic, which in turn, slowed down my superhuman healing. Eighteen months after the motorcycle crash, and I was still not fully back to normal.

"Something like that." He took another step back and then turned and walked into the supermarket.

I copped a look at his lean, muscled back—broad shoulders that tapered into a narrow waist and a really fine ass. I mean, most shifters, especially the younger ones, were all muscle, but this man was the finest specimen I'd ever laid eyes on.

He has a kid, Nikki, I reminded myself because myself had somehow discarded the information.

I really needed to break my unwelcome celibacy streak.

I got into my car, swung my bags onto the passenger seat, and swerved out of my parking spot when a chill slunk down my spine. I stared at the lit façade of the supermarket.

The baby hadn't made a peep. What if it was a prop? What if I'd just crossed paths with a murderer? I jammed my finger onto the lock button, expelling a breath when they all clicked into place, then dialed my eldest brother Nate. As Beta, he was familiar with every Boulder. He'd know who the guy was. My call went to voicemail. I didn't bother leaving a message since Nate would be at the house for dinner. The seven of us—well, nine now with my brothers' fiancées, Adalyn and Bea—were so tight that we shared meals more often than we ate separately. Especially since my dad and Nolan were the best damn cooks in all of Beaver Creek.

As I drove home, I found myself glancing into my rearview mirror more than once, my theory rooting itself so deep my nails turned into claws and remained that way until I drove past our compound's gated entrance and up the sinuous, snowy road hedged in glowing, timbered dwellings.

Being surrounded by a thousand wolves and a tall fence tipped with silver spearheads calmed my crackling nerves.

Safe.

I was safe.

CHAPTER 2

I barged into my house, tossing my coat on a hook and my keys on the console table. Yes, I was nineteen and still lived at my parents'.

Right before the accident, I'd been all set to move in with Niall in his two-bedroom pondside cabin, but I was such an invalid that I'd stayed home. Not that Mom and Dad would've let me move out weak and useless as I was.

Both my parents were the nurturing type. Dad with food and stories, Mom with her time and gentleness. I didn't always appreciate how deeply they loved and cared, especially when I was trying to be rebellious in my teenage years. Between them and my *four* older brothers, my rebellious streak died a quick death.

I tried my hardest, though, managing to check skinny-dipping, a hangover, and purple hair off my list.

Skinny-dipping wasn't that wild considering wolves weren't exactly modest, what with having to get naked before shifting, but at thirteen, it had felt totally badass.

The hangover and purple hair coincided. Adalyn and I had unearthed a bottle of Don Julio in her house and a dye kit for hair leftover from Grandma Reeves' salon. Drunk on tequila, I'd dyed her light hair blue, and she'd colored my brown hair purple. It had honestly felt like a great idea that night, but so had drinking hard liquor. Even though it wasn't all that awful, especially after her grams filled in the patches we'd forgotten to color, my brothers spent the next few weeks threatening to dye our wolves' pelts purple and blue to match.

I slid the grocery bag onto the counter, then kissed Dad's bristly cheek. "Smells delicious."

"Thanks, honey."

The butcher-block island was laden with dishes, some cooked, others raw. Amidst the chaos, Nolan was skillfully crimping the edges of a tart shell.

I dumped my bag on one of the high chairs propped under the island. "Please tell me the filling's sour cherry."

Nolan looked up at me, a streak of flour over his jaw. "Sour cherry? Now why would I bake a cherry pie in the fall?"

Where Nate, Niall, and I inherited Mom's brown eyes, the twins got Dad's blue peepers. Totally unfair. Especially considering their lashes were indecently dark and curly.

I bumped him with my shoulder. "Because you love your little sister to bits."

"It's sour cherry."

"Yes!" I grabbed a bottle of water from the fridge and was about to ask how I could help when I remembered the murdered girl and my urgent desire to talk with my cop brother about the baseball-cap wearing shifter. "Is Nate here?"

"He's helping your mother set the table," Dad replied as he heated oil in a pan, filling the kitchen with a rich-smelling sizzle.

I walked toward the adjacent dining room where Nate was uncorking red wine. "Nate, the murder yesterday—"

"Nikki, honey." Mom handed me a stack of napkins, which I folded and stuck onto plates. "No murder-talk tonight."

"Sorry, Mom, but I just want to know, was it a real wolf or a shifter?"

Nate rubbed his temple and expelled a weary sigh. "We don't know yet." Dark circles smudged the skin beneath his eyes. "But don't worry." He shot me a reassuring smile. "I have the best trackers on the case."

If he had the best trackers on the case, then why was my brother Nolan making cherry pie instead of prowling the woods? "I think I know who it is."

My brother's grip on the wine bottle turned white-knuckled.

"What?" Mom dropped the fork she'd been laying out, and it clattered raucously against the plate. "What do you mean you know who it is? How?"

"When I was coming out of the supermarket, I bumped into . . ."

The doorbell shrilled, and I jumped. Our doorbell *never* rang. Our shifter neighbors knocked, but no one ever bothered ringing.

Mom and Nate exchanged a look.

I cocked an eyebrow. "Why did the doorbell ring? Are we expecting company?"

"We are. A very special guest." Mom smoothed her denim shirt, which, in spite of her silver-streaked brown hair, gave her the appearance of a teen. Especially, since she was tall and willowy, and her face wasn't all that lined.

I got the tall part, not the willowy one.

I trailed them out of the dining room. "So, I bumped into this shifter, and I think, that maybe he was—"

"*He?*" Nate paused in the hallway, leaving Mom to greet our guest.

I frowned for a brief moment. "Yes. *He.* Wait. Did you think it was a female wolf?"

"We don't have any leads yet." Nate picked at a hangnail on his thumb, a terrible habit he'd never been able to kick. "Go on . . ."

"Well, he said he was part of the pack, but *I've* never seen him. Plus, it felt very convenient. The murder happens this morning, and suddenly there's a new wolf in town?" The door snicked open, and Mom exclaimed an exuberant welcome. Since I had my brother's full attention, I gave him mine. I'd play good hostess in a second. First, I wanted to relate my run-in before any detail slipped my mind. "He was wearing a baseball cap. I mean who wears a hat at night, right? And he had a baby strapped to his front, but I think it was a decoy."

"Nikki," Nate said.

"I know I'm not a cop, but it was all very suspicious. I doubt there was a real baby in there."

"Nikki."

"And he was tall, like 6'2" and had dark eyes, but maybe they were dark because of the hat."

"Nicole," Nate growled.

I jumped from the intensity. "What?"

He nodded to our guest.

"Fine, I'll go say hello, but please jot everything down. Actually, how about I draw you a picture of . . .?" As I finally turned, the word *him* fossilized on my tongue.

I stared at our guest, and he stared back. My mouth parted in shock. His curled in amusement.

His fingers went to the baby carrier, and he popped out one snap, then the other, and then he lifted a kid—a real one—and handed him to my mother whose fingers wriggled like a drug addict about to get her fix.

Most shifter mothers had two, maybe three werepups. Mom had five. She wanted more, but nature decided I'd be her last.

Mom hugged the child, bouncing him a little when he started to cry. "Liam, I don't think you've met my youngest yet, Nicole."

I stood stock-still as the guy unhooked the baby carrier from around his waist and then removed his cap and hooked both by the door. Mom was on a first name basis with this guy? Who . . .? Oh. *Oh*. My hand crawled up to my mouth.

I'm 6'3". Just in case you plan on drawing me accurately.

My lashes snapped higher, scraping across my browbone.

You were talking about me, right?

Oh . . . great . . . Lycaon. Had he just spoken inside my head?

Only mates and Alphas could do that, and since he and I weren't mates—I would remember having sex with a man like him—that left . . .

"You're the new Alpha?" I'd heard he was young and good-looking, but the guy standing in our foyer took handsome to a *no shade in the middle of summer* level.

"Not so new anymore." Liam smiled, and that smile filled my blood with so much heat I was afraid I'd shift right there and then.

Or liquefy.

"Excuse my little sister, Liam." Nate stepped past me and extended his arm. Liam caught it and they shook arms. Yeah. Not hands. I guess it was more manly. "She thought you were the murderer."

"Nicole Raina Freemont, you did not think such a thing," Mom hissed, which made the little guy in her arms scrunch up his brow. She kissed his temple. "Sorry, baby. No more shouting tonight." She started humming an Adele song, and the baby's brow smoothed, and then he was blinking his big eyes.

He's real. Not a decoy.

I whipped my gaze back to Liam, whose dark eyes glittered. At my expense. I guessed I deserved it.

Mom turned to Nate. "Can you call the rest of the gang and find out where they are?"

Lifting his phone from his pocket, he stepped into the living room while she vanished into the kitchen, leaving me alone with Liam Kolane.

Liam freaking *Kolane*.

I grimaced. "I apologize for jumping to conclusions."

"No offense taken, Nicole." He walked over to me and stuck out his hand.

"Nikki. Nicole's only when I'm in trouble. And when I'm in *a lot* of trouble, the middle name and last name come out, too."

A smile beat down the harsh line of his mouth.

I slipped my hand into his and shook it. His grip was strong, his palm warm, and his fingers calloused to perfection. Yes, there was such a thing. Before I started fondling them, I snatched my hand back.

"Nikki?"

Oh crap. Had he said something while I pictured petting his fingers? "Huh? What?"

"I was enquiring after your leg."

"My . . . ? Um. You know about my leg?"

"Your family told me you were in a bad motorcycle accident."

"Are there good ones?"

"Excuse me?"

"You said *bad* accident. As opposed to a good one?"

His eyebrows writhed as though he couldn't decide how to take my remark.

Well, now I'd made things awkward. "Never mind." I stuck my hands in the back pockets of my skinny jeans. "My leg's great. Thank you."

He stared down at it, which made me shift on my black, shearling-lined boots.

"So, you have a baby boy." *Great segue, Nikki.* "How old is he?"

"Nine months."

"He's very cute." When Liam didn't respond, not that I'd asked him a question, I said, "So what brings you to BC?"

"I was planning a trip out here to check on the construction, but the crime precipitated my visit." He rubbed the side of his neck. Guilt for not having traveled to BC more often?

"The cabins are sprouting like mushrooms. The Watts are very efficient."

The two hundred or so Boulders in Boulder were all moving to the compound as soon as new houses were erected. I'd heard many weren't too pleased and had demanded *we* relocate to Boulder, but Liam had decided uprooting two hundred was easier than a thousand.

Nate strolled back out of the living room. "Sorry, Liam. The last two Freemonts are on their way. Can I get you a beer? Wine?" He gestured to the kitchen doorway.

"I'll take a beer." Liam turned and followed Nate but paused in the doorway and glanced over his shoulder.

"I'll be right in."

As soon as he vanished from sight, I tilted my head back and squeezed the bridge of my nose.

The man, my Alpha, had courteously picked up my tampon while I'd discourteously accused him of murder. As far as first impressions went, I didn't think I'd made a very good one.

Playing with the ends of my hair, I pep-talked myself into going into the kitchen and pretending I wasn't a total whack job. I mean, *usually* I was a pretty level-headed person. I didn't jump to absurd conclusions that hot guys wearing baby carriers wore them as decoys so they could assault unsuspecting women.

Pasting a smile on my lips, I strode into the kitchen. *Take two.* I could do this.

I was a grown-ass woman. Of legal beer-drinking age. I walked into the kitchen and beelined toward the fridge, trying hard to mitigate my limp. As I grabbed a bottle from the door, the nape of my neck prickled. When I turned around, I caught Liam's kid ogling me, green eyes widening when I called forth my claws to pop the cap off my beer.

Yes, this lady has tricks.

I took a swig as the front door opened and shut, and in walked the two missing Freemonts along with Adalyn. I was about to lead my bestie out of the kitchen to have a word with her about the man of the hour and ask if she'd known he was coming, when she popped a stripy pink bag that said *Victoria's Secret* on the island.

"Your b-day present finally arrived." She grinned while I just gaped in total horror.

My parents were present.

Our Alpha—who happened to be a total stranger—was present.

Niall popped another bag on the counter. "And this is from me." His shit-eating grin made my stomach bottom out. Niall lived to embarrass me. "Saleslady said it was oodles of fun." He added a saucy wink.

I rolled the beer between my palms, dying a little on the inside.

"It's your birthday?" Liam asked.

"It was last week." Adalyn pushed a sharp lock of bleached white hair behind her ear. "Nice to see you back in BC, Liam, even though the circumstances of your visit suck."

"Yeah." He took a long pull on his beer.

"Um. I'll just—take these to my room." I put my beer down and went to grab my giftbags, but instead, knocked both over and out spilled the contents —a bright red lacy bra and panty set from Adalyn, and a—

"You got our sister a sex swing?" Nate glared at Niall, who hollered with laughter. "What is wrong with you?"

"Niall," Mom said sharply, while I stuffed everything back into the bags, cheeks flaming.

"Chill, Mom. It's just a gag gift."

When I straightened, strangling my giftbags, I hissed, "Next time you get skunked, Niall, you'll be sitting on the porch alone."

Nash guffawed before coughing out, "Or swinging from Nikki's new swing."

Adalyn jabbed her elbow into his ribs while I shot him my very best glower. Must not have been all that intimidating, because his blue eyes sparkled as brilliantly as his white teeth.

"There's also some sour gummies in there." Niall gestured to his gift, grin still tucked into his cheeks.

The pleasant side effect to my level of embarrassment was that I didn't even care if Liam noticed my limp.

Adalyn trailed me out of the kitchen and up the stairs into my room. "Happy birthday?"

I tossed the bags on my bed and sank down beside them. And then, because my nerves were a little shot, instead of groaning, I cracked up so hard I tipped backward on my pink comforter. I didn't even like pink, but Mom had been so excited to have a girl that I got *all* the pink.

In between bursts of laughter, I said, "First, I accuse our Alpha of murder, and then he gets a front-row seat to one of the most embarrassing unboxings of my life. He's going to think I'm nuts."

Adalyn's grin seesawed off her lips. "Rewind. Murder? Why would you accuse Liam of murder?"

After I told her what had happened, her blue eyes, which she'd accented with her usual black wingtips, twinkled as wildly as my brother's had. Lycaon, those two were going to make sickeningly pretty babies.

She laid back and turned her head toward me. "On the upside, he'll never forget meeting you."

"Ha." I dragged my hands down my face. "Did you know he was coming?"

"Nash mentioned he might, but I didn't know it would be tonight."

"Dinner's ready!" Mom called up to us.

Sighing, I rolled up and followed Adalyn back down the stairs to the dining room where everyone was already seated. For some reason, I'd missed the travel crib in the corner, but this time I saw it, the same way I saw that there were two empty seats at the table. One between Niall and Liam. The other between the twins. Adalyn went straight toward the one between my identical brothers, which left me the chair between my currently least favorite brother and our Alpha.

As I sat, Niall grinned. "What were you two doing up there?"

"Why, setting up my new present and taking turns swinging from it." I shot him a smile tighter than the sports bra I'd donned this morning in the hopes of getting a workout in. Wishful thinking.

Liam, who'd taken a swallow of his water, coughed.

Two dimples pressed into Niall's cheeks.

"Sorry about my siblings," I told Liam, as the dishes began circulating around the table.

"Nothing to be sorry about. They're a fun bunch."

"Clearly, you don't have to live with them."

He had the graciousness to smile. "I wish I'd had siblings, but most shifters aren't blessed with as many children as your parents." He spooned some green beans onto his plate, then held the dish out for me to serve myself, and it hit me how strange this all was: my Alpha sitting in my dining room, brandishing green beans. Not that meeting in fur over squirrel carcasses would've been more normal.

"They're true mates," I explained. "Genetically endowed to sustain our kind."

"I heard." He glanced over at the crib where his son was trying to reach one of the little stuffed wolves dangling from the mobile spinning over his head.

Although I had no memory of my baby days, I somehow remembered that mobile. "What's his name?"

Liam looked back over at me. "Storm."

"First Storm I've met. It's very poetic."

"His mother wanted to call him Albert, after her father. I couldn't do that to him." His lips quirked, but there was a little sadness behind his jibe.

Even though I'd never met Liam, I knew his story. Not just the one of his ascension to pack leadership but also to fatherhood. Not all the details, obviously, just the big lines: it was unplanned, she hadn't been a wolf, and she'd died during premature labor.

What with being Beta, Nate had gone to Boulder for the funeral.

"So, all of you have names that start with an N."

"How observant you are, Mr. Kolane." I added a smile to show I was teasing.

Dad, who was sitting on Liam's left, said, "It was unplanned for the first three. But once Meg and I realized what we'd done, we decided to make it a tradition."

Niall leaned over me. "You should see the discounts they get on monogrammed shit."

"Niall, language," Mom said.

My brother rolled his eyes while Liam offered us another easy smile.

"Are you and Adalyn going to continue the tradition?" Liam asked Nash.

"Leaving that up to Ads."

Dad winked at Nash. "Smart man."

As the evening wore on, my nerves began to settle. But then, Nate got a call, and since we never answered our phones at the table, when he excused himself to take it, I knew it had to be related to the case. Unless it had to do with his fiancée, Bea, who'd been notably absent for a while now.

When I heard him say, "I'll be right in," I deduced it wasn't Bea.

Liam hadn't gotten up, but he, too, was watching Nate intently. He'd picked up his son from the crib sometime before dessert, and the little guy was now passed out against his daddy's chest.

Nate plunged a hand through his hair, making it stick up in places. He looked over at Liam and expelled a foreboding sigh.

"What happened?" I asked.

My father shook his head to prevent my brother from answering.

"Dad, we're all adults here," I said.

He looked at me, and although I knew he'd always see me as his little girl, tonight, I wanted him to see me as the adult I'd become.

"Please don't keep us in the dark."

"What Nikki said." Niall leaned back in his chair, balancing on the back legs. "Leave out the gruesome deets, but at least share the big lines."

Nate's gaze unlocked from Dad's. "The girl in the morgue is gone."

"Gone?" The piece of cherry pie Adalyn had scooped up toppled off her fork and onto her lap. "Someone kidnapped the body?"

Nolan balled up his napkin and got to his feet. "I'll get my jacket."

Nate held out his palm. "Slow down, Nolan." His eyes moved to Liam, which led me to assume our Alpha was communicating with Nate using the mind link.

"Come on, you two." I rolled a lock of hair around my fingers. "What's going on?"

Nate's lips thinned, vanishing into his cropped beard. "The victim . . . she got up and left."

"Say what now?" Nash sputtered, blue eyes going as wide as his twin's.

"So, she wasn't killed?" Adalyn asked. "That's good news, isn't it?"

Liam shifted his sleepy son to his opposite shoulder and stared at Nate, who after a moment, shook his head.

Our Alpha pushed away from the table and stood. "Call the coroner and tell him we're coming."

"A morgue's no place for a baby." Mom dabbed at her mouth with her napkin. "Leave Storm with us. He's safe here."

Our Alpha seemed all at once reluctant and relieved. "Are you sure, Meg? It's late."

"Of course, I'm sure."

After kissing his son's head, Liam deposited Storm in my mother's open arms, which woke the kid right up. "Thank you."

"Please." Dad clapped Liam's shoulder. "You just made my wife the happiest person in all of Colorado."

"You did. You really did." She nuzzled the top of Storm's head while he tried to snag her ring finger, entranced by the swirly ink of my father's vow, which she'd had tattooed the day of their mating ceremony—*You are my sun, my wind, my home.*

He wore her vow on his finger—*You are my moon, my stars, my wild.*

Some packs wore jewelry; ours inked the emblem of their mating, because so many adornments were lost while shifting.

"We shouldn't be gone for more than an hour, Mom," Nate said. "Two tops."

"Don't worry about us. Just stay safe."

"We will. Dad, Nolan, thanks for dinner. Sorry I can't help with cleanup."

"We got it," Nash and Nolan said at the very same time. While they no longer shared amniotic fluid, they seemingly still shared a brain.

I got up and began to stack plates, watching Nate and Liam out of the corner of my eye. There was something those two weren't telling us. Liam caught me watching and although he tried to smile, the tension wringing his features did zilch to tame the fine hairs rising on the back of my neck.

My wolf scratched at my skin, wanting to be let loose, and it startled me since it had been a long time since she'd made her presence known. Sure, my nails and fangs lengthened, and the hairs on my body occasionally thickened, but I hadn't fully shifted since the accident. Mostly because I feared it would damage my knee.

Considering there was nowhere to run, not with a deranged shifter on the loose, attempting a full shift tonight was out of the question. The assassin may not have managed to kill the girl, but he'd tried.

I prayed it was a rogue, because the alternative meant it was someone from our pack.

Someone on this very compound.

CHAPTER 3

I stayed up with Mom and Dad until Nate and Liam finally rolled in well after midnight. They were talking in low tones as they let themselves inside the house.

They seemed almost surprised to see that none of us were asleep. Had they really been expecting us to have retired without knowing what the hell was happening?

While Mom and Dad watched a documentary, I'd started on a new commission. I didn't usually work this late, but I'd tried concentrating on the TV and then I'd tried reading a book, but my mind wouldn't focus on either. Making art was the only thing that all at once distracted and relaxed me.

"So?" I set my tablet down on the couch.

Mom turned off the television. "Nikki, I don't think tonight—"

"I'm *never* going to sleep if I don't know what's going on."

Dad reached out and gave my wrist a gentle pat.

"Mom's right." Nate squeezed the bridge of his nose. He was either really tired or really stressed out. Probably both. "Liam will call a pack meeting and fill everyone in tomorrow morning."

"Just tell me *one* thing . . . was it a shifter or a real wolf?"

Nate sighed. "Not tonight, Pinecone."

Had he really needed to use the loathed nickname? I let it slide considering everything going on. "I'm not asking for a play-by-play. I just want to know—"

"Shifter." Liam took the carrier from beside the door and strapped it on, then reached down into the crib for his baby boy who'd slept almost the entire time he was gone. As he hooked his child in, his gaze wandered briefly over my lit tablet before returning to me. "Thank you again for keeping Storm."

"Anytime, Liam," Dad said. "Anytime. Nate, you show him to his cabin?"

My brother nodded.

"It's ready?" I'd heard from Niall, who'd taken a job at Watt Enterprises, that the drywalls and roof were up, but I didn't think it was livable yet.

"Not his definite one," Mom said. "Liam will be staying in Alex's old cabin."

I wrinkled my nose. "Hope you fumigated the place."

"Nicole," Mom chided me softly.

"What? Alex Morgan was awful."

Did he hurt you?

I jerked from Liam's silent question. Had Nate told him the story or had his encounter with the hateful son of our former Alpha made him jump to that conclusion on his own? By the time I shook my head no, I knew I'd paused too long, because a muscle feathered Liam's jaw.

The truth was, Alex had tried once. I was fourteen, and he'd cornered me in the woods when we were both in fur, and I'd never been more frightened, but Niall and Nate had arrived and headbutted him. If they hadn't come looking for me. Hadn't arrived when they had . . . I shuddered.

"It's been thoroughly cleaned, Liam," Mom said, but Liam was still watching me, so I wasn't sure if he'd heard her. "And I've set up everything you need for the baby."

He finally looked away. "I really appreciate it."

"I put some food in there, but come over for breakfast," Dad said. "We're up early, and there's always a warm meal on the table."

"And my brothers wonder why I never moved out?" I said with a wink.

Even though I adored my dad's cooking, it was sadly not the truth behind my prolonged cohabitation. They knew it. I knew it. The only person who didn't know it was Liam.

Dad wrapped an arm around my shoulder and pulled me into his hulking frame. His muscles had softened a little with age, but he was still as solid as they came. He kissed my temple. "I'm off to bed. Don't stay up too late, Pinecone."

Ugh. My family really needed to retire this nickname before anyone inquired about its humiliating origin.

"Night, Liam. Nate," Dad called over his shoulder as he retreated down the hall.

For a time, when I wasn't confined to clinics or hospitals, my parents' bedroom had become mine since it was the only one on the ground floor. I'd only recently moved back into my room upstairs.

My mother didn't go after my father. Probably worried the moment her door was closed, I'd hound my brother and Alpha for more details. She was right to worry.

As they made their way out of our home, Mom said, "And, Liam, I was serious about my offer to babysit while you're here."

Liam fit his cap back onto his head, and I realized it was probably a way to disguise his identity. I was guessing he hadn't made his presence among us known to the rest of the pack yet. "I'm afraid I might have to take you up on your generosity."

My already raw nerves jangled some more at his acceptance. Clearly, this wasn't an open-and-shut case.

"Anytime." Mom's hand snaked around my arm, which had stiffened along my side, as though my bones had fused with the joint. After the front door clicked shut, she whispered, "Nikki, get yourself to bed. Everything will be okay."

I rounded on Mom. "There's something they're not telling us."

"I'm sure it's nothing."

Ha! She'd felt it too!

"A girl was attacked by a shifter. She's pronounced dead and then walks out of the morgue?" My skin prickled, my wolf pacing beneath. "Unless zombies are real, then I—" I slapped my hand over my mouth. "You think she's a zombie?"

"I don't think she's a zombie. Now put that overactive imagination of yours to rest and go to bed."

I stared at the front door. I wasn't actually planning on going back out, but Mom must've presumed I was, because she guided me to the stairs, then stayed put until I'd climbed every last one of them. After I shut my door, I walked over to my window and scrutinized the hedge of leafless aspens abutting the tall, moonlit fence.

Safe.

I was safe.

Then why didn't I feel safe?

CHAPTER 4

D ressed in workout clothes again, hopeful I'd get my butt to the compound gym today, I downed my second mug of coffee and plated a waffle from the stack my father had just taken off the griddle. I scarfed down the golden rectangle of dough, then reached out for another when Liam's voice broadcasted inside my head, making my wired mind buzz even louder.

Good morning, Boulders. Some of you might've gotten wind of my arrival last night. You've probably also guessed the reason for my trip. Although it isn't the sole reason I've come, its urgency will be taking precedence over everything else until the matter of the wolf attack is resolved. Meet me by the pond in one hour so that my Beta and I can debrief everyone at once. Attendance isn't optional.

I checked the clock on my phone screen—nine o'clock. Ten seemed like in forever from now. As I took a seat at the island, the front door opened, and three of my brothers trickled in. Nate was probably already with Liam. Unless he was driving back from Bea's where he spent most of his nights. They'd talked about moving onto the compound, but his fiancée worried about being one of the only humans around.

When my brother told her what he was—what *we* were—after he'd gotten engaged and was certain this was the woman he wanted to spend his life with, she became so skittish that she refused to come over to our house for weeks. This caused a rift between Nate and Bea, because family was everything for us

Freemonts. Mom, forever the diplomat, had finally bridged the widening chasm by heading over to Bea's and sitting her down. I wasn't sure what exactly had been said, but that night, Bea returned to our house for dinner, her fear replaced by something new—curiosity.

"Nikki, can you pass the maple syrup?" Niall rubbed his eyes.

He wasn't a morning person and usually grumpy to no end. Obviously, this had led the rest of us to devise some mighty creative ways of waking him over the years, which had run the gamut of howling into his eardrums to leaping onto him in fur to good-old foghorns and buckets of icy water.

Because I was jacked up on adrenaline and caffeine, I inadvertently knocked over the bottle, which toppled and spilled. The sticky amber syrup trickled over the wood and down onto Niall's lap. He pushed away from the island so fast he managed to tip himself over, causing a great clatter.

Dad jerked away from the sink, the griddle clattering against the metal basin, at the same time as Mom burst into the kitchen. Both hurried toward Niall, who'd already sat up. Groaning, he rubbed the back of his head, mussing his already unruly brown hair.

Nolan peered over the island's edge. "You okay?"

"Dude, it was maple syrup, not molten silver," Nash said, between puffs of laughter, which of course, got Nolan and me going.

Dad smiled as he grabbed the chair and righted it. Mom, though, neither smiled nor laughed. Even though it took a hell of a lot more to hurt a wolf—like a flaming motorcycle—whenever one of her babies got harmed, she worried. She helped him up to his feet, then went to grab an icepack from the freezer.

Niall's eyes flashed, wide awake now. "Laugh away." He balled his napkin and dunked it inside his glass of water, then rubbed at the stain on his gray sweatpants.

As he pressed the icepack to the back of his skull, he grabbed the bottle of syrup and doused his waffles, sucked the sticky remnants from his fingertips and carved up his breakfast.

"Did they tell you what the coroner said?" Nolan asked. "I tried calling Nate last night, but he didn't answer."

"No." I felt stone-cold sober again. "They just confirmed the wolf was a shifter."

"From our pack?"

"They didn't say."

As my brothers debated among themselves if the shifter was indeed from our pack, I helped clear the island and slot plates into the dishwasher.

I thought the hour would drag, but soon, Mom was clapping and hollering, "Time to go."

I grabbed a hoodie and dragged it over my gray tank top, then added my winter jacket. Although my shifter blood made my body run warmer than a human's, winter was still freaking cold up in Beaver Creek.

Instead of using cars or the main road, we crunched straight through the ankle-deep snow, winding around the timbered dwellings dotting the hill. Ten minutes later, we'd joined the lycanthropic congregation.

The massive piece of land, upon which had been built the compound, had belonged to Aidan Michaels, Cassandra Morgan's cousin. A man almost as hateful as Cassandra's son, Alex, had been. The only one in that family I tolerated was Cassandra's eldest and only surviving relative, Lori. We weren't friends, or even friendly, and not because she was closer in age to Nate than to me, but because she had little personality. Back when her mother had been alive, Lori had existed in her shadow. In her worthless brother's, too. After the duel, Lori had returned an outcast who flitted around her mother's giant log cabin like a wraith.

At some point, there'd even been rumors that she was dead. Nate, who was in charge of the shifters in our district, quickly put those rumors to rest. He also fined the younger shifters who egged her windows or urinated around her house.

I scanned the faces surrounding the pond for Lori's narrow one. Would she come out today or open her windows to listen from the privacy of her house? Since noise carried up, and her house was perched on the hill like ours, she'd probably hear Liam's speech just as clearly from there.

Sure enough, a figure as slender as a cypress and as pale as fresh snow stood between the glistening panes of an opened window.

Adalyn, who'd met up with my family during our downhill trek, guided us toward one of the large rocks we used as a diving board in the summer since it jutted over the deepest part of the pond. Adalyn's sixteen-year-old sister Gracey and their grandmother had found spots on it, along with a few others. Most elders had brought foldable chairs. The younger ones had plopped down on the thick snow blanketing the chalk-like stone that gave the creek the limpidity of a swimming pool.

However profoundly I loathed the man who'd purchased the land, I was the first to admit it was breathtaking. After his demise and then Cassandra's, Lori had inherited the parcel. Her ticket to stay alive had been to sign it over to her new Alpha.

I wasn't overly interested in real estate, but one of Liam's first acts as

Alpha had been to create a trust in which he'd placed all pack properties, made his two Betas trustees and every Boulder shifter a beneficiary, so that the acreage belonged to every wolf. That first deed had eased the anger of his detractors and the worry of those who'd found him undeserving of leadership.

His second act was to create a schooling fund, so that those who wanted to pursue studies off the compound could attend colleges of their choice without taking out student loans.

Across the bow-shaped liquid expanse, the door of Alex's former cabin slid open. The noise level died instantly, and all eyes turned in the direction of Liam and Nate. Where our Alpha had forgone his baseball cap, my brother wore one that cast his face in full shadow. Nate leaned against the cabin's wall and crossed his arms, straining his brown leather jacket.

Unlike my brother, Liam moved across the deck toward the wooden guardrail and wrapped his fingers around the railing. His hair crested around his tanned face in dark waves.

Adalyn bumped me with her shoulder and whispered, "Don't forget to breathe, babe."

"Haha."

She grinned.

My youngest brother's philosophy was to date down. Not that Niall had ever had a lasting relationship, so he wasn't some guru on the topic, but as I took in the perfect cut of Liam's physique, it did strike me that lusting after him was as futile as trying to catch flies with a butterfly net.

"Where's his son?" Adalyn squinted, but the pond, although not immense, was wide enough that we couldn't see into the cabin.

"Maybe napping?"

"Good morning, Boulders!" Liam's voice boomed through the valley, ricocheting against the watery surface and across every rock and patch of snow. "I'm glad to be back in Beaver Creek despite the circumstances of my visit."

His gaze glided across the thousand faces staring back at him, settling briefly on our rock. I wasn't delusional enough to believe he'd paused on it because of me, but it didn't prevent my wolf from murring. Thankfully, the sound didn't escape my lips.

"Yesterday, a hiker was attacked in the woods a few miles away from the compound. The police blame the crime on a wild creature, but gasoline was splashed all over the area. Animals don't cover their tracks. Humans do."

His gaze cycled around the crowd, as though looking for the culprit, which sent my heartrate into a tailspin.

"And then last night, the coroner informed Nate that the victim got up and walked out of the morgue. The police believe she was mistakenly declared dead, and we want them to keep thinking this way, but the coroner swears she had no pulse. About two hours ago, a snowshoeing couple notified the police there was a wild, naked girl fitting our risen victim's description wandering the forest."

Liam paused, and even across the watery expanse separating us, I noticed his chest puff with a deep inhale. My brother, on the other hand, was as motionless as the tawny wooden slabs at his back.

"The couple reported that the girl bared inhuman-looking fangs and sported patches of fur across her body, and no . . . not body hair . . . fur. Which leads us to believe we are dealing with a halfwolf."

Goosebumps lifted on my forearms.

"We're looking into which pack she might descend from. Once this is established, we'll be better able to understand the crime that was perpetrated on Boulder land. On *your* land." Liam paced the length of his deck like a wolf prowling a mountainous ledge. "Until we apprehend this girl and the rogue who attacked her, I urge those of you with no off-compound businesses or schools to stay put. Our best trackers will be canvasing the mountain. Hopefully, by tonight, we'll have apprehended both the halfwolf and her attacker, and you'll be able to go about your lives as usual."

"My sister and I would like to join the search party!" The voice belonged to my ex, Grant.

Liam stopped pacing his short deck and wrapped his fingers around the railing again. "I appreciate your eagerness to help and will gladly review your candidacy to join the hunt. Anyone over eighteen, come around to the cabin, and we can discuss to what effect you can be of service."

Chatter arose. So much chatter that Liam delivered his next and final words straight through the mind link.

*Boulders, whatever you do, do **not** panic. The shifter will be caught and the halfwolf will be found. Now, enjoy your day, but again, please remain calm and within the compound.*

"What if the culprit is one of us?" someone yelled.

"Then that person will be brought to justice, but don't go accusing one another!" Liam boomed.

I frowned, confused as to why he was insisting on this so vociferously, but a quick look around the crowd cleared that up. Many heads had swiveled toward Lori's house.

Poor Lori.

"The halfwolf isn't from our pack, which leads us to believe the attacker isn't either." Liam lifted his hands from the railing, then pivoted and retreated into the cabin, my brother on his heels.

"I'm going to go get Storm," I heard my mother tell my father, before turning and pushing through the loose fabric of bodies.

Nash started to go after her, but Adalyn reached out and snagged the hem of his jeans. "Babe, where are you going?"

"I'm not sitting back on my haunches all day." Adalyn's sharp intake of breath had him crouching. "I'll be safe. I'll just stick by Nolan."

"Nolan's a tracker."

A shadow fell across Nash's face. He hated that his sense of smell wasn't as keen as his twin's and abhorred to be reminded of it even more. He straightened. "I'm not useless, Ads."

She jumped to her feet and caught his hand. "That's *not* what I was implying."

"Uh-huh."

I felt the stirrings of a fight and got up. Since those two did plenty of making up, I wasn't worried. Besides, they were true mates *and* had consummated the bond, so there was no splitting up in their future.

I dusted the snow off my black leggings, searching the crowd for my family. Dad was heading toward his two best friends on the other side of the pond, and Niall was jogging toward Liam's cabin, without a doubt to volunteer his services. His sense of smell paled in comparison to Nolan's, but he was an incredibly fast runner.

I bit my lip, wanting to help, but I wasn't even sure if I could shift yet. I'd probably be more hindrance than asset. Still, I wanted to do *something*. I skirted the rocky bed, trying to catch up with my family. By the time I made it to the other shore, a long line of volunteers had formed. I didn't stand at the back. Instead, I walked right up to the front. Because my brother was Beta, our family had some privileges, and one of them was having a speedier access to the Alpha.

"Hey, Nik."

I stopped at the sound of my ex's voice. Grant Hollis stood with his older sister, Camilla, at the very front of the line, blond hair cropped so close to his scalp he almost looked bald. When we'd dated, it had hit his shoulders.

"You're not going out there, right?" His gaze dropped to my leg, and I bristled.

I was about to tell him I wasn't an invalid when Mom stepped out of the house, baby carrier and Storm strapped around her middle.

"Come." She took my arm, but I dug in my boots and peered inside the cabin.

Liam stood beside Nate and Avery, the tawny-haired male he'd almost made his Beta after the duel. The only reason my brother won out was because Avery was about to be a daddy and had informed Liam he wouldn't be able to give the job his full attention.

Since Liam was looking in our direction, I called out, "I want to help."

"Good. Because I need your help." Mom tried to steer me away.

"I meant with the search."

"You can shift again?" Grant asked.

His sister gave my leg a once-over, grimacing as though I was a sorry excuse for a shifter. The two of us had never clicked, not even when I'd dated her younger brother. Could've been because of her complete lack of empathy and kindness.

"Yes." I held out my hand and forced my claws out.

"I meant, a full shift," he added.

"Yes," I lied.

"Nikki, let's go," Mom hissed.

This time, when she tugged on my elbow, I moved my feet.

"I wanted to *really* help," I grumbled.

"You don't think that keeping a child safe is *really* helping? If our Alpha isn't worried, he'll be able to better focus on the hunt."

"Storm has you. He doesn't need me. Plus, I don't know the first thing about babies."

"About time you learn."

"About time? I just turned nineteen. Kids aren't in my near future."

"But your brothers are going to have babies someday soon, and family helps each other out."

I looked over at Storm, whose pudgy hands were pressed against my mother's chest and whose short neck was cranked as far back as the kid could manage in the carrier. Babysitting was so not how I'd envisioned spending my day.

I pursed my lips. "I know what you're doing."

"What I'm doing?"

"Ever since the accident, you've been coddling me. My leg's fine."

"Your leg's better, but it's not fine yet." Mom's pitch had gone up, startling the little guy strapped to her. She patted one of his little hands.

"What if this is as good as it gets?"

"I don't believe that for a second. Darren said we'd have to amputate it, and it healed. Then he said you might never regain use of it, but you have. So I know it'll get better, but straining it won't help. If anything, it might make it worse."

Mom rarely raised her voice, which wasn't to say she couldn't speak passionately about things. I'd learned young that words delivered placidly could make just as much of an impact as yelled ones.

"Besides, two of my sons will already be out there. Knowing the other two, they'll convince Nate to let them be of assistance on the field. Can I at least keep one child safe?" It was the fine lines bracketing the outer edges of her chocolate eyes, that palpable maternal worry of hers, that ended up placating me.

I sighed a, "Fine," then arm in arm, we climbed the snow-covered hill to the house.

After we'd stepped into the house and I'd shrugged out of my coat, Mom hoisted Storm out of the carrier. "Can you hold him a sec while I undo this contraption?"

"Um." I stared at Storm, who gaped right back. I'd never held a baby before. Babies were breakable. I especially didn't want to break this one.

"Nikki?"

I reached out and snagged him under his armpits, dangling him in midair.

"Sweetheart, he's not a pair of dirty boxers. Hold him against you."

I held him closer.

"Sit him down on your hip and keep one hand on his rump, the other on the back of his head."

"I'm scared of dropping him."

"You're not going to drop him." Mom repositioned my hold until the kid was safely perched on my hipbone.

He was way heavier than he looked.

Mom unfastened the carrier and turned to hang it, then instead of relieving me of my charge, she disappeared into the kitchen.

"You forgot Storm."

"I didn't forget him. I'm going to make him some milk."

"What am I supposed to do with him?"

"Just keep him entertained."

"How?"

"Tell him a story." Mom's voice drifted from the kitchen. "You've got a great imagination."

I peered down at Storm. Found him observing me with a disquieting intensity that puckered his forehead and made his eyebrows almost kiss. I racked my brain for an age-appropriate story. Maybe one about dragons. Or wolves. He surely liked wolves.

He reached out and seized one of my hoodie's drawstrings, his attention dropping to the gray cord.

"Yeah, it's probably a good idea to hold on, buddy. I have no clue what I'm doing."

He cracked a tentative smile. I counted eight teeth.

"You're quite a looker, aren't you?"

One side of his mouth tugged up a little higher as though he were tossing me a saucy wink.

I laughed, which made his green eyes brighten. "You're going to be a heart-breaker. I can already tell." In the back of my mind, I thought, *just like your daddy*, although I had no clue if Liam was a heartbreaker. All I knew was that he'd gotten *his* heart broken the day Storm's mother passed.

To think Storm would never know his mom. Gosh, that was sad. I couldn't imagine a world without my mother. As though sensing the tragic turn of my thoughts, Storm's own smile vanished, and he was back to being Mr. Serious.

"When I was younger, my favorite story was Robin Wolf. Want to hear it?"

His little mouth stayed locked shut.

"Right. You can't talk yet."

He didn't make a peep as my lips shaped the shifter-revised version of Robin Hood. His eyes went wider at all the key moments, which made me think he understood what I was telling him. Even if he didn't though, he was a way better audience than all of my brothers combined.

"You tell that story so well." Mom was leaning against the doorframe, milk bottle in hand.

The moment Storm spotted his meal—or maybe he'd scented it—he started squirming.

Mom walked toward us, but instead of taking him from me, she handed me the bottle. I was so surprised that I held it out of the kid's reach, which made him start sobbing. Full-on tears and all. I plopped the silicone teat inside his mouth, which made him startle, and I worried I'd choked him, but then he gripped it with both palms and gulped the contents down like a starved man.

"Feeling better, little man?"

"You should sit down with him."

I realized I was still standing in the foyer. So much for women being able to multitask.

I went to sit on the couch. "Why am I still holding him?"

"Because it wouldn't be very nice to stick him on the floor now, would it?"

"I meant, why aren't *you* holding him?"

"Because I have a kitchen to clean up and laundry to do." She slapped a dishtowel over her shoulder. "If you'd prefer switching tasks—"

"No. That's fine." She started to turn when I sputtered, "But what do I do now? Does he need to be burped?"

"Not at nine months. Once he's done drinking, he'll probably go down for a nap."

And he did. He passed out still latched onto the bottle. I went over to the crib to put him down but the moment I laid him inside, his lids sprang open in time with his mouth, so I scooped him up and held him until his lids slammed home.

Instead of placing him back in the crib, I toed off my boots and sprawled onto the couch, then kicked my legs up and let Liam's baby sleep-drool over my chest while I dozed off myself.

CHAPTER 5

Napping together must've created a bond between Storm and me, because after he woke up, he threw me a whole collection of smiles. Mom brought up cases of our old toys, which she'd kept in pristine condition, and although she sat down and played with him, she kept needing to go do something or other, making me the primary caretaker.

Mom was the sort of person who put aside everything and was a hundred percent present when someone needed her, which led me to believe her comings and goings were orchestrated. My guess: entrapment by baby. If I was stuck babysitting, I couldn't creep off the compound. My mother was smart like that. Some may even call her devious.

"Okay." I was on all fours beside Storm, poised for our crawling race. "When I say go—"

Storm burst out laughing.

I grinned. "You think it's funny now. Wait till I leave you in my dust. So, as I was saying, Storm, when I say GO."

He burst out laughing again.

Ha. It was the word that set him off. "You really like the word *go*." I emphasized it on purpose.

He laughed so hard he actually tipped over onto the rug.

"Whoa there, little man. You all right?" After I ensured he was okay, I chuckled.

He grew very serious.

"*Go.*"

He cracked up, legs and arms wriggling like he was doing the backstroke.

"You're really something, aren't you?"

Serious face.

"*Go.*"

The laughter that burst out of him was mesmerizing. No wonder Mom had never wanted to stop making babies.

"We're never going to get to that ball if you don't stop cracking up when I say the word."

"Talking about this ball?" Liam's voice made me look up so fast my neck cracked. He was crouched and tossing the red plastic ball from hand to hand.

As I sat back on my heels, Storm flipped over and crawled at lightning speed, dormant wolf genes already strong. He gripped his father's thigh and tugged himself upright, repeating a litany of, "Dadadadada."

Liam swung him into his arms and stood. "Missed you too, kiddo."

I pushed myself back up, rubbing my palms over my leggings. "Hey."

"Hi." Liam smiled at me, the calm, serious smile of a man who'd endured and hardened. I wondered if before his ex's death, before the duel, he'd slung around carefree, wolfish grins like my brothers.

"Hi." Wait. Hadn't I already greeted him? Crap. Heat crept up my neck as I grimaced. "I said that already, didn't I?"

His smile grew a little more intense. "You can say it again if you want. I can't guarantee you'll get as many giggles from me as you got from this one at the word *go*."

Storm palmed his father's scruff to get his full attention.

I smiled, still a little embarrassed. "He does seem taken by that word."

"Apparently, only when you say it." He splayed his hand on Storm's back, his fingers so long and strong. Solid. The sort of hands that kept you safe. "Looks like you and Storm had one heck of a playdate." Liam nodded to the explosion of toys.

"Oh, that we did." And now I was going to have one hell of a cleanup. I kneeled and began tossing toys inside boxes.

Still holding onto his son, Liam leaned over and helped me gather the plastic balls that had escaped the inflatable donut I'd converted into a ball pit.

"I've never taken care of a child, which you probably don't want to hear considering I spent the entire day with your son." I shot Liam a sheepish look. "So I have no point of reference, but Storm is really sweet. And funny. And enthusiastic. Okay, now I sound like a crazy person. I swear I'm not crazy.

OLIVIA WILDENSTEIN

Well, not *too* crazy." In truth, we all had a little wild in us. It was the nature of being part wolf.

Liam's brows dipped, and a slender groove appeared between them. When Storm was thinking, he made the same face, which led me to assume Liam was contemplating how much risk there'd been in entrusting his son to us Freemonts.

Biting the inside of my cheek so I wouldn't spout more nonsense, I shut a picture book and slotted it back into the book box.

"I know you wanted to go out today," he finally said.

Okay, so maybe he hadn't been pondering my mental health. "Did you catch them?"

"We got the halfwolf." He stabbed a hand through his hair, dislodged some bramble, probably from his time spent in fur. "We didn't find the rogue."

His gaze moved to the window, where the sun was spilling orange and pink light over the horizon. And all I could think of was: when did that happen? Last time I'd looked at the time, it was two.

"Thought I heard you, Liam." Mom stepped out from the basement carrying a basket filled with a teetering pile of folded clothes. "Is everyone home safely?" By everyone, she mostly meant my brothers.

"Yes. They said to expect them for dinner. Except Nate."

"Because he's with the halfwolf?" I asked.

Mom's eyebrows knitted. "You caught the halfwolf?"

"We did. Thanks to Nolan."

Mom set down the laundry basket. "And? Did she . . .? Was she . . .?"

"Is she alive?" I didn't think this was what Mom was getting at, but it seemed the more important issue. I mean, I was sure my brother was okay, or Liam would've led with that.

"She's alive."

My heart drummed a little harder. We'd have answers soon. Or maybe they already had answers. "Did you find out *why* she was attacked? Did she know the wolf who attacked her?"

"She's still stuck in that in-between stage of shifting, so she can't talk. We've pumped her full of Sillin, so she should be in skin soon."

The mention of Sillin made me grimace. I shoved the memory of those endless months on bedrest away. "Where are you keeping her?"

He nodded in the direction of the bunker, a concrete building a few miles away from the compound that was half-buried beneath a mountain. Although it boasted shelves full of unperishable items, Cassandra had transformed a part of it into a shifter penitentiary with four silver jail cells. She'd locked Niall up

34

once for having disrespected one of her many inane rules, which had made my parents go ballistic and cemented their loathing for her.

"Don't even think about it, Nikki," Mom murmured.

I whipped my gaze toward her. "I wasn't going to go out there." At least, not in the middle of the night, with the halfwolf's aggressor still on the loose. "Unless you guys want help interrogating the captive? I'm good at making people talk."

"Nikki . . ." There was a slight growl to Mom's voice.

"No one's exiting the compound tonight, Meg." Liam dipped his chin a little, staring at me over the head of his son, whose lids had fallen shut, long lashes fanning his pale cheeks. "Right, Nikki?"

I resented to be ganged up on. "Geez, I'm curious not reckless. Anyway, I have work to do." I grabbed the scattered plush toys and jammed them into their box, then smacked the lid on.

"Do you want to stay for dinner?" my mother asked Liam as I unearthed my tablet from underneath one of Dad's *Bon Appétit* magazines. "It should be ready in thirty."

"That's very kind, but I think Storm and I will head back and call it a night."

"Wait here one second then." She bustled into the kitchen. Drawers rolled.

"If you can't come to the dinner table, the dinner table comes to you," I muttered.

Did I say something wrong?

I pressed my lips together, debating whether to speak my piece or just drop it.

People can't change if they don't know what to change.

I hugged my tablet to my chest. "When I say I'm not going to do something, I'm not going to do it. The same way when I say I'll get something done, I get it done."

Fair enough. I won't question your intentions again.

"I appreciate that."

He rubbed his cheek against the top of his son's head, marking him. Dad and Mom would mark us every night when we were kids. "Once she's in skin, I'll let you know, and we can go out there together."

That thawed out my annoyance. "I swear I'm a good interrogator. Just ask my brothers. I could get them to confess to all the naughty things they did."

A corner of his mouth lifted. "You do seem to have them all wrapped around your little finger."

"One of the perks of being the baby in the family." I smiled, and then, on my way toward the stairs, I stopped by Liam to run my knuckle over Storm's velvety cheek. "Sleep tight, little man."

Caressing Storm hadn't been a ploy to get closer to Liam, but now that I was near, I couldn't help but breathe in the loamy aroma of earth and wind that clung to the male. And it did something to me . . . to my wolf. It made her want to come out and run wild. Tomorrow . . . tomorrow I'd try to shift, even if it was to loop around the compound.

I stepped back. "Goodnight, Liam."

"Night, Nikki."

Where his scent had acted on my wolf, his raspy timbre acted on my human. Goosebumps dusted my skin, increased the tempo of my heart, and altered my scent. He didn't have to be a tracker to pick up on that last one, but he'd have to be finetuned to the way I smelled normally. Since we hadn't spent much time together, he'd hopefully miss the subtle shift.

Distancing myself to dilute my attraction made me forget about Liam spotting my uneven gait. I hated that I cared so deeply about how it made me look. I thought of Ness, of the scar down her face and her sightless eye. I'd met her only twice, during her visits to the construction site with her mate, but what an inspiration she'd been. How I wished I possessed an ounce of her confidence. Especially since, unlike her, my scar was someplace I could conceal.

I sank onto my bed, my fingers tracing the skewed patch that ran down the side of my leg like a seam fashioned from melted wax. On my tablet, I could remove flaws at a press of a stylus. What I wouldn't give to be able to smooth out my scar, blend it back into my skin.

You could've been down a leg, Nikki.

I waited for this reminder to penetrate, to erase my lasting superficiality, but it just sat there like moss atop a rock, like my ruined skin over my muscle and bone.

CHAPTER 6

At the crack of dawn, I pulled on a pair of track pants, then barefoot, tiptoed down our creaky steps.

"Nikki?" Dad's voice drifted from the kitchen.

I stepped into the doorway.

He was at the stove, stirring something in a deep saucepan. "Should be ready soon."

The salt of bacon, starch of beans, and tang of tomato had my stomach grumbling. "Can't wait."

"Where are you going?"

"For a run."

He set down the wooden spoon. "Not outside the compound, right?"

"Promise."

Dad's gaze dipped to my leg, then to my bare feet. "In fur?"

"I'm going to try."

"Are you certain your body's ready to go through the change?"

"I'm about to find out. Do you mind if I shift indoors?"

"Go ahead. I'll get the door."

"Thanks, Dad." Pulling my tank top off, I retreated into the foyer. I tossed it on the console by the door, then hooked my thumbs into the waistband of my pants just as the front door opened.

I froze. A gust of frigid air smacked into me, pebbling my skin and peaking my nipples. I hooked an arm over my breasts and plucked my tank top from

37

the table, smooshing the fabric against my chest as the word *shit* raced on a loop through my mind. I didn't mind nudity as long as I wasn't the only one in the nude.

I pasted on a bright smile, even though I was dying a little inside. "You guys are up early."

Storm, who was facing out in the baby carrier, wiggled excitedly and made lots of happy sounds.

Liam cleared his throat. "Someone's excited to see you."

"Morning, Liam." My father draped an arm around my shoulders. "Breakfast's almost ready."

A door clapped behind us.

"Morning!" As Mom breezed past me, she took in my state of undress. "Maybe, next time, put on your shirt before opening the front door."

"Mom," I hissed.

"Nikki was going to try shifting," Dad explained good-naturedly

"I imagined as much, Jon." She held out her arms, and Liam unclipped his son, then handed him over. "Hello, sweet boy." As she nuzzled his head, she said, "No running outside the compound."

"I know. I know. Anyway, I may not even be able to shift."

Mom exchanged a look with Dad. "If you *are* able, you keep it short, deal?"

"Deal." I sidestepped Liam, or attempted to. We ended up stepping in the same direction twice. "Don't move this time, okay?"

His Adam's apple bobbed, and he nodded.

I slunk around his motionless body. Before heading around the house, I asked, "Hey, Liam, are you going to the bunker now?"

He shook his head. ***I'll be here when you come back.***

Content I wasn't missing out on anything, I rounded the house, the snow icing my bare feet. I ducked behind a thick rhododendron bush, stripped, and then fell onto all fours.

Please, please, please work.

For a long while, nothing happened. I tugged and tugged on the invisible cord that linked me to my other self until she stirred beneath the surface. I gave a hard yank and welcomed her out.

My bones popped, my sinews shortened, my features restructured. Thick brown and white fur poured from my pores, everywhere but on my waxy scar, which was proportionally smaller in this form. Once the change had rolled through me, I stretched and let out a low yowl of joy.

Smells, sounds, colors . . . they all intensified, heightening my already frenzied pulse. I took off at a leisurely trot toward the dense copse of naked aspens lining the fence, then increased my speed until the metal rods, slender white trunks, and snow-covered ground smeared together. The bone in my hind leg clanged, but still, I pushed myself. I'd never recover if I slowed each time the going got tough.

My breaths puffed out in milky clouds that moistened my long muzzle and dampened my fur. I inhaled lungfuls of the delicious air, exhaled ragged breaths that helped mitigate the ache growing around my stiff joint. When I reached the barren orchard, I slowed. I told myself it was to absorb the smells and check out the construction progress of the new residences burgeoning on the nearby hill, but deep down, it was because the throbbing had become too insistent.

I picked up the scent of a squirrel and trailed it to a blue spruce on the outskirts of the orchard. I circled the bristly base, craning my neck, but then remembered a warm breakfast awaited me on the stove and left the rodent to live another day. Halfway around the compound, I ran into three other wolves, one of whom was Grant. The other two were his best friends, Jared and Cane.

Grant's grass-green eyes dropped to my leg, which trembled. Damn. I slammed my paw down, and the bolt of pain that streaked through my leg almost made me whimper.

You can shift again, he commented.

Were you hoping I'd lost the ability?

Don't be like that.

I inched past him, keeping my gaze affixed to the massive log cabin which used to belong to Alaric Weathers, our Aspen Alpha, and now belonged to his brother and his children.

Shift, and I'll carry you back.

The hell I was letting my ex play hero. *You'll drop me midway and leave, so, no thanks.* I swung around and cut across the compound, taking the quickest and shortest path back home.

Even though my leg trembled, I forced my paw to graze the ground each and every time. Grant could've caught up but had enough sense not to give chase. By the time I reached the bush behind my house, I'd broken out into so much of a sweat that the idea of putting on my clothes was revolting, but I wasn't walking into my house butt naked with Liam in attendance, so I chucked them on, the fabric clinging to my slick skin. One hand pressed against the smooth logs of the outside wall, I walked to the front door and let myself in, stumbling like a drunk. I smacked into Nate, who was hanging up his leather jacket on the peg by the door.

"Nikki," he gasped. "What happened?"

I straightened, shrugging his hands off. "Nothing."

His brown eyes, which were as amber as mine were gray, took in my wind-blown locks and reddened feet. "You shifted?"

Gritting my teeth, I limped toward the stairs. "I did."

"I'll get you an icepack."

"I don't need one. I'm fine."

Nate walked up to me. "You're *not* fine."

I gripped the handrail and forced one foot in front of the other before the heat pooling behind my lids could trickle out and reveal my pain. Once I reached my bathroom, I locked the door and staggered toward the bathtub, turned on the water, then knocked back a double dose of extra-strength painkillers—our metabolism chewed through human medicine quickly—and peeled off my clothes.

Even though the icy water felt like a bed of needles, I breathed through the prickling and massaged my leg until the muscles stopped spasming, and then I stood up and showered under hot water. A half hour later, as I slid on a white thermal top and skinny jeans, the pain had faded to a dull echo. I rolled my shampooed locks into a bun and secured them with a hair tie before heading back downstairs.

"You pushed yourself too hard, didn't you?" Mom was standing in the foyer with Storm on her hip and a musical toy in her hand.

I palmed Storm's silky curls as I passed by them. "Nothing a cold bath couldn't fix."

Storm extended his arms toward me. I let him latch on to my finger and placed a kiss on his knuckles.

"I swear I'm okay." I kissed my mother's cheek.

She let it go. For now.

"I'm dying for breakfast." I glided my finger out of Storm's, whose bottom lip overtook his upper one.

Mom clucked her tongue and tapped his button nose. "How about you and I go read a book, baby?"

As she whisked him into the living room, I padded into the kitchen. I went straight for the drip coffee maker and poured myself a mug, then leaned against the counter and took a glorious sip. Nate and Liam were sitting at the island. Although they'd stopped talking when I'd walked in, tension simmered around them.

"What's with the mood? Did something happen to the halfwolf?" I ended up asking since both were alarmingly quiet.

"I got your icepack." Nate nodded to the dishtowel-wrapped cold pack he'd left on the island.

I pressed my lips together before muttering a, "Thank you." I really hoped their silence wasn't because of me. I set down my coffee to grab a bowl and ladle in some refried beans. I plopped a spoon inside, then climbed onto a chair and shoved the icepack against the side of my leg. "Has she shifted back yet?"

Nate stretched his neck from side to side, eliciting a series of little pops. "Not yet. Doc's administering a higher dose of Sillin. He'll call us the moment she's back in skin."

I poured myself a glass of water. "And the attacker?"

Nate stared out the window over the sink, at the pond shimmering like foil in the heart of the valley. "Trackers are following a few different leads, but there are a lot of scents and treads in the area. I fear we won't make much headway until the halfwolf can talk."

"How likely is it that the attack came from the pack?"

Liam put down his own coffee. "We're still leaning toward a rogue but not excluding Boulders."

A knock at the door had my gaze wandering toward the foyer. Frowning, Nate got down from his chair to see who was there.

"Probably should've done that this morning," Liam said, tipping his head to the front door.

"It could've been worse."

His eyebrows gathered.

"You could've walked in thirty seconds later and gotten a full frontal."

He didn't smile, my flavor of self-deprecating humor apparently not his thing, but then I noticed his attention traveling over my shoulder, and I glanced behind me. No one was darkening the doorway.

"She's fine," I heard Nate say.

Had someone spotted my disgraceful excursion through the compound?

"Can I see her at least?"

My good mood wilted at the sound of Grant's voice.

"She's resting," Nate said. "How about you give her a call later? If she wants to talk to you, she'll pick up."

When the door clicked shut, and Nate returned, Grant-free, I mouthed, *Thank you.*

The day Grant broke up with me in my hospital room, he became persona non grata at the Freemonts. Even Niall, who used to be close with him, distanced himself.

Nate's phone rattled on the island. He picked up. Listened. "Up the dosage, then." He grabbed his car keys. "I'll be right there."

Liam watched my brother stash away his cell phone. When Nate shook his head, I assumed that a question had been answered.

I set my spoon down. "What's happening?"

"She's not shifting back," Nate said, "yet Darren says he pumped her with enough Sillin to eradicate her wolf gene."

I knew it was a figure of speech. Sillin thankfully couldn't alter our genome. "Maybe the one he used expired?"

"Maybe. I'm going to go check it out." He squeezed my shoulder as he walked past me. "See you at dinner, Pinecone."

"Or before."

He frowned. "Before?"

I shrugged. "If she shifts, Liam said I could go help with the interrogation."

Nate tossed a look Liam's way. "That's not a good idea."

"I'm an adult, Nate. One who can help."

"I know you want to help, but until we understand what we're dealing with, I'd prefer you to stay put."

I tossed my icepack onto the island. "You all think I'm so useless."

"Nikki, I don't—"

"Yes, you do. All of you do."

Nate scrubbed a hand down his face. The skin beneath his eyes was marred with such dark shadows that I almost felt bad for picking a fight with him, but I needed everyone to stop handling me with kid gloves.

"Grant offered to carry me home. Has anyone ever offered to carry *you* home, Nate? It's humiliating; I'm not an invalid for Lycaon's sake."

He sighed and then he slung one arm around my shoulders and pulled me in tight, and I let him hug me even though I didn't hug him back. "I know you're strong, but you almost died, Nik," he whispered against my wet hair. "That's not something any of us will ever forget, all right? But I promise I don't think any less of you." When he pulled away, I read the sincerity of all he'd said inside his tired eyes. "And Grant's a fucking asshole. You better not get back together with him."

"No worries there. My knee might've gotten smashed but not my pride."

Nate stared down at me a moment longer, and for all my complaining about being coddled, I was incredibly thankful for his unwavering attention.

After he left, I looked back over at Liam. "Sorry about all the Freemont drama. I'm a little sensitive about my shortcomings."

He shifted on his chair. "What shortcomings?"

I'd heard rumors he was arrogant and aloof, but that's not the way he was coming off. If I had to describe Liam Kolane, I would use the words considerate and observant.

"Don't you owe my son a race?"

I was grateful for the abrupt change of topic. "I do, don't I?"

"Putting it off because you think you may lose?"

That got a laugh out of me. "In all seriousness, I might. Storm's remarkably fast for such a tiny person."

I shoveled down the rest of my refried beans while Liam drank his coffee, then got down from my chair. The second the balls of my feet met the gray-and-white kitchen tiles, pain sparked into my bones. If he noticed, Liam didn't mention it. Didn't even glance at my leg. Just stood and followed me into the living room.

Upon seeing his father, Storm all but flung himself off Mom's lap. She helped him down and he speed-crawled toward Liam.

"So, you're not allowed to stand at the finish line, or I'll lose for sure," I said as Liam picked his son up.

Ouch. Here I assumed I'd be more motivating than an inanimate plastic ball. My Alpha's eyes flashed with amusement while mine flashed with shock.

I rubbed my collarbone. "I just meant . . ."

"I know what you meant." His quiet words ruffled his son's hair. "Storm, you know how I told you it was impolite to beat girls? Well, forget about my teachings and show Nikki how Kolanes do it, all right?" He bent over and set Storm on the ground, proceeding to give him a longer pep talk.

I snorted and shook my head, and as I did so, I caught Mom studying me. "I'm going to go see what your dad's up to." She got off the couch. "Just call me when you need to leave. And, Nikki, Freemonts *never* lose." She winked.

I smirked as I dropped onto all fours. "Oh, the pressure we're under, Storm. Ready?"

Liam backed away, smiling.

If someone had told me I'd be racing against a baby toward my Alpha, I'd have asked them what root they'd gnawed on during the full moon. I supposed it was fitting, considering the rest of what was happening around these parts. Life in Beaver Creek had never been boring, but this took excitement to a whole new level. *Halfwolves. Near murders.*

What could possibly be next?

As though I'd willed more agitation to come our way, Ads and Nash blustered into the house a half hour into my playdate with both Kolanes. This girl couldn't get a date, but I was good for playdates.

Adalyn's cheeks were flushed in spite of the chilly temps. "Liam, Nate's been trying to call you."

My spine jammed tight. "Why?"

Nash rammed his hands through his short spiky hair. "The halfwolf just died."

"Like, for real this time," Adalyn added.

Liam went so still it was eerie.

I, on the other hand, was vibrating from how hard my heart was beating. "How?"

"Nate thinks it might be due to the injuries she sustained post attack. That there was some internal bleeding they failed to catch."

Every tendon in Liam's neck and arms twisted, every bone in his face pressed up against his skin. He set Storm gently down on the rug beside him, then stood just as Mom appeared in the living room.

"Sorry, Meg." His lips barely shifted as he spoke those words.

"Will you please stop apologizing?" She went over to Storm, whose eyes had grown as wide as my own. He was surely so finetuned to his father's mood that he sensed the alarm ringing through Liam as our Alpha pivoted and left.

Nash went after him. "Wait up. I'll come with."

I didn't know if it was the door shutting, or Adalyn's earlier exclamation, but Dad suddenly showed up in the living room doorway in his bathrobe. He looked at Mom. Adalyn looked at me. Storm looked at all of us.

"You think she really bled out, or the attacker came back to finish the botched job?" My voice bounced with anxiety.

Dad rubbed a towel over his wet hair which, like Mom's, was shot through with silver. "Let's not jump to any conclusions."

"Nolan and Avery are at the bunker, canvassing the area for unfamiliar scents." Adalyn plopped down beside me on the couch. "So, I guess we'll know soon enough."

Soon enough turned out to be *hours* later.

CHAPTER 7

Even though I tried not to worry, whoever claimed no news was good news was obviously not a shifter. In our world, silence never heralded good things. Nature never got quiet when something pleasant was about to happen.

Although Adalyn and I tried to distract each other by discussing stupid Grant, her upcoming winter wonderland wedding, the design of her mating tattoo, and Storm's total cuteness, the wait hung over us like soupy fog. We'd come up with so many conspiracy theories that Mom rolled her eyes at us and urged us to get out of the house. So we'd gone down to Pondside, the compound's one and only watering hole that Dad had opened a decade ago and whose daily operations he still oversaw, with Nolan's help now.

After several hot chocolates topped with plenty of gooey marshmallows, we finally got a message from Nash saying they were on their way home. We got up and trudged up the steep slope, my knee creaking so hard Adalyn actually heard it at some point. She insisted we slow down, and I insisted I was fine.

The scent of chimney smoke embalmed the night air, and the waning crescent moon, although crosshatched with clouds, trickled light over the white expanse.

We reached the house at the same time as car tires crunched up our driveway. I scraped the snow off my boots before kicking them off by the front door and hanging up my jacket. Car doors clicked and clapped as four large bodies hopped out of our Alpha's gleaming black Mercedes SUV.

I tried to decipher Liam's expression, but the car beams were too bright. I backed up to let him pass. His eyes held mine for a second, and I shivered.

"Meg, they're home." Dad came out of the kitchen, patting his hands on the apron I'd gotten him two Christmases ago, the one that said: *Mr. Good Lookin' Is Cookin'*.

Niall, who'd gone shopping with me that day, had suggested I buy the one that read: *I Like My Butt Rubbed and my Pork Pulled*. I'd slung him a hefty side-eye. Our father had a great sense of humor, but he was our father. Niall ended up buying the other apron for Nolan, who'd shaken his head at Niall's quirky sense of humor.

Mom emerged from her bedroom with a bathed and pajamaed Storm, who chirped at the sight of his father. Liam didn't reach out for him immediately, seeming lost in thought.

"What happened?" I looked over at Adalyn.

Her slack jaw told me she'd already gotten the lowdown from Nash through their mate link.

Liam's jaw twitched and twitched as though he were fighting down a howl. The strangest urge to reach out and lay a reassuring hand on his arm came over me. Thankfully, I reined it in. I doubted he'd want to be touched, especially by a girl who was still a stranger. In truth, he didn't strike me as someone who enjoyed being touched by non-strangers either.

He stared at his son, the silence stretching uncomfortably tight.

Finally, his shoulders loosened, and he relieved my mother of the squirming infant. "We've got another halfwolf on our hands."

I gasped. "*Another*—Who?"

Liam swung his gaze toward me. "The coroner."

"The coroner?" Mom exclaimed, looking over at Dad, who seemed just as flummoxed as she was. "He's a shifter?"

Liam closed his eyes and breathed in his son. When he opened them, they glowed a bright amber-yellow. "He wasn't. Until he was bitten."

The crackling logs in the chimney became the only source of sound in the house.

Mom stepped close to my father, who put an arm around her waist and pulled her into him. "Are you saying—are you saying wolves can be made?"

"Not wolves, Mom," Niall said, unlacing his boots. "Halfwolves."

"I don't understand," Mom said.

"Someone's been biting humans, and somehow, those humans can now transform into halfwolves." Nolan dropped an arm that smelled like wolf and snow and fire around my shoulders. I was guessing he'd spent a lot of time in fur today.

"I thought biting didn't transfer our magic?" I said.

"It usually doesn't." Liam ran his son's smooth curls through his fingers.

"Where's the coroner?" I asked.

"In the bunker. Along with his wife, who called the cops after he bit her. Nate managed to be the first cop on the scene. He's with them now."

"Shit," I whispered.

Mom must've been really shocked because she didn't admonish me.

"That's crazy," Adalyn said.

"Do you think that's why the first halfwolf was bitten?" The words rushed out of me. "Not because of a settling of scores but because the wolf who bit her wanted to change her genetic makeup?"

Liam's throat dipped. "It *is* beginning to look like someone's creating a new breed."

"We really need to find Shifter Zero." When we all frowned, Nash added, "You know . . . like Patient Zero?"

Niall shrugged out of his coat. "Looks like your trip's not going to be of the short-and-sweet nature."

Liam sighed, and although it was totally wrong of me to rejoice he'd be sticking around, my heart performed a little backflip. I burrowed into Nolan's side, hoping no one would pick up on the crash and thrum of my pulse. Thankfully, they were all much too absorbed by the fact that a shifter had managed to create wolves, which really should've been my point of focus as well.

After dinner, once the source of my attention departed with his child, I finally turned all that had happened around and around in my head.

One thing stuck out over everything else: Shifter Zero wasn't targeting wolves; they were targeting humans. Which meant wandering off the compound was no longer a risk.

CHAPTER 8

I'd worked late into the night to finish a commission, so I'd ended up missing breakfast. Dad had gone to Pondside, and Mom for a walk around the compound with Storm, leaving me home alone. My house was so rarely quiet it was eerie. I couldn't decide if I liked it or not. On the one hand, it was sort of relaxing. On the other, it was sort of lonely.

As I zapped leftover sausage links and scrambled eggs in the microwave, I called Adalyn to find out what everyone was up to. She was at the hair salon with her grandmother, having come to the same conclusion I had about it not being dangerous for shifters; Liam and Nash were at the bunker; Nolan was at work with Dad; and Niall . . . well, he was probably passed out in some girl's bed.

The youngest of my brothers was easy like that, a real Casanova. Nash had been, too, until a mating bond had snapped between him and Adalyn. Now, he'd joined the ranks of my other two brothers, who were both tight-lipped about their relationships. Especially Nolan. I'd never seen him lock lips with anyone.

"Dinner and drinks tonight at Seoul Sister?" I asked Ads over the phone.

Seoul Sister, which was owned by Bea's family, was one of the most popular places in town, a South Korean-American fusion eatery that operated year-round. This wasn't the case for most restaurants in the area that shut down the minute the snow melted.

"I really need to meet someone."

"You mean, you need to take your mind *off* someone?"

"My mind is most definitely not on Grant."

"Oh, I wasn't talking about Grant, babe."

The plate I was hand-washing slipped from my fingers, clattering against the metal basin, causing a loud, sudsy clang. "Is it really obvious?"

"To me, but I also know you inside out."

I grimaced. "My brothers also know me inside out."

"Your brothers are boys."

"Do you think Mom knows?"

"Um. Yeah. Your mother knew I had a crush on Nash before *I* even did."

"Well, shit."

Adalyn laughed softly. "Gotta finish Mrs. Mofett's perm. Pick you up at seven?"

"It's a date." I rinsed my plate and slotted it onto the drying rack, then peered out at the pasty sky. Snow was coming. I could feel the cold humidity in my bones. Especially in my damaged knee joint.

I powered on my tablet to work when the front door opened. "In here," I called out, expecting Mom and Storm.

Boy was I wrong.

My gaze scraped up Liam's denim-clad legs, black tee, and black leather jacket. Lycaon, the male was a piece of art.

"Morning, Nikki."

Even his voice was art. "Morning." I cleared my throat and focused on my lit screen, hoping he hadn't caught my once-over. "Storm's out with Mom."

That my mother sensed I had a crush was embarrassing. That my crush noticed I had a crush was a whole other level of distressing.

"Any new developments?" I bit my lip as I reworked my character's posture. When he didn't answer, I looked up, found him studying what I was painting.

"The coroner's wife shifted last night."

"Fully?"

"No. Not fully."

Another halfwolf.

"Has the coroner turned back into skin?"

Liam shook his head. "The Sillin's not affecting him."

I set my stylus down. "Why do you think that is?"

"New species? Too soon?" He leaned his hip against the island. "We have yet to understand *how* they were made. I mean, we know they were bitten, but lots of humans have been bitten over the years, and none of them have ever turned."

Had he ever bitten a human? I hadn't. Then again, we only bit humans who knew what we were or they'd call the cops on us. It dawned on me that Storm's mother was human, so Liam had probably bitten her lots since biting enhanced sexual pleasure.

Thinking of him fanging his ex made my wolf want to growl . . . my human, too. Pathetic. I was so pathetic. Liam was allowed to bite whomever he wanted. Plus, Storm's mother was dead. Being jealous of a dead woman was a new low for me.

"You okay?"

I'm jealous of your dead mate. Was she your mate? Your true *mate?* "Yeah. Peachy." *Peachy?* Had that word really rolled out of my mouth? I wasn't even aware it was part of my vocabulary.

His brows drew low.

I definitely deserved that look. I was acting weird. I was speaking weird. "Just thinking about the poor coroner and his wife." Returning to a subject that didn't make my wolf or human feel territorial over a male she had no claim on felt wise. "Where did the attack happen again?"

"About thirty miles east of here. Why?"

"Just curious of the area I should steer clear of," I lied.

His head dipped a little. "You're not planning a trip out there, are you?"

I jerked, banged my knee on the island. "What?"

"People's scents change when they lie."

"You're saying you can smell deceit?"

He crossed his arms. "I can smell a whole variety of emotions. Comes with the job."

Well, crap. "How *convenient.*" I crossed my own arms, hoping it could block my scent.

Liam's brown eyes went wolfishly amber. "Why do you want to visit the crime scene?"

"Because it's going to snow."

He glanced out the window.

"I know our pack's best trackers were out there, but I thought that maybe" —I shrugged—"maybe I'd pick up on something they hadn't."

"Leaving the compound—"

"Shifter Zero's trying to change human nature. Since I'm a wolf already, I think it's safe to assume I'm not part of the people being targeted."

"We don't know what the person's intent is, yet, Nikki."

I got up, slid my phone into my jeans' back pocket, and sidestepped him. "Where are you going?"

"Out."

Liam trailed me into the foyer where I stuck my socked feet into my boots and grabbed my jacket.

"Your brothers mentioned you were stubborn."

"Me? Stubborn? They must've had me confused with their *other* sister." I flashed him a smile.

He didn't even snicker. He was one tough audience.

I grabbed my car keys.

"Leave the keys. We'll take my car."

"*We?*"

"Either I come with you, or I tell Lorna not to open the gate." He tapped on his temple to remind me how fast he could communicate with our gatekeeper.

"Seriously, Liam. Go be with your son."

"My son's safe."

"I'm safe, too."

"And I intend for you to stay that way."

I sighed. "You're not going to drop it, are you?"

"Every member of your family would challenge me to a duel if I knowingly let you go off on your own."

"Don't say that." I shuddered at the thought of another duel. Sure, I hadn't watched Liam and Cassandra's, but I knew the technicalities of Alpha dueling —it was a fight to the death that ended when the winner ingested the loser's heart to absorb the Alpha's pack link. "You do realize I've been going off on my own for several years now?"

"Although I don't mind standing here, discussing your independence, I thought you wanted to have a look around the crime scene before it started snowing."

"I'm not going to win this argument, am I?"

"It's not an argument." He drew the door open and nodded to his black SUV.

I walked over to the car. "What is it then?"

He pulled open my car door. "It's me reminding you that I'm your Alpha, and as Alpha, I make the safety of my shifters my topmost priority."

I eyed him as I climbed into the passenger seat. "You swear you're not singling me out because of my knee?"

"Cross my heart, Nikki."

Although he sounded truthful, I wondered if he was. After all, others had left the compound. Others *would* leave the compound. Was he going to trail all of them?

As he pulled out of my driveway, I texted Mom that I was running an errand with Liam and then I called Bea's cell for a reservation at Seoul Sister, but it went straight to voicemail, so I phoned up the restaurant directly and reserved for two at seven-thirty.

Liam slid me a look as I hung up. "What's Seoul Sister?"

"A restaurant in town."

He slid me another look. "What part of *mad wolf on the loose* didn't you understand?"

I bristled. "Oh, I understood." I plopped my elbow on the window and squinted at the snow-capped land and green-gray forest. "I have four brothers already, Liam. I don't need a fifth one."

CHAPTER 9

P olice tape looped around five tall evergreens, marking off the crime scene. The snow was blemished by tread marks ranging from boots to paws to snow tires, and speckled yellow, brown, and red. My stomach heaved from the coppery scent of blood and treacly reek of gasoline.

Liam's gaze kept veering from brown to amber-yellow to dark again. I almost wished he'd shift and get some of his moodiness out. After I'd told him I didn't need a fifth brother, he'd given me the silent treatment, which was fine back in the car, but now it was maddening. I didn't like when things festered, and things were definitely festering.

I broke a branch from a nearby tree, then ducked underneath the police tape, the nape of my neck prickling as I scraped the trampled snow. I crouched and sniffed, catching tenuous threads of scents—my brothers', Liam's. I even caught Grant's. The only reason I recognized that one was because it had floated around me for two whole years. I didn't consider them wasted years—I'd learned lots about myself, about relationships, about life— but the manner in which it had ended made me regret having given so much to someone so fickle.

As I disturbed the snow around the blood, I unleashed the question shimmering at the edge of my mind. "Was Storm's mother your true mate?"

For a long while, Liam didn't answer. Maybe he wouldn't tell me. I could always ask Nate.

"No."

I frowned and looked over my shoulder. "Just your wife then?"

His arms were crossed, the leather sleeves stretched so taut I worried the seams would rip. "We were never married."

"How come?"

A gust of wind ruffled his hair. "How come you and Grant aren't together anymore?"

"Because he dumped me after the accident." I moved toward one of the trees, the only one with strips of bark clawed off. "No twenty-year-old healthy male wants a ball and chain."

Silence. Then, "Is that what he called you?"

"No. Lycaon no. Have you met my brothers? They'd have neutered him had he uttered those words." I shrugged a shoulder. "In his defense, though, Doc had just announced my leg needed to be amputated."

"How does *that* excuse his leaving?"

I brought my nose to the bark and sniffed but all I got was a whiff of sap and gasoline. "It doesn't excuse it, but it does make it understandable."

"There's nothing understandable about walking out when things get tough."

"That's why you're Alpha and Grant's not," I said, going back to foraging the snow with my makeshift rake.

Snow began falling, thick flakes that resembled goose down.

"Are you done?" Liam's voice smacked of impatience.

Even though I hadn't dragged him out here, I sighed and tossed my stick, then retraced my steps over to him, skirting the gorier area, and lifted the police tape to duck under. My knee decided it was the appropriate moment to turn gummy and haul me down onto all fours.

Nice. Not embarrassing at all.

The air around me warmed, and the minty musk of Liam's skin grew more potent as he strode over to me.

I grimaced, mostly from the pain. A little from the shame. "There was an icy patch."

If he smelled my lie, he didn't comment on it, just reached out to help me up.

My fingers crushed the snow as I scraped them into my palms. "I'm good." I pressed myself onto my knees, wincing as my weak joint sent a sharp bolt of electricity down my calf and up my thigh. As I dusted my palms, I caught the glint of something in the snow—a thin gold chain. I pinched it, unearthing a slender bracelet with a row of tiny charms.

"Did your bracelet break?" Liam asked.

I stared at the ruined clasp, enameled wolf, heart-shaped citrine, and tiny carved daisy, my heart stopping and starting, stopping and starting. "It's not mine." I sat back on my heels and cranked my neck back. "But I know whom it belongs to."

CHAPTER 10

"Whom does it belong to?"

The snow drifted so hard now that the flakes hit my eyes, stinging before melting down my cheeks. "Bea. Nate had it made for her birthday last year."

Liam crouched. "Are you sure?"

"I went to the jewelry shop with him. Helped him pick out the charms." I batted my lashes that were getting logged down with snowflakes. "Do you think Bea's in trouble? Do you think she was attacked?"

Liam slid his lips against one another. "No. All of the blood belongs to the same female. The one who's dead."

I sighed as I stood. "Maybe Nate was having it repaired, and it slipped out of his pocket."

"Maybe." He held out his hand, and I deposited the bracelet inside. "It wasn't the bracelet I wanted, Nikki."

I frowned.

He still pocketed it, then held his palm back out. "Your hand."

"My . . . hand?"

His gaze strayed to my leg.

I backed up, schooling my features to avoid flinching. "There was ice." I turned a little abruptly, and my knee screamed.

A hand closed around my elbow, and for all my stubbornness, I set aside my pride and let Liam guide me through the dense copse of evergreens toward his car. I wasn't sure if Alphas were warmer-blooded than normal shifters, but even through my puffer coat and bulky cream sweater, I could feel the heat of his skin, a mix of fire and sunshine.

He got my door and didn't let go until I was settled in the passenger seat, then rounded the front bumper and climbed in. Although he turned the key in the ignition and started the wipers, he didn't reverse onto the road, just stared straight ahead at the white land.

"We should get back," I said. "The snow's coming down hard."

Liam blinked, then clicked in his seat belt and put the car in gear.

Once we were on the way home, I pulled my phone out of my pocket. "Want me to call him?"

"Already done."

"Already . . .?"

He tapped his temple.

Oh. "What's the range on your nifty Alpha way of communication?"

Fog was starting to build on the inside of the windshield. He jabbed the defrost button. "Fifty miles."

That explained why he didn't communicate over the mind link when he was in Boulder. In six months, that would change.

"Same range as your wolf GPS?" Another gift Alphas were endowed with was the power to geographically locate their wolves.

"My wolf GPS." The terminology kicked up a corner of his mouth. "Yes."

We drove in silence the rest of the way, but unlike on the drive over, it was a relaxing type of quiet, both of us lost in thought. Mine surely nicer than his considering the sharpened contours of his features.

He put on his blinker when we reached the long road that led toward the compound. That he'd even spotted the turnoff was a miracle considering the atrocious visibility. I imagined he'd warned Lorna of our arrival, because the gate was already open when we approached.

"Niall was telling me you two were supposed to move in together after you finished high school. Is that still in the cards?"

Flashes from the accident made my lids flutter—crumpled metal, charred skin, blazing gasoline, Grant's damned fluorescent helmet.

"The accident sort of pressed pause on all my life plans, but hey, I recovered. And while I was stuck in bed, I learned how to paint digitally, and now I get to do it for a living." Not to mention, I'd gotten rid of a useless boyfriend. "All in all, it gave me more than it took away."

He pulled into the driveway and parked next to my Jeep. "You're a glass half-full type of girl, huh?"

"More of a, *as long as I have a glass, I'm filling it* type."

That earned me a smile. It wasn't very broad or very lasting, but it sanded away a little of the stress Liam carried around him like an aura. "Solid philosophy, Miss Freemont."

"Why thank you, Mr. Kolane."

As I reached for the door handle, he touched my forearm.

"Wait." His door clapped shut. Before I could tell him that I didn't need assistance, he was drawing my door open.

"You know—"

"That you're fine? Yes. I heard you the first hundred times you said it. My hearing's the other sense that improved when I became Alpha."

"Too bad your grasp of the English language didn't," I quipped.

That earned me a grin. "I'll have you know that my grasp of the English language is perfectly adequate, as is my grasp of body language. You're favoring your uninjured leg and wince when your foot touches the ground."

I eyed his proffered palm. "Cassandra Morgan used to say that holding someone's hand promoted codependence."

"She also used to say she rose to power without cheating." His eyes had darkened, or maybe they just appeared darker because the surrounding world was so very pale. "I'm not trying to make you feel weak, but don't expect me to stand back while you *try* not to fall. It's not in my DNA."

I wrapped my fingers around his forearm instead of his hand and climbed out carefully. "I'm glad you're nothing like her."

He side-eyed me. "You have a strange way of showing it."

When we reached my front door, I released his arm. Leaning on him outside my home was one thing. Inside, and my parents would put me on bedrest till the spring thaw.

The smell of freshly brewed coffee and crackling logs eased the knot of tension in my stomach. I pulled off my boots, happy they were the lace-less type, then hung up my coat. After taking his shoes off too, Liam slung his jacket over mine, and although he didn't insist on being my crutch, he matched my pace as I limped toward the living room.

Storm squirmed in Mom's arm, babbling a long string of *dada*s. She set him on the rug, and he crawled toward Liam, who was already crouched.

"They're saying we're going to get three feet of snow by tonight." Mom gestured to the window. "Ski season's going to start extra early this year."

Liam kissed Storm's temple. "Good for business."

Since the pack owned and operated all the resort lifts, it *would* be good for business.

"Is Nate here?" I attempted to make out another heartbeat in the house, but mine was pounding so fast I could barely make out the three in the vicinity.

"No. Why?" Mom asked.

I lifted my hand to Storm's neck. Caressed the little skin roll that would one day lengthen and lose its velvetiness. "He was supposed to meet us."

Don't tell your mother about the bracelet.

That hadn't been my intention. "I'm going to grab some water. Want some, Liam?"

"Why don't you sit down?" He nodded to the couch. "I'll go grab them."

I pressed my lips together. "I need to get my tablet, which I left in the—"

"Nikki, your jeans are wet, baby. Go sit by the fire and warm up." Mom glided right past us. "I was on my way to make Storm some milk so I'll grab the water and your tablet."

Liam tipped his head. "After you."

I sighed but walked to the couch nearest the fire and sank down while Liam took a seat on the rug beside a big pile of building blocks. He proceeded to stack them, and then Storm swatted the tower. As they crashed, the little one clapped, and although I had a million unpleasant things whirling through my mind, I cracked a grin.

"Lucas calls my son the Destroyer."

"I like it. Good superhero name." I eased off the couch and went to work building a tower with the blocks that had rolled my way. "Lucas is the other Beta, correct?"

"Yes."

"Are you two close?"

"He's the closest thing I have to a brother."

Mom bustled back in with two water bottles and my tablet. "Here you go."

As I spun the cap off, I said, "You forgot Storm's milk."

"I realized he ate only an hour ago. Silly me."

I sighed as she took a seat on the couch behind me and grabbed one of Adalyn's bridal magazines.

"I can't believe the wedding's next month." She flipped through a few pages. "I hope you can make it, Liam."

"When is it?"

"On the winter solstice." When he frowned, I added, "It's the anniversary of their mating bond."

"Ah . . . the infamous mating bond that *magically* snaps into place on the longest or shortest day of the year."

I added another block. "I take it you're not a fan."

"I don't think magic should factor into choice."

Was this about Ness? I'd heard they'd had a thing until she'd found her true mate.

"A mating link only exposes compatibility." Mom thumbed to the next page. "Bodies can't bind without the heart's consent."

Liam watched his son crawl over to me.

"Storm the Destroyer is on the loose," I murmured, steadying Liam's child as he climbed onto my lap. Before he could swat my tower, I tickled him.

He tucked his arms into his sides and giggled so hard he would've tipped over had I not been holding him. The second I stopped tickling him, he darted an arm out.

"Oh no, you don't." I slung him to the side just before his fingertips could graze my tower and tickled him anew.

This turned into a game. The moment I stopped tickling him, he'd reach out, taunting me with an outstretched finger while he watched, waited. Nine months, and already so clever.

"I wonder when Nate and Bea are going to tie the knot." Mom's voice tore me out of my carefree contemplation. "I assumed they'd be married before Nash and Adalyn."

The front door opened.

"Nate?" Mom called out.

Storm wriggled on my lap, commanding my attention.

Even though my gaze flitted to the double-wide entrance, I resumed our little tickle game.

"Sorry . . . this blizzard." Nate brushed the snow off his hair, then walked over to Mom and leaned over to kiss her cheek before ruffling my hair. "What's up, Liam?" He held out his palms over the crackling logs.

Liam set down the block he'd been twirling and reached into his pocket. "I was at the crime scene with your sister."

"Nikki," Mom gasped, "you went to the crime scene?"

"I apologize, Meg. I imagine you didn't want her seeing it. Anyway, while we were there, she found this." Liam slid out the charm bracelet and held it up. "Apparently, it belongs to Bea."

The bracelet shivered like a living organism.

Nate stared and stared, color leaching from his face until his complexion rivaled my wool V-neck.

Mom tossed her magazine onto the enormous chopped trunk we used as a coffee table. "Nate, honey, what's going on?"

My brother's hands began to tremble. "After I got the call about the attack, Bea—she broke up with me." The volume of his voice frayed until his next words were barely audible. "She ripped off the bracelet. Her ring, too." He dug out his wallet, then opened it and, after two unsuccessful attempts, managed to fish a diamond band out of the credit card flap. "I've been meaning to ask if you—if you could put this away in the safe."

Mom leaped to her feet and padded over to my brother. "Oh, Nate."

"The bracelet, it must've—slipped out of my pocket—when I was at—"

"Shh." Mom hugged her son, who was a full head taller than she was and yet seemed so small in that moment. "It's okay, honey." She smoothed back Nate's hair. "Shh."

I met Liam's stare over Storm's head. I wasn't sure if it was the relief of finding out Bea hadn't been harmed or a reflection of the flames snapping beside us, but his eyes seemed brighter.

Although I grieved for my brother's broken heart, I celebrated Bea's unbroken body. If she'd been attacked . . . I forced my mind not to wander somewhere so dark and depressing.

I tickled Storm with renewed enthusiasm. "I'm sorry about Bea, Nate."

"So am I, Pinecone. So am I."

How come everyone calls you pinecone?

"For no reason," I said.

I sense a very interesting reason.

Was he smiling? I tossed a building block at him, which he caught with ease.

I'd love to hear it.

"Never happening."

Storm tipped my tower, and his joy splashed over my brother's sadness. Mission accomplished, Liam's son scooted back toward his father.

It dawned on me that Seoul Sister was probably off-limits now. I shot Adalyn a text, in which I unpacked the big lines of what had happened, and asked her to cancel since I didn't want to risk getting Bea on the line, what with my brother in the same room.

That night, we ended up staying in. Partly because of the weather and partly because of Nate. When a Freemont was in pain, every Freemont stuck around to pull him or her out of it. Adalyn and I made plans to go out the following night, just the two of us.

If the blizzard let up, we'd head into town—Seoul Sister wasn't the only place to hang out if you were single and under the age of thirty.

If it kept snowing, we'd go to Pondside—not ideal considering it would be packed with shifters, all of whom I knew.

CHAPTER 11

T he weather didn't let up, so Pondside it was.

When I reached the canteen, the new barkeep, Sasha, a freckle-faced boy who'd been in my high school graduating class, gestured toward Adalyn. She sat at the head of the communal table closest to the giant chimney where poultry and lamb shanks rotated on spits, dribbling fat onto earthenware filled with sliced potatoes.

As I hung my coat on the seat beside hers, I looked around the crowded mess hall—few spots remained at the other communal tables and fewer still along the copper bar. The sleekly designed, walnut-paneled eatery worked like a members' club: compound residents paid yearly dues that compensated the staff—Nolan, Dad, and five others—and gave them access to two meals a day. Not everyone ate there twice, though, but most people caught at least one daily meal there. Alcohol was billed separately, the sole source of profit from the operation. Dad hadn't done it for the money, though, just for the love of food and pack life.

"What did people do before Dad got the idea to open up this place?"

"They ate at home?" Adalyn tossed a smile at a couple sitting at our table. "When are the babies due, Wren?"

The black-skinned shifter, who'd briefly dated Nate in her teenage years, patted her immense abdomen. "Next month, although I heard twins usually arrive early."

"Two more guests at my wedding." Ads clapped as excitedly as Storm when he caught sight of his milk bottle.

I was now familiar with most of the little guy's reactions having spent the better half of my afternoon babysitting him with Mom again while Liam dealt with the halfwolves in the bunker. Although I was dying to know if they'd made any headway in finding Shifter Zero, I'd left before he or Nate had gotten home.

Nolan walked through the flap door next to the bar, the sleeves of his black cook's uniform rolled up to his elbows. He crouched next to the fire and slivered some lamb onto a platter. When he caught sight of me and Adalyn, he sent us a wink.

After greeting our other neighbors, I leaned in toward Adalyn. "Did you ask Sasha to keep four seats vacant around us for privacy?"

"No. I told him to save them for the singles' crowd. He swore he would."

I grabbed one of the pitchers of water and filled both our glasses, wondering who was single and might come out tonight.

"What do you want to drink?" Adalyn leaped to her feet. "I'll go grab the first round."

"A beer."

She nodded, then walked to the bar and squeezed herself between the shifters sitting there.

"How's the knee?" came an oh-so-familiar voice behind me.

I glanced over my shoulder. How had I missed that Grant was sitting at the table next to us? How had *Adalyn*, with her owl-sharp eyesight, missed it?

He was balancing on the back legs of his chair.

I wasn't petty enough to wish he'd fall. "Great."

"I came by after—"

"I know." I bit my lip, then added, "Thank you. For checking up on me."

He smiled.

I hadn't meant that as an opening.

I started to turn when he asked, "Got any plans for the weekend?" His green eyes glowed in the dimly lit room, made even dimmer by the heavily falling snow beyond the picture window.

"Get your own date, Grant. Nikki's mine tonight." Adalyn pushed a cold beer bottle into my hands while giving my ex the stink eye. Where I was disappointed by how it had ended, Adalyn was downright hostile.

Grant's mouth pressed into a tight line that accentuated the oval of his face. "Always nice to see you too, Adalyn."

She flipped him the bird, then held out her beer to me. "To getting rid of deadweights."

"Ads," I whispered, wanting to nip their surliness in the bud before either of them could shift and go at each other's throats.

"Oops. I stole your toast, Grant."

"Screw you, Reeves."

The conversations around us quieted, and I assumed it was because of Adalyn and Grant, but then I noticed people looking over my head.

I followed their line of sight to Nash, Niall, and Liam.

"Out. Get out, you fucking lowlife." Nash's voice was crisper than the air outside.

Grant snorted as his chair legs clipped the slate tile flooring. "We were done anyway." He got up, then nodded at Jared and Cane, who didn't look done but who rose in solidarity. Before leaving, his palm closed around the top rung of my chair, and he leaned toward me to murmur, "The way I feel about your brothers and Adalyn doesn't change the way I feel about you, Nik."

I wanted to tell him that how he felt about me ultimately didn't matter since we were never getting back together, but I hated public drama, so instead of saying anything, I nibbled my bottom lip until he was gone, and the noise level had returned to normal.

Nash watched me as he took the seat beside Adalyn's, and I sensed the question twirling behind his azure irises, the one of whether I might be reconsidering Grant. I shook my head.

"Thank fuck." It was Niall who spoke. I was guessing the youngest of my four brothers had gathered Nash's query and my silent answer.

We were all so finetuned to each other that although we didn't possess a mind link like Nash and Adalyn, we could often surmise what the other was thinking.

Niall dropped into the seat next to Nash and right away started chatting up his neighbor, a female shifter Nate's age.

As Liam took the seat beside mine, I scanned the mess hall. "Is Nate coming too?"

"He went home early."

"My parents' place, or his?"

"His. He's taking the breakup badly."

"He and Bea were together for three years. Almost four." Part of me still hoped their relationship was salvageable. I'd hesitated to send her a message today, but in the end, decided not to meddle. At least, not yet.

Adalyn stuck her already empty beer bottle on the walnut tabletop as

Sasha came to take our order. "Actually, you guys need to find other seating. These were reserved. Right, Sasha?"

Color rose into Sasha's neck before painting his jaw and cheeks a shade of red that rivaled his hair. "Um. Well." His gaze flicked to Liam.

Telling my brothers to take a hike was painful, but his Alpha . . . inconceivable.

Before he could burst a capillary, I put him out of his misery. "It's fine, Ads."

She expelled a soft sigh. "Once the weather clears . . ."

"What happens once the weather clears?" Liam asked.

"Nothing," I said.

Nash cocked an eyebrow. It wasn't exactly a secret that I was on the hunt for a rebound. Knowing my brothers, as long as I didn't rebound with Grant, they'd be happy. Wait . . . would that even be considered a rebound?

Nash draped an arm on the back of Adalyn's chair as we gave Sasha our food and drinks order.

Once he left, my brother asked, "So, who were the seats reserved for?"

Spinning my beer bottle between my palms, I eluded the question by asking one of my own. "Where's Storm?"

"With Mom." Nash grinned. "Liam insisted on taking him home, but Mom all but shoved him down here. Said Storm was nice and cozy between her and Dad, and that Liam should go and relax, what with it being Friday night and all."

"You two better start popping out some pups"—Niall, who I thought wasn't paying attention, gestured between Nash and Adalyn—"or Mom's going to suffer from extreme withdrawal symptoms once Liam leaves Beaver Creek with Storm."

Adalyn laughed. "Yeah. Not ready for a kid quite yet. We're still enjoying the training phase."

"Perfecting our technique." Nash leaned over and placed a wet one on a giggling Adalyn.

I rolled my eyes just as Sasha returned with the drinks. After he left, I asked, "Any progress on finding Shifter Zero?"

"We're currently mapping out all the places the girl's been to and all the people she interacted with"—Liam filched one of the six fresh beer bottles on the table and leaned back in his chair—"but she's been living in Beaver Creek for the past two months, so that's a lot of places and a lot of people."

Although his legs were splayed wide, his shoulders were bunched beneath his black V-neck. Was his unease due to feeling out of place or to the case's additional complexities?

What? The word came at me like a snapped rubber band.

"Nothing." I upended my beer, then put it down. Couldn't my mother have suggested my brothers take Liam somewhere in town?

He stared at me a moment longer and I stared back, because I wouldn't be cowed by his grumpiness.

Niall's neighbor, Lena, leaned over the table and roped Liam into a conversation about the quality of life in Boulder versus Beaver Creek.

How's your leg? Liam's voice slid back into my mind, less aggressive this time.

I frowned, because his attention was on Lena and whatever she was saying that required lots of eyelash batting. *Note to self: keep eyes opened when flirting.*

"Like new," I said, unsure if he'd even catch my answer.

Adalyn cocked up one of her dark, defined eyebrows. "What's like new? Besides your hymen, that is."

"Adalyn," I sputtered, shooting her the mother of all glowers, while Nash, supportive as always, burst out laughing. I flipped him off, but that just made him guffaw louder.

"What's so funny?" Niall asked, turning away from Lena and Liam's conversation.

Hopefully, Liam had also been too focused on Lena to hear my former best friend's paltry jibe.

I shoved up the sleeves of my mustard-yellow duster cardigan. "The theme of Adalyn's bachelorette."

Niall speared his hands through his wavy chestnut hair. "I didn't even know bachelorettes were themed."

"Not usually, but Adalyn begged me for S&M."

Niall's eyebrows slammed down. He looked at Adalyn, then at Nash, and his nose wrinkled. "You're into that shit?"

Adalyn grinned, but I wasn't sure if it was at my comeback or Niall's reaction. "I can hardly wait."

Nash smiled and shook his head just as his twin arrived with a platter of succulent meats and crisped potatoes, and Sasha with a stack of plates and a utensil caddy.

"Bon appétit, guys," Nolan said, with a flourish of his hand over the beautifully-browned fare.

"Thank you, Nolan." Liam laid one forearm on the table. "Do all of you cook in the family?"

"We all know the basics." I speared a plump chicken thigh and put it on my plate, then shrugged out of my cardigan, the heat of the nearby fire and steaming food finally catching up to me.

"But Nolan and Dad are the ones with the crazy kitchen skills," Niall said, helping himself to three extra thick slices of lamb.

I reached past Liam to grab a fork and knife, my arm inadvertently brushing his. "Do you know how to cook?"

My Alpha's throat dipped with a swallow even though his beer was nowhere near his mouth and he hadn't taken a bite of food. "I can heat milk and boil pasta, so Storm's all set." After chugging down a glass of water, he loaded up his plate and dug in, polishing off his food at record speed. *You're staring again.*

I popped a potato inside my mouth, taking my time chewing it. After I swallowed, I pointed with my fork around the timbered space. "So are at least thirty other shifters."

He didn't glance around him to check, just plucked his beer and took a pull. *But why are you?*

"I was trying to decide if you were starving or in a hurry to get home."

Nash, Niall, and Adalyn had fallen into a discussion about Bea and Nate. They were presently discussing the odds of them getting back together.

"I skipped lunch," Liam finally said, out loud this time. Then, "Were you hoping I'd vacate the seat you reserved for your *friend?*"

I snorted. "You're all good, Kolane. Having my brothers around isn't very conducive to making new *friends* anyway."

He didn't reciprocate my good humor, just skated those dark umber eyes of his over my face, taking slow drags of his beer.

I placed my forearms on the edge of the table and scooted forward. "You made your point."

His eyebrows bent. "And what point would that be?"

"That staring is intrusive." And yet, I was still doing it. I averted my gaze. "Look at that. It finally stopped snowing."

Liam glanced toward the moonlit pond. *Your staring doesn't bother me, Nikki.*

Our eyes locked for a millisecond before mine flitted toward the roaring fire behind Liam. It might not bother him, but it bothered me, because I'd never been so fascinated with a male before.

The thought made me think of Adalyn's party. I wasn't actually going to go through with my threat, but we did need to discuss logistics since the original plan had been to throw it at Seoul Sister. We'd have to find a new venue and probably delete Bea's email address from the list of invitees.

At least, the party planning took my mind off Liam. I stayed hyper-aware of him for the next hour we spent sitting next to each other, but I proudly didn't look his way again. I seriously deserved a pat on the back, because his body, his smell . . . his entire aura was magnetic. To the point where I wondered if a mating bond had developed between us. But Adalyn had explained the sensation was akin to a fiery rope jutting from your navel, tying you to your intended, and my navel felt cord-and-fire-free.

My attraction to my Alpha was purely hormonal.

Damn.

Here I'd hoped I could put the blame on magic.

CHAPTER 12

O
n my way back from the supermarket with the baby formula Mom had sent me to buy, I drove in front of Seoul Sister. Hoping I wasn't sticking my paw where I shouldn't, I parked and headed inside. I'd been hoping to find Bea but got her brother Miles instead. He was standing by the front door, cell phone wedged between his shoulder and ear, tapping on his reservation tablet.

"Hey," I whispered. "Is Bea here?"

Miles raised one finger, exchanged a few more words with whomever was on the phone before hanging up and giving me his full attention. "Bea's out. Caught a bad stomach bug or something."

More like a bad breakup . . . Was it a good sign she hadn't told her brother?

"Anything I can help you with?"

"Um."

"If it's about Adalyn's bachelorette party, I actually had some questions for you."

"Yeah?" *Crap.*

"Why don't you take a seat? I'll get us two coffees, and we can go over the final details."

Discomfort made me begin to overheat. I needed to cancel the party, not have coffee to discuss it. While Miles strode toward the fancy chrome coffee machine behind the bar, I shrugged out of my coat and took a seat.

The scent of ground beans filled the brick and wood space, mixing with the aroma of baking bread.

I texted Nate: **Is it weird if we still do Adalyn's bachelorette at Seoul Sister?**

It didn't have to be weird, right?

Miles's shoulder blades bunched up the fabric of his white T-shirt that contrasted sharply with his smooth olive skin. No wolf blood ran through his veins, and yet, come snow or shine, the guy wore a short-sleeved shirt. It did quite nice things to his biceps. I placed my elbows on the bar and cradled my chin as he slid one mug beneath the sleek spout, then replaced it with another.

Nope, Nikki. Don't go there. You were almost family. You might still be family.

I shifted my attention to the bronze birdcage lights hanging around the room, each of them containing a different avian species. Apparently, it was these lights which had brought Bea and Miles's parents together. Mrs. Park had designed them for a fancy hotel in Seoul in which her now-husband had stayed. He'd become so enamored with the idiosyncratic lights, he'd asked to meet the artist.

My phone chirped, drawing my gaze down.

NATE: *Not weird.* :)

Relief spread through me. Not only did I *not* have to change venues, but I didn't have to try to find an excuse as to why I couldn't host it here.

I unlinked my fingers and sent him back: **Thanks. How you holding up?**

NATE: *Been better.*

ME: *Are you at the bunker?*

NATE: *Yes.*

I decided to stop by and check up on him on my way home. I flipped my phone over as Miles took the seat next to mine, his knee jostling my still slightly sore one.

"Sorry." He palmed my bumped joint. "I think I hit your bad leg."

"It's okay." I smiled, but then my smile wavered, because he hadn't removed his hand yet. I shifted my legs to the side, which knocked his hand off. "So, what do we need to go over?"

"The meal. Did you want platters of appetizers, plus some entrées to share?"

"Yes."

He jotted it down on a sheet of paper scribbled over with Bea's handwriting, the scratching of the lead tip the only noise in the restaurant. "Okay. And

Bea wrote something about a cake." His mouth quirked as he read what his sister had written. "Penis-shaped, correct?"

I sank into my chair. "Yes?"

His chocolate eyes met mine, sparkling with mirth. "What flavor? Vanilla or chocolate?"

I cleared my throat. "Vanilla with pink frosting."

He scrawled it down, a smile still dancing on his lips. "And balloons. You want golden BRIDE TO BE, right? Any other shape? Maybe some to match your cake?"

I palmed both my heating cheeks. "Discussing this was *way* less awkward with your sister."

He glanced up from the list. This time, a chuckle escaped him. He leaned back in his chair. "Wait till I ask Mom to help me frost the cake."

"Please don't. I'll come and do it myself."

He grinned. "Relax, Nikki. We're almost family."

"Doesn't make discussing penises with you any less weird." I dropped my hands to the bar top, then wrapped one around the mug and drank, but since I was already hot, it just made sweat bead on my upper lip.

"If you want, we can discuss breasts." He leaned back.

I snorted. "That's all right. But I appreciate your effort for gender discussion equality."

Once we were done going over the list, we chatted a few minutes about the restaurant business, which was a nice, safe subject. He'd come to Pondside once with Bea. Usually humans who weren't in a serious relationship with a pack member weren't permitted on the compound, but my Beta brother had taken some liberties with the rules.

I drained my coffee and lowered myself from the stool. "Call me if you need anything else. Otherwise, I'll see you next week."

"To frost the penis cake." Grinning, he got up too and reached out to grab my coat.

I grimaced, which just made his smile widen. As far as smiles went, his was really beautiful—teeth like Chiclets set between full lips. I must've stared a tad too long, because one of his eyebrows climbed up.

Liam was right . . . I really had an ogling problem.

The mere thought of Liam, of the hard cut of his face and body, dimmed Miles's attractiveness.

I speared my arms through the coat he was still holding up. "See you next week."

"Or earlier. In case you feel like getting out of the house now that the snow let up. There's always a free seat for you at Seoul Sister."

"I *do* need to get out of the house, so I might actually take you up on that."

"Just steer clear of the woods, all right?"

I frowned.

"I heard they haven't found the wolf yet. The one that killed that girl."

My forehead smoothed. "Oh. I'll be careful."

AS I DROVE TOWARD THE BUNKER, I WONDERED IF SHIFTER ZERO WAS EVEN still around. If smart, he would've fled town, what with an entire pack chasing after him. I sort of hoped he was still around because I sorely wanted closure.

The roads had been salted and plowed, but I was still extra cautious. More than once, my tires skidded on a patch of flattened snow, and losing control reminded me of the accident. I spent the next fifteen minutes of the drive breathing through the flare of panic constricting my rib cage.

After I parked, I trudged to the large metal door and rapped on it.

Niall was the one to open. "Nikki, what are you doing here?"

"I wanted to check up on Nate."

"You don't want to be here."

"Actually, I do." I tried to walk in, but he blocked my path.

"Seriously."

"Seriously, I do." I pressed my fingertips into his shoulder and pushed him aside. "I'm not scared of halfwolves."

He sighed but let me through.

The fluorescent tubing, that ran along the long, narrow ceiling, spilled wan light over the metal shelves full of canned goods and the silver bars of the cells at the far end. As I moved deeper into the low-ceilinged concrete space, my rubber soles squelched, garnering the attention of the four shifters on site—Nate, Liam, Avery, and . . . Who was the fourth male? I imagined he was pack, otherwise he wouldn't be here.

I heard Avery ask Nate, "What's she doing here?"

"I was passing by." I stopped next to Nate and squeezed his hand, then turned toward the blue-eyed man standing beside Liam, whose black hair was gathered at the nape of his neck in a manbun. "I don't think we've met yet. I'm Nikki."

"Ah . . . the infamous little sister." Although his arms stayed crossed, a crooked smile appeared on his face, hiking up his eyebrows. One of them, I noticed, was slashed by an old scar.

"Infamous?" I glanced at Nate, then at Niall, wondering which one of my brothers had spilled stories about me to this stranger. "I didn't know my reputation preceded me. And you are?"

"Lucas."

"Ah . . . the infamous best friend."

His grin widened. "Liam's been filling your ears about my incredibleness, I take it?"

I looked at Liam, whose nostrils flared out. "He has. I didn't know you'd be coming to help with the case." I released my brother's hand and turned toward the cells.

"Nikki, don't . . ." Nate tried to snatch my shoulder, but I ducked out of his grasp and strode toward the first holding cell.

Curled in the middle of it lay a creature with legs and arms shrouded in silver fur but with paws in place of hands and feet. Hooked, yellowed fangs protruded from pink lips that were entirely too human in a face that otherwise wasn't, in spite of the sparsity of fur coating the taut cheeks and elongated muzzle.

The halfwolf narrowed its glowing blue eyes and growled low. Although the sound raised the fine hairs on my arms, it didn't make me step back or avert my gaze, because what I felt over fear was pity.

"First time seeing one?" Liam had walked over and now stood shoulder to shoulder with me. Or rather my shoulder to his bicep.

I clutched my elbows. "Yes."

A rattling thud of the silver bars, followed by a keening yowl had me pivoting. A second, slighter half-shifted creature obscured by brown fur nipped at its front paws, whimpering.

My thumping heart decelerated as compassion bled over my distress. "Have they managed to shift back yet?"

"No. Every time we've given them Sillin, they throw it up." Liam's chin dipped, and his eyes narrowed. On me.

"What?"

You were passing by?

I tightened my grip on my elbows. "Yes. I was passing by. I went into town to grab formula for Storm."

His nostrils flared again, as though to scent whether I was lying.

"The shopping bag's in the car, in case you don't believe me."

I believe you. There was a strange crispness to his tone.

74

"Then what's wrong with your nose? Early hay fever?"

You smell like a human male.

My eyebrows jostled upward. This was about Miles? I glanced toward Nate, who was busy discussing something with the four others.

"I stopped by Seoul Sister to talk with Bea," I murmured, "but she wasn't there. Her brother was, though." My eyes locked on Liam's. "Am I not allowed to fraternize with humans anymore?"

"Until we catch the perp, you're safer interacting only with pack."

My hands bolted off my elbows. "Are you guys thinking the perp could be human?"

I must've spoken a little loudly, because the others were now looking our way again.

"Just following a few different leads." After a beat, Liam added, "Thanks for buying milk for my son."

I nodded, but then the formula I bought stirred up an idea. "Have you tried crushing the Sillin and mixing it with water?"

"We have."

"And injecting it intravenously?"

"That's what killed the first victim."

I chewed on the inside of my cheek. "So, they're stuck in limbo?"

Until we can figure something out.

My lashes slammed up. "How about Lori's blood? It contains traces of Sillin. Maybe they'd be able to absorb that."

"You mean, make them drink it?" Lucas strolled over and crouched to peer into the cage of the brown halfwolf, who tipped her elongated neck and growled. "I don't hate Nikki's idea."

I wrinkled my nose. "I was thinking more along the lines of an injection."

"They have a fondness for blood. We got them raw steaks the other day. They lapped all the blood but didn't eat the meat." Avery sounded suddenly interested in the conversation.

I swallowed, feeling slightly queasy. "We're talking about human blood, not animal blood."

"Blood is blood to an animal," Lucas drawled.

I raised my gaze to my brothers. Where Niall was bobbing his head, Nate had gone as pale as a laundered sheet. "Nate? Are you okay?"

Liam hooked a look over his shoulder at my brother.

"Good thinking." Nate rubbed the stubble on his chin, which had thickened into a short beard. "To Lori's."

I imagined this was in answer to a question we hadn't heard.

"Lucas"—Liam nodded toward Nate—"go assist Nate."

One of my brother's eyes twitched. "Lori doesn't like OBs, Liam, so with all due respect, we have better odds of her cooperating if I go alone."

Lori didn't like many people, Original Boulders or not.

Liam's jaw flinched. "Take Niall with you. In case she gives you trouble."

"She won't give me trouble. Besides, Avery's been up all night. It's Niall's shift."

Nate and Liam remained locked in a staring contest that ended with Nate lowering his head a notch.

Before the tension could escalate, I jerked toward my brother. "I'll go with Nate. I was heading home any—"

"No." Liam and Nate popped the word out in unison.

"Why not? Lori doesn't hate me."

Nate zipped up his brown leather jacket. "Mom will be pissed if she hears we're involving you."

"You're not involving me. I'm involving myself."

I heard someone snort behind me. Not Niall, who was just as protective as the rest of my brothers. Not Liam, who rarely seemed amused by anything I said or did. Not Avery, who was way too serious a person. Which left Lucas . . .

"Please, Nik." Nate scrubbed a hand down his haggard face. His beseeching tone combined with the dark circles rimming his eyes made me concede.

"Fine."

He shot me a weak smile before plodding toward the exit. "I'll be back in an hour." The door's thick hinges screeched as he shoved it open.

Once it had clanked shut, I pivoted back toward the others. Before I could even open my mouth, Liam said, "You should be getting home. Don't want my son to go hungry."

My lips pinched. I could take a hint. Especially, an unsubtle one.

It's coming from a good place, I told myself. *They're all trying to spare you.*

Why didn't it feel good, then?

Sure, I was an artist and not a cop, but I was pack, and pack helped out.

"At least, text me if my idea pans out," I gritted, before whirling around and treading out the bunker as fucking serenely as possible.

CHAPTER 13

"What a lucky guy. He gets bubbles *and* a bathing attendant."

Liam's voice made me compress one of the rubber toys I'd filled with water right into Storm's eye instead of on his chest, which was where I'd been aiming at.

"Sorry, Storm. Your daddy scared me."

Storm was a good sport. Just jerked a little and blinked a lot but didn't cry. He rarely cried actually. Only when the hunger pangs hit could he be heard halfway across the compound.

I filled the starfish, then squeezed it, sending a little jet of warm water onto Storm's chest. He squealed happily, then hit the water with open palms, splashing my tank top. "I'd offer to bathe you, Liam, but that would undoubtedly make things weird between us."

Liam went unnaturally still.

Saying it out loud had apparently made things weird between us. *Good job, Nikki.* I concentrated on Storm, so innocent, so happy. He'd eventually lose his innocence, but hopefully not his happiness.

"Besides . . . I'm still pissed at you for sending me home to feed *your* son, who couldn't starve in my parents' company even if he wanted to."

Liam's lips bent a fraction as he leaned against the doorframe. "It worked."

"What wor—Lori's blood?" The starfish slipped from my soapy fingers and plopped into the bathwater. "They're back in skin?"

He nodded.

That benched my annoyance. "And?"

"The shift knocked them out, so I don't have much more to report. We're keeping them locked up until we can make sure they don't shift back." He pushed off the doorframe and came to sit on the edge of the bathtub.

"You see . . . I'm more than just a competent bathing attendant." I cupped water and let it drip along Storm's spine.

He released a bunch of happy squeaks, and then his fingers flexed around his toy, which sent a stream of water into my eyes. I gasped, which made him break into peals of such contagious laughter that I laughed right along with him.

"You're going to pay for that, buddy."

"Are you threatening my son?" Liam sounded amused, but I glanced up at him to make sure his expression matched his tone.

He reached down and scooped out a toy, which he aimed at me. I just had time to raise my arm to deflect the spray of water. Keeping one arm in front of my face, I stuck my other one back in the bath until my fingers closed around a floating toy. I fished it out and retaliated, catching Liam in the ear.

The smile, which had tugged at his mouth, transformed into a laugh. I was so startled to hear the man produce such a joyous sound that I let down my guard and just watched him.

He raised his long fingers and swiped down the side of his face, and even though he didn't do it in slow motion, my mind decelerated the whole action and added some sexy music. He dipped his hand in the water and splashed me, effectively putting an end to my smutty scrutiny.

Oh, Lycaon, was that why he'd done it? I grabbed the towel I'd prepared for Storm and patted my face.

"I was afraid you might've tossed the baby out with the bath water." Mom stood in the doorway, hugging a bottle of lotion and Storm's PJs. "Gonna put these on your bed."

Storm raised his hand as though to show my mother his little ducky. She grinned at him and then cooed while I stared everywhere but at Liam.

"I'll go warm up his M-I-L-K." Before she left, she looked around my wet bathroom. "Not sure who's having more fun in here."

"The Kolanes are ganging up on me," I fake-grumbled. "If any of my brothers are free, send them up."

Mom shook her head, smiling. "I'll see what I can do."

Once she was gone, I laid Storm's towel on the bathmat and rose up on my knees. "Time to get out of the waterpark." I reached out for him when Liam got up.

"I got him, Nikki." My Alpha's timbre was back to its gravelly soberness. Gone was the lightness our water fight had produced.

As he leaned over, I was possessed with a surge of spontaneity, or insanity. I dipped my hand under the water and then whipped it up, drenching his face and neck.

I got to my feet, smirking down as a stream of bubbles dripped down the column of his neck and absorbed into the neckline of his black T-shirt. "You shouldn't let your guard down around me, Kolane. I may look feeble, but I was raised by wolves."

He crooked his neck and looked up at me. My heart, which was already beating fast, detonated when his eyes began to glow.

"Thinking up ways to retaliate?"

Both the yellow radiance of his irises and camber of his mouth increased.

"Should I be worried?"

"Terrified." The word rolled off his tongue like the thunder preceding prodigious summer storms, the sort that shook the sky and swelled the streams. The sort that soaked you to the bone and invigorated your very marrow.

His nostrils flared out delicately, and I swallowed, because I imagined it wasn't the powdery soap I'd used on Storm he was smelling.

Wiping my slick palms on my jeans, I skirted him. "I'll get his PJs."

The second I was out of sight, I stuck my palms against my heated cheeks and shut my eyes. I seriously needed to get a grip before I did something I'd regret.

Like make a move on my Alpha.

Inhaling sharply, I snapped my lids open and grabbed the phone I'd chucked on my bed. After shooting off a message to Adalyn to ask where she was, I dropped off Storm's pajamas and lotion.

"I need to go meet Adalyn about something concerning her bachelorette . . ." My lungs gripped my next breath in a desperate attempt to slow my careening pulse. "Will you be at dinner?"

His gaze slipped down my throat, settled on the pulse point fluttering my skin. "I think your family may need a break from me."

I didn't know about my family, but *I* definitely needed a break. I was acting more crazed than the halfwolf that had launched itself at the silver bars.

"And, Nikki . . ." He wiped his wet palm against his T-shirt, the movement slow and steady. "I apologize about the way I sent you home, but I was trying to appease your brothers."

I almost wished he hadn't apologized, because it was easier to eschew a brute than a decent man. "I figured as much." I drummed my fingers against the door. "Anyway, have a good night."

As I clambered down the stairs, I read Adalyn's reply, rooted through my bag to locate my car keys and wallet, then escaped my house and the alluring wolf upstairs.

CHAPTER 14

Adalyn locked the glass door. "I'm finally all yours. What's going on?"

I spun on the hairdressing chair I'd plopped my ass on twenty minutes ago and tossed the *InStyle* magazine Adalyn had jammed into my hands to distract me while she finished styling her last customer's short bob.

"I have the hots for our Alpha."

"What?" Adalyn slammed her palm across her chest as though she was surprised but her shit-eating grin told me she already knew, and she found it extremely amusing.

The temptation to pitch a hairbrush at her was strong. "It's not funny, Ads. And the worst part is, I think he knows it."

"Of course, he knows it."

I blanched.

"I mean, even Nash mentioned you were acting weird, and Nash never picks up on that sort of thing."

"That's it. I'm leaving town."

She rolled her wing-tipped eyes. "You're *not* leaving town."

"I can't stay."

"Of course, you can."

I leaned back in the padded leather chair, crooked my neck back, and let my lids slam closed.

"He's single and hot, and so are you."

"He's widowed and our freaking Alpha."

"Sweetie, you're not the only girl in the pack who's been ogling the shit out of him."

"Is that supposed to make me feel better?"

"Yes."

I cracked my lids open. "*How?*"

"He doesn't pay *any* attention to the others, but he can't keep his eyes off you."

"That's because I keep acting like an infatuated groupie, and I'm his Beta's little sister."

She grinned.

"Don't laugh at me. You're supposed to be my best friend. My *supportive* best friend."

"I'm not laughing."

"You're grinning."

She plugged in a flat iron, then removed the rubber band I'd stuck in my hair before giving Storm his bath.

"What are you doing?"

"Making you look less cavewoman and more femme fatale."

I stared ahead in the mirror.

"And then you and I are going out on that date we were supposed to have last night."

"I can't go out looking like this."

"Hun, you look beautiful. Now chill and let me work my magic."

A half hour later, not only had Adalyn tamed my brown mane into glossy curls, but she'd gone at my eyes with her liquid liner, making the darker rings around my pale brown irises pop. It wasn't magic yet felt magical in how much confidence it infused me with.

As she fixed her white bob, I sent Mom a message that I was having dinner with Adalyn. She asked me where. Since she wasn't the prying type, I assumed she was still worried about Shifter Zero. "Where are we going?"

"Hmm. Seoul Sister's the easiest. Is it weird, though?" She patted some serum onto her bluntly-cut ends.

"I went today to finalize your bachelorette, and it was totally fine, but that's probably because Miles doesn't know Bea and Nate broke up yet."

"He doesn't?"

I shook my head.

"Let's go there, then."

I texted Miles asking him if his free seat offer was still good. When he said yes, I told him to save me two at the bar and then texted Mom our destination.

After helping Adalyn clean up the salon, we bundled up and trekked toward Seoul Sister that glowed like a beacon in the dark night and painted the snow lining the sidewalk gold. I pulled open the door, brushing the snow off my boots. Soulful tunes eddied through the warm air. In a few hours, the place would heave with club beats and a lot more people, but the dinner crowd, even on Saturday nights, was rather tame.

Miles was just coming back toward the door when we walked in, a smile turning up his mouth. "Twice in twenty-four hours. This must be my lucky day." He leaned in and kissed my cheek, which made me freeze, because he'd never kissed my cheek before. I waited to see if he'd greet Adalyn the same way, but he just shot her a smile and grabbed two menus.

As we followed him to the bar seats he'd saved us, Adalyn pinched my waist and raised her dark eyebrows. I knew she was thinking: "What the hell was that?"

Since I didn't know what the hell that was, I shrugged.

Before leaving, Miles clicked his fingers to get the bartender's attention. "These girls have already been carded. Get them anything they want. On me."

I turned toward him as I pulled off my coat and draped it across my seat. "Miles, you don't have to—"

"Tonight, you two are my guests." He winked. "I'll catch you a little later."

Once he was gone, and we'd asked the bartender for two screwdrivers, Adalyn hissed, "Miles?"

I tucked a lock of hair behind my ear, marveling at how silky it felt. "Discussing your penis cake brought us closer."

"I'm sorry. What?"

"Wolf's out of the bag. Yes, that's the shape you're getting next week."

"Which I'm excited about, but that's not what I said *what* about."

"What did you say *what* about then?"

She leaned in real close and hissed. "The *bringing you closer* part. Nikki, that's not a good idea."

I bristled. "Geez . . . I didn't say I was interested."

"Good, because you really can't go there. Not for like a year anyway." When I cocked an eyebrow, she added, "And only if Nate and Bea don't end up getting back together, otherwise it's going to make things weird for everyone."

"Honestly, I never even considered it. I swear." I wanted to bang my head against the bar. Instead I grabbed my citrusy vodka drink and sucked half of it down.

When she didn't answer, I looked her way. She was typing something on her phone. "Sorry. Just answering your worrywart brother. You'd think we didn't have a cockblocking bond tying us."

I snorted at her terminology, however accurate it was. A mating link prevented sexual relations with anyone other than your mate.

"I wish I had a mate. It would make things so much simpler."

She flipped over her phone to give me her undivided attention. "Only if you liked the person you were bound to."

"Well, I wouldn't complete a mating link with someone I didn't like." I wrapped my lips around my straw and took another pull of my delicious drink. The fact that I couldn't even taste the vodka made me wonder if the bartender had actually put any inside.

"Real-talk: do you want me to find out if Liam's interested?"

My sip went down the wrong hole, and I sputtered, then banged my fist against my chest and coughed out a, "Don't you dare."

"I wasn't going to ask him point-blank. I was going to get Nash to weasel it out of him."

"My brother *isn't* subtle."

"How about I ask Nolan? He's the subtlest Freemont, after your mom."

"I'd rather drink deer urine."

She shook her head. "You're so dramatic."

"Please, Ads. Please don't, or I'm really skipping town."

"Fine, I won't say anything." She stared so deeply into her drink that my stomach filled with ice.

"Please tell me you didn't already say something."

"I swear I didn't."

"You swear?"

She crossed her heart.

I heaved a deep sigh, then filled Adalyn in on the halfwolf situation and my brilliant idea. After our shared appetizer was cleared, and the bartender deposited fresh screwdrivers in front of us, Adalyn's forehead pleated.

"Okay, don't kill me."

"Why would I kill you?" I was feeling so blissfully mellow that I no longer questioned the presence of vodka in my drink.

"Well, um, I sort of told Nash we were here in case he wanted to meet us for a drink."

"Three's a crowd, but I like my brother, so you're all good."

I looked over my shoulder, tracking Adalyn's gaze. When I saw my brother hadn't come alone, I whipped my head back toward my friend and hissed, "You invited Liam?"

"Not exactly. I just told Nash to mention we were out in case Liam felt like joining." She put her hand on my lap and gave my thigh a squeeze. "But can I just say one thing? He'd be at home with his kid if he wasn't interested."

"Maybe he was just interested in getting out of the house," I grumbled.

"Keep telling yourself that." She popped off her stool when the guys reached us and laced her arms around Nash's neck pulling him in for a languorous kiss.

Slapping on a bright smile, I pivoted toward Liam, because syphoning in my drink while pretending he wasn't standing there would be childish. "I thought you were laying low tonight."

The noise level had increased and was now competing with the pulse drilling my eardrums. "That was the plan."

"What changed it?"

"Your brother. He told me to stop acting like an old man, and then Lucas said he wanted to kick back with the little guy and nurse his battered heart."

"His heart is battered?"

"He and his girl are . . . on the outs."

"Shoot. I'm sorry." I folded my legs, then bobbed my foot. The alcohol, which had hushed my nerves earlier, intensified them now.

Over Liam's head, I caught Miles fording through the growing crowd. "I got you guys a table in the back. I'll have your entrées transferred there."

Nash leaned over the bar, extending a credit card. "I'll just close off the tab."

"Family's on the house." Miles flashed me a smile that soured my stomach.

Yeah. I was definitely *not* going there. The half-second I'd been interested was due to my singlehood. Was that a thing? Singlehood? Or was it singleness? Singularity? Definitely not singularity.

"Family?" Nash said, credit card still out. "Shit. You didn't hear?"

Adalyn must've yelled something inside his brain, because his eyes blew open and swung to her.

Miles frowned. "What didn't I hear?"

"That they're getting married *after* us." My brother's lame answer almost made me laugh, because the sad reality remained that for the moment, the wedding was off.

Miles blinked at Nash and then he chuckled. "Everyone knows. Nikki and I are going to be frosting a cake next week to celebrate *your* future wife." His gaze locked on me as I got off my stool and gathered my coat.

I gathered my coat, bag, and drink, then sidestepped Liam. "So, where's that table?"

As we made our way toward it, his voice lit up my mind. *He's awfully excited about frosting a cake with you.*

My shoulder blades tightened. Was that jealousy or disgust? I glanced over my shoulder, met Liam's pointed gaze, and then got so sidetracked by it that I almost bumped into Miles's back but Liam shot out his hand and gripped my hip, preventing the collision.

You should watch where you're going. Wouldn't want you to spill that pretty orange drink of yours all over our host's nice white tee. Derision tinted his tone.

"*I* wouldn't want that; not so sure *you'd* be against it."

He smirked, confirming he'd be all too happy for me to dye Miles's shirt. After releasing my hip, his fingertips scraped down my thigh.

I dropped my gaze to the skin he'd inadvertently set on fire, then raised it back up to his incandescent eyes. "A shame you have a houseguest, and I still live at home."

His smirk vanished, and his black pupils spilled over the amber.

Had I just propositioned my Alpha?

Tucking my straw between my lips, I spun and took one of the seats at the table set for four, then shut my eyes and drained my glass. Who had my celibacy turned me into?

CHAPTER 15

A minute after we sat down, Liam's cell phone rang. His expression hadn't been relaxed, not even before I'd all but confessed I wanted to go home with him, but his angular jaw was now sharp enough to hew logs. His eyes went to my brother, who sucked in a breath.

Nash scraped back from the table. "Time to go, girls."

My heart jumped right into my throat. "Why? What happened?"

Liam ended the call and stuffed his phone into his pocket. ***Nothing to worry about.***

"Adalyn and I are pack, too." The heated whisper fled my lips before I could rethink addressing my Alpha in such a manner. "Don't you dare keep us in the dark."

The tendons in Liam's neck flexed as he stared down at me. ***The coroner and his wife broke out of the bunker.***

"How? Oh . . ." My hand climbed up to my mouth. "They're not adverse to silver."

He gave the faintest of nods, then dug a wad of bills from the back pocket of his jeans, peeled three hundreds, and flung them on the table.

As I rose and grabbed my jacket, I watched the green and cream bills flatten on the varnished wood. "Liam, you don't need to—"

You let a guy pay for your dinner, and he'll expect something in return.

I slung my bag over my shoulder. "According to your logic, now I owe you."

"I'm your Alpha, Nikki. You'll never owe me a thing." He pushed his chair under the table and tipped his head to the door.

Once outside, Nash pulled Adalyn toward his ride—a souped-up, navy Audi SUV he'd spent a good chunk of his savings on. "Nikki, you have your car, right?"

I nodded. "Around the corner. I'll meet you guys at the compound." I started down the trampled snow. When I felt a presence beside me, I pushed a lock of hair out of my eyes. "You'll get there faster if you go with them, Liam."

Scanning the dark street, he said, "I'm aware."

I started to look for my keys halfway to the car, so we could get away quickly, but of course my bulbous keychain chose that moment to play hide-and-seek.

Because I wasn't watching where I was going, my boot caught on a mound of snow. I gasped as gravity slurped me up and then I gasped again as a hand cinched my bicep, keeping me from faceplanting.

In spite of the strain around Liam's mouth, a faint smile appeared. "Tell me you're steadier on four paws?" A cloud drifted over the stars, painting the man still holding me in shades of silvery grays and glittery blacks. "Nikki?"

I snapped out of my trance and slid my arm from his grip. "Um. Yeah." That did *not* sound convincing. I dropped my gaze to my bag just as a phone beam sliced across the inside. "Good thinking." The light caught on my cherry key-charm. I hooked it, then led Liam to where I'd parked in front of Hair of the Wolf.

As I stuck the key inside the handle and twisted, Liam asked, "Key fob not working?"

"Not since Niall rolled over it. But it wasn't working all too well when Nash and Nolan inherited the car from Nate." I clicked the doors open. Before climbing in, I said, "You're man enough to be driven, right?"

His lips quirked again. "Depends. Do you drive better than you walk?"

I smiled. "Yes."

He held my car door open. "Actually, how many drinks did you have?"

I bit my lip. Even with my wolf metabolism, I probably shouldn't have been driving. Not with snow on the ground and very little food in my stomach. I slapped the furry cherry into his palm and circled the front bumper.

As I strapped myself in and Liam started the car, I asked, "Wasn't there someone guarding the cells?"

He pulled out of the parking spot, gaze taped to the road.

"Liam?"

The dashboard illuminated his profile, highlighted his prominent Adam's apple.

Goosebumps rose in waves across my skin. "Wasn't it Niall's shift?"

Liam's eyes flicked to me, then back to the road. "He's the one who called. He's fine. Your parents are with him."

"Why are my parents . . .?" I couldn't even finish the sentence, because there was only one reason they'd be with my brother. "What happened to him?"

"The coroner pretended to go into cardiac arrest. Niall went in and got caught unawares. The man shut him inside and then freed his wife. To get out, Niall had to *handle* the silver lock."

My fingers wrapped around my seat belt, strangled it. "He wasn't bitten or anything?"

"No."

The breaths, which had jammed in my chest, all escaped at the very same time. "Is he still at the bunker?"

"No, he's at the compound clinic." Liam turned the car without putting on his blinkers and raced too fast up the plowed driveway.

Like last time, the gate was already sliding open when we reached it.

"So, what's the plan?"

Liam cocked a brow. "The plan?"

"The coroner and his wife are on the loose. Even if they're back in skin, I imagine you don't want them roaming around Beaver Creek."

"I've got five trackers canvasing the woods. As soon as I drop you off, there'll be six."

"Seven."

"Nikki . . ." There was a growl in his voice.

When my house came into view, I reached for my door handle. Liam punched the lock button, then swerved down the road toward the pond.

"What are you doing?"

He didn't say anything, just kept driving until his cabin came into view. The door was opened and Lucas was standing there, barefoot, wearing only a pair of sweats.

"You want to help?" he asked, before getting out of the car.

"Yes." I hopped out and followed him into the house.

Lucas's pale eyes gleamed neon-blue. "Storm's asleep."

Liam tossed his jacket on the couch, then crouched and undid his boot laces. "How's your leg? Good enough to run all night in deep snow?"

My heart caught on a beat, then slowly pulsed it out. I wanted to say yes, but it would've been a lie. "No."

"Then could you stay here with Storm so that both Lucas and I can head out?"

I looked over my shoulder at Lucas, who had his arms crossed in front of a lean, muscled torso dusted in black hair. I had no doubt he'd be way more effective out there than I'd be.

Sighing, I dropped my bag and took off my jacket. "Sure."

Liam nodded to Lucas, who stepped out of the house.

"Is there anything I need to know about Storm's nighttime routine?"

His fingers caught on the hem of his black V-neck. Was he going to get naked in front of me? Even though fear battered my chest, the slice of stomach that appeared between the elastic band of his underwear and raised shirt had a whole array of other feelings hitching my breaths.

I averted my gaze, focusing on the orchid poised on the middle of his wooden coffee table.

"He still wakes up once or twice during the night. You don't need to give him milk or change his diaper, but he likes company."

When his belt buckle clinked, I swallowed and plowed my hands through my hair to curtain off my warming cheeks. How ironic that I'd gotten my wish —going home with Liam and getting him naked. Too bad I hadn't added some fine print: *Chasing after blood-crazed lunatics not included.*

"They're on foot so they won't have gotten too far. I should be back soon."

"No worries." I dug through my bag for my phone but then remembered I'd jammed it into my coat pocket.

As Liam's jeans whispered off his legs, I reached out and snatched my jacket, then retrieved my cell. I typed out a message to Niall to ask him how he was feeling, and then to my mother to tell her I was at Liam's, babysitting Storm, so she wouldn't worry. I concentrated so hard on my phone screen to avoid the temptation of peeking at Liam that every word blurred and bled together until they resembled trails of smoke.

"Thank you, Nikki." Liam's voice was like a siren's call, and yet I resisted it.

I was so freaking impressed with myself. Especially as the air churned with his wind-musk scent. Had Grant's smell set off my pulse the same way? The fact that I couldn't remember pointed toward a *no.*

Liam's palms smacked the floor and then bones popped, transforming the man into a monstrous black creature that made my two-toned alter ego appear cute as a bunny.

A howl echoed outside the cabin.

Liam backed up, his claws clicking against the hardwood floor, then spun and leaped out the front door with almost feline grace. I went to shut out the moonless night but ended up leaning against the rough wood instead, admiring the two massive wolves racing up the hill, melting into shadows before reappearing like ink smudges against the starlit snow.

The sight of others in fur enthused my own wolf, and she paced.

"Not tonight." As though to make sure she didn't emerge without my consent, a dull ache spread through my knee, reminding her and me that we were in shifting timeout for the foreseeable future. I shoved the door a little harder than necessary.

Why had I exerted myself for a stupid lope around the compound? I should've walked. Or trotted.

When I returned to the couch, two messages illuminated my screen.

MOM: *Do you want me to come and relieve you?*

ME: *No. I've got it. Just take care of Niall.*

I switched to Niall's message thread.

NIALL: *I'm fine. Love you too, Pinecone.*

My chest cramped. Not because I didn't think Niall loved me. I knew he did. But my brother would've shot back something humorously discourteous, which led me to suspect he wasn't feeling like himself.

ME: *I'll see you as soon as Liam comes back.*

I waited and waited for his answer. Finally, two words appeared: **Don't worry.**

Yeah. Like it was something I could control. When you loved, you worried.

I was about to text Adalyn to see if she wanted to come hang out when a soft cry resounded through the silent cabin. I set my phone down and removed my boots. I'd never visited the place when Alex Morgan had been alive. Although larger than the other pondside cabins, it possessed a similar floorplan—open kitchen and living area, then a corridor that led to the bedrooms. Unlike at Niall's, this one had a third bedroom.

I trailed the sound of Storm's cries into the smaller of the three rooms where a wooden crib abutted the foot of a queen-sized bed. I was worried that when he'd see me, his cries would intensify—I mean, he was surely expecting his father or Lucas—but instead, his little lips pressed shut. I reached into the crib and gently pushed back a lock of hair that had curled and caught on his wet lashes.

"I know, I know. Me again."

He didn't make a peep, just gazed at me, tiny fists unclenching at his sides.

"Your sleep sack looks real cozy. Wish they came in my size." I flicked another lock of hair off his scrunched forehead. "So, how does this go? Do we chat a little, and you fall back asleep? Should I sing?" The few times I'd gotten him to nap was after his milk, and since Liam had told me Storm didn't drink at night, I wasn't sure what to do.

Stroking the frame of his face, I sang *Twinkle, Twinkle, Little Star*, my repertoire a tad limited. Instead of putting him to sleep, his eyes remained wide.

"This isn't a concert, little man. You're supposed to sleep."

He squeaked and then flapped his legs and arms.

I laughed, then hummed him another song, and his state of wakefulness grew more pronounced. I tapped his nose. "Thank you for being such a great audience, but you really need to close those beautiful eyes of yours and relax."

He squealed.

I grinned. I didn't speak baby, but I was pretty sure that was a negative on my shutting-eyes counsel. Sensing he wasn't ready to doze off, I looked around the room to find a chair to sit on. The room wasn't equipped with one so I started toward the door to grab one from the kitchen. The second I was out of sight, Storm released a cry so shrill his father probably heard it from the woods.

"I'm right here, Storm."

He kept wringing the life out of his lungs. I returned to him and plucked him up. He stopped crying instantly.

"You know exactly how to get what you want, huh?"

He just stared at me, and then simultaneously lifted his thumb to his mouth and gripped a lock of my hair. I tried to wrangle it from his fist, but he held on, and then he did the strangest thing. He brought the curled tip to his nose and rubbed it against his flaring nostrils. His lids dropped and dropped as though Adalyn had soaked my hair in melatonin instead of serum. When his lower lashes tangled with his top ones, his fingers began to loosen. I tried to free my hair, but his fingers clenched, and his lids lifted.

"Fine. Keep my hair. I have so much of it anyway." I pressed a kiss onto his forehead. And then I walked around the cabin, humming under my breath until his fingers unclenched and his cheeks stopped dimpling from sucking his thumb.

I lowered him carefully back into his bed. After letting go, I didn't dare move, worried that a mere shift in the air would startle him back awake. I started to turn when a little sob bubbled out of him.

I abandoned any idea of leaving the room and curled up on the foot of the bed, then reached my index through the crib's bar to stroke his open palm. He gripped my finger and flipped onto his side in spite of his cumbersome blanket.

Slowly, his lids grew heavy. This time, when he let go, I didn't. I held on to this tiny, temperamental creature, feeling so protective of him even though he was only mine to protect for the night.

"What are you Kolane men doing to me?" I murmured, watching his sleep sack puff and collapse with his quiet breaths.

His fingers cinched mine as though to make sure I hadn't abandoned him, then spread again once he'd ascertained I hadn't.

"I won't let go until your daddy comes home."

And I didn't. My index was still nestled in his fist when a warm breath fanned over my forehead and jerked me from sleep.

CHAPTER 16

I sat up so fast the dark room spun.

Shh. It's just me. Liam was crouched next to the bed, his luminous gaze steady on my blinking one.

No light lined the drawn curtains. "What time is it?" I murmured, digging the heels of my palms into my eyes.

Two.

I opened my mouth to ask a question when Liam put his finger to his lips. Even though my brain wasn't at its sharpest, it understood that conversations needed to be had outside. I edged toward the side of the bed, got up quietly, then padded into the hallway. Although Liam had a hundred pounds on me, his footfalls were just as noiseless.

As I made my way to the kitchen, my eyes felt like someone had rubbed sand into them.

"Can I use the bathroom before I go?" I whispered.

Liam nodded to the door at the end of the hallway, and I vanished inside. At first, I really was about to just use the toilet, but then I caught sight of my reflection and spent more time scrubbing off the residue of my smudged mascara than peeing. Once I'd gotten rid of my skunk look, I guzzled in some water to wet my throat and clean the lingering taste of screwdrivers off my tongue.

My eyes were red and puffy by the time I was done, but at least my hair still looked nice. Both Lucas and Liam were in the kitchen, both chugging bottles of water. Where Liam had put his clothes back on, Lucas stood bare-chested, in only sweats, an ugly bruise blooming on his left pec and shoulder, right beneath the ends of his shaggy black hair.

I leaned against the granite countertop. "Bumped into a tree?"

Lucas glanced at his purpled skin and smirked. "Close. A car."

My lids pulled up.

"They were trying to jumpstart an old truck when we found them."

"So they were still in skin?"

"Unfortunately. Not that their halfwolf physique was all that pleasant, but their dangly bits were less noticeable in fur."

I snorted at his irreverence. "Glad you found them."

"Did you doubt we would?" Lucas squashed the empty bottle and tossed it into the bin under the sink, then tapped the side of his nose. "Did Liam forget to mention I got the finest sense of smell in all of Colorado?"

"We got sidetracked discussing your ego." I added a smile to make sure Lucas knew I was kidding.

"Ouch." He rubbed his unbruised pec as though I'd physically cut him but then grinned as he stepped past me and into the hallway. "Don't know about you guys, but I'm gonna go get my beauty sleep. Night night; don't let the wolf bite." He glanced over his shoulder, past his stringy locks matted with sweat to toss us a wolfish grin. "Too hard, that is."

I frowned, until I got his innuendo. Cheeks blazing, I pressed away from the stone edge and walked to the front door. "He's . . . *witty* that one."

Liam didn't smile. Just raked one hand through his own hair, teasing the mussed mass at more odd angles. The man cleaned up nice but he also dirtied nice.

I slid on my boots and coat, then turned to grab my bag. "So, they're back at the bunker?"

Liam jammed his bare feet into his boots, not bothering with the laces. "They are."

"Are you headed back there?"

"Not tonight."

"Do you always wear boots to bed?"

He grabbed his jacket and opened the door. "Just seeing you home."

"That's really unnecessary. My car's right outside, Liam."

"Don't want you falling asleep behind the wheel. Besides, I was going to check on Niall."

"What about Storm?"

"Lucas is here." He dug my car key from his jacket pocket and handed it over.

The Jeep was still unlocked, so I got in and revved up the engine, which heaved and sputtered from the cold. This would probably be its last winter.

Liam climbed into the passenger seat.

"Did you get hurt, too?" I pulled out of the driveway and onto the shoelace road that wrapped up the hill.

"No. Lucas got the brunt of it."

He was quiet after that. Two minutes later, we were parked in front of my house.

As I killed the engine, he said, "Nikki, wait."

I looked away from the softly glowing bow window of the living room.

"You're a sweet girl, Nicole Raina Freemont."

"Thank you?" Yeah, it came out as a question.

"Too sweet for me."

My stomach felt as cold as when Adalyn and I had dared each other to slurp snow our first winter in fur. "Okay."

"Also too young."

I bristled because, what the actual hell? "Too young for what?"

He frowned. "For me."

"I'm nineteen."

"Exactly. A teenager. You haven't even been to college yet."

"I have a job. I don't need college."

He tried to reach out and touch my arm, but I pulled it out of his reach. "Nikki, don't take this the wrong way. I'm sorry if I mislead you into thinking I might be interested."

Wow. *Punch me in the heart again, why don't you?* "Got it. Loud and clear." I lurched out of the car and strode over to the house before Liam had even gotten his door. After removing my boots, I strode into the living room where Mom was curled up on an armchair, reading a book, while Niall lay on the couch.

I thought he was asleep, but his brown eyes met mine over the blanket pulled up to his shoulders.

"Hey, Pinecone."

Shoving aside my festering displeasure at Liam's words, I knelt by my brother's side. His hands were bandaged, and he sported butterfly stitches over a long gash beneath his eye.

I must've looked about ready to cry, because he said, "I heard the ladies dug facial scars, so I went and got myself one. What do you think?"

I shook my head but smiled, then licked my lips, because a tear hit them. "I'm glad to see the sense of humor has made its return." Another tear trickled out.

Niall raised one of his bandaged hands to my face but winced.

"Niall, you have to rest them," Mom admonished him.

He rested it back on his chest just as the front door opened. Imagining it was Liam, I got up and pressed a kiss to my brother's forehead. "Tomorrow, you, me, the TV, and the couch *all* day. Sounds like a plan?"

"A fucking great one."

"Niall," Mom chided him.

"A *fantastic* one," he amended with a wink that must've tugged on his wound, because it was followed by a grimace.

I pivoted, then sidestepped Liam without so much as a glance his way, and took the stairs, my emotions in a tailspin.

Mom always said the moon amplified emotions in us shifters. I hoped she was right. I hoped that in the light of day I'd be able to sort through my jumbled feelings and filter out the superficial ones, the ones that made my ego throb like a stubbed toe. Just because Liam thought I was a child didn't make me one.

CHAPTER 17

I managed to avoid Liam the entire first half of the week by spending most of my days in my bedroom or holed up at the hair salon with Adalyn. The great thing with my line of work was that I could do it from literally anywhere. I took on more commissions than I ever had, because working kept my mind off my bruised ego and the fact that Shifter Zero hadn't yet been caught.

I still saw Storm daily. Just because I was no longer a fan of the dad, didn't mean I was no longer a fan of the son.

Too sweet. How the hell had Liam managed to make something that really should've been a compliment sound like an insult? Was he only into bitches, and I didn't mean the shifter type?

"And too young," I muttered to Storm as I helped him fit animal shapes into a board that produced a jingle each time he got it right.

Mom had gone to pick up some last-minute items for the Thanksgiving feast Dad and Nolan were cooking up at Pondside, which was how I'd ended up sitting on my striped pink-and-beige rug with my back propped against my bedframe and Storm clapping happily beside me. The doorbell rang. Since Liam didn't use the bell, I scooped Storm off the floor, balanced him on my hip, and went downstairs.

I was surprised to find Lucas standing on our doormat, wiping mud off his boots. "Came to fetch my man the Destroyer."

It hadn't snowed since the blizzard, but since the air was crisp, the land

98

had stayed nice and white. Gold at the moment, since the sun was fading behind the crenellated mountains.

"Come on in. I need to get Storm's jacket from the laundry room. We had a little spit-up situation."

Lucas's head swung from side to side as he stepped inside, his short pony-tail swishing like a wolf's tail. "Nice digs."

"Thanks. It's my parents'." I caught my lower lip with my front teeth. "You probably knew that, though."

He smiled at me. It wasn't condescending. More like amused. "Yeah. I heard."

My living arrangements probably fed into Liam's belief that I was a kid. I definitely was ready for my own place. And not for Liam's sake but for my own. Maybe tonight, I'd have a chat with Niall to check if that second bedroom still had my name on it.

I rounded the staircase toward the stairs that led to the basement, Storm still on my hip. Lucas was following me. "You can wait up here, if you want."

"I enjoy visiting houses."

"Really?" Because I was incredibly insecure, I assumed he was trailing me to make sure I didn't endanger my precious, twittering cargo. Although, had he truly been worried, wouldn't he have offered to carry Storm?

"I started designing the floorplans to my future house with my girl. It's nice to see what's out there. Sometimes, it sparks ideas."

"So everything's better between you two?"

"Better?"

Shoot. Maybe I wasn't supposed to know his relationship was on the rocks. Too late now.

I wrapped my hand around the banister as I started down the stairs. "Liam mentioned you had a fight."

"Did he, now? Our Alpha is *such* a gossip."

Once I reached the bottom, I glanced over my shoulder. "He is?"

He chuckled. "Nope. The guy's a tomb. I'm surprised he even mentioned my private life."

As I headed to the stacked dryer and washer, I handed him Storm.

"Talking about private lives, haven't seen you around for a few days."

"Been busy with work." I pulled open the dryer, plucked Storm's tiny navy coat out, then turned the sleeves outside in.

Lucas nuzzled Storm's head. "*Women.*"

I narrowed my eyes. "What about women?"

"You're a puzzling bunch."

I snorted. "Hope you didn't tell your girlfriend that."

"Nah. I did way worse." He sighed. "She may never take me back."

"You're not mates?"

"Not many of those in our pack. Only Ness and August from our generation."

"Really? How come?"

He smoothed a cowlick atop Storm's head. "Probably because we eliminated girls with our gender selection root. Heard about that, right?"

"Yeah, I heard."

I took one of Storm's little fists and fed it through the armhole. "So, what did you do?"

He twirled Storm so I could get his other arm through. "I'll tell you if you tell me the truth about why you've been avoiding us."

"What do you care why I've been avoiding you?"

"Curiosity."

My ass, curiosity. "Forget it. Your love life's none of my business."

"My girl's preggers." Lucas frowned, but not at me, at the floor. "Baby's a girl."

"And you didn't want a kid?"

Lucas's black eyebrows leveled. "It was unplanned, but I couldn't be happier. Storm made me discover I have a very developed paternal bone."

"So *she* doesn't want a baby?"

"Didn't you hear the first part? Baby's a *girl*. OBs don't have girls."

My head jerked back. "It's not yours?"

"That's what I said, even though I couldn't imagine Sarah would cheat on me. I mean our sex life's—"

"Don't know you well enough to hear about your sex life."

He smirked, but it quickly morphed into a deep frown. "I asked her for a paternity test."

"Ouch."

"She told me to go fuck myself since I wouldn't be fucking her anymore, and then she moved out. Last week, I wake up to an email with the results of the test. Baby's mine. So I grovel. Buy her flowers. Lingerie. Stilettos. She loves pretty shoes. I even buy this tiny baby dress, all pink and frilly, and what does she do? Dumps it all in front of my door."

"*Wow.* Wouldn't want to be in your shoes right now."

"*I* don't want to be in my shoes right now."

I led him back upstairs, not that the basement wasn't cozy for heart-to-hearts what with its muted lighting and powdery fresh smell.

"I really fucked up, but in my defense, I didn't think I could father a girl."

"Did you try talking to her?"

"She won't pick up my calls."

"And in person?"

"She won't come out of Ness's house, and Ness won't let me in. Tells me I need to give Sarah time and space to come around. That she's working on her, but shouldn't *I* be working on her? I'm the one who screwed up. Besides, she's carrying *my* child. I want to be part of her life. Of their lives."

"Is she coming tonight?"

"Nope. Spending Turkey day with her Mom and brother. She told Ness to inform me that if I showed up, she wouldn't move onto the compound this summer or *ever*."

"Does she have a choice?"

"Yes and no. She's still at college, so she has an excuse to stay back."

"Have you tried writing her an email or a letter? Maybe if you put your feelings on paper—"

"That's such a chick thing to do."

I splayed my hands on my hips. "Maybe it's a chick thing to do, because chicks like nice words."

"I'm a man of action, not words."

"Well, your actions aren't reaping any results, so maybe try words."

He scratched his jaw that was in serious need of a shave. "Like what do I say: my bed's mighty cold since you left, and I want to see your belly and breasts get big?"

Storm was zoning out, sucking on his thumb.

"Um, *no*. That's basically telling her you miss the sex and—"

"I do miss the sex."

"*And* you're excited to see her get fat."

He cocked the eyebrow slashed with a scar. "Fat? I talked about her belly and boobs. Shit, her boobs are going to get massive."

I stared and stared at him, because he was the most uncouth person I'd ever met, and I lived among shifters, who were more in touch with their animal sides than with their human. Not to mention I had *four* brothers. "Lycaon, you really have no filter."

"I'm a fervent ambassador of honesty. And who the hell's Lycaon?"

"The god of all wolves." I frowned. "Don't you worship them, too?"

"Them?"

"Lycaon is genderless."

He joggled his head. "OBs worship the moon and our Alpha; most definitely not an imaginary god."

I was about to say Lycaon wasn't imaginary, that there were many texts mentioning our god, but didn't feel like debating this at the moment. "Look, I'm no relationship expert, but you have to make her feel loved, because you obviously love her for more than the sex."

A beat.

"Right?"

"Fuck yeah."

I expelled a breath.

"So, I need to write pretty shit?"

I tipped my head. "First things first, let's not call it *shit*."

He screwed his lips to the side. "Couldn't write it for me, could you?"

"It's got to come from *your* heart."

"My heart's not real poetic."

"How about you try and write something out and show me what you come up with at dinner tonight? And then I'll help you polish it."

His smile grew wide. "Sounds good, Knickknack."

"Uh, it's Nikki."

He patted my head. Actually, patted it. "When I like a person, I give them a nickname."

"Okay . . . but Knickknack?"

"It's an awesome sound."

"It means useless bauble."

"If they're so useless, then why does everybody have them, huh? But if you really don't like knickknack, I can call you paddywhack."

"Definitely not."

"Knickknack it is." He grinned. "So, we good?"

I hefted an eyebrow. "Up until that awful nickname, we were."

"I knew it!" He clicked his fingers, which made Storm startle awake. "Sorry, Little Destroyer." He stroked Storm's head, which lulled him right back to sleep.

"What did you know?" I asked, as Lucas wrapped a hand around the doorknob.

"I was worried you were no longer coming around because of me, but now I know it's Liam you've been avoiding."

I pressed my lips together.

"Still don't want to talk about it?"

"Nope."

He pulled the door open. "He's had a tough year, Nikki."

"He's not the only one."

His eyes dropped to my leg. "Right."

I ended up sighing. "He and I are fine, Lucas."

"I see that." His tone smacked of sarcasm. "Anyway, catch you tonight. I'll bring my heart; you bring your magical quill."

I may not have liked Liam much anymore, but I had to admit his Beta was nice. Lacked filter, but it added to his easygoing charm. More importantly though, Lucas seemed like a good friend. One who, in spite of his own troubles, cared about others.

After he left, I went to get ready for our pack Thanksgiving. I'd heard a dozen or so Original Boulders would be in attendance this year, which would make for a massive feast. Even though larger families ate at home, the singles, couples without children, and elderly would be there tonight. I wondered if Lori would show.

Last year, she'd made the trip down to Pondside, but hadn't stayed long. Nate, always the gentleman, had escorted her back to her house, which had made Bea insanely jealous. She hadn't spoken to my brother the entire meal. They'd eventually patched things up, though.

I hadn't seen hide nor hair of my eldest brother in almost a week. I imagined the case was keeping him busy.

Unless it was Bea?

CHAPTER 18

The red underwear set Adalyn had gifted me for my birthday came out of my drawer. As did my skinny black leather pants, which I paired with a tissue-soft tank top that clung to my torso like second skin. The black fabric was transparent enough to reveal the shape and color of my bra, but decent enough to wear to a family gathering.

Sadly, my hair hadn't been touched by Adalyn's magical fingers, so I tied it up in a high ponytail. Before leaving, I rolled mascara over my lashes and scarlet lipstick over my mouth to match my lacy lingerie. I stared at my reflection in the mirror beside the front door. I didn't look old, but I didn't look like a kid.

I stuffed the lipstick into my jacket pocket and took the cleared road down to the pond to avoid the crunchy snow that blanketed the hill. As I walked, I met up with a few other shifters, friends I hadn't seen in a while because most of my peers were in college. When we reached the pack eatery, I'd fallen into step with Farrah, one of Niall's exes—although could they be called exes when someone was just a one-night stand?

Like most of his other conquests, she still pined for my gigolo brother. "Would I be wasting my breath if I asked him out?"

I shrugged out of my jacket and stuck it on one of the rolling coatracks by the door. "He's never had a relationship, but I suppose the worst that can happen is he turns you down."

Would I have preferred Liam to say no instead of finding excuses? Would

104

it have rankled less? My eyes wandered over the small crowd, which had already gathered around the ten communal tables, all set up with a spread of tiny pumpkins and festive cinnamon-scented candles that must've been burning for a while because the air was thick with spice.

"Could you ask him for me?" Farrah took my arm as my gaze locked on our Alpha, who sat at the bar beside Lucas, surrounded by a skein of females.

Most were fawning over Storm, probably in order to get close to Liam. Was it petty of me to feel glad Storm wasn't putting on a show for Liam's fan club? The little guy was wedged in tight against his father's chest.

"So? Could you?"

I glanced at Farrah's wide green eyes playing hide-and-seek behind heavy black bangs. "Sorry. Could I what?"

"Ask Niall."

I bit the inside of my cheek. "Sure."

"Thanks, Nikki. You're the best." She kissed my cheek before sauntering toward one of the tables.

I worried the inside of my mouth some more because I was almost sure Niall's answer would be *not interested*. Farrah was too sweet for my—*Noooo*. I did *not* just go there. *Damn you, Liam Kolane, for polluting my brain.*

Annoyed with him and with myself, I headed to the fireplace where Niall was hanging with Nash and Adalyn.

"How's my favorite sister?" Niall's arm came around my shoulders after I'd plopped down beside him.

I rolled my eyes. "Your favorite and only sister."

"Milk the status. Next month, I'll have two sisters." Niall turned a dimpled grin toward Adalyn, who pressed her hand over her chest and *ahh*ed, burrowing closer to Nash whose lap she was perched on even though there was plenty of space on the curved leather couch.

"That was so sweet, Niall." She blew him a kiss before her gaze fell on me and lit up. "You wore my present!"

"I did."

Niall pouted. "Why aren't you wearing *my* present?"

"Sex swings are surprisingly harder to pull off," I deadpanned, which made Nash smile and Niall burst out laughing.

"Careful. Don't want your scar splitting." I glanced at the bruised skin beneath his eye. "Does it still hurt?"

"Nope. Can't say the same about my hands. Those still sting like a mother. Damn silver bars."

Before he could sink back into the night he was attacked, I broached the subject of living together.

He stared at me steadily. "The room's still yours. You tell me when, and I'll help you pack up."

"Tomorrow?"

"Let's do it."

"Have you told Mom and Dad yet?" Nash caressed the side of Adalyn's arm, over and over. Apparently, the need to touch never faded between true mates.

"No. I was waiting to find out if I still had a place to live. On a completely unrelated note, Niall, I ran into Farrah on my way here."

"Who's Farrah?"

I smacked his arm. "You're awful."

When no smile crept over his lips, I realized he was serious. "Wait. You really don't remember her?"

He pointed to himself. "Concussion victim here."

My eyes went wide in concern.

Nash snorted. "Don't fall for that. He just screws too many women to keep them straight."

"You just scared the living shit out of me," I hissed.

"Sorry, Nik. So which one's Farrah?"

"Black hair. Green eyes. Almost my height."

"Hmm. I never remember eye color, and I've been with a lot of dark-haired chicks."

"Bangs."

"Ah."

I could tell he'd fit the name with the one-night stand.

"So, what about Farrah?"

"She wants to ask you out."

He frowned.

"But she wanted me to feel out whether you'd be interested in a relationship first."

"Nope."

I didn't want to be the bearer of bad news, but I supposed it beat rejection from the source. "Can I ask why not?"

"Because I don't want to be tied down."

"So it's not her?"

"Nah. She's chill. And hot. If I had to date someone, I might just get with her."

"Niall's scared one day he'll be trapped by a mating bond." Adalyn played with a button on Nash's flannel shirt. "So he's milking his sexual independence."

"Imagine that, Niall." Nash tightened his arms around Adalyn. "Sex with the same person for the rest—of—your—life."

Niall's dimples were back. "Dude, you're gonna give me anxiety."

I laughed while Niall twisted around to cop a look at Farrah. "She interested in a second-night stand by any chance? My hands aren't at their greatest but my mouth still works fine."

I grimaced. "Eww, Niall. As for whether she's interested, go find out yourself."

"I think I will. Later, shifter." He sprung out of the couch.

"Do I really want to live with such a player?" I mused out loud.

Nash's and Adalyn's attention rose to some place over my head. I turned, hoping it was Nate, but nope, it was the other Beta. And next to him, our one and only Alpha.

Lucas dug a piece of paper out of his jeans, then dropped down beside me. "Brought your magical quill?"

"Got it right here." I tapped my temple.

Liam sat on my other side. "Magical quill?"

I didn't answer. Instead, I turned my full attention on Storm, who pushed off his daddy's chest and reached out for me. I lifted one finger, and he caught it in his pudgy fist, but then he wiggled until I lifted him off Liam's lap.

Adalyn watched me warily. She'd warned me to be careful about forming a bond with Storm, but what exactly was I supposed to do? Give a baby the cold shoulder? However painful it might be once Liam eventually settled with someone *not sweet* and *not young*, my heart wasn't hard or bruised enough to avoid affection. Lycaon, I hoped he didn't pick someone too tough. Storm deserved a little tenderness in his life.

Once I'd positioned Storm on my lap, I nodded to Lucas's paper. "Hold it out, so I can read it."

Lucas exhibited it proudly. He'd written five lines, three of which mentioned some body part of Sarah's that he really loved. "It's deep, right?"

"There's . . . *substance* to work with," I offered kindly.

"Fine. It's shit."

"It's not, Lucas. I swear it's not. But, maybe focus on *how* she makes you feel. And not just sexually."

He smirked.

"Since you guys aren't true mates, why did you choose each other?" Storm

107

caught my bra strap and pulled on it. I tried to ease it out of his grasp, but the baby had an iron fist. He relaxed his grip and the strap snapped. "Ouch," I whispered, tickling him, which of course just spurred him to repeat the whole song and dance, or rather, pull and release.

"A man after my own heart. Always go for the bra." Lucas grabbed Storm's free hand and fist-bumped him, which held his attention for a fraction of a second before he zoned back in on my red bra strap.

"To think I made you his godfather." Liam's voice curled around my neck, raising goosebumps. He was close enough to spot my skin's reaction if he looked. Hopefully, he wouldn't, or if he did, he'd attribute it to the icy draft that snaked through Pondside as Ness and August arrived along with a few other out-of-compounders.

"Your Boulder crew has arrived." I kissed Storm's forehead, then handed him to his father, adding a little *ouch* when his fingers unfastened from my strap. As he tittered, I stood. "I'm going to go check if Dad needs help. Lucas, let's work on your letter after dessert."

He folded it back up and stuffed it back into his slightly baggy jeans. "You're the bomb, Knickknack."

"Knickknack?" I heard Adalyn ask as I walked away.

The back of my neck prickled from the weight of someone's stare. I was guessing it was Liam's. He probably felt slighted that I hadn't shown him the respect due to an Alpha. If I'd done this to Cassandra Morgan—pretended she wasn't there when she was sitting right beside me—I'd have been carted off to the bunker to be taught manners.

Maybe he'd have words about my behavior later, but I doubted the silent treatment would win me a stay inside a silver cage. For all the rumors of his callousness, the time I'd spent with him showed me he wasn't morally rigid like his predecessor, merely aloof.

I almost wished he'd been more like Cassandra. Would've made flicking the switch off my attraction a lot easier. Which was why I was picking distance.

Out of sight, out of mind.

CHAPTER 19

Neither Lori nor Bea attended Thanksgiving. Nate was there, though. We had time for a quick hug before we were recruited to help carry the plates of food to the bar, which had been converted into a buffet tonight.

Before heading toward my family's table, which was also the Alpha's, Betas', and OBs', I stopped my brother with a hand on his forearm. "Are you okay?"

He parked the tray of cubed butternut squash he'd toted out of the kitchen between a wide bowl filled with green mash and a baking tray filled with herb-flecked stuffing. "Just tired."

"Because of the case or the breakup?"

"Both. It's been a rough couple of weeks."

I squeezed his arm, wishing I could take some of his stress away. "Any leads on Shifter Zero?"

"You didn't hear? Lucas confirmed it was a male from the Glacier pack." Nate's expression radiated such relief it leaped from him to me. "Liam's supposed to head out this weekend to talk to them about boundaries and an appropriate punishment for hurting a human on pack land."

"Hurting? The wolf killed a woman . . ."

"Technically, he only infected her. *We* killed her with our dose of Sillin."

"Which we wouldn't have had to administer if she hadn't been a halfwolf."

Nate flattened both his palms on my shoulders. "I agree with you. The situation really sucks, but this means Beaver Creek's safe again. This is what matters. Only this."

I guessed he was right, but like he'd said, this situation really sucked. "What about the coroner and his wife? Have they been released?"

Nate sighed. "Not yet."

"Why? I thought they were back in skin."

"They were, but it didn't last."

My pulse stuttered. "They're halfwolves again?"

My brother nodded.

This situation was *way* past sucky. "Do we know how Shifter Zero turned the first girl into a halfwolf?"

"That's what Liam's going to find out this weekend."

"Will you go with him?"

"If he asks me to. For now, he's only scheduled to leave with Lucas."

My gaze strayed toward Liam, who was entirely focused on the girl sitting across the table from him—May Weathers. I had the sudden urge to disinvite her from the bachelorette. Ads wouldn't object since she wasn't a fan of May's, but Dad would have words with me since she was his best friend's daughter.

For years, Dad had tried to get us to bond, but May was entitled and egocentric, the sort of girl who craved attention, demanded it, reminding anyone who forgot she had been the Aspen Alpha's niece, and thus, pack royalty.

"Go enjoy your night. The pack has lots to celebrate." Nate tried to fit a smile onto his face, but it tripped right off.

Before he turned away, I said, "I'm really sorry about Bea."

"Yeah. Me, too."

When his dark eyes slicked over with tears, I pushed up on my toes and hugged him. His arms came around my back and his bearded chin perched on my shoulder.

In a rough whisper, he said, "Thanks for that, Pinecone. I really needed a hug."

I smiled against his black flannel shirt. "If you keep calling me pinecone, that's the last hug you'll ever get from me."

He chuckled, and I felt happy for the first time since last weekend when Liam had told me he wasn't interested. My family was safe. My pack was safe. Everything was looking up. Besides my love life, but that would be resolved in two days' time. Well, not my love life per se, but my sex life.

Where Nate headed to one end of the table, I headed toward the other.

All ten tables had been extended to accommodate the five hundred or so shifters in attendance, making Pondside resemble a veritable banquet hall.

Adalyn had saved me a seat between her and an OB named Dexter, who was a second cousin of Matt Rogers, also present. Both were built like linebackers and both worked for August, who sat a few seats away, playing with the ends of his mate's long blonde ponytail.

Although I eyed the singles' table where Niall had elected residence, I headed toward my best friend and the OBs.

"Hi." I offered Dexter a bright smile, which he reciprocated. "Don't know if you remember me. Nikki Freemont."

His gray-blue eyes twinkled beneath brown bangs, which seemed carelessly swept to the side but probably had been styled that way. "I never forget the pretty ones." Suddenly, his forehead pleated, and his gaze flicked toward the middle of the table, toward Liam.

Was he warning males away from his Beta's little sister? He better not.

Nolan walked up to the table and set one of the thirty glistening fowls beside my plate, then wiped his hands on the kitchen towel draped over his shoulder while Dad set another turkey in front of Liam.

I leaned in and inhaled the steam lifting from the carved bird. "Smells delicious."

"Hope it tastes delicious, too. Dad and I have been at the stove since two this morning."

Freckle-faced Sasha placed another turkey in front of Liam, then strutted over. "I made the fava bean purée."

Nolan smirked. "You shelled the beans."

"Fine, fine. I *helped* make the fava purée." Sasha smiled as Nolan and him started back toward the kitchen to bring out the rest of the turkeys. "But I did shell an unholy amount of pods. Someone needs to invent a machine that does that."

"You could do it. You're good at tinkering." My brother's voice faded as Dad clapped his hands to call the pack to attention.

Standing beside Liam, he started by giving thanks to Lycaon for the bountiful meal we were about to partake in and for the gift of a generous and strong Alpha who ruled with equity and calm.

Dad would never dare criticize Liam, especially in his presence, but I wondered if he was laying it on thick or if he really was *that* enamored. I mean, objectively speaking, Liam was calmer and fairer than Cassandra, but he'd only headed the pack for a little over a year. He hadn't exactly proven himself yet.

"And lastly, we'd like to thank him and each tracker who worked relent-lessly, day and night, to uncover the source of our anguish. I'm happy to announce, on behalf of Liam, that we finally had a break in the case." Dad relayed with the utmost precision all Nate had already told me.

Cheering rang out around the cavernous space. Knowing the case had been solved was comforting, but it didn't feel right to cheer, not when one innocent had died and two more had been infected. Once they were healed—either returned to skin or turned completely to fur—I'd truly rejoice.

I looked toward Liam, curious how he dealt with so much praise. His shoulders were stiff and his gaze locked on his son, who was presently bundled in Mom's arms. Odds were, he wouldn't get him back until the end of the meal.

Once Dad said amen, and everyone had cheered with wine, water, or beer, I turned toward Nash. "What about the halfwolves?"

It was Dexter who answered. "I heard Lori's blood is losing its effective-ness. You prefer white or dark meat, Nikki?"

"Dark, please." I held out my plate, and he plopped a wing on it before snagging a giant drumstick for himself and passing the platter to Nash.

"Can't believe a Glacier was down here." Nash served Ads and himself some turkey, then passed the platter to August. "They usually don't venture out of Alaska."

"Maybe the girl was his girlfriend?" Matt suggested.

"It would explain why he was on our land, but not why he attacked her here," Nash said, around a mouthful of turkey. "Everyone knows pack land is sacred."

Ness leaned forward, planting both elbows on the table. "I was sure it would turn out to be a rogue." A loose strand of golden hair cascaded around her shoulders, veiling her scarred cheek.

"How do you guys think he made her a halfwolf?" Matt's fiancée asked.

"By biting her." Lucas delivered this with such assuredness that it sparked little fires all around the table.

Matt's girl pushed her thick curly brown hair back. "I thought biting didn't transfer your magic."

Lucas draped an arm over the back of Ness's chair. "Usually doesn't, but we're dealing with some extra special Glacier, Amanda."

One of my bra straps slipped down my shoulder. I hooked it with my thumb and snapped it back in place. "Congrats on the break in the case."

Lucas sat up a little straighter. "We got real lucky."

Opinions raged around the table about how Shifter Zero went about transferring our gene. Defective or not, no wolf, to my knowledge, had ever succeeded in passing it along to a human. Nate looked our way before getting roped into a discussion at his end of the table. As conspiracy theories were traded, I grabbed my plate and headed to the buffet. When I returned to the table, I asked Nolan, who'd just dropped into the seat beside Amanda, where he'd stashed the cranberry relish.

"Must've forgotten it in the fridge." He shrugged off his black chef jacket and draped it over the back of his chair. "I'll go grab it."

"No, you've been on your feet all day. Sit. I'll go." I wove through the long, cheery line of shifters waiting their turn to access the buffet, then pressed through the flap door.

I should've asked which fridge, considering there were four. I pulled open the largest one first, and after a quick scan of the shelves, I found a bowl filled with something red and shiny.

"Bingo," I murmured, reaching inside.

As I shut the fridge, I let out a little shriek, because standing right there, on the other side of the stainless steel, was Liam. Miraculously, I didn't drop the bowl. "For someone so big, you're awfully stealthy."

"Why are you avoiding me?"

"If I were avoiding you, Liam, then I wouldn't be standing here, chatting with you."

"You're standing here, because I cornered you."

"Okay, fine. I'm avoiding you. Happy? Can you let me through, please?"

He didn't move a muscle.

I sighed. "I guess I'll take the long way out." I started to turn when a bolt of courage streaked through me and made me ask, "Why do you even care? Do you require every shifter's attention on you at all times?"

"I don't require *every* shifter's attention, but your brother's my Beta, Nikki. I'd prefer not to burn bridges with the members of his family, and I sense that turning you down burned a bridge."

"All smoke; no fire. You and me are fine, Liam."

I pivoted in order to round the industrial-sized island.

"If you and I were *fine*," Liam replied, all low and growly, "you wouldn't be trying to escape."

I stopped. "I'm not escaping. I'm walking the other way so I don't have to elbow my Alpha. Would you rather be elbowed?"

"What makes you think I won't let you through?"

I clutched the bowl of cranberry sauce so tight that if it had been made of anything besides wood it would've cracked. "Maybe because I already asked you, and you didn't move the first time around."

"Ask me again."

Oh great Lycaon, what sort of head game was this? "I have a perfectly adequate route out of here that doesn't require me asking anything of you."

"Why are you doing all you can to avoid me?"

"Geez. You're relentless." I turned and plowed right for him, then squeezed past his imposing frame, shouldering him in the process. "Happy?"

Before I reached the door, he said, "Stay away from Dexter. He's a good guy but he's a player."

I came to a stop. I was two seconds away from telling him he was sitting in front of the female version of Dexter but bit back the words, because it would showcase I'd been watching him.

Liam padded over to where I stood, his scent slowly overtaking the sour-sweet relish I held against my drumming chest.

"At least, he's not put off by how *young* I am."

Liam's pupils dilated, deepening the brown depths of his irises. "I thought we were *fine*, but you're still angry."

"I'm not angry, I'm embarrassed. I propositioned you, Liam, and you flat-out refused." I pressed my fingertips into the door, but for some crazy reason, perhaps because I was exceptionally bitter to have been forced to relive my moment of unparalleled shame, I added, "The more I think about it, the more Dexter and his *player*ness are appealing right now." I streaked out of the kitchen, complexion surely as flaming as the relish which I slapped on the table.

"Whoa." Dexter blinked at me. "What did the cranberries do to you?"

"Nothing." I sat down so hard my tailbone whacked the bottom rung of my chair, dragging muttered curses out of me.

"Clearly." His eyes softened with a smile, while Adalyn's eyes traveled right to the kitchen door.

Her knee tapped into mine. "Bathroom break?"

"Later," I grumbled.

"Just tell me when."

It took my heartbeats a while to settle into an evener rhythm. For a spiteful second, I contemplated flirting with Dexter, but his smell didn't do it for me.

As though he'd sensed me thinking about his scent, he took a long whiff of the air, and his sunburnt forehead grooved. "Shit."

I frowned. "What?"

He focused on his food. "So, I heard you all have big parties planned for Saturday."

"That we do." Adalyn's eyes sparked like twin sapphires. "If you guys stick around Beaver Creek for the long weekend, then I hope you'll join us."

"Join you for what?" Amanda asked.

Adalyn took a sip of her beer. "Our bachelorette and bachelor parties."

"Oh, how fun!" Amanda looked over at Ness, who put her fork down and patted her mouth, glancing over at Lucas.

"Maybe we could try to come back."

Lucas stiffened, because clearly, she meant with Sarah.

August must've said something to Ness through their bond, because she raised her face toward his. She bit her lip and grimaced. He leaned over and kissed the grimace from her lips. Even though they didn't start playing tonsil hockey, I looked toward Liam to see his reaction. Found his eyes on them. Did he still have a thing for her?

"I don't have anything planned this weekend. Maybe I'll join your bachelorette party." Dexter grabbed a piece of cornbread and sponged up his plate.

Adalyn smirked. "You mean, the bachelor party?"

"Nah. I meant the bachelorette party."

Matt snorted while Amanda rolled her eyes and said, "I doubt the girls want you around, Dex."

His gaze skimmed mine as though to ferret out whether this was true.

I leaned back in my chair. "You're welcome to come to the girls' party—"

"Which will be way more fun than the guys'," Adalyn tossed in.

"But then, you'll have to partake in all our games," I finished with a teasing smile.

Dexter grinned and hooked his arm around the back of his chair. "Yeah? What sort of games are we talking?"

My smile got wider as I imagined him picking out cards from my bright pink deck of dares.

"Hey, Knickknack"—Lucas was suddenly in my face—"I'm ready to work on my letter."

I frowned. "Right, *right* now?"

"Inspiration just hit, and I need to discuss it."

Ness asked, "What letter?"

"The one you'll be ferrying back to my girl tonight." Lucas grabbed my plate. "Let me get that for you."

Was this really about his note or was this an intervention? Sighing, I indulged him and followed him to the couches. After we sat, he took out his folded piece of paper. I speared some roasted butternut squash and chewed on it as I read over the bullet points he'd added at the bottom. Not full lines, but at least he'd given me a few extra things to work with.

When I looked up at him to ask for a pen, I caught him staring over his shoulder at Liam.

"Dexter seems really nice." I made my voice go extra high on that last part, waiting for a reaction.

"He is, but he ain't for you." Lucas pushed an errant lock of black hair out of his eyes.

"How about you and Liam let me make up my own mind about who's right for me?"

Lucas slotted his fingers together and nodded to the paper, not even acknowledging my comment. "So, what do you think of my addendums?"

I was about to tell him I was serious when the seat cushion dipped beside me.

CHAPTER 20

"So let me see this love letter I'll be carrying back." Ness pushed up the sleeves of her red silk bomber and lifted the paper from my lap.

"Let's not push it, Fury. It's not a love letter; it's a lust letter."

"Fury?" I asked.

"After Nick Fury. The founder of the Avengers." At my raised eyebrow, Lucas added, "Wears this super cool eyepatch?"

"So you got a nickname too?" Ness smiled, and I couldn't help but think how strange it was to be sitting so close to someone who'd helped change the fate of our pack.

"Apparently, I qualified."

As I forked stuffing into my mouth, Ness handed me back the note. "Did you write this, Lucas, or is it Nikki's work?"

"All Lucas."

"So what d'ya think, Fury?"

"It's heartwarming."

"Is that . . . good?" he asked.

"Yes"—she leaned forward and tapped his thigh—"that's good."

He sat up a little straighter, a little prouder.

As the conversations around us grew to ridiculous levels, Ness and I turned Lucas's grocery list of heartfelt declarations into a letter that read like a poem but still sounded like it had been written by a guy. It was surprisingly fun, and more than once, we laughed at something cringily inappropriate that shot out of Lucas's mouth. Satisfied, he held his rolled knuckles up for a fist bump, which both Ness and I delivered in turn.

"And, Lucas, she really misses you, but don't you dare tell her I confessed this, or she'll put hot sauce in my mascara again."

I grimaced. "Ouch."

"Yeah, ouch."

Lucas's eyes sparked at Ness's admission. Or at his girlfriend's antics?

"Secret's safe." He gave us a two-finger salute before venturing back toward the table.

I was about to get up to help clear the eco-friendly, disposable plates when Ness laid a hand on my wrist.

"Can we talk?"

My heart catapulted against my ribs. Was she going to tell me to steer clear of Liam? Or Dexter? Or maybe to butt out of Lucas and Sarah's fight?

"Sure." I settled back in the couch and folded one leg over the other.

"We're moving here this summer, and I wanted to know how things work around the compound."

Oh. "Well, we operate like a town, but our currency isn't monetary. There's a small convenience shop by the front gate, a clinic equipped like a hospital, and a school that goes from pre-k to the end of elementary right on the premises. For middle and high school, we either head off land or use online schooling. Same for college, for those of us who go."

"Are you planning on going?"

"No." I nibbled on my bottom lip. "I'm a digital artist and make a nice income from it." I shrugged. "Maybe I'll go in a couple years from now. I heard you're enrolled. How will that work out once you're here?"

"We're keeping our houses in Boulder, so Sarah, Amanda, and I are going to commute. Spend half the week there. Long weekends here." She traced the stitching on the suede couch.

"What are you studying?"

"Business, with a specialty in accounting. I love numbers."

I groaned. "I loathe numbers."

"I'll do your taxes and you can paint something fabulous for our new house in return."

"Spoken like a true compound resident."

She smiled.

"Can I ask *you* something?"

She turned a little more toward me. "Of course."

I dropped my voice. "Did you ever want the job?"

Her dark eyebrows knitted. "The job?"

"Alpha," I murmured.

Her brow smoothed, and she relaxed back into the cushion. "No. I even turned down being one of his Betas. Too much politics and stress."

"But you challenged him back when you moved to Boulder?"

"I just wanted a place in the pack, and those bastards wouldn't let me pledge myself." She tossed a fond glance at *those bastards*. I looked, too. Found both Liam and August looking our way, well Ness's way.

She turned her attention back to me. "Don't ever let locked doors or barricaded windows stop you from getting in. There's always a rooftop access." She winked. "That's the lesson I learned when I returned to Boulder."

It was good advice. "Thank you, by the way. For killing Cassandra."

"Don't thank me. It was a team effort. I might've sank the killing fang, but Liam drained her of her energy, and August brought me back from the dead." She rubbed a spot on her collarbone, her eyes glazing over as though she were back in the arena where she'd lost her life. "That was the day I learned what it means to be pack. You're never alone."

"Still, you're an inspiration."

"Wow. Really?"

"Yes, really. Most of the girls around the compound want to be you when they grow up, fierce and tenacious." I leaned over and whispered, "Some, like May over there, just want to be you to get our Alpha's attention without needing to sacrifice her life for it."

Ness laughed. "What about you, Nikki?"

"What about me?" I asked slowly.

"Would you sacrifice yourself for your Alpha?"

Here I thought she was going to ask me if I wanted our Alpha's attention. "I'd hope that's the sort of woman I would be, but I guess one can only know when the situation arises. Hopefully, it won't."

"It's funny."

"What is?"

"That you wonder." She stood up. "Because I have no doubt that's exactly the type of woman you are."

I tilted my head. "How? You don't even know me."

"Call it a gut feeling."

"I hope your gut's right."

"My gut's always right."

"Oh, really?" I got up. "Your gut may be a little conceited then."

She laughed. "Want to know what else my gut's telling me?"

"That it wants to sample the pecan and pumpkin pies, the cherry cobbler, *and* the vanilla-bean cheesecake?"

"I believe that may be your gut talking, Nikki."

I laid my palm on my stomach, which rumbled in anticipation. "So tell me, what else is your gut telling you?"

She leaned forward and murmured, "That you're what we've all been waiting for."

My head jerked back a little. Before I could ask her what exactly that was supposed to mean, she made her way back toward August, the embroidered white words *Boulder Babe* dancing against the red silk of her jacket. Instead of her chair, she sank onto August's lap and hooked her arms around his neck. His arms came around her, and although the sight of them was beautiful, it was also depressing.

I looked over at Adalyn, who was barking out a laugh at something Dexter had just said, her fingers linked through Nash's. I'm not sure what Ness saw in me, but if she looked over at me now, she'd spot a woman full of envy. I counted my blessings—how appropriate considering what we were celebrating —until the weight of coveting lifted off my chest.

As happiness seeped back into me, burning away all the dark stuff, my gaze cycled around the room, and I swear the air felt warmer and the atmosphere cheerier. It was incredible how the entire world could change when you changed your way of looking at it.

Even when I caught sight of Liam—presently standing at the buffet with his son in his arms, circled by a few chatty shifters—my heart didn't plummet or squeeze. But it did hold still, before pulsing double-time when he caught me staring.

I smiled, done feeling embarrassed at having gone out on a branch. Sure, the branch had broken and the fall had hurt, but it was time I got up and walked away.

And so I did.

I walked away, and I didn't look back.

CHAPTER 21

I'd spent all of Friday unpacking and making the small second bedroom in Niall's cabin mine. Mom, Dad, Adalyn, Nash, Nolan, and Niall helped me lug duffels and boxes filled with nineteen years' worth of stuff, upholding the Freemont motto of '*All for one and one for all.*' The only family member not in attendance was Nate, but none of us had wanted to bother him after witnessing his level of fatigue.

When I'd brought up my desire to move in with Niall over breakfast, I'd been worried my parents would try to dissuade me, but on the contrary, they told me it was wonderful, that it would be good for me and for their wildest son. They probably thought I could tame Niall. Wishful thinking. I doubted a mating bond could tame my brother's wildness.

The following day, to make sure Mom and Dad didn't feel bereft in their big house, I went up for breakfast and stayed through lunch. I needn't have worried about them being lonely considering Liam had dropped off Storm earlier. They took turns entertaining him. While Dad cooked him homemade solids, Mom crawled around the living room floor and read him board books. I briefly wondered if I should remind them he wasn't their grandchild, but why kill their borrowed joy?

Family was everything to both of them, and when someone didn't have one, they provided. They'd done it for Adalyn, her little sister, and their grandmother after the freak avalanche that suffocated my best friend's parents. They'd tried to do it for Lori when she'd returned from the duel, motherless and brotherless, but Lori hadn't been as receptive. Probably because she was already a grown woman.

"Honey, can you bring this over to Lori's?" Dad pointed to three Tupperware containers filled to the brim with Thanksgiving leftovers.

How odd that she'd just been on my mind . . .

"I asked Nate to bring it over, but he's been so distracted these days." Dad let out a heavy sigh, clearly hurting for his son.

"Of course. Let me finish up with this little guy."

Dad stared at Storm, his eyes glazing over as though he were remembering one of us in the high chair, but then he blinked, and the corners of his eyes crinkled with a gentle smile. "He sure has an appetite. Reminds me of Niall. That boy ate more than his twin brothers combined."

I scraped the dregs of mashed carrot from the bowl and zigzagged the spoon like an airplane, complete with sound effects, into Storm's already gaping mouth, then let him play with his spoon while I carried the empty bowl to the sink.

Dad wet some paper towels. "I think a bath may be in order. Meg?" he called out, unstrapping Storm from his high chair. "I'd give you one myself, but it's the highlight of my mate's day." He carried him over to the window and pointed out a palm-sized chickadee hopping on the bare branch of a nearby birch.

The second Storm's eyes alighted on the bird, he tried to reach for it. As I slotted the bowl onto the drying rack, Dad told Storm the story of how chickadees had earned their names from their distinctive calls.

"*Chick-a-dee-dee-dee-dee.*" Dad emulated the bird cry, explaining to his captivated audience that the number of *dee*s increased depending on the predator. "You should hear them when they spot us in fur. They string a lot of *dee*s together."

I gathered the Tupperware, remembering all the times Dad had told me and my brothers this story, along with a great number of other fascinating tales on animal behavior.

Mom trundled up the stairs from the basement as I slipped on my boots and jacket.

"Bye, sweetheart. Have fun tonight, but be safe. No driving if you drink. Call us, and we'll come to get you."

"May's little sister won't be drinking. She promised to taxi us back and forth."

"Okay. Good." She kissed my cheek.

The walk over to Lori's big house took a grand total of five minutes.

Getting her to answer the doorbell took twice that long. Unlike our door, Lori kept hers locked. I was about to leave the plastic containers on her doormat when I finally heard footsteps and the scrape of metal. The elusive tawny-haired recluse squinted from the sunlight refracting on the snow, her lips as colorless as the rest of her face.

"Hey. Dad sends food."

Her violet eyes dipped toward the stacked boxes in my hands.

I held them out until she took them from me. "We missed you at Thanksgiving."

She'd never been loud and brash like Alex or their mother, but she'd become particularly quiet since her return from Boulder, as though someone had spun the volume dial on her lungs way down.

"Are you okay? You look a little pale."

"I've become a human blood bag."

I grimaced, having forgotten about that. "I'm sorry."

"Why?"

"Because it was my idea."

She regarded me a second that stretched into a full minute before shrugging. "I'm just happy I can help."

Not only was she wan, but what I could see of her narrow body had become whittled down to mere bones tented with flesh. I made a mental note to tell my father to arrange daily food deliveries or, like my car, she wouldn't last the winter.

I started to turn when I said, "We're celebrating Adalyn's bachelorette at Seoul Sister tonight. In case you feel like a change of scenery."

She raised a stunted smile. "I don't think I have the energy to make it out tonight, but thank you."

Guilt swamped me at how relieved I felt she'd turned down the invite.

Lycaon, I was a horrible person.

CHAPTER 22

Outfit folded in my bag—Adalyn had insisted all the girls get ready at Hair of the Wolf—I set out toward Seoul Sister to help Miles put the finishing touches on the party.

At the last minute, though, I took a detour toward Bea's apartment. I didn't know if she'd be home, but I decided to try my luck and parked the Jeep beside the entrance of her building. I was about to ring her doorbell when someone exited the building. They held the door open, and I slipped in.

I almost turned back when I reached her second-floor apartment, but the memory of my brother's heartbroken face made me jam my index finger into the doorbell. I waited, shifting from foot to foot, hoping I could maybe convince her to reconsider Nate, or at the very least, get her to emerge tonight. When no one came to the door, I pressed my ear against the wood, listening for a heartbeat. The door across the hall banged, making me jump.

"Can I help you, young lady?" the white-haired elderly man asked.

Guilt racked me even though I'd done nothing wrong. "I was hoping to speak with Bea Park."

"Miss Park's been absent for a while."

Had she gone home to her parents' house? That's what I would've done, but Bea wasn't quite as close to her parents as I was. I doubted many people were as close to their parents as us Freemonts.

"Did she happen to tell you where she was going?"

"No, but her boyfriend gave me the key to her mailbox and asked if I could collect her mail in her absence. Nice young man, that one. Good cop too, from what I hear."

"He's actually my brother."

"Ah. I thought I detected a resemblance."

I guessed we did look a little alike, sharing the same coloring and all. "Do you have any idea where she went?"

"He said she was visiting relatives out in California, but I don't know where exactly. Your brother would probably know."

I nodded. "I'll ask him. Thank you, sir."

"You're welcome."

As I climbed back into my car, I tried Bea's cell phone, but it went straight to voicemail. I imagined she was screening calls from my family. Sighing, I revved up the engine and headed to Seoul Sister. Maybe, just maybe, she'd be there.

She wasn't.

Miles was, though. He stood behind the bar, going over liquor inventory with the barmaid. The row of smaller birdcage lamps strung up over the bar highlighted his freshly-buzzed fade.

"Just came to drop off some stuff." I heaved my giant bag.

"Go on ahead. I'll be right with you." He nodded to the five tables he'd pushed together at the back of the restaurant, beneath the mirrored wall on which he'd taped the golden BRIDE TO BE balloons.

As I crossed the restaurant, I took out the packet of engagement-ring-shaped confetti from my bag, ripped it open, and sprinkled the contents over the five tables, then set out the eleven rose-gold Team Bride tumblers and the white Bride one—decorative and collectible. I fanned out penis-shaped straws next and blew up the giant engagement ring floatie.

By the time Miles came over, I was setting out a thick pile of dare cards. Curiosity had made me preview the deck. While some dares were tame—*drink if your hair's up in a ponytail, sing the song of your choice to five guys without laughing, dance with the worst dancer (picked by your friends)*—most were quite naughty—*ask a stranger for a condom, kiss a random guy, discuss the merits of sex toys with the person of your friend's choosing.*

Tonight would be a night to remember. Or to forget, depending on which cards I ended up with.

He scanned the tables. "Looks like you're all set." Although his expression was easygoing, his posture was closed-off, arms crossed in front of his white tee. "We just have to frost the cake."

Right . . . the cake. I heaved my bag back onto my shoulder. "Lead the way."

He took me into the kitchen, then down a set of narrow stairs toward a basement that would make a wonderful setting for a slasher flick, what with its subdued lighting and yellowish-tiled walls and floors.

"I set us up in the cellar." He entered a code on a keypad, and the door beeped.

Inset spotlights burst to life, pouring yellow beams onto the wooden shelving packed full of dusty bottles. Above the dank and woodsy aroma of corked wine rose another smell, one that made me smack my lips—sweet batter. A layered, phallic-shaped creation sat beside a large glass bowl filled with pink frosting on a tasting table.

Miles released the door, which beeped as it settled into a metallic frame.

My skin grew a little clammy, and not because of the musty chill. "Why did it beep?"

"Locking mechanism." He presented me with the spatula propped in the frosting bowl.

"Um . . . so how do we get out?"

"There's a keypad behind that wine barrel." Miles ticked his head toward an old wooden cask girdled with four shiny metal bands. "My parents have bottles worth a couple grand in here, so they upped security last year."

I swallowed, still not fully at ease with being locked in an underground cellar with a guy who wasn't family. "Could we leave the door open? I get a little claustrophobic."

Miles's lips pinched. "Dad'll kill me if the air temp varies too much."

"Can we take the cake out then? I'm sorry, I—"

"You don't need to explain yourself, but the kitchen's really busy. I'll open the door, but let's make it quick, deal?"

In under three minutes, I'd slapped pink frosting all over Adalyn's cake, and then I'd spent an extra minute smoothing it over.

"You've got serious skill, woman." Miles grinned at the uneven globs of pink icing.

As I sucked the streaks of sugary butter off my fingertips, I laughed. "Looks homemade by a toddler, but hey, it tastes divine."

His smile flickered, and one of his eyes twitched.

I leaned over and scooped up my bag from the floor, then seized the bowl. The metal spatula dinged against the glass. "Mission accomplished. Now, onto my next mission—clothes and hair."

Miles's gaze dropped to the wooden handle of the spatula, and then he was taking it from me. "You're getting frosting on your sweater."

I relinquished the bowl. "Should I get the cake?"

"No. Leave it here, so it can set." He nodded toward the door for me to go ahead of him.

I removed the broken wine rack he'd used as a doorstop, then held the door open for him. After we'd climbed the stairs, he dropped the bowl in one of the kitchen's deep sinks, then walked me back out into the dining room.

The festive decorations reminded me of our semi-formal high school graduation party at Seoul Sister. I'd danced the night away with Adalyn and Bea because Grant didn't dance, nor did most of the other male shifters in attendance. Even the human ones had preferred chugging beers and hanging with their buddies.

One week after the party, Grant and I had crashed, putting an end to my dancing days, but here I was, eighteen months later, standing on two legs, about to dance a new night away.

I sighed. "I wish Bea would come out tonight."

He leaned against the restaurant's glass door and crossed his defined forearms, bare skin not even pebbling. How was this man never cold? "You wouldn't know if she's pregnant, would you?"

My lips parted in surprise. "Pregnant?"

"Stomach issues. Bedridden. Quarantining up in the mountains."

Could she be pregnant? Heartbreak was still more likely, but what if my brother hadn't told us the full story?

"Nate hasn't mentioned anything?"

"No, but he's not the type to talk about his relationship." I nibbled on my lip. "You said she was up in the mountains?"

"Yeah. In Great Aunt Mary's hunting cabin. Bea inherited the place, what with being Mary's favorite."

I sensed resentment. Then again, favoritism among family never boded well. "Could you give me the address?"

"No address. But I can message you the GPS coordinates. Or we could head there together tomorrow? I was going to go after brunch. She keeps texting me that she's okay, doing a little better every day, but it's been three weeks, and I'm getting worried." He palmed the back of his fade. "Either way, I need to check up on her."

"Tomorrow works for me."

My assent freed his expression of its earlier tension. I hoped he didn't think tomorrow would be some sort of a date or anything. I decided not to clarify in case that wasn't where his mind had gone.

I really hoped that wasn't where his mind had gone.

On my way to the hair salon, I tried Nate's cell. It rang twice before he picked up. I was almost surprised he'd answered, not that my brother was in the habit of screening my calls. "Hey, so I was just with Miles, and he's really worried about Bea."

"Nik, this isn't the greatest time."

"Just tell me one thing. Why doesn't he know you two broke up? Did Bea not tell her family?"

A deep whine erupted from his side of the phone. I was guessing he was at the bunker. "She hasn't, no. She wanted to get her head together before she shared the news. So don't tell Miles anything. She'll call him when she's ready."

"It's between you and Bea, Nate." I was about to tell him about our plan to visit her tomorrow but bit my tongue. He'd probably ask us not to go, and deep down, I wanted to see Bea. She might not have been part of my family anymore, but I still cared about her.

"I really gotta go. Love you, Pinecone."

I started to say *I love you* back, but he disconnected before I could get the words out. When I reached Hair of the Wolf, everyone was already there.

Adalyn squealed when she spotted me. As I dug out her white *bride-to-be* sash, she trotted over in her short white dress and sky-high heels, clutching a plastic flute filled with pink champagne. Most of the girls were wearing dresses and heels tonight. I'd brought a skirt too, a pleated black one with built-in suspenders I hadn't worn since the accident, too self-conscious about my knee.

Since Adalyn had expressly asked all her bridesmaids to dress in pink—her favorite color—I'd unearthed a pink top from my closet that Mom had bought me back when I was in middle school, right before I started purchasing my own clothes and ruled out that particular color. It exposed my midriff but fit nicely with the skirt and thigh-high suede boots. I'd tried everything on last night, and decided it looked very schoolgirl naughty. In other words, an adequate pickup outfit.

Although, as I took in all the sequins, silks, and satin glimmering around me, I wondered if my selection wasn't overly academic. *Oh well.* I polished off my champagne in one gulp, then went to change in the bathroom.

When I came back out, Adalyn insisted on doing my makeup while her grandmother straightened my hair. Thirty minutes later, between my smoky eyes and waist-long, extra-glossy hair, I definitely no longer felt preppy.

We took a group shot before leaving. May tried to push her way to the middle, but Grandma Reeves shooed her off to the side and positioned Adalyn, her sister, and me between the rest of the girls.

"I can't believe you're getting married in a month," I whispered between picture thirty-two and forty-five. "Nineteen and married."

It wasn't uncommon to get married so young in the pack, especially not once a mating bond developed, but it still felt incredibly young.

"I know."

Where she vibrated with excitement, I trembled with emotion. To think this was only the bachelorette party. In what state would I be in for the wedding?

"Hey, no crying," she murmured as we wrapped up the photoshoot.

I sniffled. "Hope the makeup's waterproof."

"Aw, Nikki." She hugged me tight. "Almost sisters," she whispered into my hair. "Just like we always dreamed."

I nodded, my throat still feeling raw.

Adalyn released me and clapped. "Everyone, ready?"

A chorus of *yes*es erupted as the girls filed out. Adalyn speared her arm through mine, and we headed out into the wintry chill.

CHAPTER 23

The night started out tamely enough, but after the food was cleared, the lights were dimmed, and the music rose to eardrum-throbbing volumes, Adalyn distributed the dare cards. We got five each. Four of mine were not too awful but then I got one that made my cheeks go as bright as Gracey's neon tube top.

After reading the words on my card, Adalyn burst out laughing. "Ask a guy for his underwear. *That* I got to see."

I elbowed her.

Gracey got the *ask a guy for a condom* card. Although only sixteen, she had even less shame than her older sister, which was basically saying she had *zero* shame.

May whined. "I got *kiss the bartender*, but she's a girl."

"I'll take it," her bestie Savannah said.

"Anyone want to trade with me?" I'd been hoping to unload my underwear card, but instead, Adalyn pilfered my *order a drink in a foreign accent* card and replaced it with *kiss a random guy*. "Hey! I liked that one."

She tucked it into her pack. "My lips belong to your brother."

"You could've traded with May," I muttered.

"What could she have traded with me?" May's blonde hair swished over her shoulder, tangling with her extra-long glittery earrings.

"My *kiss a random guy* card," Adalyn said.

"Ooh. Yeah. Gimme, gimme." She wiggled her fingers.

I extended the pink card.

Adalyn thrust my arm back before I could eject my dare. "I'm the bride. That one's Nikki's."

"Boo." May pouted.

Adalyn dropped her voice, "You wanted a one-night stand. That card's your ticket to getting one."

"I'm pretty sure the underwear card could get me one, too."

May's little sister groaned. "Why did I agree to be the designated driver again? I need alcohol for this!"

"Okay, girls, listen up." Adalyn raised her tumbler filled with champagne. "You have one hour to get all your dares accomplished."

"What happens if we run out of time?"

Adalyn grinned coyly. "Why . . . you lose your place in my bridal party."

The girls shot to their feet.

"Good thing I'm the sister of the groom. Can't get rid of me even if I fail."

"I could choose another maid of honor."

I stared at her. "You wouldn't dare."

She knocked her tumbler into mine. "Are you sure? I'm pretty daring. Talking about daring, I need to go order a *drrrenk*," she said, in whatever accent that was supposed to be. She made me scoot off my chair to get up and tapped her manicured nail on my cards. "Tick tock, honey. Tick tock."

Ugh. "I should never have bought these."

"Are you kidding? They're the highlight of the evening. I mean . . ." She pointed to May who was shaking it behind some guy with disjointed dance moves.

Adalyn lifted her cell phone and taped the little jitter. May caught Adalyn filming her and flipped her off, but her smile was so wide I doubted she was truly mad.

I reread my cards, palms sweating, then scanned the crowd, looking for my first victim. When my gaze alighted on a familiar dark one, my mouth popped open. "Why is Liam here?"

"He is? Where?" Adalyn jiggled her head from side to side until she spotted him sitting at the bar beside Lucas. "Oh. I imagined those two—three"—Dexter was wending his way toward Liam and Lucas—"would be at the bachelor party. I know Nash asked them to join." She turned back toward me. "Don't let them get you off task."

"Right. Okay. I can do this." I took a gulp of champagne.

"Hell yeah." She gave me a little shove toward a dark-haired guy standing beside the table next to ours. "That one's been eye-fucking you since he arrived."

I set down my pink tumbler, heart tap-tapping.

"Use the underwear card on him." Adalyn tucked back the clip-on veil I'd gotten her.

"Come with me? Please?"

With a little nod of her head, she threaded her arm through mine and dragged me toward him. "Doesn't count if I ask him, though," she said just as we reached him. "Hi. This is Nikki. And Nikki has something to ask you."

I tugged at the collar of my top but it was sitting beneath my collarbone, so that was altogether useless.

"Hi, Nikki. I'm Jake." He stuck out his hand, and I shook it, but where my fingers loosened, his didn't.

Adalyn grinned. "I'll be right back," she singsonged, strutting away.

"So we're playing this game . . ." I snatched my fingers out of his.

"Yeah?"

I began to fiddle with one of my suspenders. "And I need to collect a pair of boxers. Any chance you'd be willing to part with yours?"

His eyes bounced to mine, and his smile graduated to a mischievous grin. "I'll give you mine if you give me yours."

"Um . . . um . . ." What the hell was I supposed to say to that? It's winter and I'm not wearing any tights?

"Only fair."

In a second, I was going to start fanning myself.

"Heard you needed a nut hut, Knickknack."

I wheeled around, found Lucas standing there with his eyes narrowed on poor Jake.

"So, I'm actually going commando tonight—don't like anything squeezing my balls, besides my girlfriend—but Liam's got some cute briefs I'm sure he'll part with if you ask nicely." Lucas dropped his arm across my shoulders and shepherded me away from Jake. "You can repay me in gummy bears. Love those things way too much."

Before I could locate my vocal cords, he plucked my cards from my hands and proceeded to chuckle as he read through them. "Fun game you girls got going. Check this out, Liam." He handed our Alpha my cards while I stood there, still a little perplexed, because this wasn't going to be half as stress-free with pack males around.

I fiddled with my suspenders again. "I thought you were kidding about the bachelorette, Dexter."

"I never kid around." He grinned wide, gaze traveling over my outfit until Lucas elbowed him hard in the ribs. Then his attention flipped to May, who was squeezing herself in next to me.

Cackling, she exhibited her forearm now inked with someone's phone number. "I'm so recycling that card at a later date. Hi, boys. Come to join in on the fun?"

"Came to make sure y'all got home okay," Lucas said.

Adalyn turned away from the bar with a fresh orange drink in her hands. "One down. Four to go. Nik, you got the guy's underwear?"

"Almost had it until this one showed up." I hooked a thumb toward Lucas.

The male exuded pride at having intervened. "The dude suggested a trade. I was protecting my packmate's innocence."

"I can protect my own innocence, thank you very much." I was completely relieved he'd butted in, but would I ever admit it? Nope. "Besides, maybe I was interested in the trade."

Liam's gaze flipped to me.

"Anyway, I still need a pair of male underwear, and since Lucas isn't wearing any . . ."

"Eww. How is that comfortable in jeans?" Adalyn grimaced as she sucked on her straw.

"He mentioned one of you"—he hadn't mentioned Dexter, but like hell I was singling out Liam—"might have a pair they'd be willing to hand over."

Dexter's gaze flicked to Lucas, then to Liam. "I'm unfortunately in the same boat as Lucas, so I can't help you there."

"Seriously?" May looked down at their crotches. "Don't zippers chafe?"

"Okay. My cue to leave." Adalyn melted into the crowd.

"What about you, Liam?" May asked. "Are you anti-underwear?"

Liam handed me back my cards. "No."

I waited for him to offer up his briefs. When his silence dragged on, I tucked my cards into the waistband of my skirt and turned to leave when I thought of something. "Aren't you guys supposed to be in Alaska?"

Liam's gaze slid to me, settled there. He was looking at my eyes and yet it felt like he was giving my soul a once-over. "We're leaving tomorrow morning."

"Were you hoping we'd miss out on all the festivities?" Lucas swiped a beer from the bar, then leaned back against it and plopped his elbows on the wood, as though settling in for a show.

"Yes," I deadpanned.

"Just pretend we're not here." Liam slung the rubber heels of his boots into the bottom rung of his bar stool and took a slow, slow sip of his beer.

Yeah . . . like that could ever happen. The room was crowded, dark, and loud, and yet all I could smell, see, and hear was him. I really needed to walk away and stay away, because walking back was ruining all my careful crush-bashing.

May popped out one hip. "Hey, Liam, I need to find a guy to serenade me. Any songs you might know?"

"Sorry, May. I don't sing, but Dex, on the other hand . . ."

Laughing, Lucas slapped Dexter's back. "Drake's got nothin' on our boy."

Dexter guffawed but indulged May by belting out a song that wounded my eardrums but made us all grin. Why couldn't Liam be fun like him? Why must he be all broody? Dexter may have had an easier life, but the capacity to let loose and make a fool of oneself was not a superpower. Just a state of mind.

After the next chorus, Dexter thankfully quit singing. "Impressive, right?"

I smirked. "Not a musical bone in your body, huh?"

"Ouch." Lucas shook his hand as though he'd been burned.

"Can't be skilled in *all* departments." Dexter winked, which transformed into an eye twitch. "Didn't know I had to ask permission." He chugged his beer. "Going to hit the head."

May tracked his retreat. "What's going on?"

"Nikki's brothers asked us to keep an eye on her," Lucas explained.

"What?" I gaped at him. "You're kidding?" My brothers would never do this to me . . . or would they?

"That sucks." May sent me a sympathetic look. "Glad I don't have bossy older brothers."

I crossed my arms. "Since when do Alphas take orders from others?"

Liam leaned back.

"We just care about keeping the peace in the pack, Knickknack. Don't take it personally."

"How could I take it any other way? You're cockblocking *me.*"

"Technically, they're cockblocking the guys who want to get with you." May held out a palm at my glower. "Down, girl."

"Well they can't possibly cockblock every guy in this club," I growled.

Liam tipped his head to the side and smiled. *Smiled!* Did he think it was some sort of twisted challenge?

"Stay. Away." I wheeled around, all the more determined to prove to these alphaholes that no one controlled me. I locked in on an easy target—Miles—and elbowed my way toward him.

CHAPTER 24

I doubt Nate would appreciate you asking Bea's brother for his tighty-whities.

I turned to glower at Liam, happy to see he was no longer smiling.

Seriously, Nikki, don't.

I'd been planning on using the shot-card on Miles, but Liam's interference almost made me change my mind.

I tapped Miles's shoulder and explained my dare: getting a guy to buy me a shot which I had to drink without using my hands. "Think you can help me out?"

"It would be my pleasure." He guided me back to the bar with a hand on my lower back.

As I passed by Liam, his anger was so palpable it rolled off him. Lucas was shaking his head as though to warn me not to do it.

After I drank my tequila under Miles's bemused supervision, he leaned over and tucked a lock of hair behind my ear. "I could get shut down for serving hard liquor to underaged girls."

I bit my lip. "Sorry. I didn't want to get you in trouble."

He raised a slow smile. "I think I'm already in trouble."

I darted my gaze around the darkened space. Were some undercover cops hanging around? Or was his bartender going to report him?

"I need to get back to the door, but if you have any other dares you need help with, come find me." His hand drifted to my bare shoulder, lingered, then slid down my arm. And then the weight of his fingertips disappeared, and he walked away.

Cheers erupted beside me as Savannah leaned over the bar to plant a wet one on the female bartender.

Her eyes glittered as she pulled back. "One card to go, and I'm done. This is *sooo* much fun." She held up a hand for a high five, which I delivered.

I stretched my neck from side to side, trying to relax so I could enjoy this game too, then scanned the club for my next victim, one I needed to take a selfie with. I spotted two guys standing against a wall, nervous and twitchy in their pressed shirts and khakis. *Not habitual clubbers . . .*

As they tracked Savannah's retreat, I walked over to them. "Hi."

One of the guys pushed square glasses up the bridge of his nose and gulped out a, "Hi."

To think I was one of the least intimidating people ever. "So, I have these dares to accomplish, and one of them is taking a picture with a random guy. Would you be game?"

He tugged at his shirt collar, color creeping into his neck. "Yeah, sure. Of course."

"Can we use your phone? I left mine at my table."

He joggled his head and dug his phone out of his jeans pocket. It took him a few seconds and some awkward body contortions to wriggle it out. After he turned the camera app on, he raised it. His grip trembled a little, then a lot when I pressed in closer.

An arm clapped my shoulder and then a face squeezed in between me and glasses-guy. He snapped the shot that Lucas had photobombed.

"Mind retaking it, man?" Lucas said. "I think I shut my eyes."

Ugh. "What part of leave me alone didn't you get?"

"I take my Beta-job very seriously, Knickknack."

I leveled the mother of all glares on Liam, who was back to looking amused—or was it pleased?—then shoved Lucas aside and stalked toward Adalyn to ask if she knew anything about this.

"I really doubt they told Liam and Lucas to babysit you." Adalyn looked over my shoulder in the direction of the bar. "I mean, your brothers are protective, but to my knowledge, they haven't held another sit-down since—"

"A sit-down? What sit-down?"

"Oh crap." She raised her palm to her mouth. "I wasn't supposed to tell you about that."

"Well, now you did."

She sighed. "I suppose it doesn't matter anymore. Anyway, when you turned fifteen, your brothers sat-down the eligible males in the pack and told them you were off-limits."

My eyes felt like they were about to rocket out of my skull. "And you knew?"

"Of course not. I only heard them talk about it a couple weeks ago."

My fingers were balled so tightly my nails were tattooing little crescents into my palm. If I didn't calm down, my claws would come out.

"Shh." Adalyn wrapped her hands around both my wrists. "Don't shift. It's in the past."

"Apparently, not so much in the past if they're having me watched."

"I really don't think it's their doing."

"Then why does Lucas show up every time I approach a guy?"

"Because he's following orders."

"You just said my brothers—"

"Not your brothers' orders."

I frowned, but then my brow smoothed. "You think Liam's behind this whole thing? He's not even interested!"

She raised an eyebrow. "Honey, he's interested."

"Did you miss our conversations about him turning me down?"

"Didn't miss a word of our multiple conversations on the subject, but I'm guessing he either turned you down because he thought it was best not to get involved with his Beta's sister or he's changed his mind."

I pulled my wrists out of her grasp. "Well, now, *I've* changed my mind." I was breathing as hard as the afternoon Adalyn and I had come across a black bear cub and heard her mother snuffle in nearby bushes. "And I'm going to make sure he understands it." I pulled my kiss card out of my deck and flapped it in midair.

"Um, Nik . . .?"

"Don't try to stop me."

"I'm not, but . . ." Her eyes rose to a spot over my head.

I wheeled around. "I swear I'll rip you a new one if you don't—" I lost my train of thought when I realized it wasn't Lucas.

If I don't what? Sit back and watch while you play your little game?

I notched up my chin. "My brothers didn't put you up to this, did they?"

Liam's throat was so veined his carotids looked about to detonate. "Adalyn, can you give us some space?"

"Only if Nikki wants space."

Best. Friend. Ever.

"It's way safer if she stays. For your sake. In case the overwhelming urge to rake my claws across a certain tender part of your anatomy overtakes me." I shot him a tart smile that made his pupils shrink.

"Nothing tender about that part of my anatomy."

Heat curled low in my belly. Because of the combo of alcohol and annoyance. "Good for you. Now, butt out." I flicked his chest with my card.

He plucked it from my fingers and read it, then flicked it over his shoulder.

"Hey. What the hell's gotten into you?"

"Consider it accomplished."

I crossed my arms. "That would be cheating, and I don't cheat."

He took a step forward, and cupped the back of my head at the same time as his lips crashed down on mine. I gasped, caught unawares by Liam's kiss. My heart pulsed out an explosion, followed by a series of sharp beats, and my arms fell from their knot.

I gripped his black T-shirt, meaning to push him away, but I neither pushed nor pulled, just held on for dear life as his mouth parted mine. A voice inside my head told me to stop whatever this was but a louder one yelled at me not to move a single muscle. Well, besides my tongue. Were tongues muscles?

As I pondered facial anatomy, Liam wound an arm around my waist and raked my body into his, which snapped my mind right onto *his* anatomy. I must've moaned because I could feel the shape of his mouth changing, curving.

Shit shit shit.

I finally regained my wits and shoved him, which just made my body dip backward since his was a freaking monolith, impossible to move. It had the desired effect though—our lips came apart like two strips of Velcro.

"What the hell was that?" I panted.

"Didn't want you to feel like a cheat." He apprehended one of my suspenders and ran it through his fingers, sliding along every piece of hypersensitive flesh on his way down.

"How obliging." Even my vocal cords had become hypersensitive it seemed considering how my voice shrilled.

"I try."

"Will you *try* to help others out with their dares?"

His hand curled around my waist, settling on the small of my back to keep me close. "No."

I swallowed, trying to calm my racing heart. A losing battle since his scent had infiltrated my body. "Whatever happened to me being *too young* and *too sweet?*"

"You still are. Both."

Again, I tried to wrench myself free, but Liam's grip was unyielding.

He dipped his face. *Is your one-night stand still on the table?*

I swallowed, stopping my wriggling. Of course, that was why he'd kissed me. To get to the sex part I'd offered. It wasn't the start of a relationship. Why was I even contemplating a relationship? Especially with a single dad who also happened to be my Alpha? That would only lead to a mountain of complications, and I wanted carefree, horizontal—or vertical—fun.

"I don't think that would be a good idea, Liam. I mean . . ." I licked my bottom lip. Once. Twice. "You're really old. Not to mention quite ornery." I delivered this perfectly straight-faced. Sure, there was truth to that second part, but obviously not to the first.

Twenty-three did not an old man make. Why was I talking to myself like an Elizabethan bard?

Liam stared at me for a full minute without speaking and without blinking. "I can't tell if you're joking or serious."

"Both."

That didn't relax his eyelids.

"Why the change of heart? Was there a shortage of old, cruel ladies?"

He finally blinked. And then . . . and then he laughed. And like when we were giving Storm a bath, I became totally transfixed by his mouth and the sound it was making, and how it was still slightly flushed and shiny from our kiss.

Walk. Away. I urged myself. *This cannot end well.*

Myself did not listen.

"Had I known calling you sweet would upset you so much, I'd have come up with some other adjective."

"The sweet part was fine. It was the adverb preceding it that did it. You don't even know me. Maybe I'm a raging bitch, and not just biologically."

"My son wouldn't be so taken with you if you were crazy and malicious." He raised his hand to my cheek, slipped his fingers to the nape of my neck. *Come home with me tonight, Nicole.*

It was strange hearing him call me Nicole instead of Nikki, but in a way, my full name made me feel older. Maybe his intent. "I *do* still need a pair of male underwear."

Amusement touched his mouth, softened the hard lines of his face.

The arm curled around my lower back glided off me, his fingertips brushing the back of my bare thigh, just below the hem of my skirt. The contact lasted a mere second, but its effect endured.

I cleared my throat. "Oh wait. I can't use the same guy for all my dares." I waited to see what my bogus rule would do to him; I waited to see just how much he wanted me. If it, at all, matched how deeply I wanted him.

If darkness were personified, it would've been Liam Kolane—his eyes went as black as a moonless sky. *The fuck you can't.*

I. Smiled.

"You were trying to get a rise out of me, weren't you?"

"No. I was trying to decide if you were worth leaving Adalyn's party for. Shoot! Adalyn." I whipped my head to where she'd been standing.

"She went back to the table when you started to moan."

Cheeks heating, I smacked Liam's chest. "I did no such thing."

"Oh . . . you did." He raised a grin so wicked it made my wolf paw at my skin to break out and rub up against his legs. *And I can assure you, I'm worth leaving the party for.*

"Careful, your *alphaholeness* is showing."

"Yeah?" His nostrils flared as he inhaled long and slow. *Your scent tells me you appreciate my alphaholeness.*

I tentatively sniffed the air but all I could smell was him and a neighboring guy's deodorant-free armpits, but mostly Liam.

"Ready to go, or do you want to hang out with the girls a while longer?"

I pushed back a lock of hair, looking in the direction of our table. Everyone, including Dexter and Lucas, was gaping at us.

I ducked behind Liam. "Shit, they all saw us."

He frowned. *And?*

"And I would've rather no one witness . . . us. Now I'll be known as one of your Alpha groupies."

"One of my Alpha groupies?" He sounded genuinely staggered.

"Don't tell me you weren't aware you had a fan club? You could pick up any girl at this bar, and they'd go home with you. Well, besides Adalyn."

I wasn't aware. And I pick you.

"Tonight. Tomorrow you might pick someone else, thus me having preferred to keep our hookup on the down-low." Just saying it out loud made me wonder if I was cut out for one-night stands. Maybe it was a gene, and although Niall had definitely inherited it, it had passed me over. "Why don't you leave first, and I'll meet you back at the compound in twenty?"

I'll get the car and idle in front. He started to turn. *You have five minutes.*

I perched a hand on my hip. "Oh really? And what if I'm not out in five minutes?"

He slanted me a look that was all at once terrifying and alluring. Terrifyingly alluring. ***Then I'll come back inside to get you, and everyone will know that you and I are going home to fuck.***

Holy Lycaon. "I see you no longer care about my brothers' input."

Did you want me to ask for their consent or does only yours matter?

"I definitely don't want any of them knowing we're going home to do . . . that."

"Fuck."

"Yes, *that*."

Grinning a tad savagely, he backed up. ***Your five minutes have started, Nicole.*** And with those parting words, he pivoted on his tawny Timberlands and pounded to the door while I used up one of my precious minutes to stare in trepidation at the beast I was about to bed.

CHAPTER 25

When I went to say goodbye to Adalyn, she pulled me aside, worry contorting her heart-shaped face. "Are you sure about this?"

"Yes. No." I hefted my bag onto my shoulder and eyed the door, expecting Liam to storm back inside any minute because I'd definitely exceeded the time limit he'd given me. "I don't know."

"Sweetie, if you don't feel—"

"I need to get him out of my system."

She snorted. "You do realize you're about to get him *into* your system?"

Ha.

She sighed, then pulled me into a hug, my enormous bag banging into her body. "If you have any doubts, at *any* point, just say stop and go home."

I nodded.

"And, Nik, thank you for tonight. It was perfect."

It had been perfect. After I let go, I snaked through the crowd, bumping into Miles on my way out.

"Leaving so soon?"

I touched my abdomen and wrinkled my nose. "Stomachache."

His gaze darted to my bare midriff. "I hope you feel better. But if you don't, just call me and we can cancel our visit."

Our . . .? Right! Bea. "I'm sure I'll be feeling better by then. Meet you here at one? Two?"

"One's good. I'll swing by the compound to pick you up."

"Or I can meet you here."

"Let's text tomorrow. Night, Nikki." I was about to turn when he leaned in to give me a one-armed hug.

The second his body was off mine, I blustered off. Even though I wore neither coat nor stockings, I didn't feel the cold wrapping around my exposed skin as I strode toward Liam's black SUV, which idled by the curb.

After I'd climbed into the passenger seat and strapped myself in, I glanced over at Liam, found a scowl tormenting his mouth. "I know, I know . . . I took way more than my allotted five minutes."

"Why do you smell like Bea's brother again?" His rough tone made me bristle.

What exactly did he think? That I'd rubbed up against another man to piss him off? "I ran into him on my way out." Because I couldn't leave well enough alone, I added, "Will you require me to shower when we get back to your place?"

His eyelashes fluttered. "I'll just have to replace his scent, although maybe I will have you shower."

My annoyance expired as suddenly as it had appeared, replaced by such potent desire that his car probably smacked of it. His nostrils flared and then a corner of his mouth curled. Yeah. He could smell it.

I tugged at the seat belt vibrating over my pounding heart. "I've never done this before, by the way."

"Had sex?"

"No, *that* I've done. I meant the whole"—I twirled my hand in the air— "one-night thing." I glanced his way, found his attention on the road that was growing progressively darker as we headed out of the heart of Beaver Creek. "Do you . . . do it a lot? Actually, don't answer that. I'd rather not know."

For several minutes, neither of us spoke.

But then the silence got to me. "Will it make things weird tomorrow?"

His grip tightened around the steering wheel. "It doesn't have to make anything weird, but if you—"

"I need to get you out of my system, Liam." I repeated what I'd told Adalyn, because, well, because it was true.

His eyebrows jumped. "And you think having sex with me will accomplish that?"

"You were a dick to me tonight, and yet I'm sitting right here next to you, because all I can freaking think about is you. Lame, huh?" I rolled my head until my left cheek was pressed against the leather headrest. "Anyway, I'm hoping that tonight can destroy the pedestal I propped you on, so I can go back to viewing you as a pretty, normal—well, sort of normal—male."

"Wow." He sounded really offended.

"Are you mad I called you pretty and *sort of* normal?"

"No. I'm a little taken aback that you think sex with me will be *that* underwhelming."

I picked my head off the headrest. "I never said that."

"Destroy my pedestal?"

I twisted a lock of hair into a long rope. "Oh. What I meant was—I'll just stop talking. I'm sure it'll be fun."

"Fun?" He popped the word out as though it were the most insulting thing I'd ever said to him.

I found myself smirking. At least, this was helping smother my twittering nerves.

He reached over and placed a hand on my thigh. My nerves revved right back up, jangling so loudly I expected them to create ripples in the air.

"It'll be more than *fun*, Nicole." He really hadn't liked that adjective.

When his hand glided beneath my skirt, I held my breath. *And* held it. His fingers were so close to where I wanted them. *So* close.

"Breathe. I don't want you to pass out before we reach the cabin."

I glowered and exhaled. "It's been a *long* time."

"How long?" His palm drifted back toward my knee, stayed there.

"Eighteen months."

"That is a long time."

"What about you?"

"It's been a while too."

I doubted our measure of time was anywhere near equal. "Like what, two weeks?"

"More like last New Year's."

My eyelashes hit my browbone. "Really?" I said this before I realized that Storm was born around that time. Well, a month later. "Shoot, I didn't mean to remind you of . . ."

"It wasn't with Tamara."

The goosebumps pebbling my thighs sank right back into my flesh. Even though I told myself I didn't get to judge him, the question leaped out before I could squash it back, "You cheated on her?"

He pulled his hand away, returned it to the wheel as he spun the car up the drive to the compound. "To cheat on someone means you're *with* them in the first place."

I frowned.

"I don't want you thinking I'm an asshole, so I'll tell you this much, but then I don't want to discuss my past again. Tammy and I tried to make it work during the first trimester of her pregnancy, but she was constantly on my case about not spending enough time together. She hated that the pack came first, and that hatred festered. Contaminated everything in our relationship. When she asked me to pick between her and the Boulders, I told her it was an impossible choice." A nerve feathered his jaw. "She said being Alpha had turned me into someone else, someone she didn't recognize, someone too difficult to love."

The compound gate ground open, and yet Liam didn't press on the gas pedal immediately, just idled in front, locked in the morose memory I'd dredged up.

Contrition made me nibble my lower lip. "Sorry for assuming you'd cheated on her."

Liam didn't answer. Just put the car in gear and drove past the gate, then past my parents' house.

Its darkened windows made me check the digital clock glowing on his dashboard—1 a.m. "What time do you need to pick up Storm?"

He kept his eyes on the road winding toward the pond. "Your parents offered to keep him overnight and through tomorrow."

"Because of your trip?"

"Yes." His knuckles whitened and didn't ease up, not even after we'd parked in front of the cabin and he'd shut off the engine.

I unclicked my seat belt. "You're second-guessing doing this, aren't you?"

He finally released his steering wheel and thrust a hand through his dark locks. "I'd be lying if I said I wasn't."

Disappointment ballooned through me and came out as a sigh. "It's okay." I tried to put on a brave front. "At least, this way, you get to keep your pedestal."

A smile finally gentled the hard line of his mouth. "Nicole Raina Freemont, you are going to be the death of my ego."

I laughed.

He reached over and pried the hands I was wringing together. As he slotted his fingers through mine, our gazes locked, our breathing quieted. I wasn't sure how long we sat in the soundless darkness of his car, but it felt all at once like an eternity and a mere handful of heartbeats.

"Are you second-guessing your second-guessing?" Did that even make sense?

"Fuck it." He set my hand down on the center console and got out of the car.

What did *fuck it* mean? Did it mean he was in or out? I was about to open my door, but Liam beat me to it. He wrenched it open, then held out his hand. After I'd hopped out, he threaded his fingers through mine, shut his door, and led me over to the cabin.

I guessed he was in.

CHAPTER 26

L iam lobbed his car keys onto the kitchen counter, then steered us down the dark hallways toward his bedroom. I dropped my bag on the floor, realizing that my eighteen-month-long celibacy was about to end, and not just thanks to some random guy but thanks to my Alpha.

My Alpha who'd gone almost a year without sex. From any other guy, I would've assumed it was a lie, but Liam was in charge of a tiny person and a giant pack of werewolves. He probably didn't have the energy or time for sex.

Once his bedroom door clicked shut, reality set in. He let go of my hand to draw his curtains closed. I admired his fluid, graceful gait from where I stood planted like a sapling in the middle of his bedroom.

When the toes of his boots knocked into mine, I craned my neck. His hands glided down my arms, then over my back, and finally around my neck.

"Is this some strange preliminary Boulder ritual?"

"Just making sure you smell like only one male."

His proprietorial act exulted the primal part of me. "Perhaps, I should mark you too, then. To rid you of any traces of other females."

"The only people I smell like is my son and you." He took my palms and placed them on his pecs. "But go ahead; mark me with your scent."

His nipples hardened as I coasted my hands over his torso and then around his taut waist and up the acres of muscle and sinew and bone that made up his back. I shut my eyes as I pursued my slow exploration of his form, committing all of him to memory.

"You can look, you know." His low voice was as heady as the scent wafting off his skin.

Keeping my lids sealed, I murmured, "I'm memorizing your body so I can paint it tomorrow."

He stiffened, which made my lids cartwheel up.

"I'll give you a different face to preserve your anonymity."

After a beat, he said, "Not much anonymity considering the whole pack's seen me naked."

My hands stilled. For some reason, I'd forgotten that detail. "Except me."

"Except you." His hands slid over the slice of bare skin between my top and the waistband of my skirt. He pressed his forehead to mine. "Do you know that the morning you opened the door to me bare-breasted has been running on a loop in my mind?"

"One of the top-ten most embarrassing moments of my life, on par with my involuntary birthday gift unwrapping."

His eyes lit up. "Have you used it?"

"What? My sex swing? Didn't you hear the part about me being celibate for eighteen months?"

"On your own, I meant."

"I'm pretty sure it isn't meant for solo use, but I brought it along in my move in case . . ." I shut up before suggesting testing it out together, because this was a *one*-night stand, which meant that come morning, Liam and I would be going our separate ways.

"You moved?"

"Out of my house and in with Niall. I'm actually six doors down from you now. My walk of shame will be short and not too shameful."

"When did this happen?"

"Friday. When you come back from Alaska, I'll give you a grand tour of my hundred-square-foot haven. If you still feel like hanging out, that is."

The night was just beginning, and I was already sad about it ending. Hopefully, he'd be a mediocre lover.

"What's with the pout?"

"I don't pout."

He ran his thumb over my lower lip as though to prove it somehow protruded more than my top one.

I sighed. "I'm hoping you're a terrible lay."

His thumb froze, and he blinked. "Why in the world would you hope for that?"

"Because if you're any good, I might want to do it again, which would defeat the whole concept of one night."

He went very still, probably second-guessing his second-guess . . . *third*-guessing himself. "You're incredibly honest."

I scrunched up my nose and slung my gaze onto the brown suede armchair in the corner. "One of my many flaws."

He pinched my chin between his fingers, angling my head back toward his. "Honesty is not a flaw, Nikki. As for your many other flaws, you'll have to point them out, because I have yet to find a single one."

I rolled my eyes. "Wait till you see my mangled knee. It's *really* ugly."

"Perhaps I should be worried what you'll think of my body then."

I frowned. "What's wrong with your body?"

He released my face, hooked the hem of his black T-shirt, and peeled it off. As he flung it onto the armchair, my jaw loosened, because the man was spectacular. So spectacular that I doubted painting him could do justice to his stacked abs, bronzed skin, and dusting of dark hair that thickened and tapered beneath his navel.

He pivoted, and I sucked in air. A myriad of scars crisscrossed the expanse of his back like railroad tracks. All were old, healed, the skin white and stiff like the one on my knee, except on Liam, none spoiled his beauty. If anything, they made the male even more fascinating, told a story of survival.

I reached out and traced the smooth edges of a scar that wrapped around his shoulder, coaxing goosebumps onto the patches of uninjured skin. "What happened to you?"

A beat. Then, "Cassandra Morgan and her silver-tainted blood happened to me."

I gasped, my fingers halting along the nastiest scar. "These are all from the duel?" His skin must've been in ribbons.

He turned back around. "Are you disgusted?"

I shook my head.

He skated his callused hands back around my waist. "I showed you mine; show me yours?"

Ice filled my stomach. "My bra's way more interesting than my scar."

He released a soft snort that smacked the tip of my nose. "You do realize I'm going to get you entirely naked very soon?" His short nails raked back around my waist toward my belly button, eliciting a full-body shiver from me. "But I'll take you up on that offer." His fingers moved over my suspenders and lowered them, then inched back to the hem of my top. "May I?"

My throat dipped at the same time as my head, and I lifted my arms.

He rolled the pink cotton off slowly, the roughened pads of his fingers running up my tensing stomach muscles before skimming my red lace bra and the swells of my breasts. "Fuck, you're gorgeous."

"Really? I mean"—I blew air out the corner of my mouth, removing a lock of hair that had fallen into my eye—"*duh*." Had I really just used the word *duh*? Wow . . . That wouldn't convince him I was a mature woman. "I really need to get myself a mouth plug." Cheeks heating, I mumbled, "That sounded dirty."

A low chuckle erupted from him. The sound combined with the feel of his palms made me shiver anew.

"Liam, how about you kiss me, so I stop talking?"

"I like your talking." Dark eyes glowing a rich amber-yellow, he tilted my neck to the side and nosed down its side, breathing me in.

I became putty between his hands. When he stepped forward, pressing his entire body against mine, I became even meltier. Was that a word? If it wasn't, it really should be, because my bones felt like they were softening, remolding themselves to fit his beautiful body.

I'd never orgasmed during sex. Well, except when Grant had bitten me, but not through foreplay or the actual act. And yet, the hard ridges of Liam's body digging into me were generating this acute, frantic throb between my legs that I suspected could be set off by a single flick.

I couldn't even remember a time I had been this hot for Grant. I set my hands on Liam's belt, unclasped it, then flipped his jeans button. Before I could pull his zipper down, he caught hold of my wrists and held them away.

"You better leave me tucked in, or this will be over much too quickly." His voice was as thick as what lay behind his zipper.

"Then we'll just do it again. It's not against the rules of one-night stands, right?"

His mouth quirked to one side. "It's even required." He released my wrists and returned one hand to the back of my head. Before capturing my mouth, he said, "Especially if one wants to preserve their pedestal."

I dragged my hands back to his spine and pressed my smile against his lips that were warm and pliant. "Let round one begin."

For a moment, neither of us moved, simply stood, mouth to mouth, heartbeat to heartbeat. Then Liam pried my lips wide and dipped his tongue through, his strokes gentle and measured, completely unlike the kiss we'd shared in Seoul Sister. My heart lost all of its solid edges, turning as fuzzy and weightless as an unspooling cloud.

As I dragged my palms up the center of his back, the muscles and scars beneath my fingertips flexed and realigned as though his body were preparing to shift. I sucked his bottom lip into my mouth, and he produced a guttural sound, more animal than human. My fangs lengthened as our kiss intensified, as his mouth ravished mine, and I nicked his damp lower lip. Snarling, he crushed his mouth to mine.

The spicy taste of his blood coated my tongue, and I swallowed it down. His chest vibrated with a deep growl. As I poured more venom into his bloodstream—it really should've worn another name, because venom sounded lethal —his thick bulge plowed into my lower belly, and his fingers dug into my scalp. Suddenly both his palms landed on my ass, and he heaved me up. I wrapped my legs around him, my underwear so damp I was probably leaving a wet spot on his stomach muscles.

I decided, then and there, that I loved one-night stands.

No awkward first date.

No need to discuss the future.

Just raw, carnal pleasure.

Nikki, what are you doing to me? His raspy voice cleaved through my arousal-muddled mind.

Since I couldn't speak into *his* mind, and speaking out loud would require me to release his lip, I decided to keep quiet until he either climaxed or flung me off.

He went with option two, tossing me onto the bed, the momentum uprooting my fangs. "Fuck," he growled. "Fuck." He swiped the back of his hand against his mouth, smearing the blood.

Heart flopping around like a beached trout, I rose onto my forearms. "I'm sorry, I assumed . . . I assumed . . ." The heat, which had been swirling through my lower half rose to my top half, splotching my skin red.

I'd never met a shifter who didn't like being bitten, but perhaps Alphas found it demeaning or something. Crap. Maybe I should've asked before assuming he'd automatically be into it.

"Sorry?" He gestured to his pants, to the blooming dark spot. "You fucking made me come. I've *never* come like that."

Fear that I'd broken some primal pack rule finally dissipated along with my blush. "Really? Why not?"

He rubbed his jaw. "Because I've never been with a shifter."

"Seriously?"

"I kissed one once, but it never resulted in"—he glanced at his pants— "*this.*"

"Well, then it was a privilege to initiate you to the pleasures of fanging."

"Fanging?"

"Fanging. Banging. Niall came up with it a few years back, and it sort of stuck."

He ran his tongue over his already healed lower lip and unbuttoned his jeans. "Do *you* like fanging?"

"It's the only way I can orgasm, so yes. Very much."

Frowning, he kicked off his boots and discarded both his pants and underwear in one fluid motion. I noticed yet another scar, dime-sized and deep, right beneath his hipbone. I wasn't a mutilation expert, but it resembled a bullet-hole.

"What do you mean, it's the only way you can orgasm?" He sprang up, thick and veiny. And hard.

"Um, what?"

He smirked, because of course he knew what had sidetracked me, and reiterated his question.

"I've just never been able to climax any other way."

"Glad to hear it."

I cocked an eyebrow. "Why would that make you glad?"

"Because I get to initiate *you* to the pleasures of fang-free foreplay."

My face filled with heat, then heated some more when he leaned over, flipped my skirt up, and pulled my underwear down my legs, over my boots, exposing me to him. "If I were you, I wouldn't waste your time—"

"Waste my time?" He *tsk*ed as he pressed my legs wide and sank onto his knees between them.

"Liam . . ."

"What?"

"You—you don't need to . . ."

"I don't need to what?" He brought his mouth so close to me I could feel the pulse of his words. "Do this?" He gave me a long, slow lick, his eyes blindingly bright.

The muscles of my legs seized. He lapped again, the wet suckling sound almost as heady as the feel of his smooth tongue.

I held my breath as I watched him watch me. As he sucked and teased, kissed and laved, never once looking away. My thighs began to tremble, and a familiar knot of heat wound in my lower belly.

He must've fanged me, but his mouth was still moving, his tongue still licking, his stubble still chafing the inside of my thighs. If his fangs had breached my skin, his mouth would be motionless. His long fingers encircled my thighs and yanked, sliding my body toward him until I smothered his face.

I gasped at his brutality, at the violence of his tongue lashing and his open-mouthed kisses. Where Grant had tasted, Liam devoured.

My spine arched as the heat and ferocity of his tongue kindled flames that skittered under my skin, banged into my marrow, and bloated my muscles. My heart distended and squeezed, shooting out a trillion beats. Moaning, I sank. Against his mouth. Against the feathery comforter. Into the sensation loosening every nest of tension and detonating every nerve-ending in my body.

"Hmm. Look at that. You can come through oral sex." There was such arrogance in his tone, and yet I couldn't even fault him for it, because that had been spectacular.

Once my heartbeats evened out, I answered, "I guess I can."

He gave my clit a hard peck, then got up, muscles swelling his burnished skin. "You know what I can't wait for?"

"No. What?"

"To feel your body climax around my dick when I'm balls-deep inside of you."

Dirty. His mouth was so dirty. And shiny.

He licked his lips. "Fuck, you taste good. As good as you smell."

I let an arm fall over my forehead, basking in the afterglow of coming. So freaking amazing. So much better than pleasuring myself. "I'm going to start doing this more often."

"Spreading your legs for me?" He sank one knee on either side of my hips, cracking open a foil packet.

I didn't even know where or when he'd gotten it. "I meant having one-night stands."

His fingers froze.

"What?"

"Nothing." He concentrated on the condom, unrolling it over his hard length.

"I'm not in heat. In case . . . you know . . . you wanted to do it skin-to-skin."

"My ex wasn't in heat either, and yet I managed to get her pregnant."

Oh.

He grabbed my rib cage, hoisting me higher on the bed, and then he picked up one of my legs and slid my boot off.

When he seized my other foot, my heart pitched into my throat, and I tried to wriggle free. "Wait, Liam . . ." Too late. The moment the suede slipped off and revealed my scar, I winced.

The small groove between his eyebrows appeared.

"Please don't look. It's going to kill your erection."

He studied the mangled flesh, then ran his thumb down the waxy span of scarred skin and lowered his mouth, kissing it from top to bottom. And although he was probably just showing my knee kindness to put me at ease, tears pooled behind my lids.

Gently, he set my leg down and dropped one palm on either side of my face. If he caught the shimmer of tears, he didn't mention it. Instead, he brought his mouth down to mine, kissing me with the same gentleness he'd shown my scar, and aligned his tip with my wet heat.

You're so fucking sexy. His compliment warmed my heart and limbs, made them soften once again. *Everywhere.*

He nosed the column of my neck, inhaled deeply, and sheathed himself into me, tearing the air from my lungs. I gasped for breath and then I gasped out his name. He covered my mouth and kissed me hard, almost as hard as he fucked.

I wasn't sure if it was his way of showing me that he didn't consider me fragile, or if it was just the way he made love, but I valued his brutal rhythm, because it made me feel normal. And desired.

CHAPTER 27

We lay in a heap of sweaty limbs and panting mouths as Liam softened inside of me.

I ran my hand down his carved chest, tracing the dips and swells of each defined ab, and then that dime-sized depression. "What happened here?"

"Silver bullet."

I whipped my gaze up to his. "Can't believe you survived a silver bullet."

"Doc got it out of me fast."

I returned my fingers to parts of his body not loaded with bad memories. "Thank you, by the way."

He twitched between my legs. "For what?"

"For tonight."

He rolled on top of me, freeing himself from me in the process, then rose to his knees to pull off the condom. "I still haven't managed to make you come through sex." After he tied a knot and tossed it on the floor, he lowered his body until his sticky lower half was flush against mine and his forearms framed my face. "Which really bothers me."

I searched the brown depths of his eyes. "Was it still okay for you?"

He rubbed his stubbled jaw over my sweat-slickened cheek. "It was a lot more than okay. Your body was made for fucking."

Helium to my ego. "Such a sweet-talker."

"I don't have a sweet bone in my body."

"You have many sweet bones, but your secret's safe with me—you have enough females throwing themselves at you."

"You're the only female throwing herself at me."

"Um." I pressed against his pecs, jimmying him off me. "I didn't throw myself at you."

He smirked.

"Okay, fine, I did."

He tucked a strand of hair behind my ear.

"You do realize you could click your fingers and almost everyone would lay back and give you free rein?"

Smirk still pulling at his mouth, he braced himself on one arm and trailed his knuckles down my front, tracing the swell of one breast and bumping against my pebbling nipple. "I'll make sure to give it a try."

My stomach tightened. I didn't want him to give it a try. Why had I planted the idea in his head?

I scooted out from under him. "Can I take a shower before I leave?"

The sky was still dark around the edges of the curtains, but dawn would creep over Beaver Creek soon, putting an end to our night together.

His answer was slow to come. So slow I looked at him over my shoulder.

He was on his side, one hand propped under his head, brow creased with a frown, dick soft but still thick and long. "Go ahead."

I walked into his slate-tiled ensuite and straight into the outsized, glass-walled shower. Once steam curled off the gunmetal-gray slabs, I ducked under the spray, closed my eyes, and tipped my head up. The water fell like silk over my body, sloughing off my sweat, but probably not Liam's smell. As I lathered up, I thought up ways I could avoid my parents until I smelled like my old, *un*sexed self. Although they wouldn't judge, I still rather they didn't find out.

Crap. What if Liam dropped by their house in a few hours before he flew off to Alaska?

Hair dripping, skin warm, I plucked a towel off the rack and wrapped it around myself. When I emerged from the ensuite, Liam had donned sweats and another black T-shirt.

"I didn't take you for a pajama sort of guy."

He smirked. "I'm most definitely not a pajama sort of guy."

"Then why are you dressed?"

"I thought walking you home naked might raise some eyebrows if anyone's up and about."

Oh. I crouched and grabbed my underwear, then slid it on beneath the towel. "You don't need to walk me home, Liam." I slid on my skirt and boots next, then squinted around the dark room for my bra.

Found it swinging from Liam's index finger. "Looking for this?"

I snatched it, then tossed the towel on the armchair. "Are you going to stop by my parents' house on your way to Alaska?"

After I'd managed to hook my bra in place, I looked up. Liam's pupils had sharpened, tiny black dots against the glowing irises.

"Liam?"

Slowly, his gaze rose, throat bobbing. "What?"

"My house. Are you going to drop by?

"No. Why?"

Relief filled me. "Just wanted to avoid my parents knowing we *hung out*."

"Do you regret seducing me, Nicole?"

I rolled my eyes. "I hardly seduced you."

Liam unhurriedly tugged up the bra strap, which had dipped off my shoulder. "Did you get me out of your system?"

Nope. He'd merely rooted himself deeper. For all my honesty, I went with a lie. "I did. I can finally move on." I backed up, moving to the armchair at the foot of which lay my top. I picked it up and put it on, then grabbed the towel and folded it. Water bled from my hair onto my top, pasting the pink cotton to my skin.

I trudged toward the door and scooped up my handbag, then turned to tell Liam he didn't need to escort me home, but instead of words, a muted gasp escaped my lips because Liam was right behind me, and I do mean, *right* there. The tip of my nose scraped across his stubbled chin. "Admit it. You're part bobcat."

He dipped his face, the corners of his eyes crinkling a little. "I'm *all* wolf."

He reached around me, and I thought he might draw me to him and admit he wanted another night. But it wasn't me he drew to him, it was the door. And not once during our five-minute walk home did he allude to a repeat performance.

In front of my new front door, he asked, "So, you live here with Nate?"

I frowned. Had I said Nate instead of Niall? It happened sometimes . . . that I confused my brothers. "No, with Niall. Nate lives on the hill." I jutted my chin toward a third-tier cabin with an unbeatable view of the sparkly pond. "Have you never been to his place?"

"Never invited me."

"Really?" I chewed on my bottom lip. "He used to live with Bea off the compound, so I don't think he considers this place home." Probably the reason why he hadn't invited Liam for a visit. "Now that they split, though . . ."

"You really liked her?"

"I did. Still do. I'm secretly hoping they'll get back together."

Liam's eyes roamed over the dark windows of Nate's cabin. The drapes weren't shut, probably because he was still at the bachelor party.

"Anyway"—I opened my unlocked door—"thanks for tonight." Hugging my arms around my waist to fend off the cold, I waited for him to say something. Anything. Even *good night* or *good day*, but he simply stared at me in silence.

Perhaps I should've asked *him* if he regretted tonight, but I feared his answer too much. Between chattering teeth, I said, "I hope Alaska goes well."

He nodded to my house. "Don't want you to catch a cold."

I guessed our evening tryst hadn't miraculously made Liam trust me with pack business. The man was as opaque as they came, and a couple hours entwined and disrobed hadn't made him any clearer to read. What had I been expecting? That a skin-to-skin would lead to a heart-to-heart? I still didn't regret tonight, but I did regret the limitations of one-night stands. For all my talk about having more, I craved a deeper connection, a lover who not only penetrated my body but also my heart and soul.

Heart thudding in disappointment, I stepped inside and was about to shut the door when he called out, "Wait."

Hope threaded through my disappointment. Was I about to get an invitation for a redo, or a front-door kiss? I'd even take a lingering stare.

Instead, I got a roll of black fabric. "I promised you my underwear. It's clean. Didn't think you'd want the ones I wore tonight."

I closed my fingers around the soft material. "I'm still down a dare. I had to speak to a random person on the phone for five minutes."

He patted the pockets of his sweats. "Left my cell phone back at the cabin, so can't help you out there, but knowing Niall, he'll probably have many interesting contacts in his phone." He backed up. "Anyway, see you around."

Around?

The threads of my hope snagged on that one word and ripped.

CHAPTER 28

I managed a few hours of sleep before my phone trilled with the alarm I'd set to meet up with Miles. After slapping cold water over my face, I dressed warmly and climbed the hill toward the compound entrance where a forest-green Land Rover idled beside the front gate.

Since Bea's brother was on the phone, I whispered a quick *hi* and strapped myself in. He flashed me a smile, then spun the car around and raced down the slick drive. His tires were wrapped in chains, so I tried not to worry about his speed. I reasoned that Miles was born and raised in these parts. Driving on snow and ice was as much part of his DNA as his South Korean heritage. Still, asking him to ease up on the gas pedal was on the tip of my tongue.

Especially when we passed the area where Grant and I had crashed. The tree, like my knee, bore the mark of our accident. I looked away from it, clutching my thighs which had begun to tremble.

"Sorry. That was Mom. She wants me to convince Bea to come home, and if I can't convince her, she wants me to resort to sisternapping."

It could very well come to that if Bea was wallowing in depression. "Is that why you're allowing me to tag along? So you have a partner-in-crime?"

"Why else?" He smiled, before nodding to my stomach. "Feeling better today?"

It took me a millisecond to remember the lie I'd fed him when I'd left Seoul Sister. "Much better, although I could've done with a few more hours of sleep." I sighed and released my white-knuckled grip on my thighs.

"You and I both."

After getting home last night, it had taken my mind and body hours to unwind and surrender to sleep. "What time did you close?"

"Five. Your friends were on fire last night. Especially that May girl."

"Ah . . . that May girl."

He looked away from the snow-packed road. "Not a fan?"

"Not really. Why did you say especially?"

"She and her friend, the one who kissed my bartender, spent the last two hours of the night dancing on the bar. Might have to hire them for future entertainment."

"Ha! I'm sure their parents would love that."

His eyes twinkled. "You had fun, though, right?"

"I did. It was perfect. Well, almost. If Bea had been there, it would've been perfect."

He sighed, then grew silent as we came to a fork in the road. After fifteen minutes of pensive quiet, I spun the music dial and settled in for the rest of the drive. I must've fallen asleep because the next thing I knew, I was being jostled from side to side.

When my head almost knocked into my window, I seized the grab handle. "You weren't kidding about the cabin being isolated."

The road we were on was narrow and dark, hemmed in by so many trees that sunlight didn't penetrate. It had neither been plowed nor salted, yet tire treads flattened the snow.

"We're almost there."

I was glad to hear it because all the jouncing made my wolf bristle and long for firm ground. I forced her back down. Miles didn't strike me as the type to be awed by our existence. More likely, he'd be the type to see us as dangerous predators and proactively welcome our annihilation.

A honeyed dot appeared amidst the tall trunks, then expanded into a doll-sized log cabin that couldn't contain more than one bedroom. As we neared it, I thought I caught the flutter of lace curtains in one of the windows.

Miles parked the car by a narrow footpath, which seemed to have been haphazardly shoveled, then got out. I unstrapped myself and climbed out, my leg muscles gummy and sore from my nocturnal activities.

"We used to come out here and go ice-fishing in the lake." He nodded to a great, glassy expanse that bordered the house. "I fell in once, when I was eight. Bea fished me out." He shaded his eyes from the sun's glare.

"Must've been scary."

"Terrifying." He shivered as though he'd slipped through the ice again. "And *really* cold."

In wolf form, I'd splashed through shallow mountain streams, but not in human form. I lowered my aching eyes to the path. Amidst large boot prints, I noticed the distinctive shape of paws. Large ones. I covered them up by stepping on them before their sheer size could worry poor Miles more than he already was.

I sniffed the air, trying to detect Nate's scent—who else would've visited Bea in fur?—but the chilled air veiled the various odors. Even Miles's mix of leafy cologne and griddle grease was less pungent out in the open than it had been in the car.

"Fuck," I heard Miles whisper right before a growl resounded through the trees, amplified by the nearby lake.

I snapped my head in the direction of the sound. A gray wolf with arctic-blue eyes appeared beneath the fence of trunks, neck lowered and teeth bared. The animal was huge and clearly not human. I tried to put a face to the fur, but couldn't remember a pure silver with such blue eyes. Instinctively, I whipped out my arm and halted in front of Miles. Of course, I didn't realize how strange he might think *me* protecting *him* could be.

"Don't worry, Nikki. I brought my gun." His low words pulsed against the nape of my neck, eliciting a layer of icy goosebumps.

"No. No gun. The wolf won't harm us."

When Gray growled again, Miles muttered, "Don't know what nature show you've been watching but animals growl when they feel threatened."

The metallic click of a hammer made me spin around. "I said no gun, Miles! Put it away."

"Have you lost your damn marbles?"

"I swear he's harmless." But then a thought coalesced in the form of new goosebumps. What if this was the shifter from the Glacier pack? What if it tried to attack Miles and turn him, and—

What the hell are you doing here, Nikki?

Shoulder blades jamming together, my eyes cut toward the giant black wolf with yellow-amber eyes prowling out from behind the cabin.

So the gray one was Lucas . . .

Get back in the car and drive away. My Alpha's command resonated inside my very bones, and yet I couldn't get my body to uproot itself.

I wrapped my hand around Miles's wrist, forcing it down. "Please put the gun away."

He didn't, but he also didn't shrug my hand off. "There are two of them now, Nik. Unless the second one's a bear."

Get the fucking human back in his car.

I wanted to grit out that I was trying, since clearly something was going on here, but I couldn't exactly speak to a wolf without raising Miles's hackles. "We should head back to the car."

"My sister's in there. What if one of these rabid fuckers found their way inside the cabin and attacked her?"

"I'm sure they didn't. They're probably just out for a stroll," I spat out, confused and angry. Mostly angry. Whatever happened to Alaska?

"Wolves don't *stroll*."

"Those two surely do." I tugged on his arm, but the man wouldn't budge. "Come on, Miles. Please."

The growling crescendoed. I wanted to snap at Liam and Lucas to quiet down, because Miles was already wired like Beaver Creek's main street during the winter holidays.

"They're on the move. Get behind me, Nikki." Before I could try to pacify him again, he dragged me behind him and then raised the gun, leveling it on the black wolf's head.

"Miles, put the fucking gun away! NOW!"

My shriek made his body jerk and arm bob. "The fuck is wrong with you?" He cocked the trigger.

I latched on to his shoulder and stabbed him with my claws. He cried out in pain and slammed his gun into my temple. It was probably a knee-jerk reaction, but damn, it hurt.

He swung the gun back toward Liam.

"Run!" I whimpered, but the idiot charged Miles instead.

The gun went off. Liam slammed into Miles, tipping him over and taking me down with him. Although the snow cushioned my fall, the back of my skull glanced against something hard and sharp that made my vision pale.

I blinked, but my already fragmented vision fissured some more as though Miles's dark goose-down parka was pressed into my corneas.

Rapid heartbeats pounded inside my skull. I tried to untangle the distinct patterns, tried to make out Liam's, but all the beats ran together, dulling to a low throb before quieting completely.

CHAPTER 29

I gasped awake in an unfamiliar bed with a searing pair of eyes fastened to me and an angry pulse at the back of my head and at my temple.

"What the fuck, Nikki?" The tendons in Liam's throat twisted like mooring lines. "What the hell were you doing with Miles Park?"

I really was in *no* mood to be growled at. "Already back from Alaska?" I clipped out, attempting to turn my head to take in my surroundings, but the pain that whizzed through my skull immobilized it.

I shakily fingered my forehead. Found an ice pack pressed against my left temple. I tried to push it off, but Liam leaned forward on the wicker chair he'd propped next to the bed and dragged my hand off.

"You need the ice." His voice was infinitesimally softer.

"The bullet. Did it . . .? Were you shot?"

Dried blood streaked the underside of his chin. His? Mine? Miles's? "No."

My lungs released all of their stored air. "And Miles? Is he . . . alive?" Again, I looked around at the bare timbered walls—one covered by a bulky, free-standing closet, one baring two small windows, and one inset with a door.

His lips, the bottom still slightly puffy from my love bite, pinched. "He's alive."

"Where is he?"

"Why do you care?"

I gaped at Liam, before narrowing my eyes. "Why *don't* you care? Has he done something to harm you or the pack?"

"You never answered my question. What were you doing with him?"

"And you never answered mine. Why aren't you in Alaska?"

"Because the wolf who started it all isn't in Alaska. She's right here in Beaver Creek."

"She?" Dread trickled through me like glacier water. Was it Lori? But if it was Lori, why was Liam at Bea's cabin?

I glanced around me again. Is this where we were? Inside Bea's cabin?

"Why were you with Miles?" he asked again.

Was Miles involved with this wolf? Was this why Liam was so interested by the company I kept?

"We came to visit Bea. To see how she was doing. I'm really confused right now. Is Miles part of this?" Whatever *this* was . . . "Is Bea part of this?"

A furrow formed between his eyebrows. "You really came to pay her a visit?"

"Yes! Why else do you think I was hanging out with him? Did you think we were looking for a place to screw?"

A nerve feathered his jaw. Shit. That was *exactly* what he'd thought.

"Can you please explain what the hell's happening? Because I'm more than a little freaked out right now."

A door clapped shut somewhere in the house and then footfalls echoed outside the bedroom. When the door creaked open, I tried to sit up but the lancing pain pinned me to the mattress like a preserved butterfly. I stifled my groan.

"Heya, Knickknack. Glad to see you're awake. You gave us quite a fright earlier when you managed to find the one jagged rock on the entire path and smash your skull into it." Lucas leaned against the doorframe, naked as the day he was born.

Liam stood, obstructing my sight of him. "Put on some clothes. And make her another ice-pack."

"Aye aye, chief." He pushed off the doorframe.

"We're in Bea's cabin, right?"

Liam turned and crossed arms swollen with muscle and irritation. To think they'd been wrapped around my naked body mere hours earlier. "Yes."

"Is she here?"

"She is."

"And Miles?"

"He's been dropped off a couple miles down the road."

That sounded ominous. "Dropped off?"

"Lucas drove his car into a ditch."

My jaw slackened. "You crashed his car?"

"In his attempt to escape the rabid wolves," Liam said slowly, "Miles took off a tad too fast."

"And left me behind?"

"He was scared for his life."

"But not for mine?"

"You really think that a man who hits a woman worries all that much about anyone else's well-being?"

I sandwiched my lips together. "That was an accident."

"Was it?"

I *really* wanted it to be. "He'll never believe he took off without checking on Bea."

"Bea sent him a message that she went on a trip out of state. Oh, and you sent him an angry text message after you woke up and found yourself stranded."

I gritted my molars. So. Many. Lies. After a fraught beat of silence, I added, "Did you really need to put him in an accident?"

"Lucas injected him with enough venom to make him woozy, but we needed him to forget, and nothing like a little concussion for that."

"Don't make light of accidents," I growled, back on the side of the road, leg crushed beneath the flaming motorcycle. "They're serious, Liam. He could sustain brain damage and—"

"I said he'll be fine, and I don't lie."

"Really? So what was your trip to Alaska? A truth?"

He dipped his chin, leveling me with a heated glare that probably should've intimidated me, what with it originating from my Alpha, but that did little to tamp down my soaring frustration.

"You said Bea was here," I bit out. "Where?"

"In the living room."

"I want to see her."

His biceps flexed, making his shoulders ride a little higher.

I released a frustrated growl. "I'm not leaving until you tell me what the hell's going on."

He snorted. Actually snorted. "You're not leaving here until I leave, because you don't have a car."

We glowered at each other until Lucas returned, dressed in sweats and a black hoodie, baring a Ziploc filled with snow. "Don't mind him, Knickknack. Liam acts like a dick when he's worried."

Liam must've spoken into Lucas's mind because the latter smirked as he levered my head up and pillowed it against the pouch of packed snow.

Tears rushed into my eyes at the awful burn and the awfuller throb. "Where's Bea?"

Lucas chucked the slush-filled pack he'd removed onto the nightstand. "Chained to the wall of the living room."

Chained? "Why is she—She was bitten by the halfwolf too?"

Lucas exchanged a look with Liam who nodded, probably to okay the explanation he wasn't giving me.

"She *was* bitten, after which your brother stashed her up here and chained her up."

"Because he's afraid we'll make her overdose on Sillin . . ." I whispered, finally understanding why my brother looked like someone had dragged him across a minefield.

"No. Because he's afraid Liam might order him to end her life."

I whipped my eyes toward Liam whose arms were still firmly tied in front of his cast-iron torso. "Why would he do that?" When neither of them spoke, I curled my fingers around the fleece comforter. "For Lycaon's sake, one of you spit it out. Please."

"Bea's Shifter Zero." Liam's voice was so low I almost missed his words.

"What?" Static rustled against my eardrums. "I thought—What about the male from the Glacier pack?"

"We didn't want to spook your brother. We were afraid he'd move Bea if he caught on to our suspicions."

Only my head was resting on the baggie of snow, and yet my entire body felt covered by it. "How?"

"Lori Morgan apparently bit her, and her unusual venom made Bea shift. Or rather, half-shift. And then Bea went ahead and took a chunk out of the hiker, who ended up ODing on Sillin, although if you ask me, I wonder if she didn't *OD*"—he added air-quotes—"on your brother."

Outrage electrified my spine. "My brother would never kill someone."

"People do questionable things in the name of love, Knickknack. The girl was the missing link to Bea. The only—"

"My brother isn't a killer."

Nate was gentle and fair. He'd *never* harm another person.

Liam finally unglued his molars. "We'll know soon enough. He's on his way over with bags of Lori's blood."

That explained her paleness. She wasn't just supplying two halfwolves but three. "How do you know?"

"She called to inform Lucas."

"You see, those two got a little deal goin'," Lucas drawled. "He keeps the fact that her bite can pass on our mangled gene under wraps, and she plays the part of agreeable blood bag."

What had my brother gotten himself into? "Was Nate trying to make Bea a werewolf?"

Lucas raised his gaze to Liam. "According to Lori, whom I had a little chat with this morning, Bea came to her after your dear brother spilled a closely-guarded pack secret, which he found out when he and Lori canoodled."

My eyes went wide. "My brother hooked up with Lori?"

Lucas's black eyebrow, the one slashed by the white scar, arched up. "You weren't aware?"

"No," I blustered. "No, I wasn't aware. When?"

"A couple years back."

I pressed the heels of my palms into my eyes. This was all so crazy. "How much trouble is my brother in?" I asked, not daring to remove my hands and look at our Alpha.

"Not life-threatening trouble . . ." Liam said. "But he is facing pack expulsion."

My hands fell away from my face. "You just said he didn't make Lori bite Bea."

"No, but he lied and kept a hazardous secret from me."

"To protect someone he loved!" Anger beat back my worry.

Both males were silent for a long while.

Then Lucas said, "The pack and our Alpha come before all, Nikki. We took an oath."

"Nate was trying to protect her," I croaked.

"Which her you speakin' about?"

"Both of them. He was trying to protect both of them."

Liam tilted his head to the side, as though seeing me in some new light, one that painted me as a traitor instead of a docile follower. "Which cost three humans their lives, Nicole."

"The coroner and his wife are dead?"

"No," Lucas popped out. "But they probably will be if we can't find a way to heal 'em, 'cause we can't exactly let them run amok and create a new breed of shifters, now can we?"

A car engine rumbled outside.

I swallowed past the lump in my throat. "If you kick him out, Liam, my whole family will leave."

Liam, who'd started to turn, paused. "Is that a threat?"

"No. It's not a threat; just a fact. Freemonts stick together, for better and for worse."

He eyed me long and hard. I tried to locate the man I'd given my body to during the night, the one who'd generously given his body back, but found only a stranger in his stead. It was as though our intimacy had never happened.

I willed myself not to look away first, but the cool intensity frightened and hurt, so I dragged my gaze to the window that gave onto the forest and watched the distant conifers drenched in burning sunshine, wondering what would become of my brother . . . of my entire family.

Would Liam be fair and forgiving, or prove as ruthless as his predecessor?

CHAPTER 30

"What the—Lucas?" My brother's stunned voice made my heart miss several beats.

I spun my gaze back toward the bedroom door but couldn't see a thing past Liam's body. Determined to get off Bea's soiled bed, I dug my palms into the fleece cover and pushed through the pain of what felt like my skull being hacked into a thousand tiny shards.

The room wobbled as I sat and slid my legs over the side of the bed. I focused on my breaths until I no longer felt strapped to a Tilt-A-Whirl. Once the floor beneath my boots stopped shifting, I stood and took a step.

My head.

My poor, *poor* head.

I raised a hand to the wound, mostly to make sure my brain wasn't protruding. When my fingers came away sticky with blood, my stomach heaved, and my vision swam.

I stumbled, holding out my hands to keep from crashing into the floor. I ended up crashing into a body that would probably have made the wood feel like foam tiles.

Liam banded one of his arms under my armpits, keeping me upright and pinned me to his side. **What exactly are you attempting?**

"I need to see my brother." I gestured to the door, bloodied fingertips bobbing in the air. Bile shot into my throat at the sight and smell. I clamped

169

my jaw shut. I would not puke. I'd keep it together. Once my insides settled, I murmured, "You can let go now."

Liam muttered something I couldn't quite catch over the blood battering my eardrums.

"Nikki?" My brother stood in the doorway, red rising into his jaw. "What the fuck did you guys do to her?"

Crap. I hadn't thought of how this would look. "It's not . . . they didn't . . ."

He stomped across the room and tried to wrench me from Liam's grasp, but our Alpha must've barked something inside Nate's head, because my brother's fingers froze a hair's breadth from my body.

"Is it true?" Nate's throat bobbed. "That you fell?"

"Yes."

He narrowed his dark eyes on Liam, brows drawn in tight. "Did someone *push* you?"

"No." His scrutiny persisted.

"I swear it was an accident."

He scrubbed a hand down his face, his palm scraping across his grizzly beard, and let out a bone-deep sigh. "Let's get the cross-examination over with, Kolane."

Liam nodded. "Living room. Now."

Reluctance slowed my brother's retreat but didn't halt it.

When Liam pivoted toward the bed, I dug my heels in. "No."

"What, no?"

"I'm not going back to bed. I'm going to the living room."

"You need to lay down."

"What I *need* is to be with my brother."

A gruff breath escaped him.

"Allowing me to be there for him is the least you can do before you kick us out of the pack."

"I'm not kicking anyone out of the pack." His growl smacked against me, rough and hot, a tongue of fire against my icy forehead.

I raised my chin and fixed my eyes on his. "I meant, before you suggest we *leave* the pack."

His jaw clenched and unclenched in time with every muscle in the arm cinched around me. "Fine." He scooped me up.

"I could've walked," I muttered.

And I could've strapped you to the bed. Probably should've done it last night. Would've saved me a shit ton of trouble and a giant fucking headache.

My mouth parted around a shallow gasp as he maneuvered us down a very narrow hallway. "You're such an alphahole."

Never pretended to be anything else, darling.

"Don't call me darling."

He smirked as he stepped into a room filled with mismatched furniture ranging from a bottle-green corduroy couch to wicker chairs, to a foldable metal table and a ratty wooden chest covered in stacks of worn books.

A soft keening stole my attention away from the decor that could've qualified as an *Architectural Digest* BEFORE-shot. Chained to the wall by a thick collar was Bea. Or rather, an animal that wore Bea's heavy mahogany hair, defined cheeks, and honeyed eyes. The rest of her features were all wrong, elongated, furred, wrinkled. Her ears were peaked like a wolf's but located where human ears sat.

Sure you don't want to go back to bed? Liam whispered into my mind.

I nodded.

He set me down on the couch with such gentleness that it almost felt like he was handling Storm instead of me. And then, as though to make up for calling me trouble and a headache, he propped pillows behind my lower back and shoulder blades.

Bea had always been curvy. Now her ribs poked through the clumps of mahogany fur dappling her abdomen and her hip bones tented her sallow flesh. Had she consumed anything besides blood in the past weeks? My stomach revolted at the contemplation, but still I held her glassy, golden gaze.

My brother perched on the lip of the couch and buried his face inside his palms. I touched his knee to remind him that I was there. Right there.

He inhaled a long breath, then dropped his hands, bringing one atop mine and squeezing my fingers. "How did you all find out?"

Liam sat on the arm of another corduroy monstrosity, a shade of puke-brown that should've been outlawed. "Your sister led us here."

I looked up so fast it felt like my head were glancing over the jagged rock all over again. "You followed me here?"

"Not quite." Lucas stood in the corner of the room, as though trying to become one with the shadows. He was doing a pretty good job of it.

"Bea's bracelet on the crime scene." Liam linked his fingers together. "It got me wondering, and I phoned up Lucas to do a little recon work."

I sank my teeth into my lower lip.

"Were you ever planning on sharing the effect of Lori's miraculous venom with anyone besides your fiancée, Nate?" Liam cracked his knuckles. "Or did you not trust me enough with the information?"

My brother toyed with a hangnail until it began to bleed. "I didn't even mean to tell Bea about it."

Bea, who'd been sitting on her hind legs, sank onto her stomach and whimpered.

Nate looked her way and winced. "As for sharing it with you, Liam, Lori begged me not to say a thing since she'd never bitten anyone before, but promised she was going to tell you once you were no longer in mourning."

"I wasn't in mourning when I took over the pack, and I haven't been in mourning for several months now, so when exactly was Lori planning on volunteering this information, and how did she even know the effect if she'd never bitten anyone?"

"Alex . . . he wasn't as disciplined, and Lori had to *clean up* his messes."

I sucked in a breath. "How many messes did she clean up?"

"Too many." Nate sighed. "But thankfully, their venom only transmits the gene during full moons and when they're in fur."

"Lori tell you that during your pillow talk?" Lucas asked placidly. "Or were you on the *clean-up* committee too?"

My brother's neck snapped very straight, and his gaze darted to me.

"It's okay, Nate." I squeezed his knee. "I heard and I'm not passing any judgment. About the pillow talk bit."

His Adam's apple bobbed. "I fucked up, Liam. I let you down. Let down the pack. Let down my fiancée." His voice caught on that last word, and then his eyes reddened, and for the second time in my entire life, I saw tears glide down my brother's cheeks.

"Does anyone else know about Lori's potent venom?" Liam asked.

"No one alive."

Even though my head throbbed every time I moved, I scooted closer to Nate and wrapped my arms around his hunched middle.

"Oh, Pinecone, I screwed up so bad."

"We'll find a way to fix it," I whispered.

"I don't think there is a way to fix it."

"The full moon's this Friday. Maybe it'll positively impact their condition." It made sense since the moon affected our shifter magic. The elders in the pack, who could no longer shift at will, had no trouble transforming into fur when the moon was bloated and bright.

My brother blinked tear-bright eyes at me. "I don't dare hope . . ."

As I rubbed slow circles over his spine, I hunted Liam's expression for a glimmer of optimism, but the corners of his lips were tipped downward.

A rattling breath snuck up my brother's torso. "What are your plans for Bea . . . and for me?"

"For Bea, she needs to be brought to the bunker. That brother of hers"— Liam eyed me as though I'd somehow plotted to ambush him with Miles— "was about to pay her a visit today. If he caught sight of her in this state . . . well, you know how that would end for him."

My brother's entire body tightened, and he nodded.

"How would it end?" I feared the answer was death but hoped—I was doing a lot of that recently—it wasn't.

"Not well," Lucas supplied cryptically.

Liam sighed. "As for you, Nate, you'll need to step down as my Beta."

Nate swallowed and again bobbed his head. "I understand."

I waited for Liam to tack on another punishment, because a job downgrade couldn't possibly be his only reprimand. Could it?

When he stood up without adding anything, I frowned.

You seem disappointed by my verdict, Nikki.

"Merely pleasantly surprised by your leniency."

He dragged his palms over his denim-clad thighs. "Nate, you do understand that if the full moon doesn't help her, we'll have to make hard decisions."

When he hiccuped a sob, my already compacted chest squeezed some more. I sent a silent prayer to Lycaon to fix Lori's mistake.

How could she have accepted to bite her knowing how it would end? "Did Bea really ask for this?"

Nate turned his reflective brown eyes to me and gave such a slight nod I almost mistook it for a tremor.

"Why didn't Lori refuse?"

"Bea threatened to expose her. Since Lori's reputation in the pack is already dismal, she accepted."

I stared at Bea in shock. Had she really resorted to blackmail to obtain what she wanted? She turned her head toward the wall and scrunched up her muzzle, just as a knock resounded in the tension-filled air. I jumped, and the movement chafed my skull.

It's Darren. You need stitches.

Lucas pushed off the wall and crossed to the door, which he drew wide open. The shifter, who'd delivered me along with all my siblings and most of my generation, strode into the room, thinning blond hair sticking out haphazardly around his face. He must've been forewarned about what he would find because pity deepened the lines bracketing his eyes and mouth.

"Sorry. I got here as fast as I could." He walked over to my side. "How you doing, kiddo?"

Way better than half the people in this room. "Not too bad."

Liam had crouched in front of Bea. I wondered if he was talking into her mind but then remembered she wasn't linked to him. Pity and fatigue tamed his irate expression. Had he even slept after he'd dropped me off? Probably not.

As he unfurled his massive body, he looked over at my brother. "Nate, you'll find Miles's car about a mile down the road. Report the accident and then follow the ambulance to the hospital. Do *not* leave Miles's side until he wakes up. I want to know exactly how much he remembers."

My brother stood, sending my hand resting on his back toppling onto the warm corduroy.

"And we messaged him from Bea's phone that she was out-of-state. In California, since that's what you told her neighbor."

So Liam had visited her apartment building also . . . I wasn't sure why that surprised me.

"Make sure to perpetuate that story. We don't want her family growing suspicious." Liam walked over to the wall and yanked on the chain, unhooking it with one stiff jerk as though it were made of plastic instead of metal. "Lucas, transfer Bea to the bunker." He handed the clanking links to his Beta, who tugged on the chain as though it were a leash, forcing Bea to stand.

"Wait." Nate dug a key from his pocket. "Here." His hand bobbed in the air.

"I'm not letting her go free."

"I know." Nate sighed. "You probably shouldn't."

Lucas pocketed the key.

"Wait." Nate vanished into the bedroom and returned with the fleece I'd soiled. He wrapped it around Bea's gnarled, naked form.

Just as I mused, "She's so much calmer than the others," her nostrils flared and her gummy lips retracted. She whipped her head to the side, running her muzzle along the bloodied stain.

When drool dripped off her fangs, Lucas rolled the chain twice more around his hand. "She's reacting to the scent of Nikki's blood!"

Bea's gaze shot to me.

I sucked in air, fear pinning my tailbone to the couch. Metal jangled as she lurched, shoving my brother into the makeshift coffee table and jostling Lucas forward. Liam sprang in front of me.

"Bea, calm down!" Nate screeched as Liam roared and cinched her elongated throat, raising her a full foot off the ground.

She let out a strangled yowl and batted at his raised arm, raking her curled yellow nails across Liam's skin, making him bleed. His fingers tightened, his knuckles turning as white as snow.

"Liam, don't kill her," Nate croaked. "Please. Have mercy."

I stared between my Alpha and my brother, my lips wobbling with the desire to second Nate's plea. But I couldn't speak. Could hardly breathe. When Bea's arms drooped, when her head lolled and her lids lowered, I unpinned my mouth and gulped in a lungful of oxygen.

"She's not dead, even though she should be." Liam tossed her at Lucas as though she were no more than a rag doll that had lost its stuffing.

"Thank you." Nate's bloodshot eyes tracked the black-haired Beta as he removed Bea from the cabin. "Thank you," he whispered again, before lumbering out the door himself, gait unsteady.

"What if she attacks Lucas?" I murmured.

"He has a tranquilizer gun in the car. I told him to use it."

"Here, Liam." The whisper of a zipper called my attention back to Darren, who was digging through his nylon bag for sterile gauze and alcohol. Not that we could get infections.

"Take care of Nikki first."

Darren delicately angled my head away, parted my clumped hair, and swiped the gauze he'd wet against the wound. As he patted the tender spot, I clenched both my eyes and fingers, desperately trying to rein in my runaway pulse.

The air churned, thickened with the scent of mint and wind, and then a warm current ribboned through the cabin's brisk air. When knees clicked and hands curled around my rolled fists, I peeked through my lashes.

Liam was crouched beside me, his face was so close to mine I could taste his breaths. Although tension traveled across his features, he exuded so much heat and calm energy that I gradually relaxed.

"Will I need stitches, Darren?"

"Depends how fast you want to heal."

I kept my gaze locked on Liam's steady one. "As fast as possible."

"Then stitches it'll be."

I gulped.

"I'll administer an anesthetic, sweetie. You won't feel a thing."

I tried to be brave. What was a little head wound considering everything else that was happening? "You can go with them, Liam. Darren can drive me home."

"They don't need me."

The words, *I don't need you either* gripped my tongue but never made their way out, because even though I *didn't* need him, I appreciated him staying. "I'm sorry I called you an alphahole," I murmured.

I've been called way worse, **Pinecone.** He popped the nickname out with a hefty dose of snark.

I was about to tell him not to call me that when the tip of a needle pricked my skull.

"So, tell me about this infamous nickname of yours. How did you get it?" he asked out loud.

I gritted my teeth, then breathed out. "A confession for a confession."

So demanding, Miss Freemont. He heaved another breath, which slid right through my parted lips. "Fine. You first, though."

My skull went pleasantly numb. I sort of wished the numbness could extend to my temple. I mean, it was in the general vicinity.

Wrinkling my nose, I admitted, "As you know, I'm the youngest in the brood. After Nolan and Nash had their first shift, I got really jealous." Darren's fingers prodded the back of my head. "Let me preface this by saying that I was eight at the time and extremely gullible." I licked my lips, because this was no less mortifying eleven years later. "Niall, who hadn't shifted yet either but insisted he was close, convinced me that eating a pinecone would activate my shifter gene early."

Darren chuckled.

"Yeah, yeah. Make fun of me, Doc."

Liam grinned. A full-on grin that made me catch my breath. "Don't tell me you fell for it?"

"Hook, line, and pinecone," I admitted.

"Had to administer some pretty strong laxatives," Darren chirped in.

I wanted to turn and scowl at him, but his fingers kept my head locked firmly in place. "You just had to share that last part? Whatever happened to doctor-patient confidentiality?"

"Doesn't extend to Alphas," Darren explained. "Thankfully, Nicole gobbled down a particularly small one."

All the blood converged inside my cheeks. "I've changed my mind. Let me bleed out."

Liam clucked his tongue. "He'd be out of a pack *and* a job if he did that."

A slight frown touched my brow. Was Liam joking or was it an actual threat? I knew he had the power to divest Darren of both, but he wouldn't . . . would he?

CHAPTER 31

"All done." Darren snipped the thread on his cranial needlepoint, then squirted Liam's arms with alcohol. After patting them clean, he put away his arsenal and rose from the arm of the couch. "Do either of you need a ride back to the compound?"

Liam swiped his palms over the hairline cuts that remained from Bea's attack. "We're good. My car's parked not too far."

Darren glanced my way, probably curious about my relationship with our Alpha who'd not only held my hands but also declared I was riding back with him without asking my opinion on the matter.

Not to mention . . . Darren's gaze had strayed more than once toward Liam's swollen lip.

I didn't make a scene while Darren was still there, but as soon as he left, and Liam and I had exited the house, I said, "Maybe I didn't want to ride back with you." The sun was still so bright it stung my eyes.

Liam, who'd been shrugging on his leather jacket, paused with the round collar folded inside-out. Slowly, he popped it flat. "I thought I was no longer an alphahole?"

"You could've asked what *I* wanted to do."

"Would you like me to call Darren back?"

"No."

"Would you have preferred to ride home with him?"

I side-eyed Liam. "Perhaps."

His lips pinched. "Can you walk or do you want me to get the car?"

"I can walk."

"May I suggest you hold on to me?"

"You may suggest it."

His eyebrows dipped. "Will you?"

"No."

He growled low, and it ricocheted off the frozen lake.

"Since we're hanging out, I'm calling in the confession you owe me."

The slant of his eyebrows increased. "Go ahead."

Heart strumming a little faster, I asked, "Do you dislike mating bonds because Ness chose her true mate over you?"

"My dislike doesn't stem from unrequited affection. Yes, Ness and I had a thing. A very brief thing, which ended because I was a dick to her." His throat moved with a swallow—grief, annoyance? I didn't know him well enough to tell. "Ultimately, I would've lost her to August, so it's probably a good thing we didn't get involved. Not only were they magically tethered, but they had history. You can't compete with history."

I picked up my pace to keep up with his longer strides. "Do you like him?"

"Who? August?"

I nodded.

"Our relationship's getting better, but he's never fully trusted I've stopped having designs on his girl."

"Have you?"

He slanted me a look. "They're true mates. Once it's consummated, there's no coming between that bond."

"But if they hadn't consummated it?"

"I don't like *ifs*. What's the point in contemplating fates that never happened? I'd rather focus on the one happening. I didn't get the girl but got the pack, and then I got a son but didn't get the mother. I've come to terms that you can't have it all, and I'm satisfied with my lot."

"That's a crappy outlook."

"Excuse me?"

"To think happiness comes at a cost."

"It does."

"No, it doesn't. Happiness isn't a transaction; it's a state of mind. You should try it." Under my breath, I added, "Although you probably wouldn't see happiness if it slapped you in the face."

His mouth's grim line gentled.

"If it isn't because of Ness, then why do you dislike mating bonds?"

His gaze swept over the tawny trunks shading us from the sun. "Because of my father."

I waited for him to elaborate.

"His true mate rejected him, which made him treat my mother like a worthless consolation prize."

"Oh." I'd heard his father was an awful man. I'd also heard rumors he'd killed his wife. However tempted I was to learn more, Liam sounded upset enough as it was.

When we reached his boxy SUV, he drew open the passenger door for me, then shut it and got behind the wheel.

"Can you drop me off at Adalyn's salon? I need to pick up my car."

"I don't think you should be driving."

I rolled my eyes. "Darren didn't perform open-brain surgery on me, Liam. Besides, it's a short drive."

"Please get it when you're feeling better. Or better yet, I'll tell Lucas to pick it up once he's done at the bunker."

The mere mention of the bunker had my stomach rolling. "Do my parents know about Bea yet?"

"I haven't told them anything."

"It's going to wreck them. They love Bea." I stuck my elbow on the armrest and watched the pallid land scroll by. "What happened to all the people Alex bit?"

"What do you think happened to them?"

"Did they not give any of them a chance?"

"You'd have to ask Lori, but I bet they were all killed immediately, or word would've spread of his clandestine abilities."

"Do you think the full moon will turn them back? Or completely?"

"I wouldn't get your hopes up."

My optimism shriveled like a raisin. I was so disappointed I couldn't muster a single other word for miles.

It wasn't until we reached the compound almost an hour later that I managed to speak again. "Now that the case is solved, will you return to Boulder?"

"Yes. But after the full moon run and the halfwolves' fates have been decided."

I'd miss having him and Storm around. Even Lucas and his stream-of-consciousness chatter would be missed.

I glanced at Liam, and our eyes held. Could he see all that was going through my mind? Lycaon, I hoped not. How embarrassing to have grown attached after two weeks. Yes, we'd spent an inordinate amount of time together and been intimate, but still . . .

"Do you miss home?" I ended up asking.

His attention reverted to the road. "Home is Storm and the pack."

I nibbled on my lower lip. "So you already feel at home here?"

"Yes."

My insides warmed as he drove up to my parents' house and parked.

Before getting out, he said, "Want me to break the news or want to do it yourself?"

"I'll do it."

I took a deep breath, readying myself to shatter my parents' hearts. Hopefully, Nate had beat me to it. They drew open the front door before we'd even reached it, faces as pale as the milk Storm was guzzling down.

"You heard?"

Mom shifted Storm to her other hip. "Nate called. He's still at the hospital with Miles but he was heading to the bunker. Your dad was about to go meet him, but I'd like to—if you don't need me anymore, Liam . . ." Her voice caught.

"Of course. Thank you for keeping my son as long as you have." Liam reached out for Storm, who released his bottle and flailed around to reach his father, wearing the drooliest smile.

In spite of the tears filming her eyes, Mom echoed Storm's smile. "Please. We had the greatest sleepover. I hope you two had fun despite . . ."

She swallowed while I sucked in a little too much air and subsequently began coughing. Liam remained perfectly opaque, answering that it had been an extremely appreciated break, and he couldn't thank them enough for their generosity.

I knew it was ridiculous to even worry about my parents finding out about the extent of *our fun*, but did it stop me? Nope. Especially since the mark of our fun was right smack dab in the middle of Liam's face. Hopefully, they imagined Liam had gotten his fun elsewhere.

Mom helped Liam thread Storm's arms through his little puffer jacket. "Why did she do this to herself? To her brother . . . to her parents . . ."

I hadn't thought about Miles in a while, but now that I did, I worried about him and his staged fender bender.

Dad pulled Mom against him and kissed her temple. "Maybe there's a way to reverse it, Meg."

Mom's bottom lip began to wobble.

"Aw, Mom." I gripped one of her hands and squeezed.

She squeezed right back. "Your head, honey. Let's go inside and—"

"My head's fine, Mom. I swear. Go see Nate. He needs you guys right now."

"Are you sure?"

"Yes." I squeezed once more.

She turned her shiny eyes toward Liam. After a few seconds, she murmured, "Thank you, Liam." And then she kissed my cheek, lightly caressed the skin around my swollen temple, and walked over to their minivan.

As they backed out of the driveway, I asked, "Why did she thank you?"

"Because I promised her I wouldn't let you out of my sight until they got home."

I jerked back, which angered all my head wounds. "Why in the world would you offer to do that?"

"So she didn't have to worry about you and could concentrate on Nate."

"Liam, I'm honest to goodness fine." I pulled their front door closed and returned to the car. "I swear."

"I promised your mother, and I'm a man of my word."

"I'll call Adalyn." I rooted around in my pocket to retrieve my phone.

Before I could pull it out, Liam handed me Storm. "Mind holding him while I drive?"

Storm grinned and squeaked like one of his bath toys. I brushed a rebellious auburn tendril out of his green eyes and smiled. I wondered if every baby's happiness was contagious, or if Liam's son had some covert shifter power.

I didn't bother strapping us in, but held on to him as securely as he held on to his drained bottle. "You do realize how ridiculous it is to babysit me?"

"You blacked out. Concussions are serious. Even for us."

I pursed my lips. "You didn't seem all that worried about concussions an hour ago when you gave Miles one."

He slung me a look, which he didn't substantiate with words. Didn't need to.

I sighed, because I was aware giving Miles a concussion was the lesser of two evils. "Thank you for not killing him," I said, just as my stomach rumbled so loudly the sound startled Storm.

Liam smiled. "How about I make you"—he stared out at the sun which sat so low on the horizon it looked propped atop Gold Dust Peak—"a very late lunch."

"I thought you couldn't cook?"

"I can boil pasta. Remember?"

After we parked, I settled with Storm on the living room rug while Liam carried over a basket overflowing with toys before heading into the kitchen.

"I didn't put much faith in this not being awkward, but it surprisingly isn't. Should've trusted the one-night stand expert."

His spine straightened. "That was pure speculation. I've never actually hung out with a girl I"—he pushed down the faucet and set the pot on the stovetop—"was *intimate* with." He rubbed the back of his neck.

Had I unsettled Liam? "If only they'd known mild concussions were the key to morning-after attention."

Liam's eyes finally flipped to mine. He shook his head when he caught my smile, but reciprocated with a diminutive one of his own.

Storm scaled my legs and jiggled his rattle so close to my corneas I blinked. "Eyes on you. Got it." I grabbed a second rattle from the toy bin and shook it to the rhythm of a vintage pop song.

Storm clapped, then remembered his own instrument and played backup. We got through three melodies before the front door opened.

"Well, isn't this cozy?" A gust of cold air accompanied Lucas's voice.

"How is everyone?" I asked.

Lucas shoved his disheveled hair back. "Cringily weepy." A heavy dose of sympathy edged his words. He walked over to the eight-person dining table and slumped in front of the giant pasta bowl Liam had just set down. "How kind of you to have made me a snack, Liam. What will the two of you be eatin'?" He managed to stab a forkful of pasta before Liam dragged the bowl away from him.

"I'll put another pot on, but ladies first, Lucas."

"It's okay. I can wait." I stood up, then leaned over to pick up Storm.

Lucas gobbled down his mouthful. "Was just kidding, although I could probably eat a whole packet. Been a taxing day."

I settled Storm in the high chair, then sat next to him. As Liam went to put another pot on, I portioned out bowls with the first batch of pasta. "Are you even fighting with your girlfriend or was that a cover story so no one would suspect your extended presence in Beaver Creek?"

"Sadly, t'was all true." He slouched in his chair, making the rungs creak.

Although I wasn't glad they were fighting, I was glad he hadn't lied. "Did Ness give her the letter?"

"Yup."

"And?"

"And she emailed me back askin' if I'd started consuming deer droppings." He grinned.

"Crap. Sorry."

"Are you kidding, Knickknack? It's the first time she's responded. Thanks to you, my dick's one step closer to redemption."

Liam let out a snort.

"So, how was *your* night?" Lucas pointed between me and Liam, eyebrows waggling.

A blush crept over my jaw but didn't chase away my smile. Focusing on cutting up a penne into tiny pieces for Storm, I deadpanned, "Had better."

Lucas laughed. "Ooh, snap."

Liam reclined in his chair. "With *Grant?*"

Even though sex with Grant had never been bad, Liam certainly knew his way around the female anatomy.

Storm slapped his plastic tray, demanding more pasta. Even though my parents had most probably fed him a three-course lunch, I pandered to his appetite. It was almost four after all.

Liam played with the tines of his fork, making it seesaw. "I guess we'll just have to schedule a redo then."

My heart fired off a beat. To avoid sounding eager, I said, "That's against the rules of one-night stands."

"Good thing I can amend pack rules."

"One-night stands are a human thing."

"I'm declaring *pack* one-night stands will now last a minimum of two nights to qualify."

Lucas was alternatively chuckling and shoveling down his food. "Lunch *and* a show."

"I'm concussed." I wasn't playing hard to get, merely making sure I wasn't too easily gotten. No wolf wanted his prey to lay back and demand to be eaten.

Although . . .

Dirty mind, there's a baby next to you and *Liam's best friend.*

"Once you're *un*concussed."

"I'll give it a think."

"Shiiit," Lucas drawled.

Liam flopped even farther in his chair, but not out of defeat. No, he slumped so that his knees knocked into mine. I didn't tuck mine to the side, because I liked the feel of him reaching for me, even if it was with just his knees.

Storm slapped his tray, and Lucas mirrored the action. "You're right, Little Destroyer. Where the hell's our pasta?"

"Softening in the pot." Liam tipped his head to the kitchen, and Lucas got up.

If you're not interested, I'll drop it.

"Don't drop it," I said, placing some more bites of penne in front of his son.

Although I didn't think Liam had taken my reluctance seriously, my answer smoothed away the ridges above his nose and brightened his dark eyes. I reveled in that look. Not to mention, a redo meant he'd enjoyed last night, otherwise he wouldn't have suggested it. It was probably the fanging and not my bedroom expertise, but I'd take whatever reason he had for still wanting me.

As Lucas toted the steaming pot of pasta back to the table, a knock resounded on the front door. Liam sat up, and the door swung wide.

Adalyn rushed in, followed by Nash and Nolan. "We were at Pondside and heard the news." Her blue eyes were rimmed red, lending them the same phosphorescence they had when she was in fur.

She sank down into a free chair, pulling my brother down next to her.

Nolan leaned against the kitchen counter, arms crossed while his twin stared at Liam, body coiled with tension. "Lori needs to pay for this. She needs to die."

CHAPTER 32

I choked on my mouthful of pasta and sputtered, then seized my glass of water and flushed down the doughy clump. "Bea *asked* to be bitten, Nash."

Nolan cocked up a brown eyebrow. "You're defending Lori?"

"Yes. How can you even suggest Liam kill her?"

"She can create halfwolves, Nik!" Nash said. "She's a danger to humankind."

"She's never done it before."

"Let me guess . . . She told you this was her first time?"

"No. Nate told me. I trust Nate. You should, too."

Nolan tightened his crossed arms. "Our brother was involved with Lori. Did he tell you that?"

I looked over at Liam, hoping his thoughts didn't align with my brothers'. "He didn't, but I found out."

"He's obviously trying to protect her," Nash insisted.

Ads wrapped her hand around Nash's forearm. "Lori basically killed Bea. Why are you protecting her?"

"Because Bea blackmailed her into doing it."

Nash snorted. "*Nate* told you that too?"

"So what if he did?" Anger shot through me. "You're talking about eliminating someone from the face of the earth because you're scared they might commit a crime."

"They *might?*" The knot of Nolan's arms tightened. "Lori did commit the crime."

I shoved my hair back.

"What happened to your head?" Ads gasped.

"I bumped it."

"You *bumped* it?" Nash repeated.

Nolan pushed away from the countertop and stalked toward me. "On what?"

I lowered my lashes. "It's not important."

"On a gun," Liam said.

I shot him a look. Had he really needed to share this *now?* My brothers were already out for someone's blood. Now they'd be out for two people's blood.

Nolan froze. "A gun?"

"Yes, a gun. Can we refocus on the main issue right now? Your bloodlust—"

"Whose gun?" Nash gritted out, his fingers curled into a fist so tight his knuckles had turned white and brown fur was sprouting over them. Over his corded forearms too.

Adalyn gripped both sides of his face, forcing him to look at her. Slowly, his fur receded into his pores.

Storm, nonplussed by the anger electrifying the atmosphere in the cabin, squealed and made grabby hands for my plate of pasta.

I sliced up two more penne on his tray. "I was on my way to visit Bea this morning with Miles when we ran into Liam and Lucas in fur. Miles freaked and took out a gun."

"And he hit you with it?" Nash burst out of his chair. So much for Ads calming him. "I will *kill* him."

Nolan cracked his knuckles. "I'll go with you."

I swung my gaze to our Alpha. "Liam, stop this insanity!"

He popped up an eyebrow, as though he quite enjoyed my brothers' impetuousness. Probably found it convenient considering his dislike of Miles.

Growling a little, I turned back toward my brothers. "It was an accident. No one's killing anyone. Not Miles and not Lori. Besides, Lucas already put Miles in a car accident. That was payback enough."

Their twin blue stares beamed right onto Lucas.

After listening to Lucas's little tale, Ads narrowed her eyes on my swollen temple. "I still don't get how hitting someone can be an accident."

"I got in his way. I was trying to block his shot of Liam to give *this one*"—I lifted my chin toward our Alpha—"time to retreat."

Liam rolled his shoulders. "You actually expected me to back away?"

I blinked at him. "I wasn't in any mortal danger."

Storm patted his tray. Instead of pasta, I got up to fill one of his bottles with water. He probably wouldn't be too happy, but more food would upset his stomach.

As I passed by Adalyn, she spun in her seat. "Why are you decriminalizing what Miles did, Nikki? The bottom line is he *hit* you. That is *not* okay."

I strode into the kitchen and started banging around cupboards in search of Storm's bottles. Found one drying next to the sink. "I know, but at the end of the day, I'm fine and he's not."

Sure, my head ached, but it would heal. How was Miles going to heal? And I wasn't talking about the car accident, but about the loss of his sister. Because he would lose her if we didn't find a way to save her.

I let the water run and run, until it cooled, then positioned the bottle under the spout. As I screwed on the lid, I turned back around. "Can we please refocus on Bea now?" I walked back over to the table and handed Storm the bottle under Adalyn's watchful gaze. "I'm aware what Lori can do is dangerous, but as long as she didn't do it out of spite, then she doesn't deserve a death sentence. Right, Liam?"

All eyes turned to him, including his son's.

Storm lifted the bottle and chugged a mouthful, drooling most of it out. His nose crinkled, but he drank some more, as though expecting the liquid to magically transform into milk. When it didn't, he held his bottle out and dropped it.

Just dropped it.

I smiled, and so did Nolan, who crouched and picked it up. I was glad that at least one of my brothers' bloodlust had quieted, even if it was just temporary.

Liam unhooked his son from the chair and picked him up. "Unless you find proof Lori's lied about this being the first time she's turned someone, she'll remain a Boulder for the rest of her natural life. Understood?" He slid one big palm up and down his son's back.

Nash muttered, "Understood."

Chair legs scraped, then Ads said, "You're about to have a mutiny on your hands, Liam."

"And where will you stand when this *mutiny* arises, Adalyn?"

I looked at my friend, at her smudged eye makeup and splotched cheeks. I waited for her to say: with him. But she didn't.

Instead, she said, "With Nash."

"Nash, Nolan, where will the two of you stand?" Liam enquired.

"On the side of justice," they said at the very same time, proving once again how nine months sharing an amniotic sac had provided them with a mind link worthy of mates'.

Nash tucked his chair under the table. "If I find proof—"

"If you find proof, you bring it to me." Liam's sharp voice made my brother's head jerk in ascent.

My gaze locked on Ads. She bit down on her lip apologetically. I wasn't mad at her, but I was a little disappointed that she'd jump aboard the *eliminate Lori train* without concrete proof.

"What about you, Pinecone? What side will you stand on if we find proof of past infractions?" Nolan asked.

"On the side of justice, too, but I still think your energy would be better spent finding a solution for the halfwolves."

Nash's blue eyes lingered on me, and although they were bursting with aggravation, they were also crammed with affection. Affection that would hopefully quench his thirst to crucify Lori. Sighing, he came over and bent down to kiss my unbruised temple.

After he stepped back, Nolan leaned over and hugged me. "Liam, you better talk to the pack before someone decides to take justice into their own hands. Everyone's pretty agitated."

Liam's jaw clenched and then his voice resonated inside our minds. ***Boulders, meeting at Pondside tonight at eight to discuss the new developments in the halfwolf case. If anyone, and I do mean anyone, misbehaves in any way, they'll be punished accordingly.***

Nash speared his fingers through Adalyn's. "See you guys tonight."

As he tugged her toward the door, she mouthed, *sorry.* I wondered what she was sorry for. Choosing Nash over our Alpha? I didn't hold that against her.

Nolan followed them out, then shut the door on the crazy world we lived in where one shifter had venom potent enough to mutate the human genome.

Fingers brushed my shoulder, stealing my attention off the shut door. ***You okay?***

I craned my neck. "You think she did it before?"

Liam's chest stilled as though he were carved from clay instead of flesh. "No."

I sighed.

Lucas pushed back from the table. "I'll just grab my phone."

I frowned. Once he'd disappeared down the hallway, I asked, "What was that about?"

"I want Lucas at Lori's until the meeting."

Storm had his head tucked in the crook of his dad's neck and his lids closed.

"You think someone might actually try to harm her?"

He laid his cheek against his son's head. "We're warm-blooded creatures."

Adalyn had mentioned a mutiny . . .

I jutted my chin toward Storm. "You should take advantage of Storm's nap to have one yourself."

"That would defeat the purpose of watching you."

"As you can see, I'm fine."

"How about you come nap with us?"

Warmth gushed into my cheeks. "I can just imagine my parents' faces if they found us in bed together, even fully clothed."

"We'll text them not to pick you up."

Dropping my voice in case Lucas was on his way back, I whispered, "I'm really not in any state for a repeat performance of last night."

"I wasn't hinting at that, Nikki. I really meant sleeping. Besides, I'll keep Storm between us to prove I have no ill intentions." He caressed Storm's back, his fingers spanning the baby's entire rib cage.

"I *could* use a nap."

His face didn't break into a smile, but his eyes glinted with quiet pleasure.

Lucas walked back out then. "Behave yourselves."

I rolled my eyes. After the door shut, Liam held out his hand. I wrapped my fingers around his, and together we walked to his bedroom.

I was surprised to find the bed made. It wasn't that I imagined Liam was a slob, but I did wonder when he'd had time to tidy up considering the day he'd had. After setting an alarm on his phone, speaking to Nate and subsequently to my parents, he placed Storm in the middle of the bed and laid down. I grabbed a towel from his bathroom and tucked it over the pillow, then climbed atop the comforter and curled onto my side.

Liam reached over and rested his hand on my hip. "Just in case you convulse."

I wasn't sure if that was his reason for touching me, but I wasn't about to complain. "What did Nate say?"

"That Miles could hardly look him in the eye he was so embarrassed about having abandoned you."

"So he doesn't remember?"

"Fortunately for him, seems that way." His thumb traced slow arcs against my hipbone, all at once causing my skin to break out in goosebumps and my eyelashes to flutter closed.

"Good," I murmured.

I didn't put much stock in actually falling asleep, but I must've been really tired, because the next thing I knew, the shower was running, the sky was pitch-black, and Storm's face was nuzzled against my chest.

He stirred, and then the corner of his lips pitched downward as though he were about to cry. But then his mouth straightened and parted around deep breaths. I smoothed out his damp curls, then ran my nose over his forehead wondering what he could be dreaming about.

"You had a tiring day, too, huh?" I murmured.

His eyelashes fluttered but still didn't rise.

"You talk in your sleep," came a deep voice behind me.

I cringed as I looked over my shoulder. Liam stood with only a towel knotted around his waist, revealing glistening, stacked abs peppered with bruises. One was particularly nasty. I imagined he'd gotten it from his altercation with Miles.

"What did I say this time? Nothing too mortifying I hope."

"Just that I was the best lay you'd ever had."

I rolled my eyes. "You wish." According to Adalyn, with whom I'd had innumerable sleepovers, nothing I said ever made sense.

Liam sat down on the edge of the bed beside me, which made the mattress dip. "I do wish."

His scent gusted off his skin, crisp and heady, intensifying as he leaned over me to stroke a knuckle down Storm's cheek. The forearm, which Bea had clawed up, brushed against my chest, and the contact woke my nipples right up. I wasn't sure if it had been intentional. Until his gaze locked on mine, and his pupils spread with lust.

I held my breath.

His head lowered to mine.

Slowly.

So slowly.

The air thickened, churned with his smell, turning my heart into a tambourine. When our mouths were an inch apart, his phone's alarm blared, ripping Storm from his peaceful slumber with an eardrum-shattering wail.

With a sigh, Liam sat back and plucked his son off the bed with one hand, then stood and spoke quietly into the little one's ear until his sobs receded.

I rolled off the bed, prodding my temple. The lump had softened, but it was still tender and swollen. "I should get home and shower." I folded up the towel, which was lightly streaked with blood.

"If you give me a minute to get dressed, I'll go with you."

"No convulsions, which means my brain is fine." I walked toward the door. "You should get to Pondside early."

Although he wasn't particularly appeased with my insistence to go back to my place for a shower and a change of clothes, he didn't put up a fight. Probably because I reeked of dried blood and resembled mangled roadkill. I hadn't even realized the extent of my resemblance to a trodden rodent until I caught sight of my reflection in my bathroom mirror. How he had even *wanted* to kiss me was mystifying.

I made sure to correct that with lots of shampoo, which stung my scalp—no way would I sport blood-crusted hair tonight though—and a hefty layer of concealer.

The nap had reinvigorated me, and by the time I made my way to Pondside with Niall, I felt ready to take on any shifter out for blood.

CHAPTER 33

Most of the pack was already present by the time Niall and I arrived. I walked up to the table my family had colonized, Lucas, Storm, and Lori in their midst. Liam was standing in the middle of the room, conducting quiet conversations with a few animated shifters. Grant's father and sister were among the disgruntled huddle.

They kept casting dirty glares toward Lori, who sat half-hidden between Nate and Lucas, while I headed toward my father.

"How's the head, Pinecone?" He bobbed his leg, making Storm jiggle as though he were horseback riding.

"All better, Daddy."

"You're not saying that because you want to spare me, right?"

"No. I swear."

As though he'd heard my father's concern, Darren walked over to us with his wife, and parted my clean hair to take a look at my stitches. "Stitches held, and you're no longer bleeding. How's the temple?"

"Much better too." I smiled to reassure him.

As he exchanged words with my father about what wine to pair with roasted lamb, and his wife fussed over Storm, a familiar voice asked, "What happened to your head?"

I turned in my chair, found Grant staring at the back of it. "Nothing. I just fell."

"You got stitches, Nikki, so it's not nothing."

For all his faults, Grant had never been pitiless. Even cowards could be considerate. "I swear, I'm fine."

As I checked the room to see if everyone had arrived, I found Liam's eyes grinding a hole in the back of Grant's skull.

Everyone, please settle down so we may begin. Liam's terse voice boomed, dimming all ambient noise.

Chairs scraped the slate flooring. The younger shifters flopped cross-legged onto the floor. Others leaned against the wall or the bar or against each other. The last time I'd been at Pondside with the entire pack was when we were still Creeks. How fast and avidly we'd adopted our new heritage. Then again, most of us had never liked being Creeks.

I'd been born an Aspen, and then, six years ago, Cassandra Morgan had walked onto the compound with her puny pack and challenged our Alpha. The fight lasted mere seconds, yet I remembered the gory battle in vivid detail. Remembered the ensuing battles, because many Aspens had challenged her. *All* had lost their lives. Grant's father had longed for a brawl, but his grandmother, a mighty frightening female, had put her paw down.

I had no doubt that, had Grant's dad been a decade younger, he would've challenged Liam. He'd apparently tried to get his kids to do it, but neither possessed David Hollis's political aspirations. Camilla was too much of an introvert, and Grant too irresponsible. I mean, the guy couldn't deal with me and my busted knee; how in the world would he have dealt with a pack and all of its issues?

"I've been accused of deception by many of you." Liam prowled the narrow space that remained between the throng of bodies. "My intentions were never to mislead you but to mislead the perpetrator to buy myself time to corner them. Although you're all entitled to your opinions on my manner of dealing with the halfwolf case, next time, voice your objections in a respectful manner."

I reached toward the center of the table, seized the water pitcher, and poured myself a glass. Storm released a little squeak, reaching for my cup. I tipped it to his already parted lips. He took one greedy sip, startled, then spat it all out, not pleased at all with the taste, just like earlier. I chuckled, but a terse look from Mom had me quieting and refocusing on Liam who'd just run the pack through what Bea, Lori, and Nate had brought about.

"Can you take him a minute?" Dad whispered, passing me Storm before getting up.

As he loped through the dense pack, I propped Liam's son on my lap and let him play with my thick braid that draped over my shoulder.

"She asked for it, my ass," Camilla grunted. "Morgans are all disgusting and fucked in the head."

I shot her a dirty glare, which she didn't catch, much too fixated on poor Lori, who sank lower in her chair, narrow face pinkening.

Nate leaned toward her and whispered something in her ear that had her eyes turning up toward his. Although the fear didn't completely melt off her features, whatever he'd said made her spine straighten.

"Too bad she didn't come back from Boulder in a body bag like the rest of her kin."

I turned in my chair this time and hissed, "Shut up, Camilla. Lori's *nothing* like her mother and brother."

Grant's eyebrows drew low over his grass-green eyes. "I thought you loved Bea."

"I do, but Bea asked to be turned."

"Into a halfwolf? Did you really fall today, or did someone hit you in the head, because you sound brainwashed?" Suddenly, Grant winced, and then his eyes brightened with fury.

Nikki, stop engaging with your asshole ex and his asshole family. My Alpha's growl made my attention snap off the Hollises.

Lucas reclined in his chair. "Can't believe you went out with this douche canoe, Knickknack."

"Betas were respectful in my time, Mr. Mason," Grant's father gritted out. "They didn't go around flinging unmerited insults."

My eyebrows popped upward.

"I respect respectable people, Hollis. Your son ain't—"

"Lucas!" Liam's command to drop it was loud and clear even though he added no other words, at least, not out loud.

Grant's father cranked his chin high, assuming Liam was siding with him. I might've smirked had this been at all funny, but it wasn't. Not even a little. It was tense and irksome, like watching fire consume the wick of a stick of dynamite.

Storm tugged on my thick braid. I didn't think he'd done it to capture my attention, but he got it for the duration of the meeting. Especially after Dad returned with a long strip of bread crust. As Storm merrily drooled over the bread, I watched him like a hawk, fishing out the pieces I deemed too big for his narrow throat.

"Boulders, don't work against me!" Liam's impassioned tone drew everyone's gazes to him. "Work *with* me. Help me find solutions to either return the three halfwolves to their former selves or aid them in accomplishing full shifts by Friday's full moon. A solution could earn you the title and responsibility of Beta."

Grant's father elbowed his kids, blatantly communicating his desire for one of them to step up to the challenge.

"What if we force them out of Colorado? Distance would eventually make them stop shifting," someone suggested.

"Apparently, this was tried in the past with the humans Alex Morgan bit. They stayed halfwolves even far from the pack. But the larger problem isn't their outward appearance. It's their feral nature and their ability to transmit the defective gene. *Born* halfwolves aren't violent by nature and their bodies don't reject human food. *Made* halfwolves feed exclusively on blood."

"So basically, they're vampires?" a ten-year-old sitting on the floor asked.

"Mighty furry and ugly ones apparently," a tween tossed out.

"Vampires aren't real," someone else hissed.

"Perhaps we should rename this new species, Liam?" a woman sitting two tables down suggested.

"New species? They're three . . . Unless others were allowed to live?" I recognized Avery's voice even though I couldn't spot him in the crowd.

"No." Nate swallowed. "The others were all dealt with."

"Just use the actual word, Freemont," David Hollis said. "Killed. The others were all *killed*."

"There are children in the crowd, David," my brother volleyed back.

David narrowed his gaze. "Werepups grow up fast."

"It *is* confusing to think of them as halfwolves, since halfwolves aren't a threat to humans," Adalyn said.

Her sister's eyes lit up. "Ooh . . . we could call them *vampwolves?*"

A chorus of *I like it* and *yes*es rang out.

Liam sighed. "Rebaptizing them won't help us *cure* them."

"What happens when they feed on blood? Do they shift back into humans?" someone asked.

"Only when they feed on Lori's Sillin-rich blood," Liam answered. "Animal blood sates and calms them, but doesn't make them slide back into skin."

"What about human blood?" I asked.

"Human blood? We can't be giving them human blood, Nikki. Can you imagine what sort of savages they'd turn into if they got a taste for it?" Avery stepped out of the crowd, his one-year-old asleep against his shoulder.

Lucas stopped rocking on the back legs of his chair, slamming back down. "Might help them shift back."

"Lori's blood helps them shift back." A lock of auburn hair fell into Avery's eyes. He shoved it back.

"Darren, you've analyzed Lori's blood, right?" I asked.

"I have."

"Can you measure the exact quantity of Sillin in her bloodstream?"

"I'd have to run a fresh sample, but yeah, I can get a pretty accurate readout."

"Maybe if we manage to reproduce her blood—"

"It'll help Lori, but it won't help the *vampwolves*," Avery's sister, Apple, interjected. "We need to find a solution that locks them back in skin."

"Lucas. Doc." Liam tipped his head to the door.

Lucas rose. "Up we go, Morgan."

Bookended between Nate and Lucas, Lori walked through the sea of shifters, who parted around her as though the very air she exhaled was toxic.

As more questions were lobbed at Liam, and Storm demolished his piece of crust, smearing handfuls on my white tank top—not so white anymore—Pondside began to empty. Soon only a hundred or so shifters remained.

David Hollis finally got up, along with his wife, son, and daughter, who shot me one heck of a stink-eye. "How long do we have to find the *vampwolves* a solution?"

Until Friday.

David nodded.

I stayed until the end of the meeting, and then throughout dinner, which Nolan and Dad had gone to prep halfway before the Q&A had begun.

The shifters who remained hounded Liam, even as he made his way to the table and took the seat Dad had vacated. He held out his arms, and I handed over Storm. Evidently tired of discussing the case, he dismissed them, promising answers after dinner.

I grabbed a napkin from the tray in the middle of the table and dipped it in water, then dabbed at my poor tank top. "Remind me not to wear white around Storm."

His lips, which had sloped downward throughout the entire meeting, finally straightened. ***You might want to stop trying to clean your top.***

I glanced down at myself, my blood warming when I noticed the spots I'd rubbed had turned so transparent the color of my black bra and the perkiness of my nipples were both visible. I undid my braid, then divvied up my hair and let it hang loosely over my shoulders.

"Got a minute, Nik?" Ads, who'd sat with her grandmother up until now, nodded to the bathroom.

I got up and followed her, sensing from her tense expression a heavy conversation coming on, one I wasn't particularly looking forward to but which needed to be had. Would it be about my stance on Lori or where I stood with Liam?

I sort of hoped it would be the former because I had no clue what the hell I was doing with Liam, besides contemplating a second-night stand and falling a little too deeply for his son.

CHAPTER 34

Adalyn locked the door behind us in the single toilet stall. "Tell me everything."

"About?"

"You and Liam, obvs," she whispered.

"So, this isn't about Lori?"

"We'll get to Lori, but first I want to know how you got from one-night stand to playing house."

"We're not playing house."

"Nik, you were at his house earlier. And then you had Storm on your lap during the *entire* meeting. And then, post-meeting, Liam heads to *you*."

"*Because* I had his son."

"Sweetie, I heard people whispering about the nature of your relationship with him."

"You'd think they'd have better stuff to talk about."

"Yeah, you'd think. So tell me. Start to finish."

As I filled her in, not leaving anything out since Ads was a detailmonger, her face went through a dozen different expressions before settling on grim concern. "Don't accept a second-night stand."

"Why not?"

"Because, Nikki, you're not the type of girl who does casual relationships."

"Maybe I am."

She raised one eyebrow.

"Just because I've never *done* casual doesn't mean I'm incapable of it."

Adalyn leaned against the sink top. "What happens once he returns to Boulder for a stretch of time?"

"I go back to living like I was before he got here." I shrugged a shoulder. "Besides, it'll only be for a few months."

"You won't miss him?"

I clutched my elbows.

"Exactly!"

A knock on the door made my heart hold still.

"Not close to being done in here," Adalyn shouted. "Use the men's room." Once the door across the hall clicked shut, she dropped her voice, "I'm all for you having fun, but I'm worried about your heart."

"My heart's not involved."

"Nik . . ."

"I swear. It's purely physical."

"Then I should totally encourage May to go after him."

My vertebrae jammed together. "Why would you do that?"

"Because she's infatuated with him, and since *you're* not attached, you don't actually care who he gets physical with."

I pressed my lips shut.

"Right?"

"Right."

She rolled her blue eyes. "You're *such* a bad liar."

"You know what? Encourage her." The very thought of him putting his mouth on another woman dissolved my stomach, but at least, it would show me where I stood with him if he accepted. "He's not mine."

"Okay."

"Okay."

We stared at each other a long moment. And then she reached around and plucked her cell phone from the pocket of her ripped jeans. "You're sure?"

My grip tightened on my elbows until the sharp bones felt like they were about to poke right through my palms. "Yep. Absolutely."

"Sending her a text now."

"Go for it."

"Nikki—"

"I'm serious. Send it."

She tapped her screen, and it felt like my heart had slipped right under her thumb. "Done." She put her phone back into her pocket. "Now, about Lori . . ."

"Bea asked for it."

"I know. Nash and I went to talk to her when she was back in skin, but do you honestly think Lori hasn't done it before? I mean—"

"She's not Alex, Ads."

"She's still a Morgan."

"You sound like the Hollises."

"That's . . ." She shuddered. "Just no."

"I'm not saying I'm not wrecked by what's happened, but I don't think Lori should be crucified."

"You really think this is her first time?"

"Yes."

"Why?"

"Because she said it was, and even though she's a bunch of things, a liar isn't one of them. Besides, I trust Nate."

"He hid the truth. From Liam. From his parents. From you, his siblings to whom he tells *everything*."

"We all have our secrets."

"What secrets do you have?"

That I'm not fine with May going after Liam . . . "None," I lied. "But give my brother the benefit of the doubt. Give *her* the benefit of the doubt. Everyone already detests her because of her last name."

"Fine, but if Nash uncovers any dirty secret—"

"Then Liam will deal with her accordingly, and I'll admit I was wrong." On a sigh, I unlocked the door.

Before I could swing it open, Adalyn gripped my forearm. "I told May to stay away from him."

My stomach took shape again, and my heart bounced back into its original cavity.

"But don't go for a second round. Not unless you're ready to have your heart broken." She squeezed once before letting go. "But in case you really *can't* resist, I'll be there to pick up the pieces."

My lips wobbled as I slung my arms around her shoulders. "If I never get a true mate, I'm glad I got a true sister."

Her arms came around me. "Stop it. You're going to make my eyeliner run."

After a prolonged hug, we finally returned to a table filled with food and crowded with people. My seat was now occupied by Niall, who was talking Liam's ear off about the itinerary for our pack run on Friday. I hadn't shifted since my lope around the compound, and my wolf was chomping at the bit. It hit me that this would be my first time running with Liam.

I took a seat at the head of the table between Mom and Adalyn, then filled my plate with the delicious food Dad and Nolan had managed to whip up in such a short amount of time. At some point, I looked up and found Liam staring back.

Everything okay?

I pasted on a smile and nodded.

His gaze slid to Adalyn, who was complimenting Dad on the roasted spaghetti squash.

Mom put her hand on mine, scanning my face in a way that made blood rush into my cheeks. Did she know? "How's your head, sweetheart?"

I expelled a deep breath, glad this wasn't about Liam. "Not hurting at all."

"I'd like you to sleep under our roof tonight so I can keep an eye on you."

I was about to tell her not to worry when I thought better of turning down her invitation. It would help me resist Liam in case he propositioned me later. He probably wouldn't because of my head wound and the insane day we'd both had, but still. "Sounds good, Mom."

She squeezed my fingers, then reached across the table for the platter of grilled salmon steaks just as Lucas trundled into Pondside.

"Nate's with her," he told Liam as he plopped down in one of the remaining free seats and loaded up his plate until the food was piled treacherously high.

"Did Darren already get the result?"

He shoveled three large forkfuls before saying, "Yeah. He's reproducin' it as we speak."

I plopped my elbows on the table and twirled a little piece of paper napkin between my fingers. "Another factor we should consider is using shifter blood instead of animal blood or human blood."

Lucas's giant forkful froze an inch from his lips and some of the food toppled onto his lap. "Good point." He pinched the fallen pieces and lobbed them into his mouth.

Liam stopped caressing the top of his son's head. "What's a good point?"

"Knickknack suggested using shifter blood instead of animal blood."

Liam's gaze slanted to mine. "Is Nate still with Darren?"

I knew he wasn't asking me.

"He was when I left."

Liam's eyes gleamed in the dimmed lighting. After a minute, he said, "I conveyed the message."

"Not just a *passably* pretty face." Lucas shoveled another bite into his mouth and winked.

I tossed a piece of bread at *his* passably nice face, which just made him chuckle and Mom *tsk* at our antics.

Thank you.

My eyes zipped to Liam's. The heat in them made me exceedingly glad to be sleeping over at my parents', because my willpower was nonexistent.

"Just hope it works," I said before getting up and piling empty plates and dishes. After two trips to and from the kitchen, I told Mom I was going to grab some things at my place and meet her at home.

Adalyn watched me, then her gaze slid to Liam. Thankfully, he made no move to follow me, yet, halfway home, I heard heavy footfalls crush the snow behind me. My heart thumped in time with my stalker's feet. I pulled in a lungful of frigid air, expecting it to be laced with Liam's intoxicating scent.

Not Liam's, but it was familiar.

CHAPTER 35

I turned around. "Why are you tailing me, Grant?"

"Saw you leaving by yourself and wanted to make sure you got home okay."

"As you can see, I'm getting home just fine. Now tell me why you're really here?"

"Because I'm sick of this."

I tilted my head to the side. "Of what?"

"Of the way it's become between us." His hands were stuffed in the pockets of his low-slung jeans. "I messed up, Nik, and I didn't realize it until—"

"Until I was no longer crippled?" I finished pleasantly.

"No. Until you got that infection, and I heard Darren utter sepsis and how the Sillin wasn't working."

My heart pumped, half from exertion and half from having to revisit that sucky chapter in my life.

"I was so scared."

He'd been scared? Nate and Dad had cried. I'd never seen either of them cry.

Because Grant clearly wanted my pity, and I had none to give, I spun away from him and bolted down the path toward my cabin.

"I tried to visit you in the clinic after your relapse, but your brothers wouldn't let me in."

Those few days had been a blur, so I didn't remember hearing about his visit. Not that it would've made a difference. I hadn't wanted anything to do with Grant by that point. I'd just managed to put my heart back together and had been working overtime on putting my body back together.

"Hey, can you quit your mad dash?"

"It's cold, and I don't want to travel down memory lane."

He grabbed my bicep and spun me around. "I heard you went home with Liam."

I shrugged him off. "It's none of your business."

"He's just using you to get information about Lori and Nate."

I crossed my arms. "What information could he possibly get from me that he can't get from someone else?"

"You're related to the perp's accomplice and was *almost* related to the victim."

I raised my chin a notch. "He figured out Nate's involvement long before I did, so I don't see what novel data screwing me would bring to the table."

The corners of Grant's lips pinched as though it hurt to hear me confirm I'd slept with Liam. Had that been the point of his conversation? To make me confess?

He swiped a hand over his sheared blond hair. "Look, I just heard him and Lucas talk about how getting closer to you would benefit the case and make him look *involved* with the NBs."

"He must be awfully disappointed then. Not only am I not useful, but I'm also not influential among the New Boulders. Anyway, I'm done talking about this."

"I hope you realize he doesn't care about you, Nik. Never will. Just like he didn't give a shit about his kid's mom. Did you hear that he didn't shed a single tear when she passed away? What sort of cold-hearted bastard stays indifferent to someone's death?"

"Not everyone expresses their sadness with tears."

"Why are you defending him?"

"Because his manner of mourning is none of our business."

"Objection. It's *completely* our business. We didn't get rid of one emotionless leader to get saddled with another."

"Oh for Lycaon's sake, Grant, Liam's nothing like Cassandra."

"Nothing like Cassandra." He grunted. "You're saying that a lot tonight. First, Lori. Now, him. I honestly didn't think you were so naïve."

"*Naïve?* Trust me, almost dying twice gave me lots of perspective. And my perspective is telling me you don't know the first thing about Liam and are judging him on hearsay."

"You weren't at the duel, Nik."

"Yeah. I remember. I was strapped to a heart monitor and IVs."

"He didn't deserve to be Alpha. Cassandra may have cheated, but Ness Clarke should've been our Alpha, and he stole the title from her, and then paid for her silence. If you don't believe me, ask him. Ask *her*."

"I did ask her, and she said he offered her the title and she turned him down."

Grant's jaw hardened. "And you believed her?"

"I did. I believe people. Maybe you should try to as well. It's way nicer than assuming everyone's a liar."

"Liam's not your hero, Nikki."

"I don't need a hero. I can save myself. Now, get out of my face, and don't you ever ambush me again." I pivoted and stalked toward my cabin so fast I missed a patch of black ice. My boot skidded, and I smacked down on my knees.

Ugh.

Grant, who was still planted in the middle of the moonlit valley, didn't run over to offer me a hand. Why would he? He hadn't offered me one when I'd needed it the most.

Whatever.

Like I'd told him. I didn't need a hero. I had everything under control.

As I picked myself up and limped past the ice, I concentrated on the trampled snow and crisp air, on the fragrance of winter smoke and the distant drum of wolf hearts.

My knee hadn't kept me down before.

The hell it would keep me down now.

CHAPTER 36

I woke up to the smell of frying bacon. My brain conjured up Niall at the stovetop, handling a pair of tongs, but that made *zero* sense. My dear brother and roommate had no clue how to work the stovetop. Maybe it was one of his sex buddies.

I turned languidly in bed, then slow-blinked my eyes open. When the oversized pink blooms on my wallpaper came into focus, I smiled. Definitely not Niall. I rolled up, regretting it instantly when a dull throb erupted at the back of my skull and in my knee joint.

Yesterday slotted back into place—Bea's cabin, Adalyn's intervention, Grant's ambush, my limp of shame home.

Sighing, I flung the covers off my legs and stretched. Once my knee felt less stiff, I wiggled into yesterday's skinny jeans, snapped on my bra, then delicately finger-combed my hair to avoid tugging on the tender skin. After a trip to the bathroom, I pulled on my graphic wolf tee that had grown as soft as tissue paper from its many cycles through our washing machine and dabbed a little makeup on the ugly bruise spanning my entire temple. At least, the swelling had resorbed itself.

When I came downstairs, I heard voices in the kitchen and a series of little squeaks. Storm was apparently in attendance but was Liam? Trying to quiet my hammering pulse before the walls of our house began shaking, I eased into the kitchen. Dad stood by the stove in his *Mr. Good Lookin' Is*

Cookin' apron beside Mom, who was pressing oranges, while Liam sat at the island with Storm on his lap.

"Morning." I walked over to my parents and kissed their cheeks. "Smelled Dad's bacon all the way down in the valley, Liam?"

I caught him eyeing my knee. Here I'd thought my gait was kind of fluid, but I guessed I was projecting the reality I wanted instead of the actual one.

"I was dropping off Storm when your father offered breakfast." He pinched a piece of banana and handed it to his son, who turned it to mush before stuffing it inside his mouth. "How's your head?"

"Great."

Mom parted my long hair with her citrus-scented fingers as though to confirm I wasn't fibbing.

"Satisfied?" I glanced over my shoulder.

"I am now." She smiled, but it didn't reach her eyes. There were as many layers to her worry as there were to the onion Dad was slicing.

After I filled a mug with coffee, I went to sit beside Liam. "Is Lucas coming over?"

Storm flapped his arms excitedly and shot me a crooked grin trimmed in smashed fruit, which I returned.

"I'm letting him rest this morning. He spent the night at Lori's."

"Who's with her now?"

"Avery."

"Where's Nate?"

"Upstairs." Mom tipped her face toward the ceiling as though she could somehow spot him through the timbered wood. "In his old bedroom. Came over after midnight."

"Did you guys manage to sleep?"

"Sleep's overrated at our age." Dad plated a mountain of golden bacon.

"Are all my brothers coming over for breakfast?"

"Who knows?" Mom smiled, a hopeful glimmer in her tired eyes. "At least if they show up, they'll be fed."

Dad slotted the plate between Liam and myself. Storm launched himself toward it, but Liam caught him just before he could seize some crispy loot.

Mom laughed. "No bacon for you yet, mister."

Storm blinked at her before desperately trying to access the glistening strips of meat. Liam presented him with another piece of banana. Storm looked between it and the bacon a few times, then, probably worried the fruit would be removed from his grasp, he seized it and stuffed it between his still mostly toothless gums.

Grinning, I filched a piece of bacon and crunched on it. Lycaon, it was good . . . I licked my lips, then my fingertips. "Where are you off to this early, Liam?"

His gaze lifted unhurriedly off my mouth, and of course, my mind rewound to another time he'd stared with such heat at it. Had I really promised Adalyn I wouldn't succumb to his charm?

He repositioned Storm on his lap. "The bunker."

"Can I come?"

The orange juice machine stopped whirring. "I don't think that's a good idea."

"I already saw what Bea looks like, Mom."

Tongs in hand, my father turned. "*Why* do you want to go?"

"To see if the blood cocktail worked."

"Liam can tell us when he gets back," Mom said.

"If it did work, I'd like to talk with Bea."

Mom sliced through an orange with such force most of the juice spilled out before she fit the cut half atop the plastic cone. "About what?"

"About how she's feeling."

"Do you really want to know?"

"She's still in there, Mom." The halfwolf who'd attacked me yesterday flashed before my eyes. I blinked to push the vision away, desperately recalling memories of Bea pre-bite. The girl who'd sat by my hospital bedside, who'd made me special dishes and told me the funniest stories. The girl whose smile and laughter came easily and often.

Mom finally sighed. "Even if we tell you not to go, you'll go."

"Yes."

She looked toward our Alpha for input. Or perhaps, for help in dissuading me.

"If Bea isn't herself, I'll get Nikki out and back here safely."

"Or I can just get *myself* out safely."

A smile grazed the corner of his lips. **You can be your own hero when I'm not around.**

My teeth immobilized against the slice of bacon. Was his hearing so acute that he'd heard my conversation with Grant through the walls of Pondside?

Before I could ask him, he roped my parents into a conversation about what sort of motor-skill toys he should get his son. I spent the next half hour hoping he'd been on his way home, because if his hearing was that good, then he'd heard my entire conversation with Adalyn, the prospect of which was mortifying.

CHAPTER 37

We left shortly after Nate descended the stairs, face matching his rumpled white tee. When we mentioned the bunker, he swallowed, but made no move to come along with us. Simply took a seat at the island and let my parents fuss over him. He was probably glad for the respite of no longer having to take care of Bea on his own.

As the compound gate ground open, Liam glanced my way. "You were uncharacteristically quiet during breakfast. Something on your mind?"

"I simply didn't have much to say."

"I have a hard time believing that."

I inhaled deeply and ripped off the Band-Aid. "How sharp *is* your hearing?"

"Sharp."

"That's not an answer."

"It was the answer to your question. If you want another answer, ask another question."

I expelled my breath. "The hero line. It's not a coincidence you used it, is it? You heard me say it to Grant."

His gaze slid to mine, lingered a moment, but then the gate's grinding stopped, and his attention returned to the road. "Yes."

"Were you still at Pondside when you heard it?"

"No. I'd just stepped out."

Relief calmed the snakes in my belly.

"Thank you by the way."

I frowned at Liam. "For what?"

"Not jumping on the *Alpha is heartless* wagon."

I pressed my lips together. "I don't know you well, but well enough to realize you aren't a heartless tyrant." I fiddled with my seat belt. "I'm sorry you had to hear that."

"I'm not. I like to know where I stand with my shifters." After a beat, he added, "Ignorance isn't bliss, Nikki; it's ruin. One of the main causes of a leader's downfall."

I thought about what he said for a moment. Turned it over in my mind. "You're quite wise for someone so young."

He grinned. "Here I thought I was old and crabby?"

I slanted him a half-smile, using the opportunity to steal another long look at his chiseled profile. Why had I agreed to turn down a second-night stand again? Oh, right . . . because I was starting to have feelings, which he surely couldn't reciprocate, since he wasn't on the market for a mate and I was.

Before he caught on to my invasive lovesickness, I changed the topic. "You think we'll be able to fix the vampwolves?"

"No."

"You don't think the blood will work?"

His easy disposition waned. "I think it'll work, but I'm afraid it'll only mitigate their shifting and thirst, the same way Lori's blood has been doing. I don't think it'll cure them. If Sillin were as common a commodity as aspirin, then it could be a viable, long-term solution, but it's rare and the quantity required to keep three halfwolves in check would deplete our reserves in a matter of months. As Alpha, I can't allow that to happen." He spun the wheel, merging onto the sinuous road that led toward the piece of Boulder land not confined within our fence. "I'm sorry if this disappoints you, but the pack comes first."

"I'm not gonna lie; it'll definitely hurt if the solution is death, but I'd understand, Liam." I propped my elbow on the armrest and cradled the side of my head on my fingertips. "And I wouldn't hold it against you." Pushing away thoughts of lives ending sooner than they should, I asked, "Do you have any idea who you want as your new Beta or are you really waiting to see if anyone comes up with a cure?"

"The only thing I have an idea about is who I *don't* want as my Beta."

"Let me guess. Any shifters with the last name Freemont or Hollis."

His eyes drifted over my face. "I'm not against taking on another Freemont, but I doubt any of you want the job."

I smirked. "Thanks for including me in the lineup, but I'd make a terrible Beta."

His eyebrows dipped. "You'd make a great Beta, Nikki."

"No. I make my decisions with my heart more often than with my brain. That would *not* help the pack."

Liam decreased his speed even though we were still a good mile away from our destination. Since the car hadn't skidded, I ruled out black ice. Maybe this conversation was making it difficult for him to concentrate on two things at once.

"Ness makes all her decisions with her heart. In my opinion, this would've made her a great leader." There was an edge to his voice—anger and regret, and perhaps even a little grief.

"She's really nice."

I waited to see if he'd nod, or add that she was the greatest female in the pack. He'd said he wasn't in love with her, but he certainly acted like she meant more to him than he claimed.

"She said the same thing about you." After a beat, he added, "Which is quite an endorsement coming from her."

That forlorn expression crimped his features, cementing my belief that he was still pining for her. It would certainly explain why his relationship with Storm's mother hadn't worked out. What could you give someone when your heart already belonged to another?

Thankfully, the bunker came into view then, interrupting my sorrowful contemplations.

Inside, four shifters were present—Avery, his copper-haired sister Apple and her mate Reese, a black-skinned shifter with peroxided hair shorn close to her scalp, and Doc.

On my way to Darren, I waved hello to the others, who seemed a tad perplexed by my presence. I wasn't a kid, and yet as long as I had the word *teen* attached to my age, the pack wouldn't see me as an adult. Where in the human world, twenty-one was the age you graduated from child to adult, in the pack, that magical age was twenty.

I came to stand beside Darren. "Hey, Doc."

He did a double take. "Nikki. What are you doing here?"

"Came to visit Bea."

He pivoted toward me. "How's the head?"

"All better."

Bea was licking what I imagined was blood from her hairless muzzle.

"Did she just drink the solution?"

"Yes."

"How long will it take to work?"

"When they ingested Lori's blood, it took them five to ten minutes to slide into skin. It's been nine." Worry wrought his features. "Mind if I take a look at your scab while we wait?"

I turned to give him better access, never taking my eyes off Bea, even though she wouldn't meet my stare. "Satisfied with your needlework?"

He chuckled softly. "I am. You should be okay to run on Friday, but I'd like to take a look at it one more time before—"

"*Should* be?" I whipped my head around to face him.

"Don't want the wound opening back up."

I sucked in my bottom lip. "I didn't know there was a possibility I *couldn't* go."

"Like I said, you *should* be fine."

My teeth sank into my lip. I was so looking forward to it that not going would be a blow.

"No shifting until then, all right?"

I nodded.

A gentle whine made us both turn back toward Bea. She stood on all fours, her skin now hairless, her fingers thin and no longer topped with claws, her mouth pink and smooth over rows of white rectangular teeth.

My pulse leaped in excitement. "It worked."

Doc set a timer on his watch. "Let's see how long it lasts."

I stood up at the same time as the woman who would've been my sister-in-law. Who might still be, if we found her a permanent solution.

I smiled at her. "Hey, Bea."

"Nikki." Her soft voice whispered through her cage as she walked toward the door and wrapped her fingers around the bars.

"Can I go inside?"

"I don't think that's a good idea, Nikki." Apple jolted her pointy chin toward Bea. "We don't know how long any of them will be in skin."

"Please."

"Up to Liam."

He turned away from the coroner, who was mid-change. After a protracted look between Bea and me, he nodded to Apple, and my heart fired in anticipation. She dug out a clunky key from the pocket of her orange windbreaker and inserted it into the lock.

As soon as it clanked open, Bea pushed open the door and stepped back to allow me in. I squeezed through, careful not to graze the silver. Once I stood in front of her, her body began to tremble, and tears slid down her hollowed cheeks. "Oh, Nikki. What have I done?"

My anticipation warped into grief. I wrapped my arms around her hunched shoulders and pulled her body against mine. "Nothing I wouldn't have done had I been dating a shifter." Truth was, if I'd been human and wanted to spend my life with someone who wasn't, I probably would've tried to change my genetic makeup. "Your skin is ice, Bea."

I pressed away from her and looked around the small cell until my eyes alighted on a blanket balled in a corner. I picked it up, then draped it around her shoulders and led her to the bare pallet nailed to the concrete wall so we could sit.

"How do you feel?"

"Like I've had a stomach flu for an entire month." Her muscles had all melted away, along with any fat. "I look horrible."

"Nothing a few meals at my house won't fix."

"I don't think I'll get another meal at your house." More tears glossed her cheeks. "At least, not the type you eat."

"The full moon's coming. We're hoping it might change you back. For good."

Her long throat bobbed with a swallow. "That'd be nice."

"You have an entire pack of shifters looking for a solution. Someone's bound to find you one."

Her lashes fanned her full cheeks, the only part of her body which hadn't been whittled by her transformation. "I heard Darren say the synthetic blood was your idea."

"It's not really synthetic."

"I meant lab-made."

"Yeah."

She stuck out one bony hand from the blanket and squeezed mine. "I'm glad Lori no longer needs to pay for my mistake. She and I may never have been friends, but I don't want her to suffer on my account."

This time, I was the one to swallow.

"How's Miles? Nate swore he was okay, but—"

"He thinks you're pregnant and trying to hide it."

"If only." A forlorn smile drifted across her face as she touched her concave abdomen. "Does Nate hate me?"

My head jerked back. "No. Absolutely not."

She leaned her head back against the dusty gray wall and closed her eyes.

"Nikki, can you make sure that, if there is no solution, he's not present when . . . when they end my life?"

My throat stung. My nose, too. I tried to form words but couldn't speak any of them.

Her eyes opened and traveled over my haggard expression. "Sweetie, it's okay. I've made my peace. I know there's not enough supply of that drug."

"Sillin isn't—can't be—the only solution. There must be another."

She sighed. "I don't know how much longer I can stand to live like this. A half-human half-monster who drinks blood."

"You're not a monster," I croaked.

"I'm worse than a monster in that other form. I attacked *you*. I've attacked *Nate*."

A loud sob leaked from the cell in which the coroner was embracing his wife.

Bea shuddered. "I can't believe *I* did this to them. To that poor hiker. Nate should've shot me the minute I shifted into that . . . *thing*." She dropped her face into her palms. "What have I done? What have I done?" She murmured this over and over, rocking back and forth.

Suddenly, she went still.

Very, *very* still.

"Nikki!" Liam roared. "Get out of there. NOW!"

CHAPTER 38

I jumped to my feet, heart walloping each one of my ribs. "Why? What happened?"

In the cell across from us, the coroner had his back bent at an unnatural angle while his wife was hunched in child's pose at his feet.

"Nikki!" Liam ran into Bea's cage and yanked on my bicep so hard I heard a shallow pop.

As he dragged me out, I peered over my shoulder at Bea, whose face was no longer human. She emitted a sound between a whine and a growl, her elongating fangs refracting the white, fluorescent light on the ceiling. "Wait, Liam. Wait."

He didn't.

Even though her elbows were bent the wrong way—the human way—Bea lowered her bony haunches, and this time, her growl was unmistakable. She launched herself at us just as Liam swung the door closed. Even though Bea made no move to jump again, he fisted the door while Apple jiggled the key in the lock.

The crackle and hiss of burnt flesh had me sucking in air. "Liam, your hand!"

Once the latch clicked, he pulled his bubbling palm away from the silver, leaving blood and pieces of skin that Bea sniffed before lapping up, reddened drool coursing down her rubbery lips.

He finally removed his vise-like grip from my arm. "I shouldn't have let you go in there."

Chill after chill swept up my spine. "How long was she in skin?"

Darren walked over with a tube of ointment and gauze. "Twelve minutes."

"Twelve minutes? I thought Lori's blood gave them hours." I clutched my elbows. Or tried to. One of them wouldn't quite bend.

"It does." Darren's chest vibrated with a sigh. "Your hand, Liam."

"Nikki's arm. I think I dislocated it."

I swallowed as the pack doctor probed it, then winced when he touched a particular tender spot. Yep, Liam had definitely popped the joint out of the socket. Bea let out a series of soft wails. I met her eyes, the only part of her that was still hers, and read remorse in them, as though she were trying to communicate an apol— "Ow."

"Good as new, but you might want to ice it. Now, show me your hand, Liam."

He raised the bloody, singed mess that was his palm, and Darren spread glistening ointment before dressing it in gauze. My Alpha didn't flinch once, even though he must've been in a world of pain.

Bea whimpered again. Whatever violence had taken ahold of her was gone, and in its place sagged a pitiful halfwolf.

I crouched so that our faces were leveled. "Bea, if you can understand me, nod."

Her oblong head topped with a curtain of human hair bobbed up and down.

"Were you trying to hurt us? Shake your—"

Home. We're going home. Now.

"No."

"Nikki . . ." Liam growled.

"Shake your head for no. Nod for yes. Were you trying to hurt us?"

She stayed perfectly still. Only her eyes moved. Straight to Liam. And then a new growl started low in her throat.

"Were you trying to protect me from him?" I asked softly.

She whined and tried to poke her muzzle through the bars but the space was too narrow.

"Let's go, Nikki."

I tipped my head toward Liam. "If you need to go, go, but I want to stay."

"I'm not leaving without you, but we *are* leaving."

I set my teeth. I understood he was rattled—I was too—but that didn't give him the right to boss me around. "She's harml—"

Snarls erupted behind me. I rose and spun.

"Get the tranquilizer gun," Liam barked at Reese.

She rushed to grab it from the wall, then rushed back just as the coroner sank his fangs into his wife's unnaturally long neck and shook his head with such violence that blood spurted from the wound.

My palm rose to my mouth, covering my gasp, just as Reese shot a dart into the man's thigh. His body froze before crumpling sideways, his fangs sliding out of his wife's mangled neck. Her body dropped in time with his, both of them smacking into the puddle of her blood.

Liam's entire body vibrated as though his wolf were about to break through his skin. "Are you ready to go home *now?*"

"Is she—is she dead?" I whispered.

Bea howled and paced on her fingered paws, her claws grinding against the cement.

"Did he kill his wife?"

"Apple, the door." Reese was breathing hard.

After ascertaining no wolf moved, Apple unlocked the cage for her mate.

Reese crouched next to the smaller of the two vampwolves and pressed her palm between the rounded breasts that were coated in velvety skin and tufts of fur. "No heartbeat."

A whimper sounded. It came from me this time.

"Nikki, please get in the car." Liam's voice brooked no argument.

Not that I wanted to argue this time. I spun and strode out, holding on to the arm that Doc had popped back into place. An eternity, which probably lasted mere minutes, later, Liam exited the bunker and climbed behind the wheel.

"When he's going to shift back into skin . . . when he's going to realize what he's done . . . Liam, you can't let him shift back into skin! He'll never forgive himself."

Liam didn't respond, didn't say a word the entire ride home, but the second we parked in front of my house, he punched his steering wheel and growled, "That could've been you. That *fucking* could've been you." A lock of dark hair tumbled into his eyes and caught on his lashes. "I should never have let you go inside that cell."

"I'm glad you did. I'm glad I got to hug her." Especially since I feared it might've been one of the last times.

No. I couldn't think like that. I wouldn't think like that.

"Are you also glad you got to see the coroner murder his wife?"

I bristled. "Of course not."

He shoved aside the lock of hair on his forehead, his eyes running the gamut of brown, black, amber, yellow. The color slideshow was slightly frightening, especially considering how robust Liam's accompanying scowl was. "Fuck. *Fuck.*"

I tugged off my seat belt and turned toward him. "I know Avery said human blood could make them feral, but maybe—"

"We are *not* feeding those creatures something with the potential to make them more violent."

"So we go back to giving them Lori's blood?"

He scraped his palms down his face, the gauze catching on his stubble but not unraveling. "That's not a solution."

Dread lashed my spine. "So, what? They die on the full moon?"

"I don't know, Nikki! I don't fucking know." He punched his steering wheel with his unbandaged hand. "All I know is that I'm done putting you in harm's way, so stay the hell away from the bunker." His serrated gaze landed on my shoulder, and the arm I'd unconsciously nestled against my chest. "And from me."

I frowned. "Why from you?"

"*Why?* Because I dislocated your fucking arm!"

"You didn't do it on purpose, Liam."

"It doesn't matter why I did it. The point is I hurt everyone who gets close to me. Ness lost her eye. Tammy lost her damn life."

"*You* didn't damage Ness's eye; Cassandra Morgan did. As for Storm's mother, how can you even blame yourself for her death?"

"I put a shifter baby in her, and that baby killed her."

I stared at his flaring nostrils a long time in the roughened silence, wondering if there was any point arguing with him when he was in such a self-flagellating mood.

"Just get away from me, Nicole. And *stay* away."

I didn't move.

"Get. Away!"

"Fine, but the only person you're hurting by shutting people out is yourself." I exited the car and closed the door.

At least, Adalyn would no longer have to worry about that do-over.

CHAPTER 39

For two entire days, I didn't run into Liam. Then again, I didn't leave my cabin, not even to pick up my car, which Adalyn ended up driving back to the compound, a handful of parking tickets wedged beneath the wiper. I wasn't wallowing or anything, simply catching up on a mountain of work.

Mom rescued my eyesight and my sanity when she came over with lunch and Storm, who took an instant liking to the luminescent garland of paper stars I'd strung over my headboard. I taught him how to click them on and off, and his already twinkly eyes twinkled some more.

Mom leaned against my doorframe, watching me guide Storm's fingers along the edge of a star. "I went to see Lori today. She's agreed to Nate's idea."

I raised an eyebrow. "What idea is that?"

"Biting Bea and the coroner on the full moon. Your brother thinks that more venom might help them shift completely."

I hadn't heard that one yet. Most of what I'd heard, all of it from my social butterfly of a brother Niall, was along the lines of killing the vampwolves and the shifter who'd made them. "You think it could work?"

Mom sighed. "I don't know what to think anymore."

"Have you visited Bea again?"

"I went yesterday."

"Was she in skin or in her other form?"

"In skin. Lori's been supplying them with her blood again. I got to talk to

219

her for a little while. She's exhausted and disheartened. Especially since the coroner won't stop crying. She feels guilty for his grief." Mom swiped a finger underneath her lower lash line, whisking away a tear. "It's so hard for me to see her hurting and not be able to do anything."

"Oh, Mom."

"I told her not to give up hope," she added thickly, "when I hardly have any left."

I walked over to my mother and curled one arm around her shaking shoulders.

Storm squeezed the back of my arm with one hand and gripped my braid with the other, anchoring himself to me as though worried I might drop him. "*Mamamama*."

I froze; Mom, too. When we pulled apart, our gazes converged on Liam's son, who looked between the two of us, drool glittering down his lopsided smile.

"Oh, baby." She caressed the edge of his face.

He repeated the syllables that had stunned us both.

She shook her head, then pointed to herself and said, "Meg."

He watched her mouth shape the word, a furrow creasing his little brow.

I pointed to myself and decomposed my name in two separate syllables, "Nih-kee."

His confusion deepened, but then his attention snagged on my lanterns again, and he tugged on my braid. Back we went.

I spent the next half hour making the lights flicker while teaching Storm the word *star*. He studied my lips but wouldn't even try to copy me. However, when I asked him to point to the stars, he extended his arm toward them.

"Smarty-pants." I kissed his temple before handing him over to Mom, who was taking him back to the house because Liam had to work late.

Hopefully, his work had to do with finding Bea and the bereft coroner a cure.

After she left, Adalyn called to find out if I wanted to grab dinner at Pond-side. Having developed cabin fever from my two-day work retreat, I readily agreed. After dabbing concealer on my faded bruise and rolling mascara over my lashes, I swapped my oversized sweatshirt for an undersized T-shirt, and my sweatpants for skinny jeans.

I grabbed my bag, tossing in stuff I probably wouldn't need or already had two of, and stepped into the wintry chill. My blood thrummed from the expanding moon. I lifted my face toward it and basked in its milky glow. Two more days, and I'd let my wild envelop and overwhelm my human.

A release like none other.

Actually, I could think of one other release that came close to the feeling of utter bliss that was my wolf form, but thinking about it led to ruminating on Liam, which inevitably strained my mood.

I shoved him out of my head as I padded up to the mess hall, inhaling the woody, wintry scent padding the air, a by-product of the slow puff of almost every chimney on the compound.

Adalyn sat at the bar, her head bent in an apparently titillating conversation with Sasha, who was pouring her a glass of wine.

"What did I miss?" I set my bag down at my feet and shrugged out of my coat.

"Sasha was telling me about the three o'clock bingo tournament. Apparently it got real rowdy and competitive. Grams almost had a throwdown with May's granddaddy. Threatened to dye what's left of his hair green when he came for his monthly appointment."

I snickered. "She'd probably do it."

"Oh, you bet she will."

"Wait, didn't she have the hots for the old man?"

"That was last summer. Remember her philosophy: a man for every season keeps the heart a beatin'."

"Your grandmother's one heck of a lady," Sasha said, pouring us some water.

With a life like hers, riddled with untimely deaths—first her mate's, then her daughter's and son-in-law's—she had to have a strong disposition or her spark would've also faded too soon. I'd asked her once how she did it . . . kept on living, kept on smiling. She'd looked over at Adalyn and Gracey and said, "By taking one breath at a time."

"What can I get you, Nikki?"

"Red wine."

After placing a stemmed glass filled to the brim in front of me, Sasha disappeared into the kitchen.

Blackberry, cloves, and woodchips curled from the burgundy liquid, making me inhale deeper. "I'm so glad you called. I needed a break from my superhero painting. I spent *way* too long drawing details on his leather bodysuit."

"Can't wait to see the finished piece."

My wine rippled as I swirled it. Before showing her or anyone else the final version, I had to rework the face, which resembled a certain Alpha's. And I wasn't talking about Cassandra or Alaric.

"Speaking of finished pieces, did you and Nash decide on your tattoos?"

"I suggested a tiny leash; she turned me down." My brother walked up to Adalyn and slung his ripped and sweaty arms around her, squeezing her against his damp muscle tee.

"Eww, Nash. You're all sweaty."

"You usually don't mind when I'm all sweaty."

"That's because I'm sweaty too." Adalyn tipped her head back to kiss him while I rolled my eyes and muttered, "TMI, people."

Once she broke their never-ending kiss, she shooed him away. "It's girl-time, Nash. No boys allowed."

"If you get bored of girl-time, join me and the guys for boy-time." He waggled his brows as he tipped his head toward one of the tables.

I looked. Probably shouldn't have, because now I was fully aware Liam was mere feet away, along with Lucas, Niall, and a handful of other guys, all of whom were dressed in athleticwear and sported varying degrees of sweat.

I returned my gaze to my brother, proud of myself for not lingering on any particular shifter. "Did you just have a buddy date at the gym?"

"Sort of. We were discussing the case, and Liam wanted to blow off some steam, so yeah, we sort of all ended up upstairs." He rolled his eyes toward the state-of-the-art gym that spanned the entire second floor and was enclosed by walls of glass that overlooked the half-moon pond. Like the eatery, it had been built under Alaric. His last project. One he never got to see come to fruition.

"Mom told me Nate's idea," I said. "About having Lori bite Bea again."

Adalyn frowned. "Why would he suggest that?"

Nash's mouth thinned. "He's hoping it'll transform her fully."

"Oh." Adalyn scooped up a handful of Dad's special cashews—made with love and a BBQ spice blend he wouldn't even reveal the ingredients of to *me*. "Don't see how that could help her."

"More venom, more pressure on her genes?" I shrugged. "Honestly, it's one of the better ideas I've heard. One of the only ones, too."

"A shot in the dark if you ask me," Adalyn said.

I folded my legs. "Better a shot in the dark than a shot in the head."

Both my brother and Adalyn startled from my emotionlessly-delivered statement.

I hadn't straight-out asked them about their stance on the subject of Lori and the vampwolves, but I didn't doubt their thoughts aligned with the majority. We may not have been dogs, but give some of us a bone, and good luck getting it away from us.

"Are you guys still looking for proof that Lori has bitten humans before or have you at least dropped that?"

They exchanged a look, and probably a couple words telepathically.

"We've stopped actively searching, but others haven't," Ads volunteered. "David Hollis is convinced he can find proof. He sent Grant out of state to follow up on some leads."

I wrinkled my nose. Even when I'd dated Grant, I hadn't been a big fan of his domineering father. Especially considering how he cowed his wife. The woman was more passive than the bear rug they had in their living room. Not to mention forever intoxicated, be it on weed or wine.

Although nothing precluded Grant from becoming like his father down the line, he'd always been rather gentle. Hopefully, he'd stay that way. His sister Camilla, though . . . I suspected she'd become *exactly* like her father.

A loud, "Fuck," had all our heads swinging toward where Liam sat with his dripping crew. He shot to his feet, along with a bunch of the others and, scraping a hand through his damp hair, stalked toward the door.

"What happened?" Nash called out.

Our Alpha turned, fur thickening along his corded forearms, fingers balling into fists at his side before snapping open as his nails curved into claws. His eyes, amber-yellow from his oncoming shift, locked on mine. Not long, but long enough for me to witness a riot of emotions—fury being the more potent one.

The coroner's dead. Used his own claws to rip one of the arteries in his neck.

Ads and I gasped while my brother muttered and went after Liam, who'd already pushed out the eatery's door. The silence that fell over the vast room was deafening. Even the music seemed to have faded. Perhaps it was because my ears were ringing from the news.

My heart hurt. Not for the coroner, whom I'd never gotten to know, but for Bea, who'd already felt guilt-ridden. What would this do to her? Even if we found her a cure, could she ever recover from all the deaths her desire to become like us had brought about?

CHAPTER 40

After over two hours of conversation and three glasses of wine, Adalyn and I parted ways. Niall wasn't home. I imagined he was at the bunker with the others or seducing a female somewhere in Beaver Creek.

I tried to phone Nate for news, but he didn't answer so I texted Nash instead.

After a few minutes, he messaged me back: *Coming home now. Bea's okay. Nate's staying with her tonight. He told me to tell you not to worry.*

Yeah. Like that could ever happen.

Heart tapping out a sullen rhythm, I wound my hair up and snapped a coiled plastic band around it, then retrieved my tablet, brewed myself a cup of herbal tea, and sat at our kitchen nook to rework my superhero's face.

It wasn't that I particularly wanted to work, but my brain was way too wired for sleep. As I painted and repainted the man's jawline until I'd thinned it out so it wouldn't resemble Liam's, there was a knock on the door.

Frowning, I walked over and drew it open.

At the sight of my sweatpants-and-black-tee wearing visitor, I leaned against the grainy wood and crossed my arms. "Your house is six doors down."

Liam's knotted eyebrows broke apart in . . . surprise? "I'm not lost, Nicole. I'm just—Can I—Can we talk?" He sounded a little lost.

The air was heavy with the smell of smoke, but not the sweet scent of charred wood. No, the odor was musky and sulfurous, like burnt hair. Like burnt flesh. The smell of a body transformed into ash.

"Niall's not here, Liam," I said slowly, still not sure why *he* was.

"I'm aware."

"Storm neither."

"I'm not here for my son." Liam nodded to my living room. "Can I come in?"

"Why?"

He blinked. "You're really going to make me stand out here to explain my reason for dropping by?"

"I am." I got more comfortable against the door, pulse lashing at my veins even though for all I knew this wasn't a friendly *I'm sorry for having barked at you* visit. I shrugged a shoulder. "You're a shifter. Can't catch cold."

A drizzle of snowflakes spiraled on the black air and drifted over Liam, caught on the thick frame of lashes lining his weary eyes.

"So . . . why are you standing outside my door in the middle of the night, Kolane?"

His jaw pulsed. "How's your arm?"

"You came to check on my arm?"

"Yes."

I extended it and rotated it. "All good. How's the hand?"

He turned it palm up. The bubbly red mess had turned into patches of skin that shone like melted plastic.

I gripped my elbows. "Anything else I can help you with, because I've got a date in twenty, and I know some people think three's an orgy but I think three's a crowd."

His hand arced back to his side. "A date?"

"You know. Hanging with a person who enjoys my company *and* proximity."

One of his eyes twitched. "Who?"

"Simon."

"Jenkins? Your dad's friend? He's fifty-something."

I wrinkled my nose. "Eww . . . not him."

"The only other Simon in the pack is eight. I'm guessing it isn't him either."

Liam's eye stopped twitching, but his mouth took over. Probably because he felt like he'd trapped me in a lie. Except I wasn't lying. I really was about to have a date with Simon. A virtual one.

"*My* Simon's not in the pack."

His mouth flattened. "Humans aren't allowed on the compound."

"Since when?"

"Since I got here."

"Well, whatever. He isn't human."

Snowflakes steamed off Liam's corded forearms and razor-sharp cheekbones. "Which pack is this *Simon* from then?"

"He's not a shifter either."

"What. Is. He. Then?" Liam's lips barely moved as he spoke. "A sex toy?"

The man had one heck of a temper. I probably shouldn't have found it appealing, yet I did. Go figure.

I snorted. "Ha. I never named my vibrator, but Simon would suit it well."

Liam growled low and long. "Can we please have this conversation inside?"

The smile warped off my lips. "You'd be breaking your own commandment."

"Fuck my commandment, and fuck your Simon, whoever the hell he is." He climbed the front step and brushed past me.

"Hey . . . I didn't say you could come in."

"Good thing I'm not a vampire."

"Or a gentleman," I said under my breath.

He smiled darkly. "Or that."

Sighing, I pressed away from the door and closed it, because it was damn cold out.

He flipped around, and although the living room was large, the space suddenly felt cramped. "You promised me a do-over."

"That was before you barked at me."

His jaw ticked as he took in my closed stance. "I'm sorry, Nicole." He stepped forward and coasted his palms over my biceps. Tentatively, at first. When I didn't swat his hands away, they settled. "Give me another chance?"

"No longer worried about my safety?"

He dipped his chin. "I'll always worry—I worry about all my shifters—but staying away . . . it's fucking with my concentration."

My pride at getting lobbed in with the *entire* pack hurt. "Get a stress ball. Heard those work well."

"I don't want a fucking stress ball."

"If you need to get your rocks off, I'm sure one of those many other shifters you worry about could accommodate you." I nodded to the door, and he released my arms.

I thought he'd leave and try his luck elsewhere. Instead, he clicked his fingers in front of my face.

I frowned. "What the hell's wrong with you?"

"You said I could click my fingers and get any female. I was testing your theory."

I snorted. "Go knock on May's door. You won't even need to click your fingers."

"You really want me to go knock on May's door?"

I tightened the arms still crossed in front of my chest. "If I said yes, would you?"

"No." He set his hands back on my arms and dragged his callused fingers down to my elbows, then back up. Down and up. Although it softened me on the outside, my insides stayed armored. "There's only one shifter I want, and she's standing right here." He dropped his palms to my hips.

"Why me? Because I'm easy?"

His head jerked back. "Easy? You're the exact opposite of easy."

We'd had sex. He'd snapped at me. And now, he was standing inside my home with his hands on my body. Sure, I still had my clothes on, but still . . .

"You may only have had one other partner, but I've had many, and I've never *clicked* with someone like I did with you. That's *why you*."

I wanted to take that compliment and store it, but doubt crept into my mind. "I'm the first shifter you've slept with. Maybe that's why we *clicked*."

His pupils shrank. "Was it the same with Grant as it was with me?"

"No, but like you said, I only have one point of reference, so unlike you, I'm no expert. I'd need a few more partners to verify your claim."

His gaze turned positively murderous.

I sighed. "Liam, I don't want one more night. I'm not cut out for"—I uncrossed my arms and made a vague gesture, trying to parse my thoughts— "*detached* sex."

His eyebrows hung so low over his eyes that the chocolate hue of his irises appeared black. "I'm not relationship-material."

"I know. You made that abundantly clear. You don't have space in your life, I get it. I really do. Which is why, even though we *did* click, even though your smell alone makes me dizzy, I'm going to say no and save us both future aggravation."

His fingers stopped trying to grind my hipbones to dust. "My smell makes you dizzy?"

I bit the inside of my cheek. Had I really needed to be that candid? Oh well. The hole was dug. "To the point where I thought you might be my mate." I tipped my face toward his abdomen. "But you're not. Which is a relief all things considered since you don't want a true mate, and had you been mine and refused to consummate the bond, I'd have been *really* ticked off."

He crooked my chin up on a bent finger. "You know what your smell does to me?" He pressed his nose into my hair and inhaled deeply. "It makes me painfully, blindingly hard." He erased the space between our bodies, probably to prove his point, because he was certainly providing adequate proof. "I could come from your smell alone, which has *never* happened to me."

Push him away, Nikki. Be heart-smart for once.

Instead of putting distance between us, I turned my head and pressed my cheek against his rapidly pounding chest, letting myself be held hostage by this intoxicating male.

"Be mine, baby. Tonight. As many nights as you want. Until you find your perfect mate, be mine."

My eyes filled with heat. My stomach, too. Because his proposal was equal amounts sweet and sad. "What exactly are you offering? Casual, on-demand sex?"

"Yes."

"Would this be exclusive?"

"Yes." He caressed the nape of my neck, coaxing out thousands of little bumps.

"Until I find my true mate?" I had a WWAT—What Would Adalyn Think —moment. Would she encourage me to accept an exclusive friends-with-benefits offer or would she tell me to run? "What if I don't get one?"

His heart stuttered. "Then until you grow tired of my ornery ass."

I smiled against the black cotton that smelled of him, of his life, of his sweat and strife and wild. "It's a really terrible idea."

"My worst one yet."

Did he not realize that, *technically*, casual and exclusive sex *was* a relationship? Maybe it was the label that scared him. "What if *you* end us first?"

His caresses stopped. "I won't."

I pressed him away. "How can you know that?"

Shadows abraded the shine of his eyes. "Because I don't want a mate, and I already know I'll get everything I need from you." His hand slid to my cheek, tipped my face up. He aligned his mouth with mine but didn't erase the thin divide of air remaining.

He'd pushed himself into my home, into my bones, into my heart, but for some reason, he was holding himself back now? Was he trying to give me the illusion that the ball was in my court? Because it was an illusion.

There was no resisting Liam Kolane's pull, however dismal the consequences of conceding and accepting a body devoid of a heart.

If the man came with a warning label, it would read: *Ticking organ not included.*

If I came with a warning label, it would read: *Caution. Breakable.*

"Damn you, Liam." I felt his forehead furrow as I closed the distance between our lips.

This was going to hurt. This was going to break me. Why did I kiss him then? Because I'd already put myself back together once and was confident I'd be capable of doing it again.

I was a phoenix in wolf's clothing.

Or just a really silly girl, but I liked picturing myself as a phoenix better.

His hands slid to my ass and scooped me up. Without breaking our kiss, I wrapped my arms around his neck and my legs around his waist, and he carried me toward the hallway of bedrooms. I didn't have to tell him which one was mine; he tracked my scent right to it.

He strode over to the bed and laid me on top, our lips breaking apart from the momentum. Panting against me, he asked, "Who's Simon?"

It took my fizzing mind a moment to make sense of his question. When it hit me, my flushed lips pulled into a wide smile. "A character on a TV show."

Liam straightened, then pulled off his T-shirt and tossed it aside. "You were going to turn me down for a fictional man?"

"I was going to turn you down because you were an ass." The wall of carved muscle before me made saliva pool in my mouth. Thankfully, Liam hadn't arrived shirtless, because there would've been zero resistance on my part.

His gaze stuck to my garland of lit stars, and he raised his nose and took a pull of the air. "Here I thought I'd be the first Kolane to visit your bedroom, but my son beat me to it." He stared at the edges of the paper stars and swiped his damaged palm down his face. "I'm exploiting your parents' kindness."

I propped myself onto my elbows. "Didn't you hear Mom say how much she's enjoying Storm's company? Besides, it's distracting her, and she needs a distraction. Both my parents do."

"Maybe, but he remains my responsibility." He plunged a hand through his hair, mussing it some more.

I sat up completely, and even though my revved-up body hated the very thought of him leaving, I said, "If you need to go get him, we can reschedule."

His gaze rammed back onto mine.

"*Or* you can let my parents revel in your son's company while you revel in their daughter's. When you think about it, it's a pretty solid trade-off."

His guilt vanished like starlight at dawn. "I'd rather not think about your parents or my son at the present moment, but I'm a fan of your logic." He ran his hands down my snug top, and I swear I could feel his calluses through the stretchy material. "This needs to come off."

"Does it?"

The slowest smile bent his lips as his fingers dipped beneath the hem and traveled up my ribs, towing up the material. I lifted my arms, and he eased it over my head before tossing it aside. I thought he'd unhook my bra next, but his fingers worked my hair tie loose, freeing my long tresses, which he combed out with such care it sent shivers through my scalp. He rolled the heavy mass up into a loose rope, then tugged on it until my head dipped backward. He leaned over me, bringing his face toward the slope of skin connecting my neck to my shoulder and pressed a kiss to my pulse point.

"Your hair is a thing of rare beauty."

I shivered, from the pulse of warm air and the compliment.

"Just like the whole of you," he added.

He released my hair, then unfastened my bra and slid it down my arms, his ragged nails running leisurely down my skin, pebbling it some more. After flinging the scrap of black lycra aside, he dipped his head and cupped my breasts, then reverently kissed each one, turning the buds sharp enough to stab his tongue.

Had I really told this man to go knock on May's door? What the hell was wrong with me?

Nerves crackling with anticipation, I stopped fisting my comforter, lifted my hands to the waistband of his sweatpants, and glided them off his narrow hips, finding him bare underneath.

He straightened, gifting me an obstructed view of his magnificent body. I wrapped my fingers around him, and then I tasted him. His breathing hitched, and his eyes began to flash as though backlit by a flame. He rasped my name, the rumble of each syllable fanning the blaze spreading through my veins like kerosene.

Humming against his taut, pulsating flesh, I stroked up the long, thick shaft. Soft curses fell from his lips as his fingers settled in my hair, his touch featherlight with the slightest, sweetest tremble. He pulled himself out of my mouth, leaving a gossamer trail of salt on my tongue, then seized the waistband of my jeans and rolled them off my legs, whisking my thong right along with them.

This time, when his dark eyes roamed over my body, over my legs, I didn't feel the need to palm my scar. I combed my hair over one shoulder, let it settle over one breast as he crouched and retrieved a strip of condoms from his sweatpants. I wished he'd trust me enough not to use them, but it wasn't me he didn't trust . . . it was himself.

He ripped one open and rolled it on, eyes roaming over my bared body, nostrils flaring fast, jaw stiff as a hunting trap. "God, you're so fucking perfect." He stretched over me, forcing my spine to yield and meet the mattress, then kissed a trail from the hollow of my collarbone to the inside of my thigh. After a long, slow lick to my core and an even longer and slower inhalation, he straightened to his full height and raised my legs, pinning the backs of my thighs to his torso before gliding into me.

Buried to the hilt, he stilled and pulled in a gravelly breath, then began to rock his hips, adding frenzied sweeps of his thumb. His heavily-lidded eyes took on the amber sheen of his wolf's as he caressed and penetrated, dragging me closer and closer to the edge of the bed, and to the edge of something else . . . a precipice I'd only ever approached with fangs, vibrators, fingers, and most recently, Liam's skilled tongue. The wet slap of our bodies overtook our quickening intakes of breath and fragranced the air with the dizzying blend of us.

"Liam . . ." I murmured.

"Yeah, baby?" When I didn't tack on anything else because I was entirely focused on the spark spreading up the walls he kept pounding into, he chuckled softly and kissed the back of my knee.

The ugly one.

That kiss triggered more sparks, this time deep inside my chest.

Highlighted only by my stars, my Alpha looked more fallen angel than predatory wolf, wingless but so full of otherworldly grace and brutal beauty. He hefted my ankles an inch higher, and the sparks became flames, which in turn became a devouring inferno.

"Liam!" I gasped his name.

He quickened his thrusts, and the angle . . . it hit something. Something that made my lips part around a hissed *yes*.

"Again. Do that again."

And he did.

My back arched, and I screamed, the ball of fire streaking from my center to the tips of my eyelashes with the force of those storm clouds that darkened our mountains, lit up our skies, and pounded our valleys.

Face tight with concentration, Liam watched me burn in ecstasy. Suddenly, he went as still as the boulders we were named for and then a tremor resonated through his bones. He snarled and roared, turning the two syllables of my name into a raw lament.

His head fell back, and his broad chest expanded as he poured himself into me. The sight was mesmerizing, a masterpiece of color and shape and sound, a wild beast trapped in the throes of pleasure.

After almost a minute, his fingers slackened and slid down my calves, releasing my legs. Still buried deep, he folded his body over mine and rested his head in the crook of my neck. Tenderly, almost like a child seeking the comfort and sweetness of an embrace. The weight of him, the girth of him, reminded me that Liam Kolane was no child.

Threading my fingers through his slightly damp locks, I whispered, "You succeeded."

"Hmm?" His breaths skittered over my skin. Breached right through.

"You made me come through intercourse."

His head lolled back, his stubble chafing my collarbone. "I told you I would."

Heartbeats swelling anew, I traced the jagged frame of his face, the slant of his cocky smile. He slid one palm beneath my head and towed my mouth to his. The kiss was delicate and sweet, so sweet I skated my mouth off his. Kisses like these were dangerous, because they sank straight through to the soul and took root.

The little dip between his eyebrows formed. "What is it?"

I wanted his tenderness just as much as I wanted his roughness, but tenderness muddled what we were supposed to be. What he wanted us to stay. "I thought I heard the front door," I lied.

If he sensed my lie, he didn't call me up on it. Merely heaved himself away and cleaned himself up while I pulled on fresh underwear and a tank top. He retrieved his own clothes and pulled them on, his gaze never leaving my profile and downturned eyes.

"If you want boxers, I may have a pair that fits."

It took him a few seconds to remember what pair I was referring to—the one he'd gifted me at Adalyn's bachelorette to help me accomplish my dare. "Those are yours. For as long as you want to keep them." Fully clothed, he padded toward me and gripped my chin, forcing me to look up. "Babe, did I do or say something wrong?"

I bit my lip and shook my head.

"Are you regretting what we did?"

"No." I slid my lower lip between my teeth. "I don't think we should kiss anymore."

He slow-blinked. "Am I that awful at it?"

I snorted. "Like you could be awful at anything."

That seemed to make him grow a few inches taller. "Then why not let me use it on you?"

I expelled an annoyed breath. I wasn't annoyed at him but at myself. "Because you don't want a relationship, and kissing"—I stepped back, skating my chin off its perch, and thrust a hand through my hair—"it feels boyfriendy, which is confusing." My fingers snagged on a knot. I forced it to surrender. "Give me a few days to adapt to this arrangement between us. Once my head gets the memo it's purely physical, we can go back to kissing."

His gaze swept over my expression twice, probably in an attempt to establish whether I was merely quirky or just plain unhinged. "Okay." He nodded. "No kissing." He backed up a step. "Anything else?"

I went back to gnawing on my bottom lip. "No hugging, hand-holding, or napping together. And definitely no spending the night."

"Noted. Anything else?" His tone was a little rigid, as though he wasn't liking my list of rules.

"I'll text you if I think of anything else."

"You do that . . ." There was a definite edge to his voice.

I released my hair. "Liam, you may not need rules, but I do."

A deep sigh relaxed the hard ridges of his body and face. "I'm so used to stipulating the law it feels strange to have someone else doing it, but I understand. And I will try to uphold all your requests."

He walked over to my bedroom door and opened it. "Have a good night."

"You too. And give Storm a kiss."

He looked over his shoulder at me. "Lucky him."

Change our status, and you'll get one too.

Thankfully, I managed to stifle those words before my bluntness could ruin this fledging tryst.

CHAPTER 41

A t dusk the next day, I finalized my painting and emailed it to my customer, then climbed the hill toward my house for dinner. I hadn't heard from Liam, not that he needed to check in. Besides, *I* hadn't texted him.

As I trudged through the snow, I thought about sending him a *hey* but then decided it might come off as an invitation for a booty call, and although I wasn't against one, that wasn't my intent. I really just wanted to see how his day had gone.

The moment I pushed through the front door of my family home, my father's stomach-growlingly delicious cooking enveloped me. "Hmm . . . what smells so good?"

"Probably me."

I froze in the doorway, and then my mouth quirked at Lucas's ridiculousness.

"Yeah. That's got to be it." I tried to peer over his shoulder, to see if anyone else was there.

"Who you looking for, Knickknack?"

My eyes zipped back to Storm, who was clinging on to Lucas's side like a koala. "No one." I reached out and scratched his chipmunk cheek. "Hey, you."

"Wouldn't be a certain *casual* friend?"

I widened my eyes and shot Lucas a couple daggers, but that just made him snicker. "You're in a particularly jovial mood."

"The full moon's acomin'. Always puts me in a good mood. Plus, all the OBs are arriving tomorrow, including my baby mama."

"Can she still run?"

"Oh, we won't be running. We'll be hanging out at home with Little Destroyer."

Storm squealed as though he'd picked up that his evening was going to be just as exciting as ours.

"Hey, honey." Mom kissed my cheek. "Dad just got started on dinner, so it'll be another hour."

"Perfect," Lucas said, "I needed some help carrying Storm home."

I cocked an eyebrow. "Can't manage a twenty-pound baby on your own?"

"The twenty-pound baby I can manage. It's the two-hundred-pound one you're better with."

I thought I caught my mother smirking as she shuffled past us and into the kitchen. I prayed I was imagining her amusement and that she didn't know, but then I thought of how Liam had gone straight to pick up Storm from my place last night, and my gut folded up nice and tight. Even if he'd showered, my mother was so familiar with my scent that she'd pick up on it.

Ugh. Ugh. Ugh.

The worst part was that she probably assumed we were dating. This was going to make for a fun conversation when it came up, because it was going to come up. I probably should have it before—

"See you later, Meg." Lucas slung his arm around my shoulder and steered me out the door.

"Bye, honey."

Once the door shut, he released me and patted the top of my head as though I were six. "You're welcome."

"For what?" I grumbled, smoothing back my hair.

"Giving you what your heart desires."

"My heart desired dinner."

"That was your stomach."

I heaved out a breath. "You do realize how unsubtle that was."

"I thought we went over this already. Subtlety isn't my forte."

"Let me guess . . . your forte involves being naked?"

He laughed. "Have you and Sarah been swapping sex anecdotes?"

I rolled my eyes. "I haven't even met Sarah yet." As we took the trail criss-crossed by footprints and paw prints, I heaved my bag that was sliding down my arm. "Are you sure Liam even wants to see me?"

"Trust me. He wants to see you."

At Lucas's certainty, my heart unspooled like a roll of gauze, all light and fluffy, filling my entire chest. That is, until we approached the cabin, and Liam's car came into view. Then all of the airiness left me and my body felt weighted with rocks.

Liam was leaning over the center armrest, his face inches from a girl's, his hands cradling her cheeks.

Lucas froze beside me.

Thud went my heart, its collapse so mighty I suspected it shook the entire valley. "I'm—I'm going to head . . . um, home."

Lucas grabbed my arm and towed me the rest of the way.

"Lucas," I hissed, "let go."

Our little disagreement must've penetrated the car, because Liam turned his head. I ground my teeth to prevent the whimper and shout building inside my throat.

The girl spun around in her seat, and damn if the whimper didn't win out, because she was stunning and *blonde*. It wasn't Ness but it was also not anyone I'd ever seen before. Was she a shifter or a human? Was Liam breaking his own rules and bringing townies onto the compound? And whatever happened to being exclusive?

I yanked my arm from Lucas's grasp just as the blonde unclicked her door and stepped out.

"Take him." Lucas shoved Storm into my arms.

I latched onto the startled baby, startled myself. Storm grabbed a fistful of my hair as though worried he might be swung into yet another pair of arms.

Together, we watched the blonde with unnerving focus. Then my gaze strayed to Lucas's ramrod posture and pinched shoulder blades. The man who was never quiet nor still wasn't budging a single muscle. I wasn't even sure whether he was still breathing. And it hit me why, before the girl's coat even swung open and revealed a slightly swollen abdomen.

Sarah.

"When did you get here?" His words came out so thinly it sounded like someone had gone at Lucas's larynx with a meat mallet.

"An hour ago."

His pale blue gaze snapped from side to side. "Where's your car?"

"I grabbed a ride with Mattie and Amanda. They're out at that restaurant . . . Seoul Sister." Her gaze traveled toward me. After a long once-over, she volleyed over a small smile that made her brown eyes glitter like my garland of stars.

I noticed one of them was slightly red, as though scratched or irritated.

Was that why Liam had held her face so close? Looking for a fallen eyelash or a stray contact lens? Probably eyelash since most shifters had 20/20 vision.

Hands lifted Storm from my locked arms. "Sarah. Nikki. Nikki. Sarah." Liam rubbed his jaw against his squirming son's head.

"So you're Lucas's muse . . ." She stuck out a hand bedecked in rings, bracelets, and bright scarlet nail polish.

Lucas still stood stock-still, as though afraid breathing might blow Sarah away.

Snapping out of my daze, I poked my hand out of my sweater sleeve and reached out. "You're the muse. I'm just the editor."

After we shook hands, she crossed her arms and tilted her head to the side, making her kinky, golden curls cascade down one shoulder. "Tongue-tied, honey?" she threw at Lucas.

A warm palm grazed the small of my back. "Let's give them a little space." Liam ticked his head toward the hill. "Your parents invited me to dinner."

My heart peeled itself off the ground and began to slink back up the length of me.

If that's all right with you, that is?

I gave a jerky nod before turning away from the soundlessly feuding lovers.

As we trekked back uphill, I glanced over my shoulder. "Are they going to be all right?"

"Those two. Give them an hour, a couple things to throw, and a bedroom, and they'll be just fine."

"Things to throw?" That sounded ominous.

"Pillows mostly. Although I have seen Sarah frisbee over a book or two. Mostly paperbacks."

My eyelashes were still glued to my browbone. My parents had gotten into fights, but neither had ever launched anything at the other.

"They never actually aim at each other." Liam gave me a reassuring smile that didn't quite do the trick. "One thing you'll eventually learn about those two . . . they're loud. When they fight. When they talk. When they laugh. When they love."

The door of the cabin shut, and just as Liam had predicted, one of Storm's plush toys sailed through the air and smacked the window above the couch.

"Hopefully, they'll have gotten it out of their system before I get home, or I'll need to find myself and Storm some earplugs."

The invitation to sleep at my house skittered to the tip of my tongue, staggered, then rocked . . . and rocked. Thankfully, I managed to gulp it back.

Storm grabbed a handful of Liam's leather jacket, babbling, "Dadadada," and the invitation tried to worm its way back up. *Nope. Don't even go there.* I pulled out a STOP sign, then a U-turn.

"How's Bea?" I blurted, desperate for a change of topic. "Anything new?"

"The coroner's suicide took a toll on her morale." He scratched the soft folds of Storm's neck. "Your brother put boxing gloves on her and cuffed her forearms. He's worried she might try to take her own life before tomorrow."

Storm gnawed happily on the zipper of Liam's jacket with his eight teeth and swollen gums.

"How was your day?"

"Productive. Quiet."

Liam smoothed down the cowlick at the back of his son's head, but it popped right back up. "I kept expecting a text message about an extra rule."

I guessed we were okay, and it made me unclench the fingers strangling my bag straps. "This isn't a rule, but I think my mom knows."

"She does. And so does your father and Nash. I believe Nolan suspects. Nate's been so out of it that I don't think he's caught on, and Niall . . . I'm guessing if he doesn't know, he'll find out soon enough."

I stopped walking. "You're kidding?"

A lock of hair fell into his eyes as he pivoted to face me. "Nash straight out threatened me. Told me it didn't matter to him I was Alpha. That if I hurt you, he'd hurt me right back."

My lips parted.

"Don't worry. I won't give him any reason to hurt me."

"That wasn't what I was worried about." I tucked a lock of hair behind my ear. "Um. What exactly did you tell them we were *doing*?"

"I let them draw their own conclusions."

"Okay. Good." I joggled my head. "I hope Mom and Dad won't bring it up, but if they do . . . just change the subject, okay?"

"If it's easier, Nikki, you can tell them we're dating. I don't much care what people assume."

Well, geez. You really know how to make a girl feel special.

"That's not a good idea. My parents have a tendency to get very attached. And considering how much they already like your son—" They'd be teaching him to say Grandpa and Grandma in no time. "I'd rather they don't get their hopes up or anything. It'll be easier on them when things end between us."

Only his fingers smoothing his son's hair moved. The rest of him had gone perfectly and terribly still.

This was going to get so messy. So, so messy. I snagged my lip and bit down so hard I drew blood. I was guessing my fangs had made an appearance. When the moon filled out, our lycanthropic nature steadily overtook our human one. For some shifters, the call of the wild was so potent they spent several days in fur around this time of month. Especially the males. Females were a tad more cautious, especially since the moon cycles influenced our menstrual cycles and our bodies became very receptive to mating.

I could already smell my own changing. Preparing. Thankfully, I'd probably be in heat after the full moon run because running with the pack in heat was uncomfortable, for ourselves and for the males surrounding us. Sometimes, the rivalry and covetousness got so violent that fights broke out, bloody ones, and females in heat were forced to fall back into clusters among other females to dull their scent.

Before our first shift, though, all of us were taught how to deal with it. If our scent was too strong, we had to sit out the run. If it was manageable, we could run, but only in what my pack referred to as *cold pods*—a group of older females whose scent tempered our young womb's allure.

Shifting Storm to his side, Liam touched my chin, disengaging my sharp teeth from my lip, then leaned forward and licked off the blood.

As he pulled away, leaving my mouth agape, he said, "Before you tell me I broke any rules, that wasn't a kiss. I was just helping clean up the mess you made of your pretty mouth."

That gauzy-stomach feeling returned with a vengeance and buoyed away all thoughts of cold pods and receptive uteruses. I swiped my own tongue across my lip, then dabbed my sweater sleeve against the puncture wound before remembering the material was heather-gray and would stain.

Nearby voices rang out, giggling, and then a stretch of silence, probably at the realization our pack's Alpha was in the vicinity. A small group spearheaded by Adalyn's sister poured out of her house.

Gracey waved at me and called out a smiley, "Hi, Liam."

Her four friends didn't so much as flinch, either intimidated or entranced by the sight of my companion. Wasn't sure which. My wolf bristled a tad possessively, making me angle my body closer to his until my bicep bumped the arm he'd curled around his son who'd started sucking his thumb as though it were his bottle's teat.

As the five finally snapped into movement and walked past us, two of them fluttering their eyelashes at Liam—had they not seen him lick my mouth?—I went back to strangling my bag strap in lieu of their necks.

Liam chuckled. "You know, there are better ways to stake your claim on a fellow wolf than stare-downs." His eyes glittered with amusement and perhaps a little lust. Not perhaps. There was definitely some lust. "You could toss that rule of yours out the window and put kissing back on the table." He rubbed his mouth against the top of Storm's head. "Would be quite practical actually and preclude certain mothers from tossing their daughters my way."

My gaze narrowed on Liam, the surrounding world fading to black mist. "Which mothers?"

Lips still soft, he tucked a piece of hair behind my ear. "I'd better not give out names when you're looking so very murderous."

Storm let out a frustrated whimper, which broke me out of my homicidal spell.

"I feel your pain, little guy. I could devour a large animal right about now." Liam dipped his head, dark eyes fastened to mine. "And a smaller one . . . if the smaller one is interested later."

My internal temperature rocketed to a degree hot enough to melt Saint Mary's Glacier. Liam inhaled and then he smiled, pleased, because my body had managed to convey, without words, just how interested I was in being devoured.

But then the smile warped off his lips, and his body locked up before beginning to vibrate. Storm must've sensed the change in Liam, because he grew very, *very* quiet and very, *very* still, head tipped back, big eyes bolted to his father's glowing ones.

With a calm that was almost frightening in its intensity, Liam pressed his son into my arms. "Take Storm to your parents' house. I'll meet you there."

All of the heat drained from my body. "Why? What's going on?"

Before he could answer, I picked up on a growl. Several growls. And then bodies. Some in skin, others in fur. All of them prowling around Lori's house. When I looked back toward Liam, he was already half a mile away, body blurring from how fast he crested the hill.

Although the shouting and snarls had calmed, Storm gripped handfuls of my sweater, burrowing his face against my chest as though to block out the frightening sounds, and then he began to cry.

"Shh." I readjusted him, then hoisted up my bag, and keeping my gaze on the tensed bodies, tucked his head under my chin and started to tell him the legend of the child who ate the moon, thus becoming the first werewolf.

Slowly, he calmed. I thought he might even have fallen asleep and stopped talking, but then he peeked up at me like a critter rousing from hibernation, so I resumed my tale, making sure to keep my voice low enough to appease his skittishness but loud enough to drown out the argument that had started up again.

By the time I met up with my parents, both of them standing on their front stoop, contemplating the rambunctious shifters, I was shivering, and not from the cold but from the dread gnawing on my insides.

I heard snatches of David Hollis's demand that Lori be put on trial for her disloyalty. "You are endangering us by keeping her alive, Liam. You are endangering humans!"

If Liam responded, he did so through the mind link.

"Let's go inside. Tempers run too high close to the full moon." Mom curled her arm around my shoulders and pulled me into the house.

The moon did heighten everything inside of us—from our moods and desires, to our senses and heartbeats—and yet, I was entirely certain that David and his cronies wouldn't abandon their fight when the sky darkened.

They'd keep demanding blood until it flowed from Lori's veins and penetrated back into the land.

Unless . . .

Unless she cured Bea tomorrow.

CHAPTER 42

D inner came and went, the compound calmed, and yet Liam didn't
return. At some point, Mom took a slumbering Storm into her
bedroom, to the crib she'd set up in the corner, and told me to go
home.

As I put on my coat, she added, very casually, that I should inform Liam
she'd taken custody of his son for the night and not to crash their sleepover.
And then she'd shooed me out of the house, claiming she was exhausted and
needed a long night's rest before the brief one we'd all have tomorrow.

On my way down the hill, I texted him what she'd said. I didn't exactly add
an invitation but hopefully he'd sense it was there. A hookup was probably not
on his agenda, though. Until tomorrow came and went with its trials and
tribulations, keeping the peace in the pack would be the only thing on his
mind.

As I brushed my teeth, staring at my reflection in my bathroom mirror, I
twisted my face from side to side. The bruise on my temple was finally gone,
but my bottom lip was slightly swollen from where my fangs had pierced my
skin. Lycaon . . . when was the last time I'd been bruise-and-scab free?

I rinsed my mouth, then splashed cool water over my cheeks and crawled
into bed. I attempted to phone Adalyn, because the two of us had a lot of
catching up to do, but it went straight to voicemail. She was probably busy
with my brother. I pushed that thought aside and curled up with the remote,

watching my virtual boyfriend, Simon, until my eyelids drooped and the world fell away.

I had some pretty great dreams that night.

All of them involved Liam. They'd felt so real that when light streamed through my blinds the next morning, I wasn't surprised to feel drained. I stretched out and rolled onto my back, freezing when my arm brushed up against an incredibly warm and solid wall of flesh.

I sat up so fast the sheets pooled around my waist and my bedroom swam out of focus. I blinked to clear my eyesight and then palmed my mouth to stifle my surprise at finding Liam in my bed, lids still closed, black lashes fanning the sharp slashes of his cheekbones.

I glanced down at my chest—naked—then peeled away the covers to check my lower half—naked, too. *Whoa.* Had I sleep-stripped? Or had he stripped me, and I hadn't woken up? How was that even remotely possible? I mean, there was no way I'd sleep through sex with Liam, not even bludgeoned or under general anesthesia would my mind not wake up for *that*.

Even though his eyes remained shut, his hand drifted to my lap, then higher, to my waist, and tugged until I was horizontal again. Trying to calm my spiky pulse, I ran through my evening, trying to locate the memory of him joining me in my bedroom.

When I couldn't, I licked my lips and asked, "Did we, uh . . . ? Did we have sex last night?"

His lids still didn't open, but a crooked smile bent his mouth. "No."

"Thank, Lycaon." I sighed in relief. "Not that we didn't have sex, but that I didn't sleep through it."

His lids reeled up, and his gleaming eyes flashed. "You offered."

Of course I had. An inanimate object would offer itself up to this man. But, wait. That meant . . . "*You* turned me down?"

That powered up his smile. "No, but by the time I came back here with condoms, you were fast asleep. You're now the proud owner of the compound shop's entire supply of contraceptives, by the way." He nodded to my desk where a pile of black cartons sat in disarray as though they'd been chucked there in irritation.

"I could open a rival convenience store."

"You'd be out of stock before you could even design the logo."

I laughed. "Oh, really?"

He rolled on top of me, pinning my back to the mattress and bracketing my face between his forearms. "Really." He slanted his mouth over mine, hovering it tauntingly close, before raising it out of reach. "I almost forgot about your rules."

I wrapped my hands around his neck. "You didn't almost forget about them. You slept in my bed, you seditious man."

The corner of his mouth twitched. "Are you saying that now that I broke one, I might as well break them all?"

Was that what I was saying? "Why *did* you sleep here?"

"You threatened to call off our arrangement if I didn't hold you all night."

My fingers froze on his blazingly warm skin, and my lips parted. "Please tell me that was a joke."

His half-smile turned into a full one. "It was, but apparently a terrible one since you aren't laughing."

I smacked his scarred shoulder as he filled my bedroom with his deep chuckle. "So? Real reason? Were you expecting me to wake up in the middle of the night and ravage you?"

"I was indisputably holding out hope for that, but initially, I stayed because Lucas and Sarah don't know the definition of fooling around *quietly*." He dropped his voice to a whisper on that last word.

Happiness welled in my rib cage. "So they made up?"

"They made up."

I studied those angular cheekbones that somehow looked sharper highlighted by first light, as though the male had been carved by the strongest of winds and the harshest of rains. "Do *you* know how to fool around quietly? I wouldn't want to wake my roommate."

The grin that struck his lips was so blinding I stacked it atop the small reel of visuals I was stockpiling of Liam for a later date when his face would no longer be the first one I'd see in the morning or the last I saw at night. The thought wrung a sad little thump from my heart.

Before Liam could get a read on my thoughts, I towed his mouth down to mine, unbuckling my thin armor and setting aside my soft shield, choosing instead to live each moment fully and without impediment.

CHAPTER 43

After Liam left to retrieve his son from my oh-so-sagacious parents, I reveled in the heat and scent of him on my sheets and worked from the comfort of my bed. At some point, I dozed off again and awoke to the cool pull of the full moon on my abdomen. Adalyn had likened this connection to a mating link. Perhaps, one day, I'd learn how similar the two were.

Or not.

Would it be so terrible if I never got a preordained mate?

The hard truth that Liam wasn't endgame material hit me, and I sighed.

As though he'd heard me thinking of him, his voice permeated my mind. All of our minds since his message was clearly addressed to the entire pack. ***The run will begin in front of the bunker in one hour. I hope to see many of you there.***

"Hey, Nik?" Niall called out through my closed door. "Ready to go?"

I frowned as I wrapped myself in a towel and pulled open my door. "Um. I thought the run was in an hour?"

Niall wasn't the calmest person, but at the moment, he was so jittery his fingers kept drumming the wall. "It is. But Lori's heading out there now. And well, Mom and Dad thought we should go. In case—for Nate—" Niall chewed up his poor bottom lip, fingers still going nuts on the wood. "Fuck, if this doesn't work—"

"Let's not think like that."

"You're right." He rammed his fingers through his spiky hair, which was the exact same shade of brown as mine, dark as walnut sapwood. "It's going to work."

I swallowed, worried my optimism was a house of cards.

Niall peered over my shoulder, and for a horrible moment, I thought I'd forgotten to stash away my teetering supply of condoms, but a quick glance confirmed I'd had the foresight to put them away. "Had fun this morning?"

I looked back at my brother, who seemed to have gone through yet another growth spurt during the night. He'd already passed the twins. Soon, he'd overtake Nate. "I did."

"Nik, I know I'm the last person who should be offering you advice, but are you sure it's a good idea? I mean, from what I hear—"

"Don't tell me, because I'm sure I've either heard it too or if I haven't, it'll just annoy me. As for whether it's a good idea, I'm a hundred percent sure it's a rotten one, but I know where I stand with him. We're just having fun. Nothing more."

"Mom doesn't seem to think you guys are just having fun." He crossed his arms, his jitteriness calming.

"Mom wants to see what she wants to see. Besides, can you imagine me trying to explain to her that I'm just with Liam for the sex?"

His dimples made an appearance. "I'd really *love* to be around if you decide to have that talk."

"I bet you would."

"Please include me?"

"Never."

"I'm your favorite brother."

I snorted. "Since when?"

"Who buys you bags of sour candy every time he goes to the supermarket? Who took you to the movies with his buddies when you were still a kid? Who—"

"Fine. You're awesome." I shook my head and smiled. "Although . . ." I scratched my chin. "I haven't spotted any sour candy around the cabin in a while."

"That'll be remedied on the morrow."

I cocked an eyebrow. "On the morrow? Since when do you speak like a nineteenth-century lord?"

"Since Farrah—" His complexion tinged pink, and he grabbed the nape of his neck.

"Farrah?" My smile strengthened by the second. "Is my favorite womanizer finally settling down?"

"Geez. No. Nothing like that." He kneaded the back of his neck, which had turned a satisfying shade of candy red now. "We're just friends, and she's really into these body-rippers, or whatever they're called."

"Are they gory or romantic?"

"Cheesy as hell."

I laughed. "Bodice-rippers then."

"Yeah. Whatever. Those."

"Yo! You guys ready?" Nash's voice boomed through the cabin, echoing against every honeyed plank.

My laughter dried up, and the blush drained from Niall's face.

"Nikki's getting dressed!" He turned and padded toward the living room.

I started to close my door when Adalyn strode down the narrow hallway, white-blonde hair swinging like twin blades beside her ears.

She walked into my bedroom and plopped down on my bed, but then sniffed the air and bounded off as though it were a crime scene. "Someone's been busy . . ."

"Says the unreachable best friend."

"Grams put out her hip, so it's been cray-cray at *casa* Reeves."

"Crap. Sorry, Ads. I'm guessing she's not running tonight?"

"Nope. Not even crawling. Should've heard her rail at Darren when he shot her up with Sillin. I swear Doc was quaking in his boots." She smirked.

I pulled on leggings and a T-shirt—without underwear since I'd be in fur in less than an hour.

"Do you realize this is my last run as a single woman?"

I rolled my eyes. "You haven't been single for a while now."

"True." She smiled, which made her blue eyes glitter like the pond's surface. "Nineteen more days. It feels both light years away and like tomorrow."

In less than three weeks, I'd get a sister.

And possibly a mating bond, if Lycaon decided to bestow one upon me this solstice.

I decided to focus on the sister part, because the latter was upsetting my stomach. Especially when I ran the list of eligible bachelors in the pack through my mind and not a single one made my heart flutter. Of course, it could be a human or someone from another pack.

"Girls, come on!" Nash's tone smacked of impatience and nerves, whisking us away from contemplations of the future and slamming us back into the present.

Adalyn and I exchanged a wary glance as I tied up my hair at record speed and left the sanctuary of my bedroom. I put on my boots and grabbed my jacket, then hightailed it toward Nash's SUV, which was already purring. Ads and I piled into the backseat. We'd barely shut the door before my brother gunned the car out of the short driveway and up the road, past my parents' house, which was eerily dark.

Pulses pounded so loudly in the car that they overpowered the heavy bass drifting from the stereo.

"Can't believe I'm finally going to meet the rest of the OBs tonight," I said, mostly to fill up the silence.

Niall spun around to face me. "Shit. I forgot you still haven't met them all."

"There are some really hot single ones." Adalyn clung to the grab handle as our fast and furious driver shot onto the main road, spraying snow and salt.

"Oh, really?" Nash's gaze locked on hers in the rearview mirror.

I tried to muster a little excitement at the prospect of meeting potential mates, but between Liam's scent that clung to my skin like lotion and Nash flooring the gas pedal, I couldn't muster a single ounce.

"Have you forgotten you're taken, Miss Reeves?" Nash added pleasantly.

She laughed, which was such a welcomed sound. "How could I forget when you keep me on such a tight leash?"

Niall made some loud gagging sounds.

"I was just reminding Nikki about keeping an open mind and an open eye."

A beat of silence resonated through the car.

"Crafty mate of mine. Part fox part wolf, I tell you," Nash finally said, even though I sensed he wanted to pass on advice or flat out tell me sleeping with our Alpha was not a sound idea.

I was glad he didn't go there though, because I didn't feel like defending my choices. No one spoke again until we parked between our parents' minivan and Liam's SUV. Five other vehicles were there. I recognized Darren's and one other one, but not the remaining three.

I imagined they belonged to OBs, considering the amount of unfamiliar sentries prowling the darkness—most in fur, a few in skin. Everyone whipped their attention toward us as we slapped car doors shut and clomped over the hard-packed snow. Adalyn threaded her arm through mine, and although I didn't think she'd done it because she was afraid I'd skid and faceplant, I was glad for the extra support and used it to minimize my limp.

Reese, who was stationed by the heavy metal door, pulled it open and held it for us. "Evening, Freemonts."

"Hasn't started yet, right?" Nash asked.

A tawny wolf slunk around Reese's denim-clad legs. I was guessing it was her wife, because although Avery was the exact same shade, he was much larger.

"No. They were waiting for the rest of the family to get here."

The second we stepped in, Mom turned away from Darren, the whites of her eyes painted red. I broke away from Adalyn and walked over to her. Bea was sitting in the middle of her cell, arms taped behind her hunched back and bulky boxing gloves jammed onto her hands. Had they already tried and it hadn't worked?

I checked the others' faces. Dad and Nate were talking quietly beside the canned fruit shelf. The lines of my brother's body were so stiff he looked like his spine had been swapped for a metal rod. Liam's features too were unsettlingly sharp, and the darkness of his eyes devouring. As I held his stare, my hope began a slow trickle out of me.

"Lori hasn't gone in yet, has she?" I asked.

Darren shook his head, and I sighed, plugging the leak on my optimism before I became as grim-faced as the rest of them.

Even Lucas's usual smirk was MIA as he pushed the key inside the cell door. "Ready, Lori?"

Like a wraith, Lori floated forward, naked body so frail it hardly made any sound as it plodded away from Liam's side. Before penetrating the cage, she dropped onto all fours and transformed from alabaster human into lanky brown wolf.

Nate and Dad approached the cell. Where Dad stopped beside Mom, Nate went as far as possible without bumping into the silver bars. Both Lori and Bea looked toward him, seeking his attention. Did Cassandra's daughter still harbor feelings for my brother? There was definitely longing in her expression. Longing and melancholy.

Nate's muscles locked up and strained his brown leather jacket. Perhaps it was because of the way Lori looked at him, or perhaps, it was because of what she was about to attempt.

Niall and Nolan stationed themselves on either side of our eldest brother, while Nash, Ads, and I hung back to witness this tragic love triangle.

Mom speared her chilled fingers through mine as Darren whispered,

"She'll have to inject Bea with venom until her heart stops and then starts again."

I balked. "Is that what she did last time?"

"Yes. Without a total system shutdown, the transformation can't run its course."

Ads wrinkled her nose. "So basically, Bea needs to be rebooted?"

Darren nodded while I throttled Mom's fingers and looked to Liam for reassurance, but our Alpha was concentrated on the two women in the cell.

A snarl made my attention slip off Liam and return to the brown wolf, who stood behind Bea, fangs glistening with drool as they inched toward the half-wolf's elongated neck. Bea tried to spin around and snap at Lori with her own serrated teeth, but Lori snatched her target and breached her skin.

Bea growled and hissed, fighting Lori's hold. For all her frailty, Lori over-powered the shackled halfwolf. A minute, maybe ten, later, Bea's honeyed eyes glazed over, and her lids collapsed.

My lungs felt like they'd transformed into saw blades, because every breath cut through my chest. The spectacle distressed me and yet I couldn't pry my eyes away.

Bea's body went limp, and Lori, without releasing her hold on the other woman's neck, delicately accompanied her tumble onto the dusty cement floor, lowering onto her belly in turn.

Niall and Nolan sidled in closer to Nate, whose big body shook when Bea's slighter one grew completely and utterly motionless.

CHAPTER 44

The irregular tufts of fur that dotted Bea's body receded into her pores. Her limbs shrank. Her bones realigned with hollow snaps.

I cinched my mother's hand tighter as she pillowed her head against my father's shoulder. They must've been carrying out a silent conversation, because she croaked, "I know, Jon. I know it might not mean anything."

The air stirred with so many pulses I couldn't pick apart Bea's. I focused on her chest, praying it would begin to pump.

"Come on," I heard Lucas murmur as he fisted the key in one hand while gripping the door with the other, a glove keeping his skin off the metal. "Come on."

Lori's eyes rolled to Nate, who'd gone so still even his hair had stopped fluttering. I released Mom's hand and stepped toward him, laying my palm between his shoulder blades.

He jumped before craning his neck and offering me a despondent smile. There and gone. "Hey, Pinecone."

"Hey." I squeezed myself between him and Nolan and wrapped my two hands around my eldest brother's arm.

Bea still hadn't moved, but her skin, although not the picture of health, seemed to have taken on a richer hue. Was it because I'd moved forward and the lighting was different where I now stood?

A snuffle followed by a resonant gasp had my brother's arm turning to steel beneath my fingertips.

My gaze cut back to the origin of the noise. Found Bea's eyes wide-open and staring at the ceiling while her body seemed to color in. Her hair, which had hung limply down her back, thickened and glossed as though someone had plunged each lock into a vat of expensive varnish. Her pale skin gleamed like a field of freshly fallen snow at sunrise.

Lori released Bea's neck and hoisted herself onto her paws, before skittering backward, her claws tinkling against the cement like hail pellets.

"Get the door, Lucas." Although his voice was calm, Liam's crossed arms and squared jaw betrayed the tension thrashing within him.

Lucas dragged the door open, wide enough for Lori to scurry through, then rammed it back into place, metal clanking against metal. After spinning the key, he lunged back.

Lori licked her crimson muzzle and dropped onto her back haunches, long lashes swathing her violet eyes.

"Did it happen exactly like this last time?" I asked my brother, who seemingly hadn't taken a single breath since Bea had taken her first.

"Yes and no. Last time, the venom deformed her features."

Bea crooked her head, and my lips parted. Although her irises were luminous like ours, the color cinching her pupils blazed red like fiery coals. I waited with bated breath for her to speak or move or do *something*, even if that something was growl. What I wasn't expecting was for her to vault to her feet like a gymnast and streak toward us at warp speed.

Her thin fingers wrapped around the bars, not a wisp of smoke forming where her skin met silver. "Nate? Baby?"

She'd recognized him. Called him baby. Stared at him as though he was her moon.

Whatever she'd been reborn as carried Bea's memories.

My brother stiffened, and although he didn't retreat, he also didn't inch forward.

"Nate?" She poked her fingertips through the bars, trying to reach him.

When he made no move to touch her, she batted her eyelashes, and a single tear trickled down her cheek, dark and red.

Was that—Was she crying blood?

My brother's throat moved with a jagged swallow, his silence resonating louder than everyone else's.

Another viscous tear beaded down Bea's cheek.

Someone had to say something.

When still no one spoke, not even Darren, I opened my mouth. "How—How do you feel?"

Her lips curved, their color so red they seemed stained in berry juice. "Incredible, Nikki."

When she turned her head to take in the rest of her audience, I searched her neck for the fang wound. Her skin was unblemished, as though Lori had never bitten it.

"Can you shift?" Liam's stance was wide, thighs as rigid as tree trunks.

She brushed her knuckles over one cheek, smearing the burgundy trail. "I'm not sure how—" When she caught sight of the blood, she gasped. "Do I have a head injury? Is that why you're all staring at me like . . . like . . ."

"You're crying blood." Nate sounded clinical.

She gaped at him, then finding no gentleness, towed her eyelashes low. "How? Why?" Mere whispers.

Darren cracked his neck from side to side. "Maybe because that's the only food you've ingested?"

That made sense. Sort of.

Bea turned wide eyes toward Lori, as though the brown wolf with the anomalous venom possessed some furtive insight on what she'd become.

My brother took a step forward, and although he didn't shrug me off, my fingers fell away from his arm. "So, can you shift?"

"I don't know, Nate. I'm not sure how to do it."

"Close your eyes. That always helps me." Darren approached the cell. "Now, do you feel something stirring inside of you? Beneath your skin?"

Bea stood very still, lids closed, chest barely quivering. "My blood. I can feel my blood. And yours. I can hear it swishing through your veins." She inhaled slowly. "I can smell it."

"That's normal," Darren reassured her. "All your senses are heightened."

"Normal?" Nolan's eyebrows dipped over his blue eyes. "I can't smell blood if it's inside someone's body."

Bea's eyes flipped open, and he flinched. Her brow scrunched at the fear dappling my brother's face.

"Eyes on me, Bea," Nate whispered, getting so close to the silver bars that Niall grabbed his shoulder.

Nate shrugged Niall's hand off. "Keep your eyes on me and try to shift."

Scarlet irises fixed on Nate, Bea concentrated on locating the supple cord that bound us to our other form. One pull, and our animal slid out. Sure, Bea wasn't a teenager anymore, but at twenty-seven, the cord had yet to begin fraying.

"The moon's high. Her wolf should be impossible to contain," I heard Lucas whisper to Liam.

"Maybe if some of us shifted, it'd help her?" Nash offered.

Liam nodded. "Good idea."

"Ads?" Nash raised a brow.

They walked toward the shelves, kicked off their shoes, and tossed off their clothes. Once transformed, they trotted back toward us. Adalyn's cream coat glistened white under the clinical strips of neon lights, contrasting sharply to my ebony brother. They stopped beside Lori and exchanged words with her that were impossible to comprehend. Then Nash howled, and the sound echoed inside my bones. The fine hairs on my arms thickened in response, my skin tightened. I needed to shift.

Oh, how I needed to shift.

I gritted my teeth and breathed, in a desperate attempt to hang on a while longer, because once in fur, I would no longer be able to speak with Bea or with my brother. Incapable of resisting the pull, my parents shuffled backward, slid off their clothes, and slipped into their other selves. Like Nash and Adalyn, they padded back toward us. Mom glided her cheek against Lori's in a show of gratitude and affection.

"Does your skin feel uncomfortably tight, your blood abnormally hot?" I asked.

Bea's forehead puckered. "No."

Nate's mouth thinned until it was a pink slash on his face.

I rounded the silver bars, stopping beside Liam. "Could Lori have returned her to her original form?"

Her irises are red. She cries blood. Not to mention she can hear and smell ours.

"So, what?" I craned my neck to look at him. "You think she made her a vampire?" I hadn't realized how loudly I'd spoken until every set of eyes locked on me.

"Vampires don't exist, Knickknack," Lucas said.

"Maybe now they do." I approached Bea's cell.

A growled, **Not too close**, stayed my feet.

"Are you hungry?"

She palmed her concave abdomen. "Yes. Very."

"How does a burger and fries sound to you?" She'd always been a fan of both, especially when Dad grilled up the meat and Nolan fried his signature shoestring potatoes.

She wrinkled her nose. "I don't think I could eat that."

"She probably needs crackers and some water." Nate walked over to the industrial sink jutting from the cement wall and filled up a glass, which he carried back to Bea.

She took it from him, their fingers brushing, which made my brother's hand jerk back.

She dipped her head dejectedly before raising the glass to her lips and taking a sip. A second later, the water sprayed out of her mouth. "I can't—I can't drink this. It burns."

"Did you brew her tea, Freemont?" Lucas quirked his slashed eyebrow.

"No." There was a bite to Nate's voice. "It's room temperature."

I glanced over at Darren. "Do you still have blood on the premises?"

"Only animal blood. The one we didn't mix with the Sillin." A glance at Liam, and Doc was walking to the blue cooler by the wall, flipping it open, and digging out a plastic bladder. He unscrewed the lid and handed it over.

Bea's pupils shrank, and her nostrils flared. She drank and drank, squeezing the casing until it crumpled. She licked her lips, catching every fugitive droplet.

I gasped. "Your teeth. You have fangs!"

She opened her mouth and prodded the pointed tips of her canines, her eyes widening in alarm.

Darren palmed his thinning hair. "If she can only stomach blood, it makes sense that her body would develop a way of obtaining it."

The wolves whined beside us.

Liam looked at them, communicating through the mind link. "Jon is asking if you feel sated."

"No. I'm still really hungry."

Darren retrieved two more bladders of blood, which she drank in great, wet gulps.

"What about now?" Nate asked.

"I feel better. Much better." As though just realizing she was in her birthday suit, she hugged her arms around her small breasts. "Any chance I could get some clothes?"

"Are you cold?" Lucas asked.

"No. Just . . ." She snagged her bottom lip. Her fangs had receded, her teeth white and blunt again. "Just feeling a little underdressed."

Nate snapped into provider mode, squinting around the bunker for something for her to wear. Besides my family's discarded clothing, there was no other piece of fabric, not even the blanket, which used to be in her cell.

"She can have my clothes, Nate." I shrugged out of my jacket and passed it through the bars.

Bea tipped me a gracious smile.

I considered concealing myself between two shelves, but everyone present, with the exception of Lucas, had seen me naked.

With a snort, he pivoted. "Fine. I'll give the little lady some privacy."

As he whistled, I mouthed a *thank you* to Liam, who'd probably asked Lucas to avert his gaze, and stripped. I shifted into fur before carrying the clothes over to Bea in my muzzle.

She grabbed them from me, then scratched the top of my head.

The bunker door creaked open, and Reese popped her head inside. "Pack's here, Liam."

Her gaze went to Bea, and her eyebrows shot up. I was guessing she was surprised to find her fully dressed. Or was it the fact that she still breathed that startled her?

Liam tugged off his shirt. "If you want to run, Nate, Lucas can stay here with her."

Bea rolled the hem of my T-shirt between her fingers. "Can't I go home?"

"No." Liam's tone brooked no argument. "Not until we understand what you've become."

She cringed.

Without breaking eye contact, Nate said, "I'll stay with her."

"Do you need Lucas to pocket the key, or will you be able to resist opening the cell?" Liam unbuckled his belt, then popped the button of his jeans open, and shoved them down.

Even though he wasn't stripping for me, and my entire family was present, albeit making their way toward the bunker's door, I couldn't, for the life of me, tear my gaze away from the man.

"I'll resist," Nate said.

"'Kay." Lucas ambled over. "Lookin' cute all two-toned, Knickknack." Lucas ruffled the fur atop my head as he walked past me on two legs.

I snarled at him, which only increased his smirk.

"Have fun tonight. I know I will." He looked over his shoulder at the wall of black fur standing beside me. "Yes, boss. Little Destroyer will remain Sarah's and my utmost priority." He winked and then he was gone.

Metal groaned as Nate unfolded a metal chair and propped it beside the cell. Bea sank to her knees in front of him and reached out until her fingertips touched his knee. He jerked, but instead of pulling back, he placed his hand atop hers.

Liam's breath disrupted the velvety fur behind my ear. ***You smell like me.***

I shivered from the feather-light tickle of his heavy breath. *I didn't have time for a shower.*

Good.

I stretched my head until my nose ruffled his thick, black coat. *Didn't have time for a shower too, huh?*

I had plenty of time, Silver.

Silver?

The color of your eyes. They're platinum. He dipped his head until it was leveled with mine. **Just like when you're aroused.**

Oh. My pulse purred. *Might not want to talk about that right now. I'm already feeling . . . sensitive.*

He ran his nose across my body, touching me with only his breaths. Suddenly, he swung his head back toward mine. **You're in heat!**

Had I gone into heat without noticing? That would be a first.

As we made our way toward the door, I twisted my head and took a deep inhale. *No, I'm not.* Relief swarmed me because I didn't want to be relegated to the cold pod tonight. I wanted the freedom to race alongside the pack, alongside Liam.

Then why do you smell like—he gnashed his teeth—**that?**

A rotting carcass?

What?

You look disgusted.

His glowing eyes narrowed. **Trust me. I'm not disgusted. I'm the opposite of disgusted.**

I nudged him with my shoulder. *I'm close but I guarantee I'm not in heat.* I dropped my voice to a slow whisper. *Stick around a few more days, and you'll understand the difference.* And with that, I scampered past him and out into the night where hundreds upon hundreds of wolves obscured the land, awaiting their Alpha.

CHAPTER 45

I trotted toward Adalyn, squeezing in between her and my mother.

Reese released the door, which clanged shut behind Liam. Like a few other shifters, she was still in skin. I assumed she was on guard duty tonight.

Boulders, I'm pleased to see so many here tonight in spite of the distance and the weather conditions. We've been monitoring the resort conditions, and although the risks of avalanches are slim, I urge you to stay in the woods and stick together. Liam's burnished amber gaze scanned the sea of fur, peaked ears, and incandescent eyes. *Six more full moons until the pack will be one. What an event that'll be.* He paced, his great shoulders rolling beneath the fur. *Before we set out, though, I'd like to share the news of what's happened beyond these walls tonight.*

An hour ago, Lori bit Bea Park a second time, injecting her with venom until the human's heart stopped. Unlike last month, when Bea resurrected, she did so in skin this time and no longer displays lycanthropic attributes.

Would he mention her eyes?

However, we will be keeping her confined to the bunker and under tight security until we are entirely certain she doesn't pose a threat to either you or humans.

The air quivered with hasty intakes of breaths and hushed whines.

The coming hours will be critical and will determine whether Bea Park has a place in our pack. And in the world.

In other words, whether she lives or dies, Adalyn murmured beside my ear, making it twitch.

Would Bea's craving for blood vanish? Would the redness of her irises fade? Would she ever be able to shift into a wolf or had Lori created a new species of supernatural? One who could heal and move at extraordinary speed and who could only stomach blood?

Vampire.

The word shimmered inside my mind.

We'd defined Bea as such, because she ticked all the criteria set forth by humans. Which led me to wonder if vampires had once existed. If they still did. Could the myth be real? After all, we werewolves were.

I'd promised that the person to find Bea a solution would become Beta. Having Lori bite Bea again was proposed by Nathaniel Freemont himself. Since I'm a man of my word, if this works, Nate has renewed access to his station.

The back of my neck prickled from the onslaught of attention directed on my family. Low growls erupted. Condemnatory. Disgruntled. Clearly, the pack wasn't pleased about a second term.

Nate knew the truth of Lori's venom and lied to the pack, a wolf yowled.

Why don't you make Lori Beta while you're at it? another snarled.

Quiet! Liam's command resonated inside my marrow. *Nate's made a mistake, but which one of us hasn't? Anyway, he's declined to be reinstated, which means the position remains open. I'll be taking candidatures as soon as tomorrow morning and will elect someone before the next full moon. Please do not come up to me tonight to discuss your desire to become Beta. Because tonight . . . we run. We run wild!*

The pack began to paw the hardened ground, anticipation bleeding over their restlessness. I had no illusions their antipathy toward my brother, and by extension, toward my family, would slip their minds, but at least, it would take a backseat for now.

Without further ado, Boulders, may the moon forever guide you home. Our Alpha tilted his head up and howled, and like an airhorn, the guttural, ancient call made our hearts blast faster, our spines snap, our tails straighten.

After a rapid look my way, he pivoted, and his wolves parted, fashioning an aisle to let him through. He took off at a jog, and then his speed increased. As soon as he'd breached the throng's periphery, the pack disbanded and took off after him, paws trampling the snow, and in turn, my prospect of running alongside Liam.

If I could even locate him in the woods amid a thousand wolves, matching his pace would be impossible. The cold fisted my still-recovering knee, tightening the ligaments and glazing the bone. I stretched my back legs as my packmates peeled themselves away like plucked daisy petals, streaking toward the conifers in a steady stream of variegated fur.

Adalyn nudged me, and we took off at a slow jog. Soon Niall and Nolan had left us in the dust, or rather the snow, but Nash stayed close to Adalyn, the same way Lori stayed close to my parents.

I tried to imagine how she could be feeling. The tightness of her gait spoke of deep-seated distress and her downturned face spoke of that melancholy I'd spotted earlier. By bringing Bea back, she'd lost Nate.

If Bea was truly back.

But even if she wasn't, Lori would remain *lupa non grata*, feared for who she was and what she could do.

As though she could feel me thinking about her, her violet eyes found mine right before we broke into the forest. The contact lasted mere seconds but confirmed my diagnosis of her poor morale. Soon, her gaze returned to the dark trunks that loomed like silent sentinels and the pale snow that cushioned our paws.

The smell of wild game threaded itself through the tall evergreens of our pack's territory, which remained untouched by humans. Not even the most fearless skier or hiker came out here, especially not in the winter. The pass to reach this land was too narrow and treacherous.

Thankfully for us, though, elks, deer, and bears were intrepid and braved the uneven terrain, providing us with glorious chases. Although I'd personally never attacked an animal larger than a bunny, I'd participated in hunts, guiding the animal we sought to its final destination, which was often my fearless brother Niall and his quick-pawed friends.

Howls erupted, signaling large prey. The wolves around me flew off like launched arrows, but I stayed put, reveling in the feel of the brisk air, of the rise and fall of the rough terrain, of the crisp scents of unsullied nature.

How's your leg, honey? my mother broke away from her group of friends and fell into stride beside me.

Stiff.

Since I neither wanted to worry her nor wanted to be sent home, I answered, *Great.*

She stared at me a long while, undoubtedly seeing right through my lie. *Well, if it hurts, at any point, you tell me and I'll walk back with you, all right?*

I nodded. After another half hour of trotting, the deep snow and muscular strain began to take a toll. However much I didn't want to show signs of weakening, I'd pay for stubbornly pushing through the pain, so I slowed to a walk.

You're limping.

Liam's voice made my step falter. I cranked my neck high and scanned the mountainside until I located him, towering from a rocky ridge. He stood so close to the edge that images of him toppling pebbled the skin beneath my two-toned coat. Sure, his vantage point gave him an unobstructed view on his vast pack, but none of us, no matter how magical our blood or how high our station, was invulnerable.

I didn't want him to fall before his time. It didn't help that I kept imagining one of the enormous wolves standing vigil behind him lunging forward and bumping him in order to steal his coveted spot, but a quick sweep of their faces told me they were all OBs, who'd sooner sacrifice themselves for their Alpha than doom him.

How's the view from up there? I called up.

Beautiful.

Adalyn yipped out my name, startling me. She'd swung around, her tail wagging as she waited for me to catch up. I took a few steps, trying not to drag my hind leg, but it dragged. Disobedient limb.

She sighed when I approached. *Hun, your leg . . .*

My leg's fine.

Clearly. She nodded to the straight line in the snow, next to my three paw prints. *Let's head back.*

Not yet.

Had my friend been in skin, her hands would've been perched on her hips. *It'll just get worse, not to mention we have a lot of ground to travel to get back to the bunker.*

It's not even midnight.

You won't be able to walk tomorrow.

Good thing I don't have anywhere to go.

Nik . . .

Fine. I huffed, my breath leaving my mouth in a compact cloud. *I'll head back, but I'm not spoiling your run, so I'll go home alone.*

A brown wolf approached, ears folded, tail tucked between her hind legs, violet eyes lidded. *I'll go with you, Nikki. I've had enough excitement for one night.*

Lori's posture spoke of something far different than excitement. Had someone bullied her?

I wanted to ask if she was okay but decided to store the question for when we weren't hemmed in by so many wolves. Would she tell me the truth, though? We weren't much to each other. Nothing really. Mere packmates.

Adalyn's gaze scrolled over the leg I'd hiked up to keep my weight off it. *Will you be able to even make it back?*

I plopped my paw down, trying my darndest not to wince. *Yes.*

Matt was on his way home. His girlfriend wasn't too happy to be third wheel to Sarah and Lucas. Liam swaggered toward our little huddle, followed by a monstrous yellow wolf and a few other equally large specimens. All males.

Females were smaller and nimbler; males larger and stronger. Except Alpha females. Not that there were any more of those in the world. As far as I knew, Cassandra had been the first and only one.

Dexter shouldered past his cousin, his blue-gray gaze seeming all the more luminous set against his deep-brown fur. *I'll escort them back, too. In case Nikki's leg gives her trouble, and she needs a ride.*

I was glad I was in fur because my cheeks would've been sizzling. *Thanks, Dexter, but I swear I'll be fine. You should stay and—*

I was due back anyhow to relieve one of the wolves guarding the bunker. He dipped his head to nip at a clump of hardened snow on one of his paws, missing the hardened glare Liam lobbed his way.

Matt gave Liam a sharp nod, then trotted past him. *Ready when you are.*

We're ready. I set out after him.

If Dexter tries anything . . .

I glanced over my shoulder, past the mahogany wolf who brought up the rear. My Alpha stood beside Adalyn, his sheer size and breadth making Ads look like a pup. If I'd had any doubts that he was jealous, one look at the twin vaporous streams jetting from his nostrils evicted them. Even though it was ridiculous, his possessiveness warmed me from heart to claw and rid my knee of much of its soreness.

CHAPTER 46

Whatever fire Liam had lit in me was snuffed out by mile three, and I was back to being cold and sore. I was so focused on pushing through the pain that I could hardly find it in me to make small talk. Not that Lori seemed all that chatty.

The only one talking was Dexter. And even he grew quiet after a few glowers from Matt, whose ears were peaked and muscles bunched. I tacked up his vigilance to Lori.

I'm going to leave Colorado. Lori's voice swam through the cold, humid air.

I swung my head toward her. *What? Why?*

You really have to ask? The fur on her forehead ruffled as she squinted in the direction of the bunker that stood beyond the forest line like a faraway pawn on a pure white gameboard.

Werewolves can be idiots. Don't listen to them. It's your home. Besides, you didn't do anything wrong.

Didn't I?

A slow wind rustled the evergreen needles overhead, dumping snow onto Lori's pelt. She wrung her body to shake it off.

I'm serious, Lori. Don't let them drive you away.

She grew silent again. Stayed that way until we sidestepped the last tawny trunk and emerged onto the field dusted in moonlight. *It's not only because of them.*

It's because of my brother?

She side-eyed me.

Just because you . . . fixed Bea, doesn't mean they're going to get back together.

She let out a short whoosh of air. *Do you know how tempted I was not to fix her? If she's even fixed. For all we know, I turned her into something worse than a halfwolf.*

I wasn't sure what could be worse than a halfwolf. *Which is another reason why you should stay. To see what happens to her. What if you actually did transform her into something else? Aren't you curious?*

I did transform her into something else, Nikki. Something Liam will probably have to put down.

A shiver skittered under my fur.

I feel guilty enough as is.

Leaving will shorten your lifespan.

She shrugged. *I'd rather live a shorter life than always have to look over my shoulder.*

You're really serious about this?

She nodded. *I've been wanting to leave for a while, but I was holding out hope that*—her long lashes swept downward—*that I'd be forgiven for being born a Morgan by more people than your family.*

My pulse ticked up in compassion. I was about to tell her that she was wrong, but was she? My own brother and his mate had jumped on the hate-Lori wagon. As for those who'd seen past her bloodline, they probably didn't anymore. Not after Bea.

Where will you go?

Hmm. Her eyes shone almost dreamily.

Unless those were tears?

I was thinking somewhere remote and tropical. I don't want to encroach on another pack's territory or live among too many humans. She turned her glassy eyes my way. *You can take the wolf out of the wild but not the wild out of the wolf.*

Will you tell my brother you're leaving?

If he asks.

The wind whistled around our lupine bodies, carrying the scent of impending snow.

Dexter spun around, walking backward. *We made it, ladies!*

Had he expected us not to? Did he think I'd collapse halfway back?

How's the leg?

Good. Thank you.

He craned his neck just as flurries began to twirl. *Aw. Geez. More snow. Just what we need. We're already behind on construction.*

A lot behind?

Nah. Two weeks. Three tops. We'll be living among you in no time. He added a smile that alleviated my mood.

You seem really excited.

I'm glad for all the new faces. Especially the female ones.

Dex, Matt growled.

What? I am. I'm sick and tired of looking at yours all day, Mattie.

I huffed a chuckle. *Whatever happened with May?*

Dexter wrinkled his snout. *She's a handful.*

Lori snorted.

Ah, that she is, I mused.

I favor laid-back.

You should favor unattached, Matt said between clenched teeth.

Don't see any tattoo around Nikki's finger. And you know Liam better than I do, Matt. He's never going to settle. No offense, Nikki, he added as an afterthought.

Matt's shoulders bunched. After a cutting glare toward Dexter, he turned his green eyes on me. *Forgive my cousin.*

For what? Squashing any and all hope that Liam may change his ways to fit me into his life? *I don't have any illusions about the nature of my relationship with Liam.*

Although I focused on the human and wolf bodies slinking around the bunker, I was perfectly aware of Lori's wide-eyed stare, Matt's contrite one, and Dexter's piqued one. I pressed back the flare of disappointment this conversation had lit behind my breastbone. But like I'd said, I had no illusion. We didn't desire the same things, which would eventually take its toll, even if I failed to bind with a true mate.

As I fit my steps into Dexter's large paw prints, he said, *Heard Amanda wants one of those tattoos instead of a wedding band.*

She wants both, Matt replied quietly.

Ha! I heard the smile in Dexter's voice. *She'll probably want to be turned next. If it worked on Nate's girlfriend.*

We all glanced at Lori, who went as rigid as an ironing board.

Out of the question, Matt ground out.

Another reason I need to leave. She laid this whisper atop a gust of wind.

One that batted the scent of . . .

I raised my nose and sniffed.

Fire!

Something was burning.

CHAPTER 47

A cacophony of howls rose; the metal door banged open. Nate stood there, wild-eyed, wild-haired. I took off at a run that had my legs stretching so far apart my belly scraped the snow. The others' paws pounded beside me.

I yelled my brother's name, but he wouldn't understand me since he was still in skin. Was the fire inside the bunker or outside? My muscles and pulse spasmed as I brushed past Nate and skittered into the concrete dugout.

Only the strips of halogen lights lit up the gray, dusty space. No flames.

"The car's on fire!"

I flipped around at my brother's shout.

He rushed toward a white Range Rover parked at the very end of the lot. Halfway there, he stopped and wheeled around. "Matt, guard Bea! I think it's a set-up!"

Without hesitation, Matt swept past me and into the bunker where Bea was pressed against the bars, her knuckles white, her complexion even paler. The fear in her eyes made my breath snag. They needed to let her out.

In case . . . in case this really was a set-up.

Dexter had morphed into skin and was helping my brother, Reese, and two other shifters toss handfuls of snow onto the flaming leather interior of the SUV. Lori stood beside me like an ice sculpture.

Roars of frustration ignited the night. Reese ran past us, disappeared into

266

the bunker, then emerged a second later hugging a fire extinguisher, which she tossed to Nate.

My brother's hands must've been trembling because the white spray shot out from the nozzle in great, shaky ribbons. "Nikki, Lori, get out of here! NOW!"

Sucking in a breath, we dashed toward the woods that divided the bunker from the compound. What took seven minutes by car took us twenty by paw. Neither Lori nor I stopped to look back or talk or breathe.

Only when the silver-topped fence came into sight did we slow. Our breathing was ragged, our pelts slick with sweat. My muscles were so hard and my bones so soft that they felt like they'd swapped places inside my body.

Tonight. She panted. *I'm leaving tonight.*

Maybe it was just an accident.

An accident? She twisted her body to get rid of the snowflakes that were coming down harder now. *That was no accident, Nikki. It was a diversion.*

You think someone was trying to get to Bea?

Yes. Just as I know they'll be coming after me next.

Dread swept a slow finger up my spine.

Didn't you hear them outside my house last night? They want me dead.

I shivered, all the while trying to reason that if anything more had happened, howls would've erupted from the bunker, calling the pack and our Alpha back. Sure, my pulse had been lashing at my eardrums, but I wouldn't have missed a howl, the same way I wouldn't have missed an Alpha broadcast. If Liam hadn't reached out through the pack link, then I assumed Nate and the others had contained the fire and foiled the threats.

The freakmaker, she whispered as we approached the compound's locked gate.

What?

That's what they're calling me now. It beats some of the other nicknames—

A sizzling pop rent the air, and she gasped.

Lori?

She seized. *Run. Get—away.*

Another pop.

Lori released a bone-chilling whine and slumped.

Lori?! I searched the abounding night for something. Someone.

Snowflakes hit my crazed eyes, made them water. Sulfur. Copper. Both hung heavy in the air.

I returned my attention to Lori's collapsed form, pressed my nose into her neck, found a pulse. She wasn't dead.

Not dead.

Warmth seeped into the pads of my front paws, steamed off the snow.

Blood.

So much blood.

Lori, where were you shot? I wasn't expecting her to answer. Not really. I was mostly trying to keep her conscious. *Stay with me.* I ran my nose over her fur until I met a spot of wetness at the juncture of her shoulder.

She let out a feeble grunt.

As long as the bullet hadn't pierced a vital organ, she should be fine. She was, after all, immune to silver. Unlike me.

I rubbed my nose against the snow, in case silver had leaked into her blood, then raised my head and howled my distress. Even in skin, the gatekeeper would grasp the urgency. Or one of the shifters, who'd stayed behind on the compound.

Nikki . . . go . . . Lori croaked.

I'm not leaving you.

Please. I don't want you to— Her long throat bobbed. *Just . . . go. Please.*

No. What I was going to do, though, was get into skin, because I needed fingers.

A minute later, I was hunched over her. Snow hit my hunched back, each flake prodding my flesh like a needle. Delicately, I handled her shoulder. She flinched.

"Sorry." My hands shook as my fingertips grazed a deep depression. Gradually, I rolled her onto her side to locate the exit wound, but her fur was so wet with sweat and snow, and my damn hair kept falling into my eyes. I shoved it back. "Can you shift?"

For a moment, nothing happened, and I wondered if she'd even heard me. But then a hollow pop dislocated her shoulder socket and her fur receded and her muscles stretched.

Her skin was as pale as the sky and land, and a wide streak of blood ran across her chest like a red sash. The sight of the entry wound, jagged and as wide as an egg, made bile rise and spill out of me. After clearing my stomach, I turned back toward Lori, wishing I had a scrap of fabric to use to fill the wound. Would packing snow inside of it help?

I wanted to yowl in frustration.

A hollow shudder raced across Lori's body as I combed back the light brown hair plastered to her forehead. Her skin was cool to the touch, her pulse sluggish, her breathing labored.

"So, what island are you thinking?" Why wasn't anyone coming? Had there been another fire? Had I not hollered loud enough? "The Caribbean? Tahiti?"

She didn't answer.

I touched her cheek. "Lori?"

A rattling cough seized her. I tried to help her sit, but I trembled so hard that neither my arms nor fingers would close around her body.

I pushed my hair out of my cold, wet eyes just as a crimson spray stained the snow beneath her open mouth.

"Help!" I roared, gathering one of her hands in mine and squeezing. "Stay with me. Lori?"

Silence.

Dread carved up my insides just as metal clanked. The gate! Someone was finally coming!

"Help is on the way. Just stay with me."

Quiet. She was horribly, terribly quiet.

I slid two trembling fingers to her neck, trying to locate her pulse point, but couldn't get my fingertips to settle. They kept bouncing off her frigid skin. I hovered my knuckles in front of her parted lips, praying for thready heat.

"Nikki!"

I looked up, squinted into the snow-flecked darkness. Saw two human bodies racing toward me, one topped with shoulder-length black hair and the other with long golden curls.

"Oh my God," Sarah whispered.

I gulped back a sob. "I c-can't find a pulse. I-I . . ."

"Are you hurt?" Lucas dropped onto his knees.

"No." Tears fled my eyes, carved hot runnels down my icy cheeks. "Is she—is she dead?"

He batted my hand away from Lori's neck, then prodded the long column of pale skin. He didn't nod, but his solemn expression confirmed what I'd already suspected.

A sob stumbled out of me. And more tears. I scraped them away with the back of my hand, not caring if her blood was tainted with silver.

She was dead.

Lori was dead.

"I sh-should have . . . sh-should . . ." *Have gone for help. Howled louder. Banged on the gatekeeper's window.* "I asked her t-to shift." I clapped my palm to my mouth as I realized it had probably disturbed the pellets, propelled one of them into her heart.

Not only was I inept but stupid.

My throat constricted, then expanded to accommodate a fresh sob.

Sarah shrugged out of her jacket and draped it around my hunched shoulders, then her mouth moved around words but my ears were buzzing, so I missed all she said.

I sat back on my heels, and my limp fists toppled onto the reddened skin of my thighs. "The shot. It just c-came out of n-nowhere."

There was so much blood everywhere. Under my nails. On my palms. Around my knuckles.

My chest cramped as more tears raced down my cheeks and plopped off my chin, drilling tiny holes into the scarlet snow beneath my bent legs.

"How come you were out here alone?" Lucas's voice reached my ears again, thumped against the quiet hush filling my head.

"There was a f-fire. At the bunker."

"Lucas, we need to get her inside. Her skin's turning blue." Sarah picked up one of my hands and rubbed it between hers, trying to drive heat into my numb fingers.

It struck me how silly her little act of kindness was considering I couldn't get frostbite.

A black speck appeared through the falling snow, growing larger and crisper until the beast with the glowing amber eyes was all I could see. My Alpha shoved aside Sarah's hands, then pulsed blistering air against my exposed skin. ***Is any of this blood yours?***

My mind ached from the volume of his voice and then ached some more when I shook my head.

"Shotgun wound to the chest." Lucas nodded to Lori's chest. "I don't smell any silver."

Not that it would've mattered since Lori was immune. Not immune to a stopped heart, though.

Liam's thick fur withdrew into his pores as he morphed into his human. Features chiseled with fury, he skimmed my jaw, then my neck.

"Long range," Lucas said. "Nikki didn't see where it came from."

"I t-told her to shift. She d-died b-because I—"

"Don't fucking blame yourself."

"But I told her—"

"She didn't die because she shifted back; she shifted back *because* she died." Liam surely said this to reassure me, but reassured or not, guilty or not, Lori died while I'd just sat there, gagging.

My teeth chattered so hard their clicking could probably be heard by every Boulder, even the ones still on the other side of the mountain.

"Canvas the area where the shot came from," Liam ordered.

"Wh-what if the k-killer is still out there?"

"Then I'll catch'em." Lucas's blue eyes flashed as he stripped.

Before shifting, Sarah stepped up to him, gripped the nape of his neck and dragged his head down. "You be careful. I'm *not* raising this kid alone."

When she kissed him, I looked away, but then I thought of Storm. Weren't they supposed to be watching him?

I must've uttered his name, because as soon as Lucas was in fur, Sarah turned toward me. "He's with Amanda."

More people arrived then—some in skin, most in fur.

Before I could see if Nate or my parents were among the horde, Liam scooped me up. I raised no protest, because my legs felt all at once like hard candy and jelly. I doubted I'd have been able to walk. I rested my cheek against his hard chest and closed my eyes.

After a few minutes of punitive silence, he growled, "I can't fucking believe Matt let you go off on your own. I gave him one job. One fucking job."

I raised my lids. "It's not his fault, Liam. There was a fire—"

"I know about the fucking fire!"

"Nate asked him to guard Bea."

"*I* give the orders, *not* your brother. And I don't give two shits about Bea. That bullet was meant for Lori but if the shooter—" He shuddered. "If he'd missed, or if you'd seen him—" Again he stopped talking abruptly, but this time, he didn't shudder.

"Could be a woman."

The look he fired at me might've made me smile had a body not lain prone mere feet away.

I touched his granite jaw. "Look at me. I'm unharmed."

Like the rest of his face, his glowing eyes didn't soften an iota.

I swallowed. "Who set the fire?"

"We don't know yet, but we assume it's someone from the pack." Each one of his heartbeats punched my cheek.

"Is Bea okay?"

"Yes."

"Do you think the fire and"—I licked my lips—"what happened to Lori are related?"

"Yes."

Liam pushed a door open, and I realized it was the one to my family home. Without turning on any lights, he stalked up the stairs, then burst into my pink-tiled bathroom. With a gentleness that was so at odds with his brutal movements, he set me down inside my bathtub, plugged in the stopper, and twisted the tap until water gushed out.

He took my hands, inspected my fingers, which were swollen and purplish, then raked his gaze across the rest of me. He pumped soap into his palms and rubbed my skin, the groove between his eyebrows deepening as he worked up a lather.

Voices erupted downstairs. And then my mother stood in the doorway, her long hair snarled, her eyes shiny and red-rimmed.

Her lips began to tremble. She slammed them shut, then inhaled deeply. "I'll go get dressed. I'll be right back."

I drew my knees into my chest as Liam drained the bath and turned on the shower nozzle, spraying my curved spine to keep me warm. Once the sullied water emptied, he jammed the plug back in place and one-handedly shampooed my hair. I rested my cheek against my knees, gazing at this strange man who surely had more important things to do than rid my body of foreign blood. Not that I wasn't grateful for his quiet ministrations.

I was tremendously grateful.

And moved beyond words.

I almost wished he'd stop and leave, though, because how was I supposed to not fall completely in love with him?

My mother returned as he was combing his fingers through my long hair, attempting to coax out the multitude of knots. I'd need conditioner. A lot of it.

"I got her, Liam." She placed a palm on his scarred shoulder. "Go."

When he didn't, she extricated the shower nozzle from his white-knuckled grip. He rose slowly, eyes glazed and unfocused.

"Thank you for bathing me." I tried to smile. Managed a fleeting one.

He gave a sharp nod, rammed a wet hand through his chaotic locks, and backed up. And then he wheeled around and was gone.

I met my mother's tired gaze, and the dam I'd erected around myself crumbled, releasing all my pent-up tension. "Oh, Mom." My voice splintered. "Mom."

She hung up the shower nozzle and then leaned over and wrapped her arms around my shoulders.

"You're getting all wet," I croaked.

"You think I care? All I care is that you're breathing. That you're safe. Oh, sweetie . . ." She muffled a sob against my neck. "When your daddy and I heard the gunshot, and Nate said you'd gone home with Lori . . ." Her whole body shook.

I laced my arms around her back, soaking her T-shirt. "Lori was going to leave tonight," I whispered.

And she had, but she hadn't made it to any island.

I raised my gaze toward my skylight and shut my swollen eyes, feeling the moon on my face through the white tempest.

I hoped Lycaon would transport her to an island.

Even if it was one in the sky.

CHAPTER 48

I woke up where I'd fallen asleep—on the couch in the living room, with my head on my mother's lap. All four of my brothers, my father, and Adalyn were there, sprawled helter-skelter over the rugs and armchairs.

We'd talked long into the night, all of us too wired to sleep, yet too exhausted to head to our respective beds. In all honesty though, it wasn't exhaustion which had tethered us to the living room but a visceral need for one another, to monitor each other's breaths and heartbeats.

I took a moment to gaze upon all these faces I loved.

Niall, with his gaping mouth and arms butterflied behind his head.

Nolan, with both his hands tucked beneath his cheek.

Nash, with his nose pressed against the crown of Adalyn's head.

Nate, with his snores that could wake a hibernating bear.

Dad, with his head lolling back on the seat cushion he shared with Mom.

And Mom, with her head tipped toward Dad's and her hand resting on my shoulder.

My own little pack. How lucky I was.

I'd never taken a single one of them for granted, and never would. Especially not after last night. If that bullet had hit one of them instead—

I shuddered, which woke up my mother. Dad awoke next with a snort-grunt. And then the rest of the Freemonts yawned and stretched.

Only Niall remained passed out a few minutes longer. Took Nash tossing a leftover tortilla chip at him before the youngest of my brothers jerked awake, grunting a, "What the fuck, man?"

Mom shook her head but smiled, her hand combing through my hair over and over.

Dad pinched the bridge of his nose. "What time is it?"

Nate checked his phone. "Eight." He pressed the heels of his hands into his puffy, red-rimmed eyes. "I need to check on Bea." When he'd arrived home last night, his complexion had been ashen, but his eyes had been clear, slick with shock but not with tears, which told me he must've wept after I'd fallen asleep.

Mom exchanged a look with Dad, and probably several words. "The funeral's this morning, Nate," she finally said. "You can go see her after you've paid your respects to Lori."

My brother flinched. I didn't think my mother had meant for it to sound accusatory. Or maybe she had. After all, it was in part Bea's fault that Lori had been gunned down.

I'd assumed Mom had forgiven Bea, and maybe she had until last night. Until one woman's ambition ruined another woman's life.

As though he'd felt us stirring, Liam's voice sounded into all our minds. *Boulders, I expect you all at the graveyard in one hour. For anyone twisted enough to use a funeral to access the bunker, you'll be sorely disappointed by what you find there.*

Nate's gaze jerked to Nash's. "He moved her?"

"Yeah. Last night."

"Where?"

Nash shrugged. "Don't know."

"I'm going down to Pondside to get last night's food ready for the wake," Dad told Mom as I headed for the stairs. The big feast we'd planned on devouring to celebrate the full moon would now be consumed to commemorate a fallen shifter. "I'll meet you at the cemetery."

When she wound her arms around his waist and kissed him, I turned away.

"Ew, get a room," Niall said.

I smiled while my other brothers snickered. But my delight vanished when I started up the stairs, because my overexerted joint felt welded to both my shin and thighbone. I broke out in a cold sweat but powered through the pain. Inside my bedroom, I swapped my sleep tank for a long-sleeved black tee and my leggings for stretchy jeans, then sat and took a few minutes to massage my leg, trying to soften the tendons and warm the muscles. Time slipped away from me, and soon, Mom was knocking on my door.

One look at my hands cradling my knee made her purse her lips and head into my bathroom. She returned with four white pills and a glass of water. I shot back the anti-inflammatory drugs, then stood up and inched back toward my closet for a dark gray fleece that had once belonged to Niall. It swallowed me up but afforded me the warmth and softness I'd need to get through the day.

After offering me her arm, we treaded back down the stairs and out the door. It was no longer snowing, but ice crystals twinkled on the skinny branches of the birch trees, tinkling every time the wind bent them to its will.

Although the cemetery was only a half hour walk, Mom insisted on driving. Clearly, she was doing it for me, though she claimed she'd need the car to help Dad lug stuff back from Pondside.

The temperature inside the minivan was almost harsher than outside. As the car curled down the road, crunching over yesterday's ice-crusted snow, we passed other shifters making their way to the graveyard. We even picked up a few on the way—mothers with bundled-up toddlers and pregnant bellies, and older shifters with brittle hips.

The conversation of who the shooter was cropped up. I supposed it was unavoidable, especially since no suspect had been found. Then again, Lucas and Liam had known who'd attacked the hiker before the rest of us had, so maybe they did know and would unmask the killer in the graveyard.

"David Hollis was a sharpshooter in the military back in the day," Corinne Goldberg, one of the eldest shifters on the compound, said. "His father too, for that matter."

"Tommy said David and his wife were running alongside him last night when the gunshot went off," a still-pregnant Wren said.

I picked my head off my fingertips. "What about Camilla and Grant?"

"Camilla was there with her friends," Corinne said. "As for Grant, he's out of state. Well, *was*. He's probably been called back for the funeral."

Right. David had sent him to dig up damning information on Lori.

Mom sighed as she pulled up along a stone wall made of flat rocks that everyone on the compound had supplemented at least once in their lifetime, a memorial of sorts. "Sadly, too many of our people are good with guns."

The tragic irony was that it was Cassandra Morgan who'd forced us to learn to handle them. She'd wanted us to be capable of protecting ourselves in case of a human insurgence. She was so convinced that it would happen some-day, that word of our existence would spread and paint targets on our backs.

I wasn't naïve enough to think it *couldn't* happen, but I was optimistic enough to hope that if it did, the majority of humans would be accepting.

Hundreds of shifters were already amassed in the graveyard, and many more were heading down the winding path that cut behind the orchard, beehives, and chicken coops. The compound wasn't completely self-sufficient, even though that had been Alaric's dream. Our old Alpha had been the one to add the chickens and the hives. I realized I'd never asked Liam if he had any interest in making the compound fully autonomous.

Thinking about Liam spurred me to look for him. Between his height and commanding presence, it didn't take me long to find him. Most shifter males were tall, but few had such a prodigious aura. Part of it was due to his position in the pack, but another part of it was due to the man himself.

As I approached on Mom's arm, Liam's gaze found mine across the deep pit. Purple halfmoons stained the skin beneath his eyes, and his cheeks looked as though someone had taken a chisel and hollowed out the skin.

Mom squeezed the arm I'd threaded through hers before releasing it. I wasn't sure if it was her way of telling me to go to Liam, but I chose to stay next to her. It wasn't that I didn't want to go to him, but I wasn't sure he wanted me at his side in public.

As Lucas leaned over to whisper something in Liam's ear, I cast my attention on the pale-blue fleece wrapped around the baby carrier, then lower, on the sheet that ensconced Lori's body. Even though the coppery, sulfurous scent of death clung to the air, no blood stained the white cotton.

My ears began to ring with yesterday's gunshot, her gasp, my screams. I shut my eyes and shivered so violently Mom snaked her arm around my waist. I rested my cheek against her shoulder and focused on breathing until my pulse calmed and my mind cleared.

When I finally dragged my lids up, the crush of bodies had thickened, and although I'd never felt claustrophobic, I suddenly felt like I couldn't breathe.

Nikki? Concern creased Liam's brow.

I patted my throat, hoping it would convey how I was feeling, and pulled away from Mom. After spotting Nate standing beside my maternal grandparents' headstones, along with the twins and Adalyn, I limped toward them.

Nate was sporting a pair of aviator sunglasses that made him look like the cop he was, even though he'd worn them to hide the grieving man that death had turned him into. I wrapped my arm around his middle and leaned into him, taking in the myriad of dry eyes. However troubled by the manner of her death, most Boulders wouldn't grieve Lori's passing.

"A penny for your thoughts?" Nate's breath ruffled the flyaways that had escaped my ponytail.

"How many people around here actually care that she's gone?"

Adalyn sighed. "Many."

"Do you care?"

Ads gasped. "Of course I care. No one deserves to be murdered. Not even her. Actually, I take that back; her brother and mother definitely deserved it."

Boulders. I'd say good morning, but it isn't. Last night, a great act of hatred was perpetrated within our pack. We may shift into animals, but we are not animals. And yet someone, perhaps the person standing beside you, forgot this and assassinated one of us. Many of you aren't stricken by the passing of Lori Morgan, but all of you should be stricken, outraged by the way her life ended.

I'm ashamed to be standing out here today. Ashamed of your festering contempt toward a woman who, for all her differences, never once used them to hurt her fellow packmates or her fellow humans. Lori Morgan didn't deserve your hatred, the same way she didn't deserve to be shot in the heart.

After you pay your respects—because you will pay your respects to our fallen sister—each Boulder in possession of a firearm will head home and gather it. I want them all brought to Pondside during the wake.

Boulders, we are wolves. We have claws and fangs. We do not need bullets and guns.

People squirmed and kept squirming even after Liam had stopped doling out threats about evicting gun owners who refused to surrender their weapons.

Soon, it was time to toss handfuls of dirt over Lori's body and wish her departed spirit safe travels back into the land which had birthed us all.

While the pack lined up, I stayed back with Nate. "Can I ask you something?"

"Anything, Pinecone."

"When were you and Lori together?"

Nate sighed, and although his lenses were dark, I caught the flutter of his eyelashes. "We had a fling about a month before Bea and I started dating."

"So, you never cheated on Bea?"

His gaze snapped to mine. "No. Never."

It was silly, but I was happy to hear Nate espoused the values we'd been raised with. "Good."

Arm in arm, we made our way toward Lori's final resting place. I raised my clenched fist over the hole and fanned out my fingers, watching the grains of dirt drift toward the growing mound of soil. Swallowing, I looked up and met Liam's stare. I took a step back, then circled the grave.

"Hey." I offered him a thin smile, which he didn't return, the corners of his mouth cemented downward.

I saw movement beneath the sky-blue fleece, and then a sliver of skin appeared between the blanket and a woolen hat pulled so low it skimmed Storm's auburn eyelashes. He wriggled and writhed, pushing his palms against his dad's chest.

"He really hates facing in."

"Tell me about it." Liam palmed the carrier. "He's been slugging me since he woke up."

"Want me to take him?"

His gaze dipped to my knee, which made my heart pulse out a sullen beat.

"Liam?" Reese waved him over.

Before heading to where she stood with Avery, he said, "I'd love some help with him when we get to Pondside."

"Of course." I was about to limp my way there but took a minute to bask in the sunshine and let its warmth burn away the darkness of the night.

If it hadn't snowed, would I have seen the murderer? And if I had seen them, would they have gunned me down to cover their tracks?

"Hey, Nikki."

I cracked my lids open, found Grant swiping a hand over his sheared blond hair. "You're back."

"I am. Returned as quickly as I could." He took another swipe at his bristly do.

"Anxious to celebrate with the fam?"

His palm froze on his hair. "That was uncalled for."

"Was it?" I stepped up to him and poked his chest. "Tell me you're not happy she's gone."

"I'm relieved but not happy." Grant caught my wrist.

I snatched it back, smacking my face in the process. *Nice, Nikki.* After I got over the shock of punching myself, I took a calming breath, but my inhale failed to soothe me.

Instead, it made my heart clap harder, because . . . I took another whiff. Over Grant's familiar scent, I picked up hints of something else, something acrid and sweet, smoky. Had he been drinking? His family was strictly against the consumption of alcohol.

I stepped in closer to see if the smell of alcohol was also on his breath. "Did you hear I was running right next to her when it happened?"

"I did. When Dad told me, I . . ." He rubbed his chin, scraping his week-old stubble. "I'm so sorry, Nik. I can't imagine how scary it must've been."

The alcohol wasn't on his breath, it was on his skin. He lowered his hands, and the smell grew fainter.

"Who would do such a thing?" I made my voice squeak and my eyes produce tears, even though what I really wanted was to shout. Demand why his hands smelled like rubbing alcohol. Like gasoline and fire.

I gripped his palms and rested them on my cheeks as though I were looking for comfort in his touch.

His thumbs stroked away the dampness. "I'm so sorry you were there, Nikki. So fucking sorry."

I shut my eyes.

He was about to be a hell of a lot sorrier.

CHAPTER 49

"Knickknack, a word."

I sighed, feigning annoyance at Lucas's intervention even though I couldn't have been happier for it. I wiped my eyes. "I'll see you at Pondside?" I pasted on a smile that was entirely for show.

Grant's Adam's apple jostled, and so many little things hit me at once. The perfect oval of his face, the lankiness of his shoulders screwed into biceps swollen with muscle, the blond hair on his forearms that was so thick it hid the galaxy of freckles stippling them.

But most of all, what hit me, was how he made my skin crawl.

I limped toward Lucas. "What is it?"

"What the actual fuck are you trying to achieve?" he hissed, while glaring over my shoulder at Grant.

"I was trying to find comfort in the arms of an old friend. You have a problem with that?"

"What I have a problem with is your choice of buddy."

"Are you the friend police, now?"

His eyebrows drew together. "You're acting real weird right now."

"I'm in shock, Lucas, so give me a break." I made sure to sound annoyed with his meddling. "But hey, if you're dead set on discussing my weirdness, at least do so while giving me a ride to the mess hall."

His eyebrows popped up, hopefully in understanding.

"We were just leaving, so we can give you a ride." Ness walked up to us, hand clasped in August's, golden hair piled high on her head in a haphazard topknot.

Even though I wanted to talk with Lucas, I reluctantly accepted her offer to avoid making a scene and hobbled alongside them toward a navy pickup. I briefly attempted to even out my gait, but between my drumming heart and crackling nerves, controlling my limbs proved an impossible feat.

As August got my door and offered me a hand up, I looked over to where Liam stood, still talking with Reese and Avery, and caught the feverish twitch of his eyes. I lowered my gaze before it could convey my thoughts. The last thing I needed was for Grant to catch on and get spooked. Although, if he did, it would conveniently confirm his guilt.

Once August backed out of his parking spot, I scooted to the middle seat and leaned forward. "Can you drop me off at Liam's and then get Lucas to come over?"

Ness looked at August, then at me, her pale iris so white compared to the colorfulness of the other. "You think he has his cell phone on him?"

"Don't see why not?" August spun the wheel, circling around the orchard, before driving alongside the hill dappled with all the new cabins.

Ness pulled her phone out of her jacket pocket and typed out a message. A moment later, she turned in her seat to face me again. "He'll be there in ten. *With* Liam." Sounded like a warning.

I tucked a fugitive strand behind my ear. "It's really not what you think."

"I hope not, because I don't like what I think."

August reached over and clasped Ness's hand to calm her.

"He's been through a lot, Nikki. He's still going through a lot. He doesn't need head games."

I pressed my lips together, a little annoyed that, out of everyone, the girl who'd broken his heart was judging *me*. "Good thing I'm not into head games," I ended up saying. And then I stayed quiet until we reached the cabin. Before shutting the car door, I thanked them for the ride.

I headed inside and beelined toward the kitchen for a glass of water. After hydrating, I handwashed the glass and set it to dry before returning to the living room. The front door opened, letting in a ribbon of frigid air.

Ness tugged on the zipper of her black puffer, bringing it up to her chin, then back down. "Just came in to apologize. What I said in the car was uncalled for."

Yeah. It had been, but she didn't know me. Not really. The same way I didn't know her. We knew *about* each other. That was all. Perhaps someday, trust would spring from our mutual affection for Liam.

"Look, Ness, I know you care about our Alpha. So do I. Even though he and I aren't together *together*, I'd still never use some other guy to get a rise out of him. That's not my style."

"I didn't think it was. And what do you mean, you aren't together?"

"We're just friends." I left out the *with benefits* part.

The door bounced open, almost smacking Ness, who had the good reflex to lunge forward.

In strode Lucas, face flushed almost as brightly as his eyes. "Better have one hell of an explanation for your little show, Knickknack."

Liam stepped in behind his Beta, each footfall deliberate, each movement measured. He unclipped Storm's carrier methodically, then set him on the floor while he rid himself of the contraption, knuckles white from how hard he clasped the navy fabric.

Storm made little sounds of delight, but they were much too swiftly blotted out by the wall of tension going up around the room.

I crooked my finger at Lucas. "Come here and sniff my face."

"Gotta work on your insults, because that one's plain-ass weird."

I rolled my eyes. "It's not an insult. I need your olfactory input."

His eyebrows drew together, but at least, he stepped closer. I gestured to my cheeks. He leaned over and took a long drag, then pivoted my face and smelled the other side.

"Ho-ly fuck," he muttered. "That little piece of shit."

"You smell it too, then? I'm not delusional."

"Can one of you enlighten me?" Liam asked as Ness crouched and picked up Storm, who cooed at her.

"Come smell your girl's face," Lucas chirruped.

"I'm not his girl," I mumbled as Liam pushed in between Lucas and me and tilted my head up with his fingertips, then dropped his nose to my cheek and ran it so slowly over my cheekbone that my lids drifted shut.

This isn't foreplay. It's a serious matter. And yet my veins swelled. If Liam didn't back up soon, my desire for him would overpower the evidence I'd collected.

"Maybe you should tell the gatekeeper to seal off the compound?" My voice was so thick I was surprised it managed to squeeze out. "In case Grant gets suspicious. Like Lucas said, I *was* acting out of character."

Liam's fingers drifted away from my jawline. "Gate's already sealed. People can come in, but no one can go out."

"What's going on?" Ness asked.

"The fire at the bunker was started by a Molotov cocktail." Lucas pointed to my cheeks. "Grant's touch reeks of all the ingredients."

Her lids climbed high. "Do you think he shot Lori too?"

"I don't smell sulfur, so no, but he'll know who did."

"Grab him, Lucas." Liam's teeth didn't separate as he spoke. "Grab him and bring him here. Take Ness and August with you."

Lucas stopped next to the door. "Weren't Fury and Watt off to replace Sarah and the others at the safe house?"

Ness set Storm back on the rug and pulled out a few toys to keep him entertained. "Sarah said not to hurry. She's making a killing at Texas Hold'em."

Lucas drew open the front door, grinning. "That's my girl." He tapped the wood. "Ready?"

Before leaving, Ness said, "I'm sorry I jumped to an unfair conclusion, Nikki."

I was drowning in too much anxiety to honestly care about her awry judgement.

"What was that about?" Liam asked, once the door shut.

I lifted a brow as I walked over to Storm and sank onto the floor beside him. "Ness assumed I was a hussy. Lucas too, for that matter. And from the way you looked at me back at the graveyard, I'm guessing your thoughts aligned with them."

A nerve feathered his jaw.

"I may not be *your* girl, Liam, but I'm also certainly not Grant's or anyone else's."

His already dim expression darkened further.

Storm picked up a book filled with textures and climbed on my lap, brandishing it excitedly. I took it from him and opened it to the first page. As he ran his fingers over the scaly leather insert on a cute green dragon, Liam dropped onto the couch and leaned forward, propping his forearms on his spread thighs and linking his fingers together.

"What are you going to do to Grant?" I turned the page for Storm, who grabbed fistfuls of the pink fur sticking out of a fat, fluffy cat.

"Kill him and his accomplice."

Horror raced up my spine as I flipped to the next page.

"Unless you'd rather do it," he said slowly.

The fuzzy yellow duckling Storm was stroking blurred. I'd known the second I carried the evidence back to Liam that I was condemning Grant, but I hadn't thought I was condemning him to death.

"If he's not the one who pulled the trigger, then—then—" I swallowed multiple times but couldn't get my throat to work and beg Liam to alleviate the punishment.

Liam sighed, then got up and came to sit on the floor beside me. Storm glanced over at his dad but made no move to leave my lap.

I wiped my eyes. "I hope I'm wrong. I hope he didn't start that fire."

Liam slid his arm around my shoulders and pulled me against him. "You do understand that if he did, I cannot let him get away with it, right?"

I rested my head on his shoulder and let the tears glide down. "But death?"

"Death is kinder than many other punishments."

Storm squirmed on my lap, and Liam reached out to flip the page.

"That asshole doesn't deserve your pity," Liam said in a voice so low and rough it raised the hairs on the back of my neck. "Or a single beat of your heart." He slid his palm over my wet cheeks, catching my tears and smearing them, stripping my skin of Grant's scent, replacing it with his own.

Storm yanked at the board book, trying to turn the page himself since I was doing a substandard job. When I didn't provide the requisite help, he pressed his palm against my cheek to redirect my attention.

"Sorry, baby," I murmured, stamping a kiss to his open palm before turning the page.

As Storm stroked the feathers stuck to a peacock's cartoonish backside, Liam stroked the side of my neck. "You're wrong, by the way."

"About what?"

"About not being my girl."

I picked my head off his shoulder to stare up at all the soft slopes and hard bones that made up his face. "Being the girl you bed and bathe doesn't make me yours."

His fingers tightened, along with the line of his mouth.

"You're not on the market for a girlfriend, remember?"

The door flapped open then, putting an end to our conversation.

CHAPTER 50

L iam's grip faded as Lucas gestured with a flourish to the open
doorway. "Your package has arrived."

Grunts and clapping car doors glued my fingers to Storm's book.
"Shall I bring it in or keep it outside?"

It. Not *him.* How degrading.

Liam rose to his feet fluidly, then stalked toward the door.

"Wait. I want to go with you." I nodded to Storm. "Can anyone come in
here and take over?"

"Fury?" Lucas called out. "Your godson needs you."

Godson?

As Ness stepped through the open doorway, I stood up and handed Storm
over. He let out a frustrated little whimper but quieted when she carried him
over to the kitchen.

"How about we find you something to nibble on, cutie?" she singsonged.

My heart began to bang harder as I walked into the brightness beyond
Lucas and Liam. It took my eyes a second to adjust to the harsh sunshine
beating down on Grant's blond head. He'd been shoved to his knees, his wrists
and ankles bound with duct tape. Two of my brothers pinned down his shoulders while the other two restrained a screaming David Hollis.

None of his words registered in my throbbing eardrums.

Grant stared at me, then at Liam, then back at me. Slowly, he shook his
head and let out a crazed chuckle. "Should've known. Should've known."

I stepped off the front step of the cabin and approached him. "What should you have known?"

"Why you touched me at the funeral. You planted evidence on me to make me look guilty."

I froze. "What?"

"Rubbing your fucking face on my hands—"

Niall gave Grant a hard kick to the ribs that made him grunt and list forward. "You pin your fuckupness on my sister one more time and my next kick will have you regurgitating your own balls."

"Doubt he owns a pair," Lucas drawled.

I crossed my arms in front of my chest. "Is this really the man you want me to remember you as?"

"Talking about me as though I were already dead, doll? Was that what you and Liam were doing in there?" He nodded to the cabin. "Or were you too busy fucking and high-fiving about nailing me?"

Niall released Grant's shoulder and hit him so hard between the legs that my ex gasped and wheezed. "I warned you not to disrespect my sister."

Grant's eyes took on the phosphorescence of his wolf. If he shifted, he'd probably manage to break free from his restraints, but he wouldn't get far, which was probably why he remained in skin.

I schooled my features, refusing to give him the pleasure to see how deeply his viciousness was affecting me. "Did you kill Lori, Grant?"

His nostrils flared. "No. Same way I didn't start that fire, 'cause I wasn't even in Beaver Creek last night."

"Actually, you were." A blond, burly guy, who looked like an older version of Matt, pulled a lit cigarette from his mouth and blew out the smoke. "We have footage of your car cruising in town around midnight."

Grant's face took on a pasty sheen, before red dots of color stained his cheeks. "Of course you do. After all, you need to make my guilt look real."

David Hollis hollered, "My son's innocent!" while his wife stood at his side, rigid and quiet as a rake.

Two OBs broke through the monochromatic rainbow of onlookers and strode toward Liam. I heard one say, "No sign of her."

Her?

"Camilla Hollis is out of my blood link range." Liam's voice was hard as bone. "Now, why would someone flee Beaver Creek in the middle of the night?"

I choked on my inhale as it hit me. Sputtering, I looked back toward Grant, caught him exchanging a look with his dad.

"*She* killed Lori?" I whispered.

Grant's gaze slammed back into mine, fear sparking in his eyes.

The crowd began to whisper, heads swiveling, eyes rounding.

David snarled, "Here you go accusing my daughter! You really have it in for us Hollises, huh? What'll we be guilty of next? That my son's motorcycle crash wasn't an accident but an attempt on Nicole Freemont's life?"

All the soft tissue inside my body toughened. Not because I actually believed it was staged, but because it was such a hateful thing to say.

Liam stepped in front of me. "Leave Nikki out of this, or I'll make sure the entire Hollis line dies out today."

Grant's face drained of color while David's filled with it.

"What an Alpha you make; taking a whore's word over—"

Nolan slammed his elbow against the man's temple, then whispered something I didn't hear but which made David's eyes burn with more hatred.

My mother shoved her way to the front of the crowd, rounded on David, and punched him square in the nose. "How dare you, David. How fucking dare you." She shook out her fist as blood dribbled down his lip and chin. "Rotten to the core."

Then she stalked toward me but stopped halfway there and whirled around. "Oh, and, David, if Liam doesn't kill you today, I will."

Whoa.

She took my hand and pulled me toward the cabin. "They've got this handled. You don't need to be here for the rest of this."

A snarl rent the air, and then Lucas was lunging past me. I turned just in time to see David sinking his fangs into Nolan's forearm. Blood splattered everywhere. Onto my stunned brother's face. On the snow beneath their feet. Nolan paled and started to fall. Nate released David to catch Nolan. Amidst the chaos, Grant's father shifted and then leaped past Lucas, shooting straight for Liam, bloodied fangs bared.

I screamed; Mom screamed, then released my hand and raced back toward Nolan while I stayed planted there, watching David's lupine body bullet toward our Alpha.

Liam dropped onto all fours, his clothes ripping from the speed of his change. And then he lurched straight for Grant's crazed father, slamming into him so hard they both went down and the very earth beneath my boots quivered. A soft whine rose, followed by the wet snap of a tendon or a vein or Lycaon only knew what Liam's fangs had sectioned.

He released David's neck, and the ash-brown wolf thudded onto the ground, blood oozing and steaming off the snow. I palmed my stomach, trying to keep its contents from fleeing my gaping mouth while Grant yowled and his catatonic mother dropped to her knees.

"Go." Lucas stepped over to Nash, whose skin had gone as gray as Nolan's, as though he were experiencing his twin's pain on a physical level.

"Thank you," Nash whispered, moving as soon as Lucas took ahold of Grant's bicep.

Viscous blood trickled off Liam's muzzle as he unhurriedly strolled over to Grant. *If you don't want to be next, tell me where your sister's hiding.*

"Fuck you, Kolane." Grant's green eyes shimmered. "You're gonna kill me anyway."

"He won't. Not if you give up Camilla," I found myself saying.

Liam eyed me, probably deeming me nuts to think he'd let Grant live, but didn't contradict my claim.

"I'm not like you, Nik. I'd never betray someone I love." My ex's gaze draped over his father who was shifting back, a chunk of flesh dangling awkwardly from his throat. "I always thought it was a miracle you'd survived the crash, but now I see what Dad always saw. That it was a great, fucking misfortune."

I gasped.

His body jerked, and sweat poured down his blond sideburns. "Yeah, well fuck you too, Kolane."

Liam stared at my brother.

"With pleasure." Niall reeled his fist back and smashed his knuckles into Grant's temple.

My hateful ex didn't even flinch, just pivoted his head back onto its axis slowly.

Any last words?

Grant tipped me an unhinged smile. "I. Ruined. Her. First."

My eyes blazed with tears I refused to shed.

Liam grew so terribly still that I half expected him to pounce on Grant and make this breath his last, but he kept himself in check. *I was talking to Nikki.*

I swallowed once. Twice. "No," I whispered. "I have nothing left to say to him." Liam had been right . . . my heartbeats had been wasted on Grant Hollis.

If only I could reclaim them all, erase every minute I'd spent loving someone so undeserving.

My throat swelled, then thinned as I turned toward Nolan, who was sitting on the blood-strewn snow, his forehead grooved in pain, surrounded by Doc,

Adalyn, and my family. While Darren tended to Nolan's mangled arm, Dad and Nate spoke to him softly.

Take the traitor to the bunker and lock him up.

I froze.

"What? You're letting him live?" Niall sputtered, voicing my thoughts.

Camilla will come back for her brother. Liam's wolf stood a full head taller than kneeling Grant, as imposing on four legs as on two. *That's what people who love each other do, right? They return for one another?* He pivoted but twisted around to add, *Make sure he can't harm himself.*

"You asshole! Using me to get to my sister is . . . is . . ."

"Ingenious?" Lucas supplied while he and Niall hoisted Grant to his feet none too gently.

"Cruel! Disgusting!"

Liam slanted his head to the side. *Funny how our view on justice and cruelty differs, but I guess that's why I'm Alpha and you're . . . you.*

Reese detached herself from the quiet crowd. "Go to your brother, Niall. I'll take care of the traitor."

"Nah. Not ready to say goodbye to this asshole just yet." He looked at Liam and jerked his head in ascent. "Understood."

As they hauled him off, Grant snarled, "What will you do with my father's body?"

Feed it to the coyotes, burn it, spear it on the fence so Camilla can see what happens to traitors. The possibilities are truly endless.

"You fucking degen—"

Lucas jammed his fist into Grant's jaw, which not only cut him off but knocked him out. His head lolled and jiggled as they shoved him into the trunk of Liam's car. Niall climbed in beside him, then Reese jumped into the passenger seat, her wife in the backseat, and Lucas took the wheel. The crowd parted, lining up along the road. Their faces ran the gamut of shocked to saddened. I was glad to see that Mrs. Hollis had been escorted away, or maybe she'd gotten up and walked, realizing that her days of subservience to a belittling asshole were finally over.

Even though David Hollis had been somewhat popular, no one came forward to claim his body. Most people just turned away and headed to Pondside. He'd attacked our Alpha, so his death was understood, even if his life would be mourned more than Lori's.

Lucas backed up the SUV, rolling over David's body, not once, but twice. The crunch of bone and squish of flesh made me squeeze my lids shut and hold my breath.

The wind swirled around me, kicking up the ends of my hair and rattling the frostbitten trees separating the cabins. I raised my face, daring to breathe again. I regretted it immediately, because the reek of charred carrion smothered my lungs.

The blond, who resembled Matt, was holding a lighter against the tattered remains of clothing—David's and Liam's—which he'd lobbed over the fallen man.

Soft fur tickled my limp fist. I looked away from the funeral pyre and met a glowing amber gaze. ***The day I shred Grant's body, I'll make sure he understands what being ruined means.***

Although I appreciated Liam's desire to avenge my honor, the form of retribution was decidedly gruesome.

After addressing the pack and telling them to head to Pondside, he strode up to his front door and morphed back into skin. Besides a trickle of blood running the length of his neck, and the galaxy of old scars covering his back, his skin was unblemished.

After you check up on your brother, come and see me. You and I weren't done talking.

He stepped over his threshold and shut the door before I could even respond.

CHAPTER 51

After accompanying Nolan back to our family home where he'd be convalescing—whether he wanted to or not, since one didn't argue with our mother when bedridden—I sat by his side while Mom fussed with his pillow and Dad cooked up some comfort food. It pained Nolan to eat, but he knew it would pain our father if he didn't, so he spooned in the chicken broth.

When Mom went to fetch him a painkiller, and Dad went to tidy up the kitchen, Nolan touched my shoulder with the arm not strapped to his torso. "I'm sorry those two assholes targeted you, Pinecone."

"I'm sorry you just called me pinecone."

He shot me a lopsided grin. "You secretly love the nickname."

I rolled my eyes. "Yeah. Yeah."

"So, you and Liam, huh? Is that something I need to get used to?"

"Nope." My cheeks began to prickle.

"You sure?"

"Yep."

"In case my opinion matters, I like him."

"How fortunate for him, considering he's your Alpha."

"I meant, I like him for you."

"Well, it *is* a step up from Grant."

Nolan's blue irises dimmed. "Don't ever speak that bastard's name again. He never deserved you, and he knew it. *Everyone* knew it."

"Except me." I sighed. "I wish I'd listened to all of you when you told me not to date him."

"Hey, we all make mistakes. He was your mistake."

"Did you ever make a mistake?"

His mouth curved. "More than one."

"Really?"

"Yes, really."

"With someone from the pack?"

"Maybe."

"Do I get a name?"

"Nope."

I fake-pouted. "Not even for your favorite sister."

He grinned. "Look, I swear that if I ever get serious with someone, you'll be the first to know."

"Cross your heart?"

"Cross my heart."

I got up from the seat I'd dragged over to his bed. "And no dying, 'kay?"

"No dying. Now get out of here so I can pretend to sleep before Mom barrels back in and tries to get me *more* comfortable."

I laughed, then pressed a kiss to his forehead. "Love you."

"More than you love Liam?"

"Shut up."

In my head, I floated down the stairs and down the hill. In reality, I limped all the way to Liam's cabin, averting my gaze from the six-foot ring of blackened snow.

When I let myself in, I came upon more people than I'd bargained for. Liam, along with at least a dozen OBs, had colonized the living room. Considering the amount of snack food littering the coffee table, getting rid of traitors sparked appetites.

"Hi?" I closed the door a little hesitantly, wondering if maybe this wasn't the best time to resume that conversation which Liam and I had apparently not finished.

"The she-wolf of the hour is in the house!" Lucas whooped before slinging a look at Ness, who was huddled against August. "Notice how I didn't use the anatomically correct word for the female of our species, Fury?"

Sarah, who sat on the floor with her legs extended, slapped Lucas's knee, while Ness gave him an eyeroll. The others either grinned or snorted.

Storm released a little squeak, clambered off Sarah's lap, and speed-crawled toward me.

Even though my knee let out a squeak of its own, I crouched. "Hey, you."

He sat back on his heels and wiggled as though he had ants in his pants, then latched on to my bent thigh and heaved himself up. "Look at you." I put a steadying hand behind his rump.

In spite of my pintsized welcome committee, my encroaching discomfort grew from everyone else's muteness.

Matt cleared his throat. "How's Nolan?"

I could've kissed him for breaking the silence.

"He's cracking jokes and wiggling all ten fingers, so he's good." Storm wobbled and wobbled, his knees more springs than cartilage. I smiled at him, which won me a mighty proud and mighty drooly grin in return.

"Want a beer, Knickknack?" Lucas stood up and headed to the fridge before I could even answer. I supposed it was five o'clock somewhere. After he'd handed it over, he scooped up Storm with one arm and blew raspberries against his belly, making the little one giggle his heart out.

"Don't break him," Sarah chided Lucas, big brown eyes filled with hearts.

"Break the Destroyer? Impossible."

I stood back up, awkwardly holding on to my beer, wondering if I should maybe pull up a chair.

"Dave, up." Ness elbowed a guy with a birthmark beneath his eye, who popped off the couch, freeing the seat beside Liam. "Sorry. We're still trying to teach our males some manners. You know what they say about old dogs and new tricks?"

That earned her a couple snickers from around the room and the bird from Lucas.

"You mean young wolves and old tricks." Amanda gathered her highlighted brown curls and wound them in a bun.

As I made my way over to the freed seat, her fiancé bounced his leg, as though supremely uncomfortable. "I'm really sorry I abandoned you last night, Nikki."

"You don't have to apologize." I was perched on the edge of the couch, not really daring to lean back because leaning back would put me in contact with Liam's arm. "Camilla would've shot at us whether you'd been around or not."

Liam, who still hadn't moved or said a thing, chugged down his beer, leaned forward, and slapped it on the table.

"We'll nail the bitch, Liam," Lucas said as Storm tried to grab on to his nose. "We made lots of noise about Grant being locked up." He nodded to Matt's doppelganger. "Cole's tracking their mama's phone and monitoring cameras in town. Not to mention, Dex, Niall, and a couple others are out on the prowl."

As Liam leaned back, I swigged down some beer, hoping it would hit my veins and loosen my nerves. "How's Bea?"

Sarah tossed a handful of gummy bears into her mouth. "We let her play poker after she promised not to bite any of us, and not only didn't she bite, she was annoyingly good."

Lucas bounced Storm on his long legs. "You're still the best, babe."

"Well, obvs."

A girl with short black hair grabbed a handful of tortilla chips before reclining against the great bear of a man. "If your baby girl's anything like you, her head probably won't fit through your birth canal."

Sarah flipped her off.

Why are you sitting a mile away?

I glanced over my shoulder at Liam and brought the beer to my lips. *Because I'm not your girlfriend and sitting any closer would give that impression.* Wordlessly, I turned back toward the others. "So, who's who?"

After the six shifters I wasn't familiar with introduced themselves, Cole's girlfriend Haley, pointed between Liam and me. "When and how did this happen?"

I looked over at Liam again, waiting to see what he'd say. When he didn't offer an explanation, I yanked up some courage and quipped, "He was bored; I was bored. We decided to be bored together."

Lucas grinned. "Shit, it's like our story, babe."

"It's nothing like our story, honey." Sarah patted his knee. "You were whipped; I held the whip." She tipped her head back for a kiss, which he delivered.

Laughter rolled over the room and did away with most of my awkwardness. What did away with the rest of it was when Liam snared my waist and dragged me backward, parking me against his body.

"Isn't that better?" he murmured into my ear.

Yes and no. Like I'd told Ness, I wasn't into games, and pretending I was his girlfriend felt like one.

"How are you feeling?" I nodded toward the window overlooking the front lawn blemished with David's ashes.

"Like a giant splinter has been removed from my side."

"You know, babe," Lucas drawled, "I'm feeling mighty bored. Want to go be bored together?"

Sarah guffawed and sprang off the rug surprisingly lithely.

"Just do it against the far wall of the bedroom this time." Haley tracked them with her blue gaze. "I thought you were going to go straight through and land on us last time."

Lucas swung Storm into Ness's already opened arms. As she propped him on her lap, August dug into his pocket and produced a little wooden palm tree keychain, which he twirled in front of Storm's mesmerized gaze.

"Hey, Ness?" Liam scooted forward. "Keep him for a bit?"

"My godson and I haven't had a proper playdate in over a month." She ran her finger down the slope of Storm's nose. "If you don't mind, I'd like to keep him for more than *a bit*. How does overnight sound?" Liam must've asked her if she was sure, because she smiled and said, "Yes, I'm sure."

"Okay, but no playing with August's sanding machines this time."

She scoffed. "Storm wore a helmet *and* goggles."

"What about my collection of chainsaws, Kolane?" August asked. "Can I introduce your son to those?"

Liam grunted as he scooted forward, pressing me upright with a palm on the small of my back. "Let's avoid all contact with sharp-toothed objects and people. At least, until his first shift."

I put my beer bottle down, stroked Storm's silky curls, and walked past Ness and August and the two other shifters sprawled beside them, Liam radiating heat along my taut spine.

Your place?

I nodded as I made my way to the front door. When Liam drew it open, letting in a blast of frigid air, Storm began to wail. August seized him under the armpits and raised him like an airplane, adding sound effects to enhance the experience.

This morning, when I'd woken up surrounded by my parents, brothers, and best friend, I'd felt a twinge of pity for Liam and his son, but as my gaze cycled around the room, I realized he did have a family. Had they always been this tightknit or had Tamara's death woven deeper, indelible bonds?

I pressed my lips together to avoid bringing her up. I wanted Liam all to myself for the next hour, or two, or however long we had before someone inevitably called upon him.

"So, what is it we still needed to discuss?" I planted my hands into the pockets of my oversized polar fleece sweater, mostly to keep my fingers from reaching out and wrapping around Liam's.

His attention, which had been on the road, moved to my face. "Hmm. Let's wait until we're indoors to have this conversation, all right?"

The nerves the beer had quieted revved anew.

"Don't look so alarmed. It's nothing bad."

A few minutes of copious silence later, I turned down the path that led to my dark and empty cabin. As I unzipped my bulky sweater, Liam reached out and held the collar. The staticky material clung to my black T-shirt and pasted it onto my skin. I plucked at the sleeves to get them unstuck and to give my twitchy fingers something to do.

I knew Liam intimately, and yet the man still had the power to make me nervous. Go figure.

"I'm going to preface what I'm about to ask by saying that I still want to take it slow." Liam rubbed the edge of his jaw, the sound of his calluses catching on his stubble.

"Okay . . ."

"When you pointed out you weren't my girl, it really ticked me off." He started on the nape of his neck, scouring his skin like Dad scoured the bottom of his giant pots. "So? Would you?"

I frowned. "Would I what?"

He blew air out the corner of his mouth, then mumbled, "Officiallybemygirl?"

It took my mind a minute to parse out his inarticulate sentence. When I did, I smiled so wide my cheeks hurt. "You want to date me?"

In slow motion, his hand fell away from his neck and settled loosely at his side. "Is that a yes?"

"Is my smile not wide enough?"

"It's pretty wide, but you're a generally very smiley person."

I took a step forward and wrapped both my hands around his neck, pulling his face down toward mine. "I can't believe how nervous this made you. I didn't think anything could rattle my stoic Alpha."

"Apparently something can. *Someone*." He enclosed my waist between his large hands.

"I always dreamt of having a superpower."

A smile finally eased onto his face, brightening every shadow. "You *are* aware you can transform into a wolf, right?"

I laughed. "I am, but I wanted an edge."

"I saw your art. That's definitely a superpower."

I cocked an eyebrow. "Where?"

"On your tablet once. Then I might've stalked your social media." He bumped my nose with his.

"Huh. Imagine that. A great pack Alpha using Instagram. Let me guess . . . your handle is BigBadAndSexy or MisterBigBad?"

This time, he laughed. "No. And I don't have an account, but Sarah does for her deejaying. I borrowed hers." His hands dipped into the back pockets of my jeans and squeezed. "And I really mean it. About you being talented."

"You're not just saying that to get laid?"

"Isn't getting laid a prerequisite in a relationship? Speaking of . . ." He tipped his head toward the hallway. "I'd really like to get bored with you right now, Miss Freemont."

I laughed as he walked me backward into my bedroom.

Behind my closed door, our lips collided and our clothes came off. Fingertips and tongues met bare skin. Every place Liam tasted blazed, every spot his calluses scraped tingled, every area his breath struck heated.

This beast caressed and kissed as ferociously and calmly as he killed, as consummate in the wild as he was between the sheets. I flicked a lock of his hair off his forehead as he hovered over me, the word *mine* repeating on a loop, amplifying each thud of my heart.

Until a mating link did us part, Liam Kolane would be exclusively, publicly, and emotionally mine.

Unless . . .

Baby steps, Nikki. There was a vast difference between life mate and boyfriend, and assuming we could turn into more was like believing the sun could suddenly start shining at night.

I'd take the sun-filled days and settle for starlit nights.

CHAPTER 52

I woke up to rapping on my bedroom door.

"Nik?" Niall called through the wood.

I stretched my arms over my head, bumping a warm body. My gaze snagged on Liam, sprawled out beside me. "What is it?"

"Can I come in?"

"No!" I tried to vault out of bed, but Liam strongarmed me back into his warmth.

"I need to talk with Liam."

I froze. How did my brother know he was here?

Liam sighed, then rolled up, located his sweatpants, and tugged them on. I just had time to drag the sheets to my shoulders before he drew open the door.

An amused glint entered Niall's eyes. Fortunately for his mansack, he didn't comment on my state of undress or the fact that our Alpha stood half-naked in my doorjamb.

"You found Camilla?" At least, Liam got straight to the point.

"We found her rental car but then lost her trail. Dex thinks she took a heavy dose of Sillin to dull her scent." He rammed his fingers through his distraught locks. "Nate dropped by the station and put out a clear alert with her description, so we have cops on the task force."

"What happened to her cell phone?"

"Left it in her cabin."

"Time to open the gate," Liam said.

"What do you mean?" I asked.

Liam looked over his shoulder. "She had friends in the pack, right?"

I nodded, combing out the knots in my hair.

"I want a list of any person the siblings were buddies with."

"It's a short one, but I'll get it to you," Niall said. "Pack's gathered at Pondside by the way. Everyone's expecting you."

I eyed the clothes strewn over my bedroom floor. "What time is it?"

"Eight."

Liam sighed. "Time to get to work. Thanks for the update. I'll let everyone know I'm coming. Might incite some to venture out. Who's on gate duty?"

As they talked logistics, I picked up my phone. Adalyn had blown up my screen with worried messages. She must've figured out I wasn't in any harm, because she told me to call her when I was done cuddling Liam's eggplant. She hadn't written the word, just added the cute emoji. I snorted and told her I was on my way to Pondside.

"What's so funny?"

Liam was stalking back toward me, the door shut again.

I grinned. "Nothing."

"Uh-huh." He tore the sheet off my body, eliciting a gasp.

Then he extended his hand. "I need a shower and I believe you need one too." He leaned over and ran his nose across my collarbone, making a giggle pop out. As he dragged his nose lower, he froze, and then his nostrils flared.

I propped myself up on my elbows. "What?"

He dipped a finger inside of me, then pulled it out and smelled it. His pupils dilated, diffusing over his irises. "Hope you've got lots of episodes with your little Simon lined up because you're going to wait for me—right—here."

"Um, why?"

"Because you're in heat."

"So?" I pulled my legs to the side and stood, then walked past him into the bathroom.

"What do you mean, so? If I can smell it, the whole fucking pack can smell it."

I turned on the shower. "You do realize I'm in heat four times a year, and it's been happening for a while now."

He stared at me as though I'd grown an extra head. "Four?"

"Once per season. Wait . . . you didn't know?"

"I didn't exactly grow up around female shifters."

"Well, then let me educate you, Mr. Kolane. We're in heat every three months, and when that happens, we don't hole up."

He leaned against my doorframe. "What about cold pods?"

"When we're in wolf form, we take extra precautions, what with being naked and in touch with our wild, but in skin, males are surprisingly civilized."

He grunted, then pushed off the wooden frame. "I'm in skin, and I'm not feeling very civilized."

I grinned up at him as he approached. "Good thing you're not required to be."

"It is, isn't it?" He hooked my waist and pulled me against him. "How long does it last?"

"Three days."

His pupils shrank to pinheads. "You think it'd fly if I tell the pack I don't feel like alpha*ing* for the next seventy-two hours?"

Laughing, I turned and stepped into the shower. He followed me inside, not laughing.

Water streamed down the sides of his face, dripped off his rough jaw. "Any chance your parents would keep Storm tonight?"

I grabbed on to his shoulders and touched my lips to his. "The problem with my parents won't be the handover; it'll be the *getting him back*."

Such potent hunger blistered his gaze that my stomach performed an entire gymnastics routine. "May Storm forgive me for all the abandonment issues he's going to have."

"You're not abandoning him, Liam; you're increasing the number of people who get to love him."

He tipped my chin up and slanted his mouth over mine. "So sweet," he rasped. "Everything about you is so fucking sweet, Nikki."

My lashes lowered with the weight of his affection.

"What the hell are you doing with a man like me?"

"Trying to prove to him that he's allowed happiness, even if he doesn't believe he deserves any."

CHAPTER 53

To call the ten days that ensued blissful would be a pretty stretch. There was much to love about them, but there was also much to hate.

Liam was growing increasingly frustrated because we had yet to pin down Camilla, and Nate was becoming progressively annoyed because he had yet to convince the pack that Bea could live freely among us.

"You really can't stomach food anymore?" I asked her, during one of my visits.

"I really can't."

"Only blood?"

"Only blood."

"Do you have a preference for its *source*?"

"You don't want to hear my answer."

I chewed on my bottom lip. "But does it ever get out of hand where you think you might attack someone?"

"Not as long as my daily ration is met." She toyed with the green silk scarf she'd braided into her heavy mahogany hair. "Three square meals."

I wrinkled my nose, because her version of square meals were blood bags. "And you still can't shift?"

"Not even a little." She held out her arm to demonstrate. Her skin remained smooth and hairless.

Although she was no longer in a cage, she was under house arrest with an anklet to monitor her whereabouts and an alarm system that would blare if she tried to leave the compound. Not that she'd ever tried. Between her scarlet irises and still-erratic manner of moving, she'd risk more than lockup if she were caught out and about. Once she gained control over her altered body, she could purchase colored contacts and wander the streets of Beaver Creek.

She dropped her hands back to the book cover of her newest paranormal read, something to do with vampires from the looks of the male biting the female on the cover. Bea had always loved fantasy novels, but the teetering pile of paperbacks gracing my brother's bookshelves revealed an increased appetite for them.

"Doing research?"

She glanced down at the cover as though she'd forgotten what she'd been reading. "Ha. No. Just restless from being cooped up. But there are some details in these books that are alarmingly accurate. I'm thinking that series over there"—she pointed to a trilogy about werewolves—"must've been written by someone who knows a pack, or who is pack." She distractedly flipped through the pages of her vampire novel, making the tissue-thin paper snap and pulse air against the potted stems of lavender. "How's Miles?"

Last week, for the first time since our trip out to Bea's cabin, I'd crossed paths with him in the cereal aisle of the supermarket. He'd spent half of our run-in apologizing for having abandoned me, and the other half, firing questions about his sister's trip. "He misses you."

"I don't think he believes I'm backpacking through Asia to nurse my broken heart or to research our heritage." That was the story Bea had fed him through text messages, and which I'd supplemented with photoshopped pictures of his sister in various settings.

"Why'd you say that?"

"Because he keeps insisting on flying out to meet me, and I keep having to tell him that I need to make this trip on my own, and he doesn't understand why." She stopped toying with her book. "If only I could tell him the truth. Just him."

"What truth, though? That you're some sort of new and improved vampire?"

She arched an eyebrow. "Improved?"

"You can walk in the sun. Neither garlic nor holy water affects you."

She grinned. "That was quite funny."

"It was. Nate's face was priceless."

We'd sat around this very table. Bea had pinched a raw garlic clove and taken a small bite. Besides her eyes watering and expelling reddened tears, and my brother wincing, she didn't combust, or whatever it was vampires supposedly did at the contact with garlic. That same day, Niall had bottled up some holy water at the local church and sprinkled it on her hand. Great beads of sweat had rolled down Nate's temples, and he'd squeezed his eyes shut until Bea had patted his hand to reassure him that she wasn't burnt to a crisp.

I slid the magnetic lid of my travel mug open and shut, open and shut. "Do you regret it?"

She gazed out the window at the glossy surface of the pond slicked over with ice. "I regret four innocent people died because of me."

"*You* didn't kill any of them."

"What I did killed them."

"Not Lori. A close-minded shifter killed her."

Bea reached over and wrapped her hand around mine, skin as cold as snow. "You're such a sweetie, Nikki, but I'm a big girl. I take full responsibility for my actions. Those deaths—all of them—are on me, and I will spend the rest of my life attempting to make up for them. I don't know how yet, but I'll find a way." Her mouth parted, then shut, and she eyed the door. "Nate's coming."

Her senses were so acute she could map out everyone's whereabouts within a ten-mile radius. We'd tested this a few times already with my brothers. They'd run off to a random corner of our ten-thousand-acre gated property, and once immobile, they'd phone us up and Bea would focus on them.

She'd never been wrong.

Not once.

The realm of Liam's grasp was five-times broader, but Bea's remained impressive.

A full minute later, my brother walked in, brushing the snow from his boots on the bristly doormat. He didn't seem surprised to find me with Bea. Probably because I'd been visiting almost every day, bringing my tablet along to work beside her as she read a book or flipped through TV channels. Often, Adalyn joined us. On rare occasions, Mom stopped by. But where Ads was always ecstatic to hang out, Mom was a tad more cautious, a mix of fear and blame mitigating her mood.

"Hey, Pinecone," Nate chirped, pulling out the chair beside Bea's.

Her hand slipped under the table, probably to grip his. I suspected the engagement ring in my parents' safe would be brought back out very soon.

"You're in a chipper mood." My gaze swung between the two of them, and then down to Bea's left hand, which remained atop her book. I half-expected a diamond to twinkle back at me, but her long fingers were bare.

Nate leaned forward, brown eyes sparkling. "Because Liam didn't shoot down my idea."

Bea's eyes widened. "He didn't?"

"What idea?" I asked.

"Roping Bea into the pack by linking her to him. If he can communicate with her, then that would mean she has lycanthropic magic, even if she can't shift. And if she has werewolf magic, then he'd consider letting her roam free. Well, through the compound."

My heart took off like a flock of geese at the sound of a gunshot. "By linking her to him, you mean through a blood pledge?"

Nate nodded so enthusiastically it tossed a lock of hair into his eyes.

"What if her blood poisons him, or transforms him into . . . into what she is?"

"It won't."

His conviction didn't temper my apprehension. "How can you be so sure?"

Nate and Bea exchanged a long look followed by a long smile. "Because she and I . . . experimented."

"Experimented?" I shrilled.

They both turned toward me.

"What do you mean *experimented?*" I was trying to wrangle back my annoyance. Especially since my brother seemed like his usual self, if not more high-spirited.

"You didn't tell her?" he asked Bea calmly.

"I was waiting for you to do it."

He settled back in his chair, still holding onto her hand. "A week ago, I tasted Bea's blood."

"Why?" I exclaimed. "Why would you do that?"

His broad smile chipped. "Because I was trying to understand what she's become."

"And it didn't make you sick?" I scanned his features, looking for changes. I found only positive ones—the circles under his eyes had all but vanished and the fine lines rumpling his brow were gone. I'd assumed it was the effect of sleep, but perhaps it was the effect of her blood.

"Not only does her blood taste like ours, but it has enhanced properties."

"Meaning?"

"Meaning . . . check this out." He lifted their linked hands to his mouth, dragged the sharp tips of his canines across both their wrists, then pressed the weeping wounds together.

I hissed, expecting Bea to leap onto him and sink her fangs into his flesh, but only her pupils stirred, distending until a lone ruby rim remained. Nate pulled apart their wrists, then licked his clean, and displayed his wound.

Or the place where his wound should've been.

I snapped my eyes to his. "There's no scar!" I looked at her wrist next. Not even a faint line remained either. "And you can still shift, Nate?"

He pushed his leather jacket sleeves up and coaxed out his fur.

"So her blood isn't toxic," I mused.

"It's magical." My brother's smile was back with a vengeance.

"What about her venom?" I asked.

"We haven't . . ." Her tongue darted out and swiped her upper lip as though hunting for residues of Nate's blood. "We haven't experimented with my venom yet."

"Will you?"

"Yes," Nate said at the same time as she shook her head *no*.

I breathed out a sigh of relief.

My brother frowned. "Babe, Lori's venom was innocuous to shifters."

I assumed he knew this because she'd fanged him. I wrinkled my nose, still finding it strange that they'd had a thing.

A shadow fell across Bea's face, and I couldn't tell if it gathered there because of guilt or jealousy. Perhaps a mixture of both. "We're still not experimenting. If I took away your ability to shift, I'd never forgive myself."

Nate sighed. "We'll discuss it later."

"There's nothing to discuss."

The air simmered between them.

Before an argument could break out, I said, "Your restraint was impressive."

They both turned their attention to me, moods as tight as their bodies.

I gestured to my brother's arm. "When Nate bled."

She crossed her stiff arms. "I drank before you arrived."

Nate sighed. "As long as she's sated, she's in complete control." He placed a hand on her thigh, and although she didn't cover his hand with hers, her posture relaxed. But then her shoulders squared. "We're doing it now?"

I frowned. "Doing what now?"

"The blood pledge. Your boyfriend's on his way."

Nate's eyes sharpened. As much as Niall and Nolan were enthusiastic about my fledgling relationship with our Alpha, Nate and Nash remained cautious.

I wished they'd both come around and accept it, but I supposed only time would soften them up.

A minute after Bea had predicted Liam's arrival, the cabin door opened and in he stalked along with Lucas and Reese.

Liam's already drawn features tautened further when he noted my presence, but he thankfully didn't ask me to leave, probably sensing it would be a waste of breath. He ambled over to where I sat and dropped a warm palm on my shoulder.

I reached up and covered his hand with mine. He didn't kiss me, and I didn't kiss him. We weren't quite *there* yet, but his hands always strayed to my body. And once they found purchase, they stayed.

Bea's elegant throat bobbed with a swallow as she tipped her head back, the silk scarf gleaming like a strand of emeralds in the milky light streaming through the window. The tempo of her heartbeats, which usually matched ours, quickened.

"If we do this, and it works, you'll be a Boulder until the day you die. This means, you live with the pack, you work with the pack, you breathe with the pack. We are your family; we are your everything." Liam's deep voice rumbled through the high-ceilinged space. "Do you understand?"

"Yes."

"You're certain you're ready to commit, Bea?"

"Yes."

Where Lucas leaned against a nearby wall with his arms crossed, Reese stood in Liam's shadow, ready to spring forward. Ever since he'd made her Beta, she'd been sticking to him like gum. I was really glad she wasn't into men. I was much too jealous to accept another woman getting so close to my man, even if it was for professional reasons.

Liam removed his hand from my shoulder to pull off his jacket and T-shirt. As always, the sight of his bare torso made my stomach morph into a beehive. He slid out one of his claws and slashed the skin over his heart, right over the thin pale scar that remained from his first and only Alpha pledge when he'd taken over the Boulders.

Bea froze. Even the vein in her neck seemed to have stopped pulsing.

Clasping her hand, Nate pulled her up and around the table. "Ready?"

She nodded, following the dribble of blood streaming into the grooves of Liam's six-pack. I was staring too, but not quite for the same reasons.

"Repeat after me," my brother said. "I pledge myself to thee, Liam Kolane, to guide me for as long as I shall walk this earth."

When Bea's fangs lengthened, Reese stepped forward, fur already darkening her arms and corded neck.

Liam extended an arm to keep her back. "It's all right."

Bea sank her teeth into her wrist and twisted her head, creating a wide gash, probably so it wouldn't zip up before she could finish speaking the pledge, and then she lifted it to Liam's chest and repeated his words, her voice thick, her pupils enlarged.

Even though her blood hadn't harmed my brother, it hadn't come in contact with his heart. I held my breath and focused on each beat of my Alpha's thudding organ, willing it not to speed or slow. It did neither, and when Bea dropped her arm, his skin, like my brother's was unblemished.

Suddenly, her irises flared, bright as taillights, and a single bloodied tear ran down her cheek.

My brother paled. "What? What is it?"

"I heard him," she murmured. "I heard him."

A peal of delight rang, shearing my eardrums. Nate grabbed Bea and swung her around like a child, his laughter spilling over her sobs.

I raised my palm to Liam's chest, to the bloodied smear, and touched his skin, needing to feel his heartbeats pour out of him. "Are you okay?"

He wrapped his fingers around my wrist. *I am.*

Lucas, who must've walked over to the kitchen at some point, dangled a soggy ball of paper towel. I took it from him and delicately wiped Liam's torso.

Got any plans this afternoon? he rasped into my mind.

My eyelashes fluttered as I met his luminous gaze. "None whatsoever."

He pulled the pinked paper towel out of my hands and tossed it on the table, then slid his fingers through mine. Not bothering to put his clothes back on, merely slapping them over his shoulder, he turned toward the others. "Reese, get Bea's anklet off."

"I'm free?"

"Yes, but no leaving the compound. Is that clear?"

A couple more tears raced down her quivering cheeks. "Yes." She swallowed. "Thank you."

Liam gave a sharp nod.

As I hooked my bag and grabbed my travel mug, my nerves finally settled, and I smiled. Liam's heart was intact, as was my brother's, and although Bea's entry into the Boulders had been far from smooth, she'd made it in.

"Welcome to the pack, Bea," I called out as Liam towed me out the front door.

She wiped her cheeks and mouthed another *thank you*. And then she turned toward my brother, wrapped her arms around his waist, and bloodied his blue shirt with her joy.

CHAPTER 54

The pack didn't accept Bea overnight. They didn't accept her after several nights either. But talk eventually veered to Adalyn and Nate's upcoming nuptials, and the oddity that was Nate's fiancée— the ring was back on—skidded to the backburner of everyone's minds.

"So what will you do if Lycaon binds you to someone?" Adalyn and I were scrolling through Pinterest boards filled with elaborate hairdos, because she was still unsure of what she wanted for her big night.

My veins filled with ants at her question. "I don't know."

"Good thing you'll have six months to decide."

I glanced at Storm, who sat in between my legs, hard at work composing a symphony on his colorful plastic piano. The mere thought of a mating link made me sick to my stomach. I didn't want to lose Liam, but I wasn't naïve enough to believe he'd stick around if we couldn't be physically intimate. It would merely precipitate the inevitable.

I rested the back of my head against my mattress and shut my eyes. "I hope Lycaon forgets about me this solstice."

Adalyn was quiet, but I could hear her thoughts. Well, not actually hear them, but feel them whirring, loud like Storm's toy instrument. After a long while, she said, "Mating links happen for a reason."

My lids flipped up. "Please don't, Ads."

"I'm just saying—"

"I know what you're saying. I also know you think I'm too attached to Storm and to his father."

"I'm just looking out for you, Nik."

"Good thing I'm a phoenix, huh?"

Sighing, she gathered my hand in hers and squeezed. "You are."

Storm twisted around and gazed up at me, his chin shiny with drool. I smiled at him and stroked the frame of his still-round face.

He turned and pressed his two palms into my chest, lifting his wobbly self up. "Mama."

I wrapped one arm around him to help him balance. "No, baby." I pointed to myself. "Nih-kee."

"Mamama," he babbled.

"Nih-kee."

Adalyn released a whistling breath. "You see? Even *he's* too attached."

I side-eyed my friend. "He doesn't know what he's saying."

"Are you sure about that?"

"He's ten months, Ads. He's just mimicking everything he hears and since he spends so much time with me and Mom, he hears me call her that."

Storm offered me one of his signature lopsided grins as though he sensed I needed a smile. I offered him one in return.

"How does Liam react when his son calls you that?"

My heart fired off a beat. "He's never heard him say it." *Thankfully.* I couldn't imagine he'd appreciate it.

Storm rocked a few more times, then looked over his shoulder at his piano.

I helped him twist back around. "I wish he didn't hate the idea of life mates." Every time someone so much as mentioned the word, even if it wasn't in connection to me, he tensed up.

"Maybe he'll come around."

"Maybe," I murmured with little conviction, but then inhaled a long breath and shoved away my negativity. I'd never been a pessimistic person before. No way was I becoming one now. "So"—I tipped my head to Ads' tablet—"have we narrowed it down?"

"Nope, but we should, shouldn't we?"

"Well, you *are* getting hitched in five days."

Her eyes lit up at the reminder. "I feel like I've been planning this wedding forever."

"You have been planning it forever." Ever since she'd scraped her knee climbing the tree under my window when she was eleven, and my brother had carried her back into the house and dressed her wound with Minion Band-

Aids. For all her talk of abiding by Lycaon's wishes and marrying her prese-lected mate, Adalyn would've ended up choosing my brother even if he hadn't been chosen for her.

An hour of hairstyle browsing set to Storm's Symphony Number Six later, Adalyn had finally narrowed it down to two looks, which she set off to try out.

Once she was gone, I texted Liam to find out when he'd be back from Camilla-hunting.

On my way now. Should be there in fifteen. Sorry. Heard you got stuck with Storm.

ME: *If by stuck, you mean I got the privilege to spend my afternoon with your son, then yes, I got stuck with him.*

The audacious girl who'd propositioned her Alpha reared up her head and typed out: ***I'm hoping to get stuck with his father next.***

A chuckle came through the mind link.

Smiling, I went back to playing with my ward. After foam ball tosses and a few crawling contests, Storm yawned and fished out a board book from the box of toys in the corner of my bedroom.

He held it out, babbling, "Mamama."

I shook my head as I reached over to take it from him. Before I could correct him, he squealed, dropped the book, and speed-crawled over to my doorway. He seized Liam's shins and hoisted himself up, spilling a litany of *dada*s.

Liam's dark eyes lowered to his son. Flattened lips hinting at a bad day, he bent and hoisted Storm into his arms.

I picked up the book. "Still no luck finding Camilla?"

Without lifting his gaze off Storm, Liam asked, "Why did he just call you that?"

That was the source of his foul mood? "Because he apparently deems Nikki too hard to pronounce."

"So you taught him to call you Mom?" His tone was so scathing my fingers garroted the book.

"Of course I didn't."

"Then *why* did he call you that?" he repeated between barely parted teeth.

The hand not holding Storm's picture book perched on my hip. "Maybe because he hears me call my mother that way, and since he spends so much time with us, he thinks it's what you call people who take care of you."

Liam kept staring at me, and not in a nice way. It was the way he looked at people he didn't trust. Or like.

"I correct him all the time for your information."

"Didn't hear you correct him just now."

"Because you walked in, and I got sidetracked." My knuckles whitened around the book. "What exactly would I gain from Storm calling me Mom? In case you forgot, I already have a family, Liam. I'm not looking for another one."

"What you're looking for is a life mate, and once you find him, you'll be out of our lives." He readjusted his grip on Storm, shifting him to the side.

I wanted to remind Liam that we were pack, that I'd always be part of their lives.

"This needs to end now."

"Storm calling me Mama?"

"No. Us, Nicole."

My lashes rose so high they grazed my browbone. "You're breaking up with me because of two syllables your son strung together in place of my name?"

"They're not just two syllables."

My shoulders snapped back. My heart, too. It struck my spine before slithering down. "His coat is hanging by the front door." I kept my voice placid so as not to worry Storm, whose head was swiveling between his father and me.

"I'm just trying to protect him."

"Yeah. Sure. Whatever." I pivoted before my burning eyes could expel any tears. "Please leave."

"Nik—"

"I said, *leave.*"

When Liam's footsteps petered out, when his heartbeat decreased in volume, I tossed the book on my desk and yanked on my blinds, and then I curled up on my bed and lamented into my pillow about what a fool I'd been to believe I could bend an inflexible man.

CHAPTER 55

The next morning, when Niall stopped by my bedroom to see if I was ready to head up to Mom and Dad's for lunch, I faked stomach cramps. Considerate boy that he was, he placed a glass of cold water and a bottle of aspirin on my nightstand. If only that could cure what ailed me. I should've listened to Adalyn and stayed away from our Alpha whose trust issues were so big it was a wonder he could see past them.

After Niall shut the door, I closed my eyes and forced my whirring mind to switch off. I woke up to a cool hand gliding across my forehead.

"She doesn't feel warm," Mom was telling someone.

I cracked my lids open, found her and Adalyn gazing worriedly down at me. One look at my swollen eyes and both grasped it wasn't my stomach that ached but my heart.

Mom crouched next to my side of the bed, her palm combing locks of hair off my forehead. "Sweetie, what happened?"

"I don't want to talk about it."

Her face puckered.

"Not yet."

Adalyn touched Mom's arm. "Meg, let me talk to her."

Even though I didn't want to discuss Liam at all, sending both away with zero explanation was as impossible as asking the sun not to set.

Mom straightened and walked away, her gaze lingering on me before she softly shut the door.

Adalyn plopped down on the bed beside me, making the mattress jiggle. "*What* happened and *when?*"

I hugged my pillow and shut my eyes. "You know how Storm was calling me *mama?*" I swallowed past the huge lump which sat inside my throat like one of Storm's toy balls. "Liam thinks I taught him to say it."

Resentment dimmed the brightness of Adalyn's eyes. "Jerk."

I pressed my lips together.

"I'm disinviting him from my wedding."

"I don't think you can disinvite your Alpha."

"Watch me." Her smile was so wicked it made my trembling lips curve.

"I appreciate the solidarity, honey, but you really don't need to do that. It's not like I can avoid him all that long anyway. Besides, the great thing about mating ceremonies is that the whole pack will be there, so he'll just be one face in a thousand."

She stared at the garland of stars I hadn't bothered lighting. They reminded me of Storm, which reminded me of Liam, which was silly because I'd had them long before I'd met either Kolane.

"Nash told me Liam left for Boulder this morning, so fingers crossed, he might not get back in time."

"He's gone?"

Ads pushed a peroxided lock back but it sprang from behind her ear, swinging around the gentle camber of her cheek. "Apparently, he had some business to take care of."

There was no *apparently* about it. It wasn't heartache that had driven him away. For hearts to ache, they had to be involved, and Liam's had never been part of the package.

"Did he take Storm with him?"

"He did."

"And Lucas?"

"Lucas went home with Sarah the other day, but they promised Nash they'd be back for my big day."

"What about Camilla? Is anyone still looking for her, or did everyone just give up?"

"Last I heard, Reese had a meeting with every tracker on the premises. If anyone can locate the bitch, it'll be our new Beta. She *really* loathes the Hollises."

"I have the absolute worst taste in men."

Adalyn laid her hand atop the one not buried underneath my pillow, then scooted down until she was horizontal. "Thankfully for you, the solstice is coming, and the choice could be taken out of your hands." She added a smile, even though I wasn't feeling very smiley in return.

"With my luck, if Lycaon binds me to someone, it'll be another crappy male specimen."

Adalyn's lips quirked. "Lycaon will choose only the best for you."

"From your lips to their ears."

She brought her index and middle finger to her lips, placed a kiss on them, then flicked them with her thumb to send the kiss soaring upward. It was something her superstitious grandmother had always done, a quirk which she and her sister had picked up.

"You know what you need?"

"Pouches?"

She chuckled. "Forgot about those."

"A smarter heart?"

"Guess again."

"A shower?"

She laughed. "You need a spa day with yours truly. What do you say I book us a whole afternoon of pampering?"

I sighed. "I'd say that sounds really nice."

"Consider it done." She fished her phone out of her jeans and dialed up the best hotel in town. After a few minutes, she hung up. "We're all set for tomorrow. 3 p.m. Now, what do you say I pop some corn and pour us some candy, and we fry our brains with hours of television?"

"You have a million better things to do, Ads."

"I have *zero* better things to do."

"Are you sure?"

"You really have to ask after almost two decades of friendship?"

The lump expanded again, but this time, from gratitude. It swaddled the grief, preventing its ragged edges from tearing me up further. Although I didn't feel fully healed when Adalyn left that night, I felt better.

And the following morning, I felt better still. And when Miles asked if I could meet him at Seoul Sister for coffee—probably to grovel some more and discuss his sister's trip at great lengths—I decided to pay it forward and said yes.

CHAPTER 56

I tugged my duster cardigan closed and heaved my bag farther up my arm as I walked through the sun-drenched streets of town toward Seoul Sister. The sky was a shade of blue so bright it seemed surreal. Not a cloud marred its limpid expanse.

I inhaled a slow breath, filling my lungs with its blueness. Maybe I'd go for a run before my spa date with Adalyn. Not maybe. I'd definitely go for a run.

When I'd awakened this morning, I'd decided today was going to be a good day, and since we were the architects of our moods, today would be awesome.

The aroma of milky coffee and baking bread whirled into me as I entered the restaurant. Miles was standing behind the bar, the only soul in the dining room at this early hour. Besides the cooks, who I assumed were already tucked behind the stoves, prepping Sunday brunch.

"Something smells delish." I swung my heavy bag onto a barstool, then sat on the one next to it. "Please tell me your coffee invite includes breakfast."

Miles, who was standing at the sink, blinked a few times, as though he had something stuck in his eyes, then turned off the water, wiped his hands on a kitchen towel, and rubbed his twitching eyes.

"You okay?" It was a stupid question considering how red the whites of his eyes were. Lack of sleep and worry had clearly taken their toll.

"I made you a mocha." He slid a tall glass striated with coffee, milk foam, and cocoa powder in front of me.

"Thank you." I wasn't all that picky about how I took my coffee, but I usually preferred it black. Not that Miles would know.

I doubted Liam even knew that.

The mere thought of my Alpha stained my mood, so I scrubbed his name from my brain and tipped the drink to my lips, drowning my smarting insides in sweetness and warmth. "Mmm. This is really good."

Miles stared and stared at my face, then averted his gaze and joggled his head. "Glad you like it."

Wow. Poor guy was several steps beyond frazzled.

I drank some more. "Miles, Bea and Nate made up."

His eyes rammed back into mine with such violence that I felt my eyeballs dip. "You're just saying that to make me—" He rubbed the back of his neck a tad spastically. "Please don't lie to me, Nikki."

"Lie? I'm not lying."

His sharp Adam's apple bobbed.

I wrapped my hands around the warm glass. "I swear, Miles."

He shut his eyes and pinched the bridge of his nose. "Is he going to fly out to meet her in . . . where is she again? Cambodia? Or is it Bhutan? Or is she back in South Korea visiting our cousin three times removed?"

I chewed on my lip, then took another sip of my mocha, trying to buy myself time to decide how to answer. In the end, I went with the truth. "No."

His lids flipped up. "They made up over the phone?"

How I wished I could just tell him the truth, but since I couldn't, I said, "Yes," then chased the bitter aftertaste of lying with more coffee.

He snorted, gripping the edge of the bar, muscles shifting like taut riggings.

"Phone her up right now and ask her, and she'll confirm it."

"I'd do it, but even though I'm not the little shit who broke up with her, Bea doesn't pick up my phone calls."

"Hey." I set my glass down hard. "That was uncalled for."

"Uncalled for?" He shoved away from the bar, his body vibrating from his cocktail of anger, stress, and fatigue.

"Yes. Uncalled for." I jolted to my feet.

The ground felt soft.

I reached out and grabbed ahold of the bar to steady myself. "Bea's the one who screwed up their relationship, *not* my brother."

He watched me with those narrowed, red-rimmed eyes of his.

"I came to share the good news, not to listen to you insult my family." I reached out for my bag. Instead of closing around the slouchy leather, my fingers carved through air and slapped the neighboring seat. "What did you—"

The sunlit room spun around Miles.

The barstool tipped, and tipped, and then its weight was towing me down. Down.

Down.

The realization that Miles must've dosed my coffee hit me at the same time as the floorboards of his restaurant.

CHAPTER 57

I tasted salt, copper, and sawdust.

Smelled pine and damp icy air.

I jerked awake.

Thin sunlight pressed against my eyes. Although they stung, I kept them open. After a couple sweeps of the room, the realization of where I'd been brought slotted into place.

The ratty corduroy couch.

Rattier table.

Mismatched everything.

Miles had drugged me to bring me to Bea's cabin? What the hell was wrong with him? Anger pulsed behind my lids. I tried to heave myself up, but the asshole had bound my wrists behind my back. He'd done the same to my ankles.

Gritting my teeth, I pulled on my arms to pop the duct tape off, but he'd wrapped it around so firmly it was a wonder blood still flowed into my fingertips. I growled my annoyance, then invoked my wolf, urged her to come forth and take over my weak human body.

However hard I tugged on that strand which connected my two selves, fur didn't sprout from my pores, fangs didn't sharpen my teeth, claws didn't curve from my nail beds.

Fear overtook my anger and pebbled my skin, because there was only one way to keep a werewolf in skin—Sillin. Not only did Miles know *what* I was, but he also knew how to weaken me.

How?

And what exactly was his plan? To use me as a bargaining chip to get his sister back?

I listened for voices, heartbeats. Caught the thump of one.

No. Not one . . .

Two.

A slow, human one—Miles—and a fast, lupine one.

That explained how he knew what I was: his werewolf companion must've filled him in. Now to understand who that companion was. I'd never been one to wait for things to come to me, so I opened my mouth, which he hadn't duct-taped—I suppose there wasn't much point in shutting me up when surrounded by miles upon miles of trees and lake and snow. I didn't even think that in wolf form, my howl would carry back to the compound.

"Miles?" I screeched. "Miles?"

The human pulse quickened, and then footsteps trampled snow and twigs. A second later, the doorknob spun and the front door squeaked open. I turned my head and watched my captor approach.

"What the hell? Why did you kidnap me?"

His jaw ticked. And ticked. He pursed his full lips, pressed them together, parted them. "You lied to me. You lied to me about Bea." He looked toward the door he hadn't shut, probably at his shifter companion.

"What exactly did your *friend* tell you?"

His eyes snapped to me. "What?"

"I know someone else is out there." I spoke this loud enough for the person to hear. Come to think of it, considering what they were, I could've whispered it and they'd still have heard me.

Shock momentarily warped Miles's crazed expression. He shifted on his heavy boots, then crossed his arms, creasing the sleeves of his winter jacket. "You lied to me, Nikki."

Even though I was curled up on my side like some hapless larva, the anger careening through me made me feel indomitable. "Yeah. And you fucking kidnapped me. On a scale of one to ten, what you did rates *way* higher than what I did. So now tell me what the coward hiding from me told you I lied about." I glared in the direction of the heartbeat pounding out of sight.

"You really aren't in any position to make demands."

"For Lycaon's sake, Miles, just tell me why you kidnapped me."

"To get your fucking brother to release my sister, that's why!"

"You could've gotten that without kidnapping me!"

He took a step closer and put one knee to the ground. "Don't you think I tried? I know Bea isn't traveling the world in search of herself." His voice was so loud it echoed between the low-timbered ceiling and beetle-eaten floor-boards. "I may be human, but I'm not an idiot."

Even though my brain felt like it was grinding against my skull, I twisted my neck to look up at him. "Call Nate. Call him and ask him to put Bea on the phone. She'll explain why she faked her traveling. I bet you, she'll even come out here and tell you herself."

He fisted his fingers, and his knuckles cracked. Was he going to hit me? Was whacking me with a gun *not* an accident? Was Miles the type of man who hit women? "You don't think I tried phoning your brother already? You don't think that was the first thing I did when your friend told me he was keeping her in a cage?"

"My friend?" I spat. "Obviously, your informant's not my friend, or I wouldn't be shot up with Sillin and tied up like some criminal." I glared at the door, wishing I had X-ray vision. "Bea's alive, Miles. She's alive and well. And *not* a prisoner."

Doubt sparked in his dark gaze, but it was quickly snuffed out. "If she were alive and *well*, then why doesn't she pick up my phone calls?"

"Because she was told to cut all contact with people outside the compound." I licked my lips, found the lower one swollen. I licked it again, tasted copper. I must've bitten it or hit something when I'd fallen. "Call her from my phone. She'll pick up."

A nerve ticked along his jaw. "I can't do that."

"Why not?"

"Because I didn't bring your phone, that's why. Didn't want anyone tracking you."

I blinked at him and then shook my head, probably picking up every dust mote in the process. "I'm guessing you know what I am. What my family is. Right?"

He dipped his chin, lips ironed shut.

"Do you really think my brothers and my *real* friends need cellular service to track me?"

A floorboard creaked, and then boots topped with slender legs came into view. I didn't need to trail my gaze any higher to figure out who'd filled Miles's head with lies.

CHAPTER 58

"They haven't tracked *me* yet," Camilla said pleasantly.

"But they will now," I replied, just as sweetly.

She smiled that disdainful smile of hers. "The only person who can get a read on our whereabouts is in Boulder. *Way* too far to locate us."

My mouth went dry because she was right. We were out of Liam's range. But then I remembered my appointment at the spa with Adalyn. The second I didn't show, she'd know something was wrong. And then my brothers would know, and they'd come looking, and they'd find my car parked in town, and they'd track my smell to Seoul Sister. Renewed confidence extinguished my flare of panic.

As though she'd caught on to my train of thought, the raised corners of Camilla's lips flattened.

I turned my attention back to Miles. "Bea isn't a prisoner, Miles, and Camilla would know this if she hadn't fled with her tail between her legs after she gunned down the woman who saved your sister's life. Did Camilla happen to mention she's a murderer when she roped you into whatever little scheme you two came up with?"

Miles stiffened. Even the bags underneath his eyes seemed to firm up. He swung his head around to look at the blonde, green-eyed traitor. "What is she talking about?"

Camilla's answer was slow to come, the same way her gaze was slow to lift from me and settle on Miles. "You want your sister back or not?"

He gave an almost imperceptible nod.

"Then just stick to the plan. Nikki's your ticket to getting Bea released from her cage."

"She's not in a cage! She's not a prisoner!" Losing my temper was probably not the wisest plan of action considering my prostrate posture, but I was a bargaining chip, and bargaining chips were useless dead. The conviction that neither of my captors was going to kill me gave my tongue wings. "Do you know the full story? Has Camilla told you everything?"

"She told me your kind imprisons and kills their human exes so your existence isn't revealed."

"That's a lie."

"No, it isn't." Camilla stepped farther inside the house. "I can list a whole bunch of humans who died unexpectedly around these parts over the years."

She was bluffing. She had to be bluffing. But that was besides the current point.

"Bea's neither Nate's ex nor his prisoner. But yeah, she's not supposed to leave the compound because, what she also *isn't*, is human. Your sister, Miles, wanted to become one of us, so she asked a shifter named Lori to bite her."

Miles's eyebrows writhed, knitted, lowered.

"Except wolves can't be made; they can only be born. I can prove it." Camilla plucked one of Miles's arms from their knot and raised it to her mouth, then sank her already elongated fangs into his skin.

Startled, he didn't push her away. And then his eyes glazed over. Of course, she'd injected him with her venom to make him pliant. Camilla was a lot of things but unfortunately not stupid. When she unhooked her teeth from his body, he'd gone so limp I worried he'd collapse. But he didn't. Just blinked at Camilla as though she were the most fascinating being he'd ever laid eyes on, while his blood dripped onto the floor beside my head.

When he finally snapped out of his daze, he snatched his arm up, cocooning it in front of his heaving chest. "What have you done?"

"I bit you."

His eyes rounded in terror, and he backed up, hitting the couch and falling onto it.

Camilla smirked. "Chill, Miles. You're not a wolf."

"How—how do I know that?"

"Can you do this?" She rammed her hoodie sleeve up. Her fingers retracted until her hand morphed into a paw and yellow fur sprouted from her skin.

He blinked at her, no longer so enchanted, then squinted at his hand.

"See. Human. Just like your sister."

"Miles, call my brother. Call him and put him on speakerphone, and he'll confirm everything I told you."

"Of course he will." Camilla dropped into a crouch and patted my cheek with her bloodied fingers. "He'll say anything to keep you on the line while he tracks his beloved sister."

"Miles—"

Camilla slapped me, the violence and shock cutting off my breath. "If you want to save Bea, stick to the plan."

As I stared into the mossy depths of her eyes, I saw Grant. "This is all about her brother, Miles. Camilla doesn't care about Bea. She made you kidnap me to get her brother back."

A smile sawed across her face. "Miles knows I have a vested interest in all of this."

"Liam will never release your brother."

Her hand stilled on my cheek, and her smile strengthened. "If I'd wanted my brother to go free, I would've kidnapped Liam's son."

The mere idea of her taking Storm made me want to slash her face. "Then why did you kidnap me?"

"Why, to help Miles get his sister back, of course."

My confusion shot up a notch. "You expect me to believe you orchestrated this whole thing for nothing in return?"

"Oh, I'm getting something in return. My freedom. My *true* freedom."

"How—" My lids slammed up. "You're going to kill Liam?"

She hooked her thumbs under a strap which I realized was hooked onto a shotgun. The one she'd probably shot Lori with. She pulled it away from her chest and threaded her head out.

"Miles?" I yelled. "Are you hearing this? She's insane!"

She glanced over her shoulder at where he sat, hands clasping his knees, lashes fluttering, eyes fixed on nothing. "That's not a very nice thing to say, Nikki."

I glared at her, then cranked my head back. "Miles!"

She kicked me in the stomach, and I gasped.

"Quit shouting already."

"Or what? You'll kill me? That'd ruin your whole plan. You need me alive."

She hit me again, this time with the butt of her rifle and straight in the knee.

I cried out, then gritted my teeth as the crate-sized living room went in and out of focus, and sweat dotted my forehead. "She's going to get you killed, Miles. Don't you see that?"

Camilla grinned. "He doesn't see that, because he's not smart like you, Nikki." Her words were still registering on his face when she shouldered her gun, racked it, and fired off a shot that went right through his torso, blowing it wide open. She lowered the gun. "He was surprisingly efficient, though."

Miles's chin slumped against his chest as though he were checking out his injury, and then his whole body listed to the side, and he toppled, blood and intestines spilling onto the couch and slinking to the floor.

I screamed. Bile soared up my throat and spewed out.

"Then again, you're an easy girl. You should really work on that. Not being so"—she wrinkled her nose—"promiscuous."

"He was my friend."

She regarded him again with her head cocked to the side. "You should probably pick better friends."

Another bloodied piece of him slithered from the crater of his chest.

"Anyway, time to get setup so we can welcome all your saviors properly."

"Liam won't come, Camilla."

"Sure he will."

"We broke up, so no, he won't."

"Shit. Grant was right. You really are *loose*." She looped the strap of her shotgun back over her head. "Doesn't much matter whether you two are screwing. You're his shifter, and like the good Alpha he believes himself to be, he'll come to save his little wolf."

"He won't." *Please, please, please, Liam, don't come.*

"Maybe at first. But eventually, once the dead bodies start piling up, he will."

"How many people are you planning to kill?"

"However many it takes to get to him." She retrieved her phone from her jacket pocket and held it out. I was guessing she wasn't looking for a signal. She tapped her screen a few times. "There. The video's in both Liam's and Nate's inboxes. How long do you think it'll take them to come? Fifty minutes? An hour?" She tugged her ponytail free from the strap of her shotgun. "Probably less. Your brother . . . brothers are *really* crazy about you. Might take Liam longer since he's in Boulder, though."

Terror seized me. I shook so hard my teeth chattered. "Camilla, don't do this. Don't—I'll help you free Grant."

She snorted a chuckle. "My brother's a dumbass. I told him to run after he planted the Molotov cocktail, and what does he do? He returns to the compound. I mean . . . Darwinistically-speaking, our species is better off without him."

The rancid smell of death pressed in around me, made my insides heave anew. I wondered, as I expelled the remaining contents of my stomach, if the Sillin was out of my system. I called upon my wolf. She didn't rise.

"He's your brother. He loves you. If the situation were reversed, he'd do anything to break you free."

"If the situation were reversed, I'd be as good as dead considering his ineptitude." Camilla's ponytail flopped over her shoulder as she crouched beside me again. "Enough talking. Let's get you situated." Her claws curled from her nail beds, sharp as shivs. She slashed the duct tape around my ankles but not the one binding my wrists. "Don't feel like dragging you, but if you try anything, I won't hesitate to blast off your leg. The one that still works," she added with a curl of lip.

Camilla Hollis had always been borderline—the *shoot-first ask-questions-later* type—but cruelty was new. Or maybe it wasn't. Maybe she'd always been inherently vicious. Apples, after all, didn't fall far from the tree.

"Get up, Nikki!"

Between my trussed hands and the slippery floor, getting myself upright proved tricky, but the acrid reek of vomit and hemorrhaging body spurred me into motion. I rolled myself to sitting and then to standing.

My throbbing knee caused my legs to wobble. I probably would've crumpled had Camilla not clasped my bicep and hauled me out the door, toward the blinding-white arena in which she planned to wage her war against Liam. Against our pack.

A war which I prayed to Lycaon no one would charge into blindly.

CHAPTER 59

Camilla dragged me out onto the icy lake. Where her steps never faltered, I skidded in my sneakers. The wind whooshed around us, bending the crowns of the evergreens that cinched the enormous lake, burning my skin through the thin cotton sleeves of my long cardigan. My coat was at home, and my hair, although loose and long, offered little protection from the brutal elements.

I tried to coax fur from my pebbling skin, but the dose of Sillin I'd been given still stymied my magic. Perhaps I could fool my body into believing the air was a balmy seventy degrees if I repeated *I am not cold* enough times.

"So, what's the plan? A round of figure skating?" I was trying to crack the tape on my wrists but was merely succeeding at making it bunch up and cut into my flesh.

A low swish lapped at the hardened crust beneath my rubber soles. I kept my eyes on it, trying to decide if I wanted it to crack or not.

On the one hand, it would destabilize Camilla.

On the other, I'd go down with her, and without the use of my arms, getting out would be challenging. I reminded myself that seals didn't have hands, and they managed just fine.

Camilla whistled as she hauled me along, stopping only once we reached the very center of the lake. "So the plan is, we're going to get comfortable out here. I want to make sure Liam can see us."

Or rather, that she could see him.

The barrel of her shotgun poked out from behind her shoulder, blazing silver beneath the bright sun. If only I could grab it and pry it away from her. Trying to keep my shoulders stationary, I worked my hands harder, trying to create space where there was none.

Unhurriedly, Camilla rooted around the giant pockets of her knee-length puffer coat and fished out two pairs of cuffs. "It's not that I don't trust you, but yeah, I don't trust you."

She kneeled and slapped one cuff around my ankle. I almost kicked her with my free foot, but her threat of shooting my leg off hadn't sounded like a bluff. Alternating waves of heat and cold smacked into me as I pulled and pulled on my hands.

As she snapped the second cuff in place, the duct tape rolled to the widest part of my hand.

Almost.

I was almost free. Another few seconds and—My hand slid out. I slammed my fist against her jaw, right at the juncture of her mandible. Her face jerked to the side, but somehow . . . *somehow* the impact didn't tip her.

Niall had made me practice this move over and over. He'd sworn that a well-placed punch to the jaw was as potent as one between the legs.

Why hadn't it worked? Had I not hit hard enough?

Camilla lunged back and swung her gun, leveling the muzzle on me. "I said, don't try anything, and what do you do? You go try something. Now what part of your body are you willing to live without? How about your hands? You need them for your fancy artmaking, don't you?"

Blanching, I hid them behind my back. They trembled. All of me trembled.

"Pull your hands out."

"I won't try anything again. I swear."

"Pull your fucking hands out from behind your back."

"If you blow off my hands, you won't be able to cuff me."

"If I blow them off, I won't *need* to cuff you. Your hands, Nikki."

"You want my hands? Then you'll have to go through my body. The second you do, Liam will feel I'm dead, and he won't come."

Her nostrils flared. "You're a real pain in the ass, you know that?" She tossed the cuffs at me, whacking me in the stomach. "Put them on, or I *will* shoot off your legs. Both of them."

Afraid to reach down and expose my hands, I shuffled around the cuffs, so that my back was to her, then crouched as best I could with bound ankles and picked up the metal bracelets.

"What the hell are you doing?" she barked.

"I'm putting the cuffs on."

"Turn around."

After I snapped both loosely in place, I turned, making sure to keep my hands leveled with my heart.

She took a step forward, then prodded the cuffs with the muzzle. When they didn't clatter off, she settled the gun astride her spine again and stepped forward to squeeze the cuffs until they were jammed so snugly around my wrists I had no hope of freeing my hands.

"That's better." Her phone rang. She backed up a step to extricate it. After a cursory glance at her screen, she raised the cheap mobile and said, "Cheese." After sending off the picture she'd taken of me, she explained, "They wanted proof of life."

Which meant Liam hadn't left Boulder yet, or he'd have sensed my heartbeats.

Maybe he wasn't coming after all.

Maybe he trusted that his new Beta and my brothers would accomplish this rescue mission just fine without him.

I refused to be dismayed if he didn't show.

After all, I'd prayed to Lycaon he'd stay away.

After pocketing her phone, Camilla pulled her coat open, revealing not only a Kevlar jacket but a holstered gun, the type my cop brother carried—small, black, automatic. "You may want to sit down. It's going to be a while."

I remained standing, wondering if she'd picked this spot because of its unobstructed vista of the surrounding land or because she planned on using the ice against me.

Against the pack.

"Suit yourself." She retreated to the shore and crouched next to it.

The crush of nylon followed by the rustle of a zipper animated the stark silence. Camilla straightened and jammed a bright-orange helmet onto her head, then turned and lowered the visor. The sight of it dried my tongue and propelled me back to a time and place I yearned to forget. The looming tree trunk flickered in front of my lids, the bang of metal reverberated inside my ears, the reek of flames chewing through fuel and flesh assaulted my nostrils.

I forced back the memory by focusing all my gray matter on the ice's subtle pops and groans, on the water's sporadic gurgle and muted slosh, until my dire present smothered my dismal past.

A crack, thin as a hairline fracture, veined the translucent whiteness between my shoes. I held my breath, fearful that so much as breathing in its

329

direction might tear my raft apart. But then I glanced back in Camilla's direction, found her lumbering back toward me, bulky in her makeshift armor.

My limbs might be bound, but I wasn't weighted down like Camilla. I began to shuffle again. When that didn't widen the crack, I hopped in place, gritting my molars against the brutal ache in my knee.

"What the hell are you doing?"

Come on, ice. Come on. "Trying to keep warm."

Something glared and clanked in one of her fists. It took my sore eyes a second to make out what it was: a heavy chain. That would help her sink nicely.

I hopped harder and faster, a bunny on LSD.

What sounded like faraway cannon fire roiled around us. The lake was awakening.

Camilla grinned, maniac that she was. "You're impatient."

To be rid of you.

My rubber sole landed on a particularly slick spot, and I lost my balance, smacking down so hard I heard a crack. I figured it was my tailbone since the ice beneath my smarting ass held.

I could feel the roused water beneath me. Could feel its lapping tongue and liquid entrails. If only it could split open and swallow Camilla. I fixed my gaze on her cleated boots, wishing hard for each step to be her last. Soon, she was standing over me, her helmet casting my face in shadow.

I licked my split-lip. "What are you planning to do with that chain?"

"Why . . . secure us, so that if we go down, we go down together."

Although I could no longer see her eyes through the mirrored visor, I could feel their malevolence. "We don't need to go down at all. We can stay up."

She grabbed the links between my handcuffs and hauled me to my feet. "Your fate rests in Liam's hands, Nikki, not in mine." She looped the chain around my waist twice, then spun me so that my back was to her front, and proceeded to wrap it around her waist before securing the ends with a heavy metal padlock. "He lets me shoot him, and you and I live. He fights me. And we both die."

Heat billowed off Camilla's body, warming mine. At least, I wouldn't freeze to death.

Unless the ice cracked.

Then I'd freeze.

And quite possibly die.

I tried conjuring up my wolf again. Failed. So I conjured up the next greatest weapon I possessed: my notorious optimism.

Camilla was too close to turn me inside out with her shotgun, and the ice was really very thick.

"I'm not dying today." I said this out loud, not so much for Camilla's sake, but for mine.

Her helmet pressed uncomfortably into the back of my skull. "Then I guess I'm not either."

Even though there was nothing romantic or magical about my connection to Camilla, I finally understood why Liam was so against being bound to another.

Because this was how he perceived mating bonds.

Two bodies shackled together for better or for worse.

CHAPTER 60

Time became elastic as I stood pressed against Camilla with the song of the wind on my skin, the caress of the sun on my numb cheeks, and the slap of the water against my eardrums.

Minutes passed. Some stretched into full hours; others snapped like mere seconds.

I spent each one analyzing how to use our proximity to Liam's advantage.

"Finally," she whispered, her breath pluming out and dangling like a cloud in front of my face.

A single heartbeat, that was neither mine nor Camilla's, stirred the air.

While my gaze plundered the shoreline and the shadows coalescing between the dense evergreens, Camilla readjusted her stance. Was she reaching for her shotgun?

How I wished I didn't have my back turned, because not knowing what was going on wreaked havoc on my cortisol levels. I discovered what she was up to soon enough, though. She jammed a cold, cylindrical object against the underside of my jaw.

Crap.

The handgun.

The foreign heartbeat quickened, and a twig snapped. I swiveled my head in the direction of the noise, finding only the darkened air of the forest.

Was Liam here? Or one of my brothers?

Another wooden crack, this time behind us.

More than one shifter had come.

Camilla spun me around, the gun never moving off my throat.

Adrenaline spiked inside my veins, sharpening my senses. Something odd struck me. There was only one *other* heartbeat, not two. Even at full speed, a shifter wouldn't have been able to circle the lake that fast. Not even an Alph—

Bea! Bea could move that fast!

"Of course he sent a scout ahead of him," Camilla gritted out. "Probably one of your brothers. Such a fucking coward."

So she too knew it was only one shifter, and yet didn't she find their velocity odd?

She jammed the gun harder into my throat. "Whoever's out there, you can report to Liam that if any attempt's made on my life, I won't hesitate to shoot Nikki or break the ice beneath our feet and sink her."

"You'd sink with me," I reminded her, surprising myself with how cool and collected I sounded.

"I have a tiny secret weapon," she breathed into my ear. "A key."

And I had a huge secret weapon: my vampiric future sister-in-law who could move and heal superfast.

Could she heal from a gunshot wound, though?

There was no room for fear inside my brain, but somehow, there was room for doubt. And that doubt gnawed at me. What was Liam planning? Had he even sent Bea, or had she come of her own free will? How long had it been since Camilla made the call?

Maybe he'd sent Bea, so he wouldn't need to endanger any of his shifters' lives.

Even as I thought it, I realized how unlike Liam that would be. Sure, he was good at delegating, but he always got involved.

Another twig snapped. This time, I was facing the right portion of forest and caught the human shape streaking between the trunks. Camilla did too. She whipped the gun off my skin and fired a shot, the gun so close to my ears, it felt like my right drum shattered.

I leave Beaver Creek for one day, and what do you do? You go ice-fishing with a criminal? I can think of several better ways to spend a pleasant Sunday afternoon. None of them involve frozen lakes or guns.

I snorted.

Oh, and before I forget, Lucas told me to relay that he's pissed, because you made him lose the bet he's got going with Reese. Apparently they wagered a large sum of money that he'd be the one to locate Camilla.

I didn't want to laugh, but my nerves were so shot the sound leaped out of me.

"What the hell are you snickering about?" Camilla growled.

Searching the darkness for Liam, I said, "You never had much of a sense of humor, so you wouldn't get it."

She jammed the gun into my jaw. "Try. Me."

"Fine. Fine. Liam made a joke, and it was surprisingly funny even though his sense of humor's not all that great either."

Ouch.

I squinted to see where he was, but the sun glaring off the ice blackened the forest beyond. "I admit I was wrong and you were right, Camilla. I didn't think Liam would come."

You didn't think I'd come?

I pressed my lips together, hunting the darkness for glowing yellow eyes.

"Since you're here, Liam, kindly show yourself!" Camilla bellowed.

The crunch of hardened snow echoed all around us.

The gun muzzle dug harder into my skin.

"How kind of you to come to us, Camilla." Liam's voice resonated, human and deep.

Massive furred bodies rocketed around the tawny trunks, moving too fast for me to make out whom they belonged to.

"Plan on hiding for much longer, Liam?" Camilla screeched beside my still-ringing ear.

How do you feel about swimming, babe?

Better than I feel about being called babe. I telegraphed my thoughts through a pointed glower, but then realized he might construe my look as reticence for his aquatic plan.

I directed my eyeballs downward toward the metal chain around my middle, then shuffled a step to make the cuffs clink. I imagined he was already aware I was trussed up like Dad and Nolan's Thanksgiving turkeys, but it didn't hurt to bring my poultry status to his attention.

You think you can hold your breath for two minutes?

I gave the faintest nod, my heart fluttering wildly in my chest.

"Li-am," Camilla singsonged. "I'm losing patience."

A muted pop whispered through the ice, followed by a pale laceration.

I inhaled a deep breath.

Not yet. I'll tell you when.

Another wet grinding.

Camilla's body hardened. "If you don't quit whatever you're doing, I'll put a bullet through your girlfriend's skull before she hits the water."

"I'm not his girlfriend."

"What is it I'm doing, Camilla?"

She pivoted toward the sound of Liam's deep voice, forcing me to turn. "I'm going to count down to three."

Out of the corner of my eye, I caught the flurry of movement. A lithe body running wide circles around us on the ice, stopping every few feet to crouch, explode upward, and land so hard the ice trembled beneath us.

"What the hell's that?" Camilla slid the gun off me and leveled it in the direction of the blurred form.

That, ladies and gentlemen, is Bea, I thought proudly.

Camilla fired off three bullets. One of them resulted in a whimper that made the fine hairs on my arms rise. Bea crumpled on the ice like a tissue.

"Shouldn't have let the vampwolf out of her cage," Camilla murmured, compressing her finger on the trigger.

I jammed my shoulder into her raised arm, jostling it. The shot went wide. I prayed it didn't hit anyone.

She swung the gun back toward the bloodied ice upon which Bea had lain only a moment ago. She was gone. Had someone collected her, or had she gotten up and sped away?

Grumbling, Camilla rammed the barrel of her gun into my neck. "Come the fuck out, Liam, or the next bullet's for Nikki!"

The ice shifted beneath my feet. I tried to look down, but Camilla's gun was keeping my head tipped back.

"You win, Camilla. I'm coming out."

He was bluffing. He had to be bluffing.

A tall, broad figure materialized in the darkness of the forest, stark naked. Camilla snapped the gun off my chin and pointed it at the body.

"NO!" I screamed.

Now!

She fired.

The bullet hit its mark.

Blood spurted.

The body listed.

Toppled.

I screamed.

The ice webbed beneath my feet.

Split.

I fell backward, splashing into the frigid water, and sank like an anchor.

335

CHAPTER 61

I snapped my mouth shut, trapping the measly amount of oxygen nestled inside my lungs.

The image of the blood spraying from the naked male coupled with the shriek of the bullet made me convulse.

The chain around my waist jangled.

The cuffs too.

The surface glittered with sunlight and shifting sheets of ice as we drifted downward.

How deep was this lake?

Camilla twisted behind me, her helmet biting into the back of my skull. Tiny air bubbles fled my nostrils as something brushed against my legs—a fish, pondweed? Metal clicked, and then the weight digging into my waist slipped off when Camilla untied us. I imagined it wasn't to save me.

Sure enough, the second we hit the sandy bottom, she propelled herself away from me, tossing off her helmet, which fell like a bowling ball next to my leg and raised tongues of gray particles. She tried to grab the shotgun strapped to her back, but her movements were clumsy and slow, made even more so by her heavy jacket and Kevlar vest.

My lungs squeezed. Soon, they'd start burning, and the countdown to their emptiness would begin.

I set my teeth and stared upward, past my hair which floated like dark seaweed around my face. I estimated the depth was thirty-something feet. All in all, not insurmountable. If I pushed off the sand and wriggled like a worm on Speed, I could probably surface in under a minute, but I'd have to get going now.

Something landed beside me—the shotgun. Camilla saw me peer at it. Probably thinking I was going to seize it, she flipped around and swam for it, fingers already outstretched. Perhaps I should've gone for the gun, but bullets didn't travel as accurately or speedily in water as they did on land. Not to mention, I could hardly rack a shotgun with bound hands.

I stared at my cuffs and then stared at the girl within my reach.

When her fingers closed around the barrel of her firearm, I made a split-second decision.

One that would cost both of us greatly.

I stretched out my arms in front of me, levitated onto my knees, and snared Camilla's downturned head. She jerked, then bucked, but not before I managed to yank my elbows back and crush her larynx with the chain linking the cuffs.

For better or for worse, Camilla.
Looks like it's going to be for worse.

CHAPTER 62

M y lungs had gone past burning; they blazed. And still I didn't loosen the noose of chain and arms around Camilla's neck. She thrashed, grabbing fistfuls of my hair, pulling. I held strong.

Silt and sand shimmered around us, thickening as Camilla fought. I blinked, but the world didn't brighten. It was as though the sun were setting, but the sun wouldn't set over Colorado for a few more hours.

Over me, though . . .

I smooshed my lips together. I wasn't ready to let go. Not of Camilla and not of my life.

Camilla threw out a jerky kick that didn't meet its mark, unless her mark was a clump of pondweeds. My lungs tightened, folding in on themselves like an origami, desperately trying to trap the last crumbs of oxygen.

The current shifted, shoved against me. As I tipped, as the light waned and the lake became overcast, Camilla's fingers slackened around my hair.

Ah . . . that felt nice.

Bubbles popped against my cheeks.

I saw Liam then, but it was probably only in my mind, because his face was chalky and gray as though I'd lowered the saturation and applied a blurry filter.

I hoped Camilla's bullet had missed his heart because Storm needed him. The pack needed him. I tried to feel the Alpha tether, but my body felt as unsubstantial as a fern caught in a summer breeze.

The weight of the lake, the gallons and gallons of water sat on my lids, on my ribs, on my lungs. I parted my lips to alleviate the pressure, and icy slush snaked into my chest, doused the fire in my ribcage.

My body rose, weightless, numb, empty.

Was I on my way to Lycaon's den of stars?

I still had so many goals I wanted to accomplish. So many people I wanted to hold. So many *I love you*s to speak. Had I told my parents recently? My brothers? Adalyn?

I tried to fight the ascension but had depleted my strength on the lake floor.

Was Camilla rising toward Lycaon, too?

I couldn't see her.

Couldn't see anything.

Or hear anything.

But I could feel something.

A repetitive pressure on my chest.

On my cheeks.

On my lips.

And then a deep growl resonated inside my skull, **Come back, Nikki. Come back to me.**

Liam? He was alive?

Did hearing him mean I was as well?

Or were we both dead?

My lungs seized and thrust a jet of liquid up my throat. I gasped. Vomited. Gasped again. Vomited some more.

Oxygen streaked down my throat like sunlight, puffed up my shriveled lungs. My chest heaved again, but nothing more came out. Everything was now coming in.

Air.

Noise.

Light.

Pain.

Someone wept softly beside me.

I blinked my heavy lids open. Blinked them some more.

The first face I saw was Liam's, complexion pale, lashes clumped, black V-neck plastered to a rapidly heaving chest. Rivulets of water ran off his hair and dripped against my neck.

"You're alive," I murmured. "How are you alive? Camilla shot you."

"It wasn't me." His chin dipped as his gaze raked over my bruised lip, my wet clothes, my wounded wrists and ankles.

"But I saw—"

A muffled sob carried my attention away from my Alpha, who was rising to his feet.

"Oh, Nikki," my mother croaked, her eyes so red they almost resembled Bea's.

"Mom . . . you're here."

"Where else would I be?" Her lower lip overtook her upper one. "Oh, Nikki. Oh, sweetheart."

Dad draped his arm around her, his face pressing in close. "How many times are you planning on testing the durability of our hearts, Pinecone?"

"I'm sorry, Dad." I tried to extend my arm to touch my parents, but my wrists were still bound. As were my ankles.

"What the actual fuck, Nik?" Nash and Nolan said at the very same time.

Niall stabbed a quivering hand through his wet hair, turning it as spiky as the twins'. "Can you quit hanging with people wearing the last name Hollis?"

Adalyn, whose eyes and cheeks were smudged with mascara and tears, shoved between the twins to reach me. Her mouth opened as though she was about to say something. Closed. Opened. Closed again, before settling into a smile-sob combo.

Nash draped his arm around her shoulders and tugged her to him.

I swallowed as my gaze cycled around the circle of familial faces. One was missing.

"Where's Nate?" My pulse quickened as I remembered Bea's prone form, the bloodstained ice. "And Bea?"

Niall leaned back, and I caught sight of my eldest brother and Bea.

"We're right here, Pinecone." Both Nate's white shirt and undershirt were plastered to his torso and pinked with blood.

"I'm so sorry, Nikki," Bea whispered, playing with the hem of her steel-gray tee which bore a hole under her left breast. "I tried to get to you before you went under, but—"

"You were shot," I said. "She shot you."

"Yeah." Bea wrinkled her nose. "I didn't factor in how good she was with firearms."

I propped myself up on one forearm, teeth chattering. "How are you—standing right now? How are you—alive?"

"Easy there, girl." Nolan put a hand to my spine to help me sit while Dad draped his jacket around my shoulders.

"I'm okay, Nolan."

Niall added his hands to the mix. "Five minutes ago, you weren't breathing, sis."

That set Mom off again. She burrowed her face against Dad's neck and honked like a goose.

"Niall," Nolan chided him softly.

The youngest of my brothers grimaced.

"Any chance someone can get these off me?" I held my cuffed wrists out.

Nash's glassy blue gaze flicked to where Liam had retreated. "Li—"

"Why bother him when the woman who single-handedly cleaved open a frozen lake, is sitting right here?" Adalyn shot me a meaningful look. "I bet cuffs are putty in her hands."

Bea looked at Liam. When he nodded, giving her permission to undertake the job he could've accomplished in a heartbeat, she kneeled beside me. Her slender fingers wrapped around the cuffs and ripped them open.

"Like I said . . . putty." Adalyn sat back on her heels.

I rubbed the violet circles of injured skin. "Now can you tell me how you're seemingly fine after being shot in the chest?"

Bea tipped her neck back to look at Nate. "The bullet . . . it sort of . . . *popped* out on its own. And then my skin sealed."

My bloated eyes widened. "Did it injure your rib cage? Or any of your organs?"

She shook her head, her gaze straying to the cabin. When a scarlet tear raced down her cheek, I stopped trying to piece together what had happened.

Later.

I'd get a play-by-play later.

I reached out and covered one of the hands she'd curled atop her thighs. "Bea, I'm sorry about Miles."

The pop of the shell, the rip of flesh, the dripping organs. I shook my head to rid my mind of the macabre memory.

"My fault." A tremor raced through her body, blurring all her toughened edges. "My goddamn fault." She swiped her cheeks, spreading the red paint of her sorrow. "I didn't deserve to survive that bullet."

Nate scowled. "Don't say that, Bea. *Don't.* All that happened since the full moon run was entirely Camilla's fault. Not yours. *Hers.*"

Her lashes swept down over those peculiar ruby eyes of hers.

Nate crouched beside her and wrapped an arm around her hunched shoulders, drawing her trembling body against his and kissing her rumpled brow.

I squinted at the lake beyond them, at the crowd of shifters in fur and skin milling around. "Is she dead?"

My question had some darting glances my way; one stared steadily—Liam.

She is. "Would you like to see her?"

"Liam," Mom and Adalyn hissed in unison.

"I don't think—" Mom started.

"Yes." I stood. Wobbled. Found my balance thanks to Niall and Nolan. Kept it too, thanks to them, since neither agreed to release me when I told them I was good.

In truth, I probably wasn't.

After fitting my shaking arms through the sleeves of Dad's coat, they led me to the water's edge where Camilla's supine body bobbed against icy shards and wet pebbles.

Without flinching, I observed the bluish tint of her lips, the unseeing green of her irises fixed on the sky, the purple bruises circling her throat like those plastic chokers Ads and I used to wear as tweens.

I guess it was for the better for me and the worse for you.

Slowly, I lifted my eyes off her and twisted around to look at Liam. I scanned his chest, his stomach, looking for the telltale shape of a bandage. "If she didn't shoot you, who did she shoot?"

"Grant," Niall said.

My head jerked back. "She shot her own brother?"

"I know." Niall sighed. "I was really looking forward to ending his life myself."

"Niall!" I gasped.

"What?"

"You're not a killer."

"Don't want to share the spotlight?" He hefted a dramatic sigh. "Fine."

I froze as his words cemented themselves onto my skull.

I glanced back at Camilla, willing myself to feel regret.

I didn't.

Not only was I a killer, but I was a coldblooded one.

Shame heated my cheeks and curdled my heart.

Extricating my arms from my brothers' grip, I limped away from Camilla and the girl she'd turned me into.

CHAPTER 63

"How do you want your eggs, honey?" Dad asked as I took a seat at the island, in front of an already consequential amount of food.

"Fertilized?" Niall coughed under his breath.

I rolled eyes that a full twelve hours of uninterrupted sleep hadn't managed to deflate.

"How old are you again?" Adalyn flicked the back of his neck as she walked past him, carrying a mug of coffee which she set in front of me. "Black."

"Just like her murderess heart," Nash quipped from where he was dutifully cutting up strawberries and tossing them into a giant bowl.

"Nash!" Adalyn's eyes widened.

"What? Too soon?"

She placed a protective hand on my shoulder. "It will always be too soon."

As everyone grew silent, unsure how to proceed around me, I tipped the mug to my lips and drank a scorching sip of coffee. It didn't taste like the coffee I'd had yesterday, yet it propelled me to Seoul Sister, to the cabin in the woods, to the lake.

Gunshots clamored inside my skull.

My hands began to shake. Coffee sloshed over the rim and singed my skin. I set my mug down and dried my fingers on my napkin just as the front door opened, letting in a gust of frigid air and the scent of . . .

Liam stepped into the kitchen doorway and removed his baseball cap. "Hi."

I lowered myself from my seat.

His dark eyes sparked as I approached. Little did he know I wasn't going to him. I limped past where he stood, my knee purple from where Camilla had hit it with the butt of her rifle. I clung to the handrail, using it to hoist myself up the stairs and back into my bedroom.

Hushed conversations erupted in the kitchen. My father, forever the homemaker, asked Liam if he wanted anything to eat. Liam turned him down. Mom asked after Storm. Did he need help later on? I cinched my lids shut, hoping he'd refuse. I wanted to see Storm but if he called me mama, it'd rip all the tape I'd pasted on my heart.

I leaned against my bedroom door, curling my shaky fingers into fists.

The stairs creaked, and then Liam's smell billowed around the edges of the wood. *Nikki, can we talk?*

I closed my eyes.

"Nikki?"

"Go away."

"Babe, please."

"Don't call me that," I snapped.

His frustrated sigh seeped into the wood. "I just want to talk."

"And I just want to be left alone."

Silence settled between us, as thick and heavy as the heat hissing from my radiator.

"When?" Liam added no other word.

I licked my bottom lip. Still a little swollen. "When what?"

"When will you be ready to talk?"

"To you? Possibly never. I'd rather save my breath for people who actually listen."

The floorboards creaked outside my bedroom. "I deserved that."

I pushed away from the door and went to stand by my window, my socked feet skimming the pull-out mattress on which Adalyn had spent the night. She'd claimed it was tradition to avoid the groom until the wedding night, but I knew this had nothing to do with a time-honored custom.

Nikki?

I didn't answer this time. I'd told him I didn't want to talk and yet I'd talked. I was done talking.

After several long minutes, he loosed another breath and left. He must've felt my stare on him as he walked away from the house, because he turned around and craned his neck. I backed up. When my calves hit the mattress, I sank onto it.

A KNOCK ON MY DOOR DIVERTED MY ATTENTION FROM THE PLAY OF shadows across my striped pink-and-beige rug. "Honey, can I come in?"

"Sure, Mom."

She entered, holding a steaming mug of tea and my handbag. "Nate and Bea brought this back." She put it on my desk chair. "And they drove your car back."

"How is she?"

"Brave. She's being extremely brave." Mom walked over and handed me the tea.

I scooted up, resting my back against my headboard, and took the proffered mug. "When's the burial?"

"There isn't going to be one."

I frowned.

"They burned the cabin down after we left. Too many dead bodies to cover up."

"But there'll be a ceremony, right?" Minty steam curled off my tea and warmed my cheeks.

"After the wedding." Mom traced the vow tattooed on her finger: *You are my sun, my wind, my home.*

"Have you forgiven her?"

Her thumb slid off the word *home*. "Misguided love is still love."

"What's that supposed to mean?"

"Bea was afraid of losing your brother, and her fear drove her to act rashly." She paused. Then, "A little like Liam."

I towed my lashes down. "What he did and what Bea did aren't remotely the same."

"Aren't they, though?"

"No."

She leaned forward, cupped my cheeks, and pressed her lips to my forehead, held them there. Her familiar scent of cloves and caramel enveloped me, sweetening some of the leftover bitterness. "Not everyone is as emotionally intrepid as you are, my darling girl."

Emotionally intrepid? More like emotionally naïve.

Her strange compliment replayed inside my mind long after she left. I feared losing people just as much as the next person. Just because I didn't try to alter myself or push others away didn't make me brave.

CHAPTER 64

The compound was aflutter with wedding preparations. Boxes of
tinsel and fairy lights were being toted out of cabins and carried or
driven over to Pondside. Laughter rang out from every home, and
easy smiles were being tossed around like snowballs.

From great tragedies sprang great joy. Such was life, an alternating series of
peaks and valleys.

I was glad we were on the uptick and secretly hoped we'd plateau, because
I could do with a few years of uninterrupted happiness.

When I reached Pondside at sunset, Grandma Reeves, who'd requisitioned
her entire bingo team to decorate, and Mom, who'd called up all her friends
and their husbands, were in full stage-director mode. Standing in the middle
of the dark, glittery room, I slow-twirled to take in its beauty.

I offered to help and was sent to assist Sasha behind the bar to uncork the
wine. Not an especially challenging task, even though there were close to a
hundred bottles to open. Perhaps sensing I wasn't feeling especially talkative,
Sasha filled the silence. He told me about his latest invention—a knitting
machine for his mother—and his grandfather's garage band—*The Grandpops*—
which played electronic bluegrass. Apparently, they'd offered to perform
tomorrow. Sasha hadn't known how to turn them down, so he'd asked Nolan
for help. My brother had been so impressed he'd ended up hiring them.

"I'm not sure what electronic bluegrass sounds like," I admitted.

"It's like instrumental country."

"That's neat."

Sasha grinned.

Niall arrived then, along with Sarah, Lucas, and Ness. As my brother helped Sarah set up her deejaying equipment in one corner of the room, Lucas and Ness took seats at the bar in front of me.

"Didn't know you bartended on Tuesdays, Knickknack. What's your Wednesday gig?"

"Maid of honor."

"You see, Fury? It never gets boring around here." He tightened the black elastic he'd tied around his hair, then fiddled with the button on his blue dress shirt, as though supremely uncomfortable.

"I see that." Ness was studying me, that one eye of hers lingering on the split lip I'd brightened with gloss. "How are you feeling?"

Because she didn't strike me as a person who was after a generic answer, I gave her question actual thought.

"Happy," I ended up saying.

Happy to be alive.

To be here tonight.

To have all my limbs attached and operational.

I'd heard I owed Liam my life. Heard he'd been the one to reach me and swim me back to shore at a velocity that rivaled Bea's, to administer CPR, purging my saturated lungs.

I hadn't even thanked him yet.

I would.

Eventually.

The door opened, and a dozen shifters breezed in, most in fancy attire—cocktail dresses for women, button-downs over jeans for men. My heart quickened as I scanned their faces. I didn't find the one I was looking for.

Why was I looking for it again?

Oh, right . . . To say thank you for rescuing me from a frozen lake.

I returned my attention to Ness and Lucas. "Can I get you guys something to drink?"

Ness, who'd turned toward the newcomers, redirected her attention to me. "I'd love some sparkling water."

I poured her a glass. "Lucas?"

"Another one of those for my baby mama—no ice—and a beer for me."

After sliding both over, he stood. "I told him to get his dick out of his ass BTW."

I raised an eyebrow. "Um . . . what?"

"When he got to Boulder. Before, you know, the whole Nikkinapping incident, I told Liam to get his dick out of his ass and catch up to Little Destroyer, who's decidedly the more astute of the two Kolanes."

My pulse tripped. I knew they were like brothers, yet couldn't imagine Liam discussing our failed relationship with Lucas. With anyone, for that matter.

"His head, Lucas." Ness sipped her drink. "Not his dick. His head."

Lucas shot us a crooked grin. "I like my expression better."

"I don't doubt it." Ness popped her elbow on the bar and propped her chin on her closed fist. "To think you're going to have a daughter soon. You think her first word will be dick or ass, Nikki?"

I managed a half-smile even though my mind was still stuck on what he'd said, about Storm being astute.

"Not funny, Fury." Lucas scrubbed a hand across his forehead as though he were mopping off perspiration. "My daughter will *never* speak the words dick and ass. *Never*. She won't even know what the former means until the ripe old age of forty."

"Uh-huh." Ness crunched on an ice cube. "Let's revisit that when she hits puberty."

Lucas scowled at her before taking his drinks and walking over to Sarah.

Ness's eyes were so shiny they rivaled the fairy lights strung up between the row of naked bulbs illuminating the bar. "His hair's going to go gray fast."

Smirking, I stole a pitted maraschino cherry from the bowl of garnishes behind the bar and popped it inside my mouth. "Where's August?"

"He went to pick up his parents from the hotel."

The one where Adalyn and I had been supposed to meet. I heard Liam had privatized it for the pack.

Her palm drifted to her stomach. "They're driving up to the gate now."

"Is it weird . . . to feel him?

"It is, but it's also comforting."

I rolled the candied stem between my fingers. "Do you ever regret it?"

"Consummating the bond?" Her hand drifted off her navel and closed around her glass. "I know love can exist without mating links. I mean—" She gestured to Lucas, who was standing behind Sarah, arms draped around her middle, chin nestled in the crook of her neck. "But the connection you get from a mating link . . . it's something special. So, no."

The door opened again, letting in an icy draft and additional cheer.

"Tomorrow night's a big night. The winter solstice."

I bit down on my lip, forgetting it wasn't quite yet healed.

"Did you know that only thirty percent of us have true mates?" Ness asked.

"I thought the number was higher."

"Crazy, huh? I'm pretty sure our pack single-handedly dragged that number down." She drained her water. "Want another statistic?"

"Sure."

"Seventy-five percent of true mates consummate the bond."

"I didn't know that."

"I'm full of useless statistics. What can I say? I like numbers." She got up. "My second favorite wolf has arrived. I'll catch you later?"

I looked toward the door.

Of course . . .

Liam.

My brooding expression led her to add, "I meant Storm. In case you were wondering." Winking, she set off, blue dress flouncing around her bare thighs.

I lowered my eyes toward my own legs. Adalyn had tried to get me to wear a dress, but between my scar and my bruise, I'd gone with leather pants and a simple navy camisole.

A pat to my wrist made me startle. Sasha nodded to the room. "Better get out there or you'll be stuck serving drinks all night."

"I don't mind."

"Nikki, it's your brother's party. Go have fun."

I glanced at the crowd, willing my eyes to surf over Liam, who was depositing his son in Ness's arms.

After the handoff, Liam turned toward the bar and then he started walking.

"Um. I'm going to go check on the food." Sasha scampered into the kitchen.

As Liam neared, I eyed the end of the bar and the crowd which had amassed alongside it. If I strode off now, he wouldn't be able to catch up with me. At least, not without jostling people. They'd probably part for him, but I'd still have gotten away and melted into the throng.

Hesitation cost me my escape plan. May and Savannah bustled up to the bar and asked for two Pinots, gushing about how gorge Pondside looked. By the time I'd filled two long-stemmed glasses and handed them over, Liam was standing before me, palms flat on the bar. He'd swapped his usual black V-neck for a black dress shirt, opened at the collar.

Would there ever come a day when I didn't find him attractive?

Keeping my gaze on his Adam's apple—I would not look any higher because eyes were a direct conduit to hearts, and I didn't want him glimpsing all that was going on in mine—I asked, "What can I get you to drink?"

"Surprise me."

His answer made my gaze bounce upward. So much for keeping my eyes to myself. "Since when do you like surprises?"

"I don't but I trust you."

"Really?" I raised my chin and crossed my arms. "That's new."

The girls sipped their wine, absorbed by my exchange with our Alpha. Suddenly, they both jolted. I imagined Liam had commanded them to leave, because a second later, they were gone.

"It's my defense mechanism, Nikki. I push away people who get too close."

"That's not an excuse for acting like a hot-headed alphahole."

"No. It's not an excuse."

A song ended and another one began.

"You did warn me, though," I finally said.

His eyebrows slid toward one another.

"You told me to stay away. Told me you hurt all those you got close to. I didn't believe you. Then again, I also didn't believe I was too sweet. But as they say, you live and you learn." I unknotted my arms, plucked a beer bottle from the little fridge beneath the bar, uncapped it, and placed it in front of him.

"Beer?"

I drummed my fingertips on the bar. "Surprises are overrated and much too often disappointing." And then I finally walked away from Liam Kolane.

It didn't feel good, but it felt necessary.

CHAPTER 65

I woke up with stomach cramps. *I* wasn't the one getting married, and yet my insides felt as twisted as wisteria vines. I assumed it was because of the looming solstice. I wasn't in the right mindset for a mate. I had so much more healing to accomplish before I let anyone, blessed by Lycaon or not, anywhere near my body and heart.

By the time noon rolled around, my cramps had gotten so violent I could barely look at the platters of finger food Nolan dropped off at Grandma Reeves's place. I'd eat after the ceremony, once the stars were bright and the crescent moon was high and my fate was mine and mine alone.

Ness's statistics returned to me—thirty percent. I looked around the living room littered with gowns, makeup, hot irons, and animated bridesmaids. Out of the twelve single women in attendance, possibly four would get mating links at some point in their lives, and one of them would choose not to consummate it.

As though thinking about Ness had conjured her up, she arrived with Sarah and Storm.

"We come bearing gifts," Sarah announced, a shopping bag thrown over her shoulder.

"Something blue?" someone quipped.

"Adalyn's already got Nikki for that," May said.

I rolled my eyes but smiled, because May wasn't wrong . . . I was still quite blue. On the inside and outside.

Sarah smirked as she rooted around the black paper bag. "No. What Ness and I have to give you all is red."

"*Very* red," Ness confirmed.

May clapped her palms as Sarah handed out black silk pouches to every girl in attendance. My mind automatically jumped to lingerie, and although I liked pretty underwear, having Sarah and Ness purchase some felt a little odd.

Unless outrageously padded, the contents of the pouch were much too bulky for underthings, though.

Giddy squeals erupted as the gifts were unpacked.

Bea and I were the last to unwrap our gift—a red silk bomber jacket with flowy white embroidery on the back that read *Boulder Babe.* The same one Ness had worn at Thanksgiving, and which Sarah was wearing presently under a raccoon fur vest.

"This. Is. Gorgeous." Adalyn's eyes glittered like the delicate rhinestone and pearl headband woven through her bleached hair. She hugged Sarah, then Ness, and in her effusiveness, even gave Storm's cheek a quick kiss.

As she shrugged it on, I pushed back one of my sleek curls and traced the white embroidery on my own jacket with my index finger. It was incredibly pretty and incredibly meaningful.

"Hey. It matches your eyes, Bea." Although, for once, I didn't think May had meant it as an insult, it made Bea fold the jacket back up.

"Everyone needs to put it on so we can take a picture." Ads clapped her hands eagerly. "Grams?"

Grandma Reeves set down the curling iron she was using on her own hair and took out her cell phone.

"I . . . uh . . ." Bea bit her lip.

After putting mine on, I filched the pouch from Bea's fidgety fingers, retrieved the jacket, and held it up, so she could spear her arms through.

"One day, those eyes will be on my niece or nephew. Be proud of them so they'll be proud of being different, too." This was me being hopeful again, because no one actually knew, not even Doc, if Bea would be able to reproduce, biologically or even *venomously*.

She hadn't been able to bring her brother back, but maybe, for her venom to take effect, the person had to be alive. During one of my many afternoons spent at Nate's, I'd heard her and my brother discussing biting terminally-ill people. Liam had vetoed it. For now.

With a little sigh, she gathered her thick hair and indulged me. I clasped her hand to remind her that she was one of us, no matter the shade of her eyes or the genetic makeup of her body.

After the photoshoot, Ness approached me, Liam's son balanced on her hip. "How are you doing today?"

Storm stretched out his arms as though assuming he was about to be chucked my way. I hesitated for all of a second before taking him from Ness.

Just because Liam and I were done didn't mean Storm and I were. We were both Boulders after all. I inhaled his sweet milky scent and whispered, "I missed you," into his amber curls before answering Ness. "I feel like I'm about to throw up, and I'm not even the one getting married."

Storm pressed his cheek against my collarbone, his little body going slack the way it always did when he trusted the person carrying him, but then he caught sight of my long earrings—rose-gold chains interlocked with diamond stars—and he eased off my chest to paw at the sparkly jewels.

"Sympathy nerves," I added when Ness's gaze drifted to my abdomen.

"Or solstice nerves?" Adalyn suggested with a wide smile.

I went as white as her gown, which still hung from the top of the living room door in its garment bag.

"You'll know in"—May checked the time on her phone—"two hours and three minutes."

"You have a timer on?" Gracey asked, as Grandma Reeves rolled her grand-daughter's dark hair into twin buns at the top of her head, Princess-Leia style.

"No, but I looked it up this morning." May slid her phone into the back pocket of her jeans. "Solstice begins at 4:58 p.m. this year. Right smack during the ceremony." She placed her hand on her own stomach. "My stomach's been acting weird all day."

Savannah rolled her eyes. "Every solstice you say that."

Storm yanked on my earring, which made my attention slip to him instead of my spasming abdomen. "Easy there, baby." I pried his fingers off and headed to the kitchen table to find something else to busy his little hands. After a quick scan that made my own stomach shrivel and hide, I grabbed a celery stick from the crudité platter.

Storm seized it excitedly and stuck it inside his mouth. The grimace that followed his first taste made my nerves release and a chuckle escape. He flung his arm out as though he were holding a stinky sock and dumped the green stick.

"Fine. Let's go for the unhealthy option." I peeled the bun off a slider and placed it inside his open palm. Delighted chewing ensued.

As I poured myself a glass of water, my phone buzzed with a message from Niall begging me for a ride back from the worksite. He'd gotten stuck finishing something in one of the cabins, and apparently everyone else in my family was too busy to taxi him around, and he couldn't shift because he was already in his vest, shirt, and trousers.

Why in the world had he gone into work today? And why in his nice clothes? My brother was sometimes such an enigma.

After a quick kiss to Storm's squishy cheek, I relinquished him to Ness, thanked her and Sarah for the gift, promised Adalyn I'd be right back, then got into my car and drove up the hill toward the cluster of brand-new cabins. The tawny wood glowed amber in the already low sun and the windows glistened like cut topaz.

From the outside, the new homes looked almost finished, but apparently the insides were still bare concrete.

I called Niall's phone as I reached the new path spiraling up the hill. "Which house are you in?"

"Number ten."

"Which one is number ten?"

"The one with the best panorama."

"That doesn't help me much, Niall. They all have great views."

"The one with the curved living room window and 360 view. Kolane's."

Oh. "Could've led with that."

"I was afraid you might not show if I'd led with that."

"My dislike of him doesn't extend to his future home."

I bumped along the unfinished road till I reached the giant cabin and parked in the giant driveway. "I'm out front."

"Come inside. You need to check out this view."

"Niall, what I need is to get back so I can finish getting ready. I'll go inside some other time."

Or not. I didn't see myself dropping by for a visit or a tour in the near future.

"Come on, Nik. It's really something."

I sighed a, "Fine," and disconnected the call. "Niall?" I called out as I stepped past the unlocked front door, ducking beneath scaffolding and exposed electrical wires.

My stomach went back to acting up, probably because I was trespassing even though I doubted Liam would mind I was visiting the empty shell of his house.

I was about to call out my brother's name again when I spotted him standing by the strip of curved glass, decked in jeans and a black T-shirt. "What the hell? You said you were wearing . . ." The rest of my sentence faded into breath as the man turned.

It wasn't my brother.

CHAPTER 66

"Um. Sorry. I didn't know you'd be here." I hugged my red jacket close as though it could somehow shield me from Liam's intent stare. "I was looking for Niall." Something occurred to me then, and I cocked my head to the side. "Did you also forget your car?"

"No."

"So why did he call *me* for a ride?"

"Because I asked him to." At my frown, he added, "I needed to talk with you."

My jaw went slack. Niall was such a traitor! Liam may have been his Alpha, but I was his sister. Sister trumped Alpha. "Liam, I told you already—"

"Give me ten minutes."

I chewed on the inside of my cheek and eyed the front door, digging through my mind for ways to get Niall back, because my brother would definitely pay for setting me up.

Please.

"Fine. Talk."

Liam rubbed his jaw, slid it from side to side.

I waited a minute.

Two.

It was only when I started to turn that he spoke, "I hate solstices."

I glanced over my shoulder. "You dragged me up here to complain about

356

your distaste for the shortest day of the year?" Or longest, depending on the season.

"No." He cupped the back of his neck, peered down at his scuffed Timberlands, then back up at me. "Nikki, what happens if you get a mating link tonight?"

"I don't know." My stomach squeezed as though speaking those words had somehow activated one. "Honestly, I'm sort of hoping Lycaon forgot about me this season."

"I thought it was your big dream."

"It used to be. Might still be. But I'm currently not ready for . . ." I licked my lips, trying to slow my breathing in order to absorb less of Liam's intoxicating smell. "Another partner."

"Why?" He stepped toward me.

I stayed rooted in place, not willing to be cowed into pedaling backward. "Because my last one screwed me up pretty badly."

His neck stiffened. "You said you'd leave me if you were given a true mate."

I raised my chin up a notch. "I only said I'd leave, because you made it clear you didn't want me to stay."

That slender, vertical groove formed between his eyebrows. "You would've resisted a bond to stay with me?"

"Crazy, right?" I stared past him at the valley still burnished in sunshine with its gilded orchard, polished pond, and lavender puffs of chimney smoke.

"If you're given a mate tonight, what will you do?" He moved again, blocking my view of the outside world.

"What are you really asking me, Liam?"

His Adam's apple bobbed in his rigid throat. "If you're given a mate tonight, will you choose him?"

I stared beyond his lowered lashes at the eyes, which had captivated me from the very first instant I'd caught their gleam beneath his baseball cap in a dark parking lot. I'd spent weeks willing those eyes to see me. And now . . . now I wanted those eyes to look anywhere else than into mine, because I feared they'd discover the shield forming over my heart had yet to harden.

"I won't consummate a link for the sake of having a mate, but I also won't hold out for an emotionally-stunted, commitment-phobic male."

Liam's mouth softened. "Emotionally-stunted?"

I needed to look away from that mouth before I did something stupid and allowed it to soften me in turn.

He took another slow step toward me, and another. Until he was so close the beats of his heart unsettled the air between us. "You smell like my son."

I glared up at him. "Am I not permitted to see him anymore?"

The bite in my voice made his gaze slide to a hardhat someone had left behind. "I was scared, Nikki. He already lost one mother; I didn't want him to lose another."

So Mom had been right . . . fear had prompted Liam to break up with me.

Didn't excuse the insensitive way he'd gone about ending things.

"He's *your* son, Liam. Not mine. I never forgot that, and I never tried to use him to pin you down."

Still scrutinizing the hardhat, he asked, "Could you ever love him like your own?"

My saliva solidified, and so did the oxygen in my lungs. "What sort of question is that?"

"The night I picked him up from your place wasn't the first time I heard him utter the word Mom. He'd said it twice in his sleep, and once when he got really upset with me. I thought he was asking for Tamara, but he never knew Tamara, so why would he ask for her?" Liam pushed a lock of hair out of his eyes. "It frustrated me at first, because I wanted to be enough for my son, Nikki. And I thought I was until I got here, until you and your mother helped me with him, and he just lit up. He was always such a quiet baby, happy and sweet, but quiet. Now he's so . . . *alive*."

His throat bobbed, and my already soft shield grew downright spongy.

"Anyway, one of the times he said it, it got me wondering if you—but you're so young . . ."

"And too sweet?" Sarcasm coated my tone.

A smile. And then it was gone. "Yes, Nikki. And because of that, I couldn't imagine you'd want a kid, especially one you hadn't created with that perfect, preordained mate of yours. And then you said you didn't want another family, and—"

"I want a mate, Liam. A mate who loves and accepts my family, because they'll be his too."

He closed his eyes. Inhaled. "Would you take me?" Opened his eyes. Exhaled. "Even if you get a true mate at nightfall, would you take me as your mate, Nicole Raina Freemont?" There was something so wounded in his tone, as though he pictured the ledge he'd walked out on already crumbling beneath him. "Me and my baggage?"

"Your baggage?"

"My son. My trust issues. My—"

He stopped talking when I took a step forward.

Stopped breathing when I captured both sides of his face, my thumbs dipping into the hollows beneath his cheekbones.

"Do you swear to *never* walk out on me again? If you're angry or scared, you talk, you yell, but you don't. Walk. Out."

He turned his head and placed a kiss inside my palm. "On all the storms and stars, I swear to never walk away from you again."

His promise snatched up all my heartbeats and compressed them into a giant one that made my body shudder.

"On all the storms and stars, huh? Didn't peg my rugged Alpha as someone who waxed-poetic." The lightness of my tone smoothed away his lingering worry.

His hands found purchase on my waist and crumpled the red silk. "Better not tell anyone or I'll lose all my pack cred."

I laughed, then pulled his head down to mine.

"My mate," he murmured against my mouth.

I stopped laughing.

I was someone's mate.

Not just someone's.

Liam's.

"I've been feeling sick to my stomach all day at the idea of getting a mate," I confessed.

One of his hands drifted to my belly, stayed there stroking slow arcs over my T-shirt. "Do you still feel sick?"

"A little, but I doubt it'll just poof away."

His eyebrows tilted toward one another. "You're not pregnant, are you?"

"Pregnant? Ha. No. We used protection." A little blood drained from my cheeks. "But now you're freaking me out." *Could* I be pregnant? I listened for another heartbeat, but Liam's and mine were creating quite the din.

He crouched and replaced his palm with his ear. After a second, he looked up. "No pulsing. Just lots of bubbles."

"Thank, Lycaon." A mate was one thing. *A baby* . . .

He raised the hem of my tee and pressed a kiss against my navel, which seemed to react by throbbing harder. "You should be thanking condom makers." Liam straightened from his crouch and kissed the tip of my nose but must've decided it was too tame a place to kiss, because his mouth coasted lower, sealing over mine.

At the taste of him, my pulse detonated, raining glitter inside my veins. I threaded my hands through his silky hair and tugged him close, and then closer, wondering if he'd ever feel close enough.

When my lower belly began to spasm like someone had hooked it up to an electrode, I pulled away. *Please, Lycaon. Please overlook me.*

Liam combed back a strand of my hair, his lupine eyes dimming. "It hurts when I'm close?"

Breathing hard, I croaked, "It doesn't hurt, but it feels . . . funny." Anguish slicked my eyes. "What if it is a mating bond in the making?" After laughing, now I felt like crying. "I don't want you not to be able to touch me for six months."

His brown eyes flashed. "You don't have to worry about that."

"Really? You're going to be fine with six months of celibacy?" I supposed he'd already gone that long without sex.

He brought one hand up to my face, his knuckles grazing the delicate chain of twinkling stars. "I meant it won't be a problem because I'll be sending your mate on a diplomatic mission into another pack territory. The Rivers, perhaps. Their Alpha and I are on excellent terms." His thumb stroked my lobe. "Leading a pack has its perks."

"And that'll be far enough?"

"Yes." There was no hesitation in his tone, as though he knew this for a fact. Maybe he did.

"What if *you* get a mate?"

"I already got myself a mate."

"I meant, a real one."

He stepped in until his hard body dented my soft one. "You feel very real to me, Miss Freemont."

"I'm serious."

"She'll also be sent away. Nothing and no one will come between us. Never again. You're stuck with me for life, and if I can help it, for the afterlife too."

He laced his arms around my waist and hugged me, just hugged me. And although my navel kept thumping, it no longer pained me, because Liam had a plan, and I had Liam.

CHAPTER 67

The sun dipped and tinged the snow rose-gold to a version of the Wedding March like none I'd ever heard. *The Grandpops* with their banjos, fiddles, and guitars, turned the soulful melody into one which felt shaped by the earth and trees themselves.

Last night, I'd wondered how my mother and Grandma Reeves could outdo themselves, but as I moved down the aisle strewn with pine needles and lined with crackling tiki torches, I marveled yet again. They'd even adorned the frozen surface of the pond with candles shaped like water lilies.

My long copper dress snapped around my ankles as I walked arm in arm with Nolan, absorbing the splendor of the evening.

"So, I'm guessing you said yes?" he asked.

"To what?"

"You mean, to whom?"

"You were in on it, too?" My jaw must've dropped a little because he pressed it back up on a bent knuckle.

"Well, he did come to all four of us to ask for our permission." He squeezed my arm, as he flicked smiles at the crowd of shifters lined up behind the row of torches. "After he got our parents' blessing."

I didn't think Alphas asked for anyone's permission. What if my brothers hadn't given it to him? Or my parents? Would he still have pursued me?

"Better shut your mouth before someone decides to launch a snowball at it."

"Only Niall would do that, and he's behind us."

Nolan chuckled as he released my arm and took his place beside his twin under the wedding arbor. I eased in opposite him, then turned to watch Nate and Bea approach. Her eyes shone fire-bright and her full cheeks shimmered with a pearlescent sheen that matched her metallic dress. Beside her, my oldest brother glowed in his own way—tanned, smiling, with a freshly-trimmed beard and gelled hair. The picture of health and bliss.

As Bea sidled in beside me, she stared open-mouthed at the swaths of glittery tulle draped over the simple wooden structure, braided in with heavy garlands of white blooms and strings of lights.

"Beautiful. So beautiful." Her murmur was edged with heartache.

Was she thinking about Miles? How he wouldn't be at her side when it was her turn under the arbor? How he'd never get to exchange vows himself?

A gunshot went off, and I startled.

I looked over at Nash, at Nolan, at Nate. Their postures were relaxed. Their expressions easy.

The gunshot had been in my head.

I closed my eyes, trying to rein in my runaway pulse.

Babe? What is it? Liam's voice broke me out of the spell.

As I searched the torch-lit obscurity for him, I licked the little dots of sweat coating my upper-lip. I found him standing at the very front of the assembly, flanked by his OBs and my parents, Storm bundled in his arms.

Nikki?

I'm okay, I mouthed.

Is it your stomach?

I shook my head.

A breeze caught in the tulle draped around the columns. The gauzy fabric billowed and grazed my back, a gentle caress reminding me that Camilla was gone and I was here.

As the other bridesmaids and groomsmen took their places beside us, my pulse quieted. The music, too, calmed. And then it stopped. When *The Grandpops* launched into a melody of such beauty that tears warmed my lids, everyone turned to watch my best friend take her first step toward my brother.

Almost everyone.

Liam hadn't turned around. His attention remained on me, his eyebrows drawn, his forehead grooved. He evidently didn't trust that I was okay. I smiled, then turned my smile toward Adalyn and her grandmother, and the sun igniting the sky behind them in dabs of oranges and pinks and periwinkle.

I took a mental snapshot of that moment, because I wanted to paint it for Adalyn and Nash, to immortalize tonight. Even though they were already mates in Lycaon's eyes, tonight they became mates in everyone else's.

Grandma Reeves released Ads into Nash's care and retreated to where my parents stood, her eyes as glossy as Mom's, as Gracey's too. Adalyn reached out and squeezed her sister's hand, mouthing a quick *I love you*, which made Gracey's tears brim and spill over her cheeks.

As Nash and Adalyn exchanged their vows, the moon rose, and with it, my heart, as though someone had filled it with helium and set it adrift among the stars. My stomach, though . . .

I dropped my hand to it. Unlike my chest, my abdomen felt as though someone had sucked all the air out and stomped over it. I breathed through the discomfort.

Was I about to be sick? What if I'd contracted a stomach bug?

I gritted my teeth and lifted my bouquet to quell the nausea, but instead of lavender, I smelled Liam. The man had not only gotten under my skin but all over it. Then again, we had made out in our future kitchen, bedroom, living room, walk-in closet.

Our . . .

"Are you okay?" Bea murmured.

I swallowed and gave her a quick nod that didn't seem to reassure her in the least considering her thin eyebrows remained smooshed together.

A flutter behind my navel, followed by a gentle tug, robbed me of my next breath.

Oh . . . no.

No, no, no, no.

Horror surged behind my breastbone as my childhood dream turned recent nightmare came to fruition.

I turned wet eyes toward Liam, the ruckus of applause and howls ensuing Adalyn and Nash's first kiss as man and wife fading to static.

He was smiling, that slow, steady smile of his. Soon, my news would snip his smile. Even if he had a plan, no male wanted to hear that the female they wanted was intended for another.

CHAPTER 68

I kissed Adalyn's cheek, then Nash's. My friend thankfully assumed my tears were joyful, because she didn't question them. By the time I made my way toward Liam, my dress felt like a corset made of spikes.

He didn't speak, didn't ask what was wrong. He must've known, though. Must've already smelled my fated mate on me. That was one of the first signs. I raised my shoulder and sniffed my skin, but couldn't pick up another scent over Liam's.

Oh, Lycaon, why? Why would you do that to me? Are you testing my affection? Is that it?

Liam extended one of his arms toward me as I trampled the pine-needle encrusted snow.

"It happened," I croaked.

He curled his arm around me, dragging me into his big body, squashing Storm's little one. "I know."

Storm squirmed, probably a little freaked out by how close we all were.

I attempted to muster up a smile for his sake, but my lips wobbled too harshly to shape one. "It's not fair . . ."

"Here I thought it would delight you."

"Delight me?" I pressed away from Liam. "Why in the world did you think it would delight me?"

His eyebrows gathered, spilling shadows into his eyes.

"Liam, hand over the Destroyer before you smother my smallest friend."

Lucas plucked Storm right out of Liam's grip, a smile toying on the edges of his mouth.

If he knew what was happening, he wouldn't be smiling. He'd be patting my back or Liam's, offering his condolences. Then again, he didn't have a true mate, so maybe for him, what had happened wasn't all that momentous.

"Nikki, I know you think I don't want this, but I want you, so I want this."

Sniffing, I scrubbed the tears off my cheeks. "None of what you just said makes any sense."

He frowned. "What part didn't make sense?"

"Why would you want me mated to someone else?"

"Why *would* I want you mated to someone else?"

"Why are you repeating what I just asked?" I palmed my cheeks again, hoping the makeup I had on was really waterproof or I'd scare away the man I was desperately trying to keep close in spite of a stupid mating link.

Suddenly, his forehead smoothed. "Babe, who do you think you're linked to?" He dropped his gaze to my navel.

A hard tug had me stumbling into him.

I froze, my fingers clutching the lapels of the tuxedo jacket he'd worn over a white button-down. "You? Lycaon linked me to *you?*"

"You sound positively appalled."

I pressed a fist to my mouth and didn't blink for such a long time that tears crystallized along my lash line.

One of his hands settled on the small of my back, the other played with the ends of my hair. "Apparently, my wolf's the ideal match to yours." His forehead dropped to mine. "But we already knew that, didn't we?"

My mouth was parted, yet I hadn't breathed in almost a minute. "You really want this, Liam?"

"Yes."

"I mean, you accept to consummate it?" I whispered across my knuckles.

"Well, I was planning on consummating you," he said all low and gravelly, "so might as well consummate *it* at the same time."

Heat splotched my cheeks.

He curled his hand around my fist and towed it off my still-gaping mouth.

Just tell me when, and I'll be there, hard and willing.

"Tonight."

He chuckled. "You don't waste a single minute."

"I don't want to chance you changing your mind."

He raised my hand to his mouth and kissed it, then rolled his cheek against my knuckles, marking me with his scent even though his scent was already on me, would forever be on me. "I'm not going to change my mind."

"You swear?"

On every storm and every star.

"We're still doing it tonight, because I cannot wait to speak into your mind." I pushed up on my toes to seal his vow between our lips.

"I forgot about that detail."

"Only fair."

"I suppose it is." Gentle. His voice was so gentle.

As I took his hand to lead him toward the twinkling reception, I asked, "You think I desired it so much I made it happen?"

A corner of his mouth ticked up. "You *are* incredibly persuasive."

"I knew I had a hidden superpower."

The other corner joined the fray. "Have you *again* forgotten you can transform into a wolf?"

I laughed as he pulled on my hand, spinning me back into his arms.

Beneath a sky swathed in stars, with our very own Storm watching on nearby, Liam pressed a kiss to my lips that promised many more to come.

EPILOGUE

FIVE MONTHS LATER.

I burst into the house we'd moved into a week earlier, Storm balanced on my hip, even though at fifteen months, he was perfectly capable of walking on his own.

"Liam!" I breathed hard even though I'd only run from the swing set in our backyard.

He careened out of the living room, eyes repeatedly raking over Storm and me, muscles writhing beneath his tanned skin. "What? What is it?"

She's here. "She's here," I repeated out loud for Storm.

His future best friend had arrived.

Or mate.

Unless he was like my brother Nolan and preferred males.

Here I went again, wanting to matchmake *everyone*.

Tears slipped out from how incredibly and perfectly happy I was. Sure, I'd been this way since the winter solstice, but the birth of another werepup had just added a whole new layer of happiness to my world, a stroke of bright color to something already beautiful, a filter that made everything twinkle.

Liam froze. "Is Sarah . . . is she . . .?"

His dread tempered my joyous outburst. We all had triggers—gunshots and motorcycles for me; births for Liam. As much as we both wanted to add children to our family, I worried he wouldn't take a breath the entire time I was pregnant.

"Heard her cursing Lucas out for putting such a huge baby inside of her, so I assume she's fine. I'm more worried about Lucas."

Liam finally relaxed and strode over, simultaneously kissing my wet cheek and stealing Storm from my trembling arms.

"They called her Lark."

Storm watched me shape her name, then gave it a whirl. "Lock."

"Almost, buddy." Liam smiled. "Shall we go introduce ourselves?"

I clapped, which made Storm clap, which made Liam roll his eyes.

I pinched his ribs as he curled his arm around my waist. "You know, you're not too male to clap."

"I'm entirely too male to clap. Not to mention, I'm an Alpha. Alphas don't clap."

"The world would be a better place if they did."

"If it makes you happy, I'll clap a certain part of your body later."

That shot a bolt of heat through the tether.

"Is that a suitable concession, Miss Freemont?"

Officially, I would become Mrs. Kolane next month in a large celebration, which Mom and Adalyn were planning relentlessly. Both were possibly more excited than I was.

Not true.

No one was more excited than I was.

Even though Liam was already mine in all the ways that mattered, next month I'd stake my ownership of the man in front of our fellow Boulders and the heads of six North American packs, four European ones, and two Asian ones.

I wrapped my arm around his waist and squeezed. "It'll do. Now let's go."

"You do realize," he said, as we walked down the road to the next cabin over, "that Lark's not going anywhere."

"I know, but I'm *dying* to see who she looks like."

We reached Sarah and Lucas's front door at the same time as Ness and August. I guessed they'd heard Lucas howling his joy from his balcony too. Or they'd heard Sarah barking at him.

Ness's eyes were as shimmery as mine, and her smile just as bright. August, too, exuded delight. Unlike the stoic man at my side, who still deemed displaying too much emotion a sign of weakness.

Ever since Liam had taken me as his mate, I'd been instantly inducted into the tight circle of OBs. Ness and Lucas had even gotten me an *Original OB* T-shirt, which I'd worn so often in the past five months, it was becoming as soft as my silk *Boulder Babe* jacket.

We barged right into Sarah and Lucas's love nest that was so new the walls were still unadorned and the surfaces bare of the tchotchkes that turned houses into homes. They had their entire lives to fill it with things. Already they were filling it with people.

Lucas met us on the threshold of the master bedroom, grinning so wide his molars were on display. Nestled in his giant arms was this tiny thing with a tuft of black hair, a button nose, and lips as pink as the blanket she'd been swathed in.

"Ready to get your minds blown by what my swimmers can do?"

Ness wrinkled her nose. "You did not just say that."

"All your doing, huh?" Sarah huffed from somewhere in the bedroom, which made me laugh.

"Come on closer and feast your eyes on the very definition of perfection." His voice dropped to a reverent whisper as he lifted the infant and nuzzled her pink cheek.

I tipped my head to the side. "Lucas, are you about to cry?"

"The hell's wrong with you, Knickknack?" He sniffed. "Real males don't cry."

I crowded in to stroke Lark's soft hair. "Like they don't clap?"

"Exactly."

"You clapped at Storm's birthday." August pressed in close behind Ness to get a better look at the newest werepup. "Got it on video. I can pull it up if you'd like."

Instead of one of his usual barbed comebacks, Lucas went back to grinning.

Storm's birthday had been bittersweet for all those who'd known Tamara, since it was also the anniversary of her death. Nevertheless, the OBs had all mustered bright smiles and plenty of cheer to make Storm's celebration extra special.

"Can you bring the party inside the bedroom? You all know how I feel about missing out," Sarah bellowed just as Matt and Amanda blustered in, along with Cole and Haley, all of them weighed down by gifts.

Sarah's family strode in next. First her mother and sister-in-law, both armed with designer babywear giftbags, followed by Sarah's brother Robbie, carrying his twin fifteen-months-old daughters.

Where the men stayed out in the living room with little Lark, the women gathered around the new mama's bed, which resembled a crime scene yet smelled like new life—sweat, sunshine, and blood.

The balcony windows had been thrown open, and the May sun streamed in, illuminating Sarah's flushed cheeks and golden curls.

"That's one pretty baby you popped out, lady," Ness said around a smile.

"Let this be known, Lark didn't *pop* out. She came out slowly and painfully."

Her sister-in-law smirked, probably reminiscing on when she'd given birth to not one, but two babies.

"She's beautiful, honey." Nora kissed her daughter's forehead.

"Thanks, Mom."

One of the twins, Evie, or maybe it was Daphne, toddled toward the bed. Sarah reached over to clasp her niece in a hug, but then Storm appeared in the doorway, and the child lost all interest in her aunt. Storm rushed over to me, taking refuge behind my legs as the twins crouched around him to entice him to play.

I threaded my hand through his curls that had grown so dark I was beginning to think he'd end up with his father's coloring.

"Since everyone's here"—Ness inhaled deeply—"I have an announcement."

Sarah and I exchanged a look because we already knew. Lucas, with his insanely sharp hearing, had picked up on it last week when we'd eaten Seoul Sister takeout on our brand-new terrace overlooking the compound.

"Ugh. Here I thought it would be a great surprise, but of course you guys already know."

"We can act surprised," I offered.

"You're pregnant?" Amanda squealed, her eyes lighting up as though she, too, had shifter blood. She was still hoping Matt would come around and allow Bea to alter her genetic makeup, but Matt refused to let Amanda be a guinea pig, especially since Bea had yet to test her venom on humans and shifters alike.

"Babe, you said you'd wait for me to tell all of them." Matt stood in the doorway as though unsure whether it was safe to step past the threshold.

"Wait . . . what?" Sarah sat up in bed so fast she winced and slid right back to her propped-up position. She leveled her gaze on Amanda's abdomen. "How did I miss that?"

"Probably because Lark's heartbeat was *loud*," I suggested.

"You guys are having a baby, too?" Ness gasped.

"Matty!" Amanda shook her head.

"Oops," Matt said before a big hand snagged his shoulder and pulled him backward into the living room. The sound of loud shoulder pats echoed throughout the house.

A second later, he popped back into the doorway. "If you weren't telling them about our news, who else is preggers?"

Ness pointed at her still-completely flat stomach.

"Little Wolf's having a baby! Whoop!" Matt burst in and swung her around.

Ness laughed, cried a little, then laughed some more, and then she hugged Amanda and congratulated her as all the men finally trickled into the room.

Arms laced around my stomach. ***Not jealous?***

I reclined my head, pillowing it on Liam's shoulder. ***I've already got a baby.***

Liam's gaze dropped to his son, who was sitting at my feet, eyeing the toys Sarah's nieces kept dropping at his feet. ***Not so much a baby anymore.***

Storm's lower lip snagged his upper one when one of the twins pulled the rattle the other twin had just given him right out of his hands. He twisted around and scaled up my bare leg, his head almost leveled with my scar now. I crouched and hoisted him up the rest of the way.

Liam ran a knuckle under his son's eye, catching a big tear. "Females can be so cruel."

"Oh shush. You love females."

I love one female. I tolerate the rest of them.

I nudged him with my shoulder. ***You adore my mother and Ness, and you even have a soft spot for Sarah and Adalyn. But your secrets are safe with me. Wouldn't want to tarnish your pack cred.*** I winked at him.

Do you have any idea how much I love you?

A faint one. Very faint. How about you refresh my memory?

He leaned over and placed the longest, sweetest kiss on my lips just as Lark let out a cry worthy of a much larger set of lungs.

"Nights are going to be fun with this one," Lucas drawled, relinquishing his daughter to Sarah and taking a seat beside his girls on the bed while birds chanted outside, shifters chattered inside, and laughter rang out everywhere.

LARK'S STORY IS UP NEXT.

Be sure to sign up for my newsletter to stay up to date on all my future releases.
Sign up on www.oliviawildenstein.com

Or join my Facebook Reader Group for teasers and giveaways:
Olivia's Darling Readers

WANT MORE PARANORMAL ROMANCE?

DISCOVER MY COMPLETED FAERIE SERIES THAT BEGINS WITH
ROSE PETAL GRAVES.

OR HEAD OVER TO THE CITY OF LIGHTS WITH MY ANGELS
IN FEATHER.

ACKNOWLEDGMENTS

I hope you've enjoyed this new addition to my Boulder Wolves series and that it has redeemed Liam in your eyes. I had so much fun seeing all my characters again and even more fun crafting new ones. Most of the heroines I write come from broken homes, so it was a breath of fresh air inventing Nikki and her loud, loving family.

Although so many of you rooted for Ness and Liam, I always believed Liam needed someone who offered him stability and unbridled affection. And for me, that was his polar opposite, "too sweet" and "too young" Nicole Raina Freemont.

Now onto the gratitude part.

First off, Anna Missa. What a godsend it was to work with you. Thank you for diving back into my shifter world alongside me. Your love for my wolves, your thorough fact-checking, and your keen attention to plot scrubbed and polished my manuscript to a beautiful, high-shine. Better get ready for Lark, because she'll be in your hands next.

Secondly, I'd like to thank my wonderful beta readers, Laetitia Treseng, Rachel Theus Cass, and Jessika Livengood. Your feedback was truly invaluable. A Pack of Storms and Stars turned out the way it did thanks to you three.

Thirdly, Rose Griot. One of my favorite readers, and now one of my favorite proofreaders. I'm so grateful we bonded over our shared reverence for epic love stories.

To Courtenay Oros, thank you for coming up with this beautiful title, which fit Liam's story to perfection!

To my family, whom I neglect when I fall deep into my imaginary worlds. Forgive me, and please remember I love you more than all my characters combined.

Lastly, thank YOU, for filling your day(s) with another one of my wild romances.

ABOUT THE AUTHOR

USA TODAY bestselling author Olivia Wildenstein grew up in New York City, the daughter of a French father with a great sense of humor, and a Swedish mother whom she speaks to at least three times a day. She chose Brown University to complete her undergraduate studies and earned a bachelor's in comparative literature. After designing jewelry for a few years, Wildenstein traded in her tools for a laptop computer and a very comfortable chair. This line of work made more sense, considering her college degree.

When she's not writing, she's psychoanalyzing everyone she meets (Yes. Everyone), eavesdropping on conversations to gather material for her next book, baking up a storm (that she actually eats), going to the gym (because she eats), and attempting not to be late at her children's school (like she is 4 out of 5 mornings, on good weeks).

oliviawildenstein.com
olivia@wildenstein.com

ALSO BY OLIVIA WILDENSTEIN

The Lost Clan series

ROSE PETAL GRAVES

ROWAN WOOD LEGENDS

RISING SILVER MIST

RAGING RIVAL HEARTS

RECKLESS CRUEL HEIRS

The Boulder Wolves series

A PACK OF BLOOD AND LIES

A PACK OF VOWS AND TEARS

A PACK OF LOVE AND HATE

A PACK OF STORMS AND STARS

Angels of Elysium series

FEATHER

CELESTIAL

STARLIGHT

Standalones

GHOSTBOY, CHAMELEON & THE DUKE OF GRAFFITI

NOT ANOTHER LOVE SONG

Masterful series

THE MASTERKEY

THE MASTERPIECERS

THE MASTERMINDS

CPSIA information can be obtained
at www.ICGtesting.com
Printed in the USA
LVRC100912070521
686270LV00027B/641/J